STEPS TO THE HIGH GARDEN

STEPS
TO THE
HIGH GARDEN

Colin Duckworth

CALDER PUBLICATIONS · RIVERRUN PRESS
Paris · London · New York

First published in Great Britain in 1992 by Calder Publications Ltd
9-15 Neal Street, London WC2H 9TU
and in the United States of America in 1992 by
Riverrun Press Inc
1170 Broadway, New York, NY 10001

BRITISH LIBRARY CATALOGUING IN PUBLICATION DATA
is available on application

LIBRARY OF CONGRESS CATALOGUING IN PUBLICATION
DATA
is available on application

ISBN 0 7145 4155 9
ISBN 0 7145 4229 6 pbk

Set in 11/12 point Times by Spooner Graphics, London.
Printed and bound in Great Britain by
Dotesios Limited, Trowbridge, Wiltshire.

Mon amie, mon coeur,
songe à la douceur
D'aller là-haut vivre ensemble,
aimer à loisir, au pays qui te ressemble.
Là, tout n'est qu'ordre et beauté,
luxe, calme et volupté.

Le soleil couchant revêt le jardin
d'hyacinthe et d'or.

Tout s'endort dans une chaude lumière.

My love, my heart,
think how sweet
To live together yonder,
loving at leisure, in the land
where, as in you, prevail
Order, beauty, delight, calm and ecstasy.

The setting sun bathes the garden
in hyacinth and gold,
warm light lulling
everything
to sleep.

**(adapted from Charles Baudelaire,
L'Invitation au Voyage.)**

1

Late October. A fine Spring evening. The golden sun forced its way through Simon's polaroids, and he pulled down the sun visor. In England the setting sun had never seemed so blinding as it was here.

'I told you not to bring the car,' Prestcott grumbled. 'You know what it's like in the rush-hour. Every car on the move but not one vacating a parking space.'

'It wasn't worth the risk of having you complain about coming in by tram,' Simon countered.

'Nonsense! I love Melbourne trams.'

'But not when they're hot and sticky and overcrowded, right? You know perfectly well you'd rather cruise around by yourself in your own private little space looking for a spot to park this old heap.'

Simon suddenly thought of the parking lot on the corner of Collins and Elizabeth. A long walk from the club, but still... Turn left out of Little Collins, there it was... no it wasn't. Somebody had bombed it in the night, it was just one gigantic hole in the ground.

'Another high-rise office block going up,' said Prestcott.

'Perhaps it'll be a multi-storey car park?'

'Too late though.'

'Yeah. Let us carry on the search, resolutely and with as few complaints as possible, shall we?'

'That's just the point, isn't it? Turn left here, Simon.'

'Left. Right. What's the point, Prestcott?'

'I couldn't have put it more succinctly myself. Here you are, an academic approaching middle age... Yes, let's be honest... And you're already having a mid-life crisis. You think you can cover old mistakes by going through the Cambridge thing again. Mark my words, no good will come of this, my dear chap.'

'You are a sanctimonious old fraud at times, Prestcott. There's one!' Simon jammed on his brakes, and a taxi driven by a Serbian bandit screeched to a blaring halt right behind him, making it impossible for him to back into the meter space, so he drove on. Prestcott was in a relentless mood, however.

'Why *are* you going back to the Cambridge part of your life, Simon? Why not move on, go to California, or better still get out of the academic rat-race? You're not even a useful academic. The government thinks you and your ilk are a drain on the public purse, so stop draining and do something real, like television commercials. They at least sell things.'

Dr. Simon Prestcott had had this conversation many times in recent months. He felt he had reached a crucial point in his life, but he could not see more than ten yards along any of the roads open to him.

Then came the explosion. He had just turned into Russell Street and was proceeding in a northerly direction when a flash and a large blob of billowing smoke materialised some way ahead of him, followed by a thump like a giant firework. The cars ahead swerved and stopped and began to bank up. Resisting the temptation to find out immediately what had happened, Simon took the next left turn back again towards Bank Place, which he now had little hope of reaching in time for the start of the Cambridge Society meeting. In the distance he could hear police or ambulance sirens. He turned on the radio just as the pips went for a news update.

'The dollar... Unemployment figures... Canadian anti-terrorist forces accused of involvement in Air India disaster... President Bush has declared a goal: to colonise Mars within thirty years. The project, called "mission architecture", involves physics, mathematics, engineering, robotics, and cybernetics... *(Rustle, rustle.)*... News is just coming in of a large bomb explosion in the centre of Melbourne. It occurred outside the Magistrates Court and opposite the

Central Police Station. One policewoman is known to have died and other casualties are feared...'

Simon felt slightly queasy. If he had gone straight up Russell Street to look for a space, instead of down to the bulldozed corner lot, he may not have had any more worries about his direction in life.

Third time round the block Simon Prestcott glimpsed a parking spot, just pipping a BMW which, in a rage, roared off in further search of sanctuary, catching the bumper of the car parked in the adjacent space. This afforded Simon some momentary pleasure. Not that he didn't feel sorry for the chap who would come back and find his bumper bent. Before leaving his car, Simon took a pad of paper out of his glove compartment, scribbled a short note in pencil, and tucked it under the wiper blade of the offended car. It read: 'Just thought you would like to know a shiny new BMW hit your bumper. It did him more damage than you.'

He had hardly lowered the blade upon the piece of flapping paper, rather clumsily leaning on the bonnet in the process, when an ear-splitting wail rose up from the bowels of the car, causing him to jump back in alarm, the word is well chosen, his posterior causing the car behind him to rock visibly. It too began to wail, but in a different key. As luck would have it, a police car was at that moment ambling past on some errand of mercy.

Twenty minutes later, and rather pinker, he walked through the warm evening sunshine along Collins Street, going straight past Bank Place with his mind still on what had just transpired, realised his mistake, and retraced his steps. Bank Place, one of the more picturesque little spots in Melbourne, was jammed with a noisy, apparently happy throng of shirt-sleeved yuppies and yuppas, all clutching glasses which would miraculously find their way back into The Mitre sooner or, more likely, later. One extremely attractive girl caught his eye and smiled at him as he tried, not too aggressively, to steer through the ebb and flow of beer, ginantoner and Schweppervescence, in descending order of popularity. He smiled back and said 'Excuse me', with genuine regret as he would have liked to respond with equal sociability, but his destination was not among this hedonistic mingling of hopeful stockbrokers and broke young barristers of all sexes and sizes; it was within the portals of Number 12. His Agenda said:

The Annual General Meeting
of the Cambridge Society of Melbourne
will take place
at the Melbourne Savage Club, 12 Bank Place,
at 6.15 p.m. on 25 October.

Simon had hesitated at first about joining the newly-formed Cambridge Society. Was there any point in trying to keep alive an experience which had been both exquisite and excruciating? He blinked in the semi-gloom as his eyes settled down after the sun's October glare, and tentatively edged towards the bar. Most of the others seemed older than he: greying professors in blazers whose buttons didn't meet any more, dowager doyennes who had no doubt blazed a trail for the feminists of whom they now heartily disapproved because they took for granted what they had had to fight for. Perhaps they were none of these; he liked to weave imaginary lives round other people — they were usually more interesting than the real thing.

A face he knew moved towards him, preceded by outstretched hand.

'Simon! So glad you could come!'

'Thank you very much, Michael. I thought I'd never get through. In fact, I thought that lot outside must be the Cambridge meeting, it's just like May Week.'

It was Professor Michael Bristow who had encouraged Simon to come, and he had agreed to devote an evening to this strangely nostalgic activity largely because he had

10

recently received the surprising news from his old college that they would be glad to welcome him back as a Visiting Fellow for the following year when he would be on leave. A room in college at incredibly low rates, and free dinners in Hall. You had to take your hat off to the Oxbridge system, they did remember their own. And it had been a few years now since he had left — 'Gone Down', as if fallen back into the world from some transcendental Olympian Heights or Elysian Fields — with his brightly-coloured certificate confirming he was a Doctor of Philosophy. He wasn't sure if his professor had had anything to do with the visiting fellowship, and did not quite know whether he should broach the subject. But not here and now, anyway. He liked Bristow well enough to be sincerely affable, without a thought of being accused of sycophancy.

'Do you know anyone else here?' asked Bristow. Simon looked round. There were several he recognised from one or other of the three Melbourne Universities, and a few greeted him with a smile or raised glass.

'Actually,' Bristow went on, 'I particularly wanted you to meet our guest speaker.' He led him over to a man who was already surrounded by several of the younger women at the gathering, either wives of Cambridge men or Cantabs. in their own right. They made way for Professor Bristow with something remarkably and anachronistically resembling respect.

'Do excuse my breaking in, we only have a few minutes before the tedious part of the meeting begins. The elections I mean, not your speech, Dr. Schoenheimer! I'd just like to introduce a colleague of mine: Dr. Simon Prestcott. He's a bit of a hybrid: part psychologist and part historian. You know Dr. Schoenheimer's work, of course, Simon. He's a historian too, in a way.'

'Um...' Simon sent a frantic search command to his brain.

'Hypnotic regression,' said Schoenheimer helpfully. Simon's mind clicked. Of course. Well, if I'm a hybrid, what's that make Schoenheimer, he thought. At that moment, the Secretary of the Society called them all to order, and the tedious part began.

Simon sat himself in a capacious armchair obviously designed for someone at least six foot six and fifteen stone, next to a young lady whom he had briefly observed among the admirers clustered round Schoenheimer earlier. He smiled and raised his eyebrows at her. As she leaned across towards him, the neckline of her simple, elegant dress (his French mother had taught him not only her language but an appreciation of style) performed the function it was intended to perform: raise hopes marginally and other things positively.

'Hello, I'm a visitor here. My name's Anna.'

That was clearly as far as any introductions were going to get at that juncture.

'Fellow members of the Cambridge Society and guests,' began Michael Bristow, 'it gives me great pleasure to welcome you all to this A.G.M. of our society, especially as it takes place in the Melbourne Savage Club, of which I also happen to be a member, which is hardly surprising as it is the most anarchic club in Melbourne.'

Simon knew that Bristow was one of the most well-ordered people imaginable, so could afford to label himself as a member of an 'anarchic' club. His mind suddenly, and for the first time, attached itself to his material surroundings. The walls were covered with an array of primitive armaments: spears, assegai, shields decorated with weird designs — all the accoutrements of warlike savagery one could imagine. A haven for some Aboriginal Returned Servicemen's League maybe? But in that case, what was the ultra-civilised Bristow doing as a member?

Bristow continued, the committee were re-elected unopposed, and the assembled audience were invited to recharge their glasses at the bar before the main interest of the evening began.

'Would you like another drink?' Simon asked Anna. She stood up lithely and indicated it would be a good idea.

Between leaving their seats and reaching the barman, he had extracted a certain amount of vital information. Anna was here as a guest, not as a Cantab. or spouse. A guest of whom? The guest speaker. The guest of a guest, then? The partner of a guest, say. An absolute stunner, anyway, Simon concluded.

'Tell me about Schoenheimer,' he said. 'I know his name, but I can't honestly say I've read anything by him.'

'He hasn't actually written all that much,' she replied. 'Five or six books and fifty or so articles in journals that can't be found anywhere but in medical libraries.'

Simon began to feel slightly chastened, thinking of the one book and twenty articles he sometimes blew the dust off to remind himself he had the glimmerings and beginnings of an academic reputation. Anna was going on speaking, as they edged towards the alcohol dispensary.

'He spends nearly all of his time in practical work, helping and counselling people. That's very time-consuming.'

'You're obviously quite a fan of his?' — Simon tried hard to keep any trace of jealousy out of his voice.

'I suppose I am.' Anna paused. 'But then, I am his daughter.'

By the time Schoenheimer had given his lecture, which was not a learned paper but a lay exposition of his work, as was right before a highly intelligent but nevertheless non-specialist audience, Simon understood why his boss, Professor Bristow, had been so anxious for him to be there. The guest speaker was in Melbourne briefly from London, Bristow explained in his introduction, to launch a new television series entitled *Being Past and Present*, for which Dr. Schoenheimer had contributed half a dozen impressive but controversial cases of hypnotic regression — not simply taking the subjects back to their birth, or to their pre-natal state, but to purported previous lives, former reincarnations. Bristow, a highly literate and musical mathematician, maintained a level but cool attitude towards the whole proceedings, without hostility but without enthusiasm either. The cases Schoenheimer quoted were, in themselves, impressive, but it was not easy to convince those present that it was really possible to take a person back to a previous incarnation under hypnosis.

'Even if you do find the cases in the T.V. series fascinating,' Schoenheimer concluded, 'I very much doubt whether the naturally sceptical Cambridge graduate would be willing to admit the objective truth of the cases. After all, all you have to go on is my word for the fact that you are not being conned, that the whole thing is not an elaborate hoax perpetrated by a B.B.C. and an A.B.C. desperate to improve their ratings. We all know Uri Geller fooled people for years. Why shouldn't I?'

His honesty was either the bravado of an accomplished showman, or the resignation of one well accustomed to being ridiculed and doubted. Simon stole a glance at Anna, at his side, and saw her with head back, eyes closed, relaxed and unperturbed. She obviously knew her father could cope. After polite applause, Bristow, as chairman, cast the first stone.

'Dr. Schoenheimer, those working in the field of psychology and of parapsychology know that almost any phenomenon can be faked by a determined operator. The patients you have shown us in the video extracts are truly impressive: the woman who told you under deep hypnosis that she had been immured as a nun in a particular building in France in the sixteenth century, and actually led you and your T.V. crew there, and we saw the wall being opened up before the cameras — that was very impressive. But how are we to be sure you and the B.B.C. will not say in a few months time, "Ha! Got you there, didn't we! It was just a T.V. drama like any other. Pure fiction!" How are we to be *sure*?'

Murmurs went round the room as physicists, surgeons, historians and lawyers nodded gravely. This was the sort of question they would also have asked. Schoenheimer stood in the centre of the rostrum with his chin resting in his hand for several seconds. Then he said:

'I can convince you only by appealing to your sense of logic and of probability. If I were to admit to one such fraud, that would be the end of my career. I am not an entertainer, but a healer. I studied medicine and psychiatry at the Universities of Utrecht and Cambridge before I had any inkling of the, how shall I say, additional sensitivities that have been wished upon me without my consent or even desire. My life would have been simpler, and no doubt richer, had I simply continued the conventional path as a clinical psychiatrist in Harley Street. In fact, I do have an office in Harley Street, but life is not as simple as I would like. I don't like being controversial. I should prefer to be a safe, solid, sometimes successful doctor of the mind, curing some schizophrenia here and some manic depression there, with a big house in the country and a Rolls Royce to take me there. But other forces outside myself keep intervening. Cases which earn me no fees, or very few, force themselves upon me, and I usually cannot refuse if I sense they are right. I find myself drawn to strange places for no apparent reason, but the reason always reveals itself. The person I am meant to help always shows up, and neither of us knows why to begin with.'

His quiet matter-of-fact statement had produced the kind of rivetted silence that follows the end of a classical tragedy. He looked out at his audience, and with a helpless sort of gesture and a wry smile, he concluded:

'Within the last half hour or so I have sensed that the real reason for my coming all this way to Australia was not known to me before. It is not just to launch the television series — that could have launched itself without me. The real reason lies with some person in this room.'

Simon felt an unpleasant tingling in the back of his neck as he realised that Schoenheimer's eyes were fixed upon him.

15

2

The questions that flowed rapidly after Bristow's opener covered most of the controversial ground that Simon had heard or read previously. What surprised him was that even in that rather unrepresentative gathering, so few had heard of regression hypnotherapy. Those who had, thought of it as some oddball 'alternative' belief, like astrology or numerology or Tarot. Simon himself was far from convinced, simply because, he felt, this was a phenomenon that had to be experienced. No amount of talking about it would win over people who were being constantly bombarded with arguments and documentaries showing why they should believe in UFOs and the Nighness of the End of the World. It did not enter his own world-view at the moment, anyway. He had quite enough trouble trying to orientate himself in the here and now; and more specifically in the History of Science and Ideas Unit.

Michael Bristow had reigned over the Unit as its first professor for ten years, since its establishment, and despite his ebullient nature he sometimes found bitterness creeping into his mind because the Unit still lacked the status and (above all) the security of a fully-fledged Department. He had attracted some good staff, and had managed to keep the jealousies and rivalries of the younger ones (striving to make a future for themselves in a rapidly shrinking academic world) just below boiling point, by his own good humour and civilised benevolence.

Bristow had been particularly successful at getting funds for eminent visiting scholars capable of drawing wide audiences — a way of making more people aware of the Unit's value as a link between the apparently disconnected worlds of arts and sciences. On the evening after

Schoenheimer's talk to the Cambridge Society, Bristow had to introduce the most eminent speaker of the year in the Faculty's series of lectures devoted to *Issues in Contemporary Society*. This was to be given by none other than the cineast and semiologist, Jean-Claude Merdrillard, famous for his avant-garde films, which seemed to the uninitiated to be fairly straightforward mixtures of drug-running and prostitution in Marseilles and Paris. In fact, they were, but Merdrillard, being highly intelligent, had realised very early in his career that two simple ploys would mark him out for success on both the commercial film circuit and the lucrative American university lecture circuit: first, he carefully jumbled up all the scenes in his films, so that only people who went to see them ten times could work out what was going on and could then write about them superciliously in art film journals; secondly, Merdrillard mastered the jargon of semiotic and deconstructionist terminology created by the French as part of what George Steiner had acutely identified as the French intellectuals' response to the humiliation of the German Occupation. Bristow could make little of this kind of pseudo-scientific gobbledegook, but recognised it as characteristic of a society which respected ideas only if they were wearing technological emperor's clothes.

Merdrillard was an absolute master of the French Aesthetic Newspeak, and excelled even more when he had to deliver it in English. Simon therefore took a book with him to read during the lecture. He was furtively turning a page when his attention was unavoidably caught by what was being said by the famous man, whom a couple of hundred students had come to hear — mainly from the various Melbourne Departments of Media and Communication Studies, Simon guessed.

'Eet does sy we one prematory major of the gas chambers,' Merdrillard was saying. 'At the ghost of few cheers. Forgetting affidation. We move that mortgage of Auschwitz. Televised tailends attempt to re-heat the cooling systems of the cold war. Dissuaded ant daze, forêt, tactueux. TV is no longer any mage. Mirrow of the greemy moj. Holocaust Stevens, saltoric terror, stereotypes of sevotree. We have already been irrugating. It doesn't muffly. I do not believe in images worthy television. It is show secret with reality. Life,' he concluded with a flourish, 'is a travving shot. You reach Scarbytown in a muzzical ambience.'

The medium was clearly the message, for Merdrillard received a rapturous ovation. Simon swore he would remember the technique in future for overseas conferences. If a Frenchman who tortured the English or French language (he wasn't sure which) for an hour and a half with aplomb and panache, could be accepted as an authority worth paying out good money for, he would give up trying to be a model of logical clarity. Perhaps, the horrid thought suddenly assailed him, perhaps, people were happier not to understand.

Trying to make a brisk getaway after the performance so that he would not be obliged by the Vice-Chancellor to make polite conversation with Merdrillard (even though he had been looking forward to a chat in French), he was slightly put out to find Bristow on his heels, flanked by Dr. Crow. Victorine Crow had been appointed to the Unit at the same time as himself. There had, in fact, been three of them, but the third, a rather nice nun from Sydney, working on the history of witchcraft since the nineteenth century, had withdrawn from the rat-race after being subtly but consistently hounded by Dr. Crow with the argument that God's handmaidens should not try to get the best of this world as well as the next. She therefore resigned and went back to her nunnery, leaving in peace quite a few adepts in the black arts out in the bush. In his more paranoid moments, Simon thought it just possible that the Crow might have been in league with them.

'Fascinating stuff, that,' Bristow was saying, 'but quite beyond me, I'm afraid. Did he make it up on the spot, or does he have an autocue, do you think?'

Dr. Crow glanced at Simon and gave a little smirk. 'I think you must have missed the key thought, if I may say so,

Michael,' she said.

'And what would that be, Vikki?' asked Bristow.

'Well, I'm sure Simon will correct me, if he can, but it seemed to me fairly clear that the spatial discontinuity of the image deconstructs the spurious continuum of outmoded art-forms, and this is best rendered by the film, which can re-train the eye for a genuine semiotic re-appraisal of social reality. Robbe-Grillet had already said it all years ago.'

'I see,' Bristow nodded sagely. 'Would you agree with that, Simon?'

Simon was tempted to put in a claim for Bergson as having said it before Robbe-Grillet, but was suddenly quite overwhelmed by a feeling of nausea. Outside there were vast problems to be solved; millions who were starving; there was the large hole in his own pavement that the City Council had not had the organizational powers to get filled in for six months, and Dr. Crow was drawing good money from the government to convince herself and her students that the deconstruction of reality was a topic of major concern to humanity, and even to the university. And was he much better himself? His momentary revolt contained a hefty element of guilt.

'Frankly,' he contented himself with saying, 'I think Dr. Crow is labouring under a misconception of dimensions inversely proportionate to the importance of the subject. Surely Monsieur Merdrillard, whose name is in pre-established harmony with his ideas, was saying that the mirrow of the greemy moj, which was obviously a virtual image created by Holocaust Stevens ... Well, it's all strictly in line with the quantum theory, the doppelgang sevotree being muffly right through the travving shot. Surely you got that, Victorine?'

'Well, if your only response to a serious attempt at understanding is to take refuge behind facile mockery, there isn't much more we can say, is there?'

Simon assumed a mien of contrition.

'Oh dear, I think we're getting our wires crossed, Victorine.' (He knew she hated the name and responded only to Vikki.) 'You think I'm being trivial about something serious, but I'm not, honestly. I'm treating a triviality in such a way as to show it *could* lead to something serious.'

She gave him the sort of look that made it clear what kind of nunnery she was consigning him to. A bunch of noisy, chattering students elbowed past them, and disappeared in the direction of the Union caf.

'I may not know *what* is serious,' Dr. Crow said coolly, 'but I'm pretty damned clear about *who* is not.'

'I think Vikki wins that round on points,' Bristow interjected.

Simon was inclined to agree. He must curb his growing disenchantment with some of the more recondite activities of his colleagues. Sometimes he felt that it was only his sense of the absurd that kept him sane.

'All right,' he went on earnestly, 'let's assume Merdrillard was talking about reality and appearance. Now I come to think of it, I don't think he mentioned Swedenborg...'

'Swedenborg!' Dr. Crow snorted. 'A brilliant scientific brain that went through a mid-life crisis and turned psychic!'

'You might get a learned paper out of it, Vikki,' Simon mused. 'How about "Fantasies of Heaven and the Male Menopause, from Swedenborg to Merdrillard"? Or "Mid-life Crisis and the Cosmos as Hologram, in Merdrillard and Bohm".'

'Bohm?' Michael Bristow pricked up his ears. 'The physicist? Colleague of Einstein's?'

'The very same. Even Black Hole Penrose thinks he's "*serious*". Perhaps one day we'll find Heaven and the physical universe are all part of the same cosmic hologram, an infinite three-dimensional illusion.'

'Ah, but whose illusion?' asked Bristow, 'God's, or ours?'

Or Dr. Victorine Crow's, thought Simon with a shudder.

Ambling home on foot across the tree-lined campus and past the gastronomic paradise of Lygon Street, Simon began to sing quietly to himself:

The time has come, the walrus said,
To speak of many things.
Of holocausts and holograms,
And angels without wings.

But the song and the smell of garlic swirling about him in the warm air barely served to sooth his irritation with Merdrillard and the Crow. As he put his key in the door of his flat, his telephone was ringing.

'Yes?' he barked.

'Oh dear, you don't sound in a good mood.' It was Anna.

'I'm sorry. It's very good to hear you, Anna. I was going to phone you this evening. I've just had a rather nerve-shredding time, listening to an incomprehensible Frenchman.'

'I thought you prided yourself on being bi-lingual.'

'English and French, not Franglais and Frubbledidub.'

'...and what?' she laughed.

'I'll give you an example.' Simon dragged out of his jacket pocket the envelope on which he had scribbled notes of Merdrillard's remarks, and gave her a very accurate rendition. By the end they were both collapsing with laughter, and he felt better.

'I'm sorry I had to dash off last night. I hope you didn't find my father's talk as irritating.'

'Of course not. Even if I had, I'd have been perfectly happy looking at you out of the corner of my eye.'

'I was wondering if you could bear our company again this weekend. We've been invited to a place out in the country, and I am allowed to take a friend. Perhaps I'm presuming?' She was misreading Simon's silence.

'No, good heavens, I'd be delighted! I was just lost in a little fantasy: you and I out at a country-house party, and suddenly everybody else disappears. Just the two of us left. Lovely thought.'

'I'm not so sure. You might find out too soon that I'm a rather boring person to be alone with.'

This was a revelation to Simon. She had appeared completely self-possessed and self-confident up to that point. He began to feel less nervous, and was grateful to her.

'The only reason you feel free to say a thing like that is that you know it isn't true. Where is this place?'

'Somewhere near... Healesville ... yes, that's right. Is that far?'

'No, about an hour and a quarter. The only trouble is...' — he had just remembered — 'I'm having my car serviced by a chap who does it cheaper at weekends.'

'That's all right. I'll pick you up and we'll drive up together, if you like.'

He certainly did.

The doorbell of his Carlton flat near the university rang at two minutes past nine. Intuition had warned him to be ready on time. They shook hands formally, and laughed at the formality. So he bent forward to kiss her, just as she began to turn away, giving her ear the benefit.

'Are you trying to bite my ear off?' She smiled, and pushed her flaxen hair back.

'Yes, I love the crunchy, waxy bits. But I really prefer lips.'

She obliged. The ice was broken. They went down the short garden path hand in hand, and Simon suddenly stopped short. Before them, with its driver's door open, stood a shiny new BMW. It had an ugly graze, about twelve inches long, over the back mudguard. She saw his look, and smiled ruefully.

'Pity, isn't it? That's what comes of lending one's car to a headstrong young man.'

Simon felt both relieved and annoyed.

'I'll tell you about it on the way,' Anna said.

As they purred through the greens and silvers of the Victorian countryside, they caught up on one another with avidity, as though each had been kept in ignorance of the other's life. Anna had been brought up in London. Her father had been smuggled over to England from Holland during the war as a child and cared for by a wealthy uncle. Simon, she learned, had spent his childhood in France, his parents had divorced when he was twelve, and his mother had remarried, a very pleasant Englishman, whom he had soon come to like and love and emulate — so, he could pass as an Englishman and as a Frenchman, just by adopting different body language.

'But what brought you to Australia?' she asked.

'Flight,' he answered. 'No, I don't mean Aeroplop or Luftwaffe: flight. Fugue. From an unpleasant reality. You see, I was married, much too young, and fell into the same trap my parents had. It was a terrible mistake. In fact, I'm wondering if I really ought to go back to Cambridge next month. It might be rather painful.'

'Is your ex-wife still in Cambridge, then?'

'No, she's happily married in Surbiton or Cheam, I hear. I just don't know why I still feel as I do. Humiliation, I suppose.'

'Then it's time someone took your mind off it.'

'Oh, don't get me wrong. I don't brood about it at all. It's because the whole Cambridge thing has come up again.'

At traffic lights before Healesville, a car drew level with them, and zoomed ahead the moment the amber appeared.

'So someone grazed your lovely new toy for you?' he asked casually.

'Yes, it was pretty annoying. The car hire firm is going to charge me the access...'

'Excess.'

'Sorry. Apparently, it happened while Blake was at the Cambridge Society lecture. You must have seen him? A tall, fair-haired chap with a floppy bow tie. He said he had parked the car just round the corner in Queen Street, and when he came back the damage was done.'

Can't really blame the fellow for lying, thought Simon. Or was he? Perhaps the car the BMW hit was also a BMW?

No. The parked one had had its bumper bent; Blake was certainly the one who had got his (or her) car grazed.

'What was he doing in your car, anyway? Don't answer if you don't want to.'

'It's quite simple: my father and I drove in together, and I needed mine straight after the lecture, so he offered to drive it in for me. It'll be the last time. He's a bit wild, as you'll see.'

'You don't mean he's going to be there this weekend!'

'I fear so. But he's quite harmless. He has problems with his sex life. That's why he drives like a demented bluebottle.'

'Just leave the psychology to me, will you?' said Simon. 'You stick to... to what, exactly?'

'Music. I'm a musician. A pianist of sorts. That's why I've been invited, I suspect. I'll have to play for my supper. It's worth it, though, to have a chance to get out of town. In good company,' she added, glancing at Simon.

'Whose, though,' he said gloomily. 'Mine or this guy Blake's?'

'I was thinking of our host, actually.' She gave her head a little shake and smiled. 'He's a sweetie.'

Simon decided she was not to be trusted.

3

Connie had awoken that same Saturday morning with a thick head and puffy eyes. She groaned as she peered at the unsympathetic mirror, and swore under her breath at the Great Creator of Allergies. It was the time of the year when everything that could get up your nose did. Including Anna.

'Whoja say she was bringing?' she yelled at Bryce, busy with his Braun in the en suite which had been carved out of a maid's closet when they bought the place ten years before.

'Who?' he yelled back. He knew perfectly well what she meant, and knew she knew he knew, but this was a way of prolonging conversation that might otherwise falter so early in the morning.

'You know damn well. The Showhammer girl.'

'Schoenheimer.'

'Oh, he's a relative?'

'Not of mine, he isn't. Is he one of yours?'

'No, you said he was another Shinehammer.'

'I don't know who he is. Something at the university. Couldn't very well refuse, could I? It's not as though we're short of bedrooms or spoons.'

'Well, I think it's a pity, it'll make us thirteen, and mess up the table, and he'll get in Blake's way.'

Bryce strolled barefoot and betowelled into the white, cool bedroom. 'Bit of competition never did any harm. He's always had his own way too easily, your darling boy.'

Connie decided that this old bone of contention was not worth throwing back.

'I just think,' she said, taking her still shapely torso through into the en suite, 'that if he can find himself a nice, rich girl, it'll be about the cleverest thing he's ever likely to achieve. Messing about in theatre'll get him nowhere.'

Bryce reflected on the appropriateness of Anna Schoenheimer's being labelled as a nice, rich girl. Nice-looking, and rich-looking, yes, but the reality behind the appearances depended on the credibility of her father, and he was possibly a ringer. Fascinating fella, but distinctly dodgy, till proved otherwise. Bryce had not trebled his considerable fortune in the last eight years without having a few gifts of intuition of his own. When he had first met Floris Schoenheimer, he had recognised that there was a lot of vibe-reading going on that was not so very different from his own.

He set about disguising the idiosyncrasies that age had imparted to his physique, by means of the best that Savile Row had been able to suggest for hot summer wear, on his most recent trip to London. That was when he had first set eyes on Floris and his daughter. In a way, he was responsible for their being in Australia now.

Simon bent over the hand-drawn map again. 'If there's a road on the left about a mile up, we take it.'

'What's a mile? Never 'eard of it, mite,' she smiled across at him.

'Now, don't you patronise us poor new immigrants who are trying hard to innergrate ourselves,' he whined. 'You're only a foreign visitor, an alien, so be careful. I could have your passport shredded. Hey, you'd better tell me something about these people we're going to meet. Are they humans, or astral projections, or Schtroumphs, or what?'

'I don't know who else has been invited. Our hosts are the Trevelyans. Sir Trevelyan and ...'

'Sir Trevelyan Trevelyan!' It was the first time she had betrayed her non-Englishness, if one didn't count the excess-access slip. She gave a slightly sheepish grimace.

'Sir...what is it now...Bruce... no, Bryce. And Lady Constance. He was enknighted or whatever it is before Australia stopped giving people honours.'

'Oh, they didn't stop, they just do it their own way,

26

instead of creating a separate class of people. Anyway, what did he do for it?'

'I've no idea. You'll have to ask him. I expect he's used to being quizzed about it. Something financial, big business, takeaways or takeovers, I don't understand all that.'

Simon looked out at the wooded hills flanking the road, and suddenly remembered they should have turned off. But neither of them had seen a turning off to the left. Ahead of them was a tractor. Its driver was applying a spanner to its innards. Anna pulled up alongside him.

'Excuse me, we're looking for a place called Whitegates. We seem to have missed it.'

The man straightened up and looked at her with a grin. 'My oath, you've missed it all right. Coupla kays back, on your right. Keep your eyes skinned this time and you'll see her, good as gold. The road, that is, yer won't see the house, 'cos it's over the rise, but just keep goin' and hope yer don't meet nothin' comin' the other way! Wouldn't be good to get that nice new paintwork scratched.'

They thanked him and turned round. Two kilometers back, they found the road off. But it was easier to see from this direction, as it was not at right-angles to the main road. A single track between hedges, it rose up quite steeply for another mile or so. About a coupla kays. Then all at once it rose no more, the hedges dropped away. In front of them were two gleaming white double gates, five-barred with a curved piece arching elegantly over each from the hinged sides towards the centre. Just as Simon was about to get out to open them, they glided open of their own accord. It was then that he spotted the video-camera discreetly housed in one of the gate-posts.

From here on, the path was laid with fine white pebbles and curved through well-cut lawn on each side. After another five hundred yards, the masking trees slid to one side, and before them lay the house. There was a sharp intake of breath from Simon.

'Stop a minute, will you?' he whispered.

With an inquisitive glance at him, Anna complied.

'Beautiful, isn't it?' she commented after a few moments of silence.

'It's more than that. It's... I don't understand this.' His voice faltered and she focused on his eyes.

'You recognise it?'

'Yes. I don't know. I just feel I've been here before, but I know I haven't.'

Anna turned to look again at the house. It was uniformly white, apart from the roof of deep red tiles. There was only one storey, so far as they could see, but of great and apparently unpredictable shape and proportions. The late morning heat was making it shimmer. The only sound to be heard was the gentle put-put-put of the tractor on the road. To his consternation, Simon realised there were tears in his eyes. He furtively wiped them away. Anna put her hand on his and squeezed it.

'It's exactly like a house I have dreamed about for years and years,' said Simon. 'I had never been able to place it before, it's just rather weird to see it really exists, right there, in front of me.'

Through the wide arch spanning the driveway they now saw a figure, beckoning, as if puzzled at their slow advance. The pebbles slooshed under the tyres. From up in the trees came a burst of ribald laughter.

'There's a welcome for you from our well-trained kookaburras,' said Bryce as he stepped forward, arms outstretched, to greet them. Anna introduced the two men.

'You're not the first to arrive,' said Bryce, 'Blake got here a little while ago. You must go and join him in the pool and freshen up after your journey.'

He looked up at the cloudless sky. 'Make the most of it. There are storms forecast for later on.'

It seemed unbelievable at the moment, but that was the way in Victoria. One minute Spain, next minute Wales.

'Anna! Darling!' Blake Pascoe waved his flute at her and rose from his chaise-longue, spilling champagne over his stomach as he did so. 'Don't kiss me too passionately,' he instructed her, 'or I'll come off on you. The oil, I mean.'

'Blake, I'd like you to meet Dr. Simon Prestcott. Simon, Blake Pascoe-Trevelyan.'

'Quite a mouthful,' said Blake apologetically. 'Blake will do. Goodday, Simon. You two ought to get your bathers on, it's great in the water.'

Simon felt as though they were being urged to go through some kind of cleansing process, or purification by total immersion. They were taken by a maid to their rooms, which were next to each other (Connie had not had her way over this, except to the extent that Blake's room was the other side of Anna's), overlooking the rolling countryside to the east. Simon undressed, showered the travel dust off him, and lay down on his bed to ponder about the dream-house. With his eyes half-closed, it was only after a short while that he realised he was being observed by someone on the verandah outside his window. It was Anna, in a sleek, black one-piece. She motioned for him to slide the glass door open. As his own swimming apparel was still in his case, he felt he could not reasonably keep a lady waiting outside if she wanted to come in. Who cared if she was to be trusted or not? Here she was knocking his bedroom door down. The glass panel slid silently sideways and she glided into the room with a bright smile and a small toss of her fair hair. He suddenly felt very embarrassed and put his hands coyly in front of him. Anna noticed the movement, and burst out laughing.

'I do believe you're going to blush!' she teased.

'You make me feel indecent. Actually, no, *you* look indecent, all covered up like that.'

'So why don't you do something about it?' She threw her small white handbag on to a chair.

'Me? No, I think I'll just lie here and look at the view while you bring yourself up to the standard of dress expected in this establishment.'

'Very well. But you promise not to look. Out at the view, I mean.'

'I've suddenly come over all short-sighted. Funny, I can't focus on anything more than six feet away.'

29

'Just as well you're in the front row of the stalls then.'

Anna stood perfectly still for at least a minute, letting her gaze travel downwards from Simon's tousled brown hair, over his rather spare body, strangely vulnerable in its whiteness, noting the curly texture and darker brown of the hair that began just below the navel. She leaned forward and placed her fingers on his knee, pushing it slightly to one side. His other leg responded also, in the opposite direction. Simon had never gone through this kind of appraisal before, but recognised it as the perfectly legitimate feminine equivalent of male pleasure in the sight of a lover's body. But how few women ever allowed themselves to admit that the sight of a man's body could arouse them. He loved her directness, openness, absence of hang-ups. His approval showed itself as the pink bud emerged from the nest. Anna reached up and undid the thin strap that ran from the bottom of her deep cleavage to the nape of her neck. But instead of lowering the top, she stood there with her fingers intertwined behind her head, and began to shake her breasts, at first slowly, and then with a faster rhythm. The flimsy material, finding no reason not to respond to gravity, inched its way down over the rounded contours, rested momentarily upon her nipples, which boasted surprisingly large, tan areolas, then came to rest on her hips. She transferred the gyration to the only area still covered, but turned her back to Simon, who watched with intense concentration as her small firm buttocks shook off their gauze. The garment fell to the floor. Still with her back to him, Anna slowly bent down and released her feet from the encumbrance. Then she swivelled round and did a deep curtsey. Simon clapped his hands silently.

'That was beautiful.'

'I can see you liked the performance. It's good to be appreciated.'

He held out his hand to her, and she lay down beside him. Now it was his turn to move. His lips brushed the lightly perfumed skin of her neck, shoulders, in between her breasts, around the navel, as far as the mass of very blond

30

pubic hair. Then he turned round, straddled her, and kissed her shapely ankles and legs, lingering behind her knees until his tongue made her laugh, and then on to the final lap. Anna began to moan as his tongue parted her lips, but he silently indicated the need for quiet. Some inquisitive rival might come and ask if she was feeling ill. This only served to make her response even more passionate, as her mouth and tongue reciprocated his explorations. Their mutual desire to give pleasure as much as receive it, and the long moments spent simply gazing into each other's eyes whilst he moved minimally within her, were an expression of human warmth and tenderness which neither had experienced before.

It was some time before they appeared beside the pool, looking very pleased with themselves.

The remaining guests, including Floris Schoenheimer, drifted in during the afternoon, and either retired semi-prostrate with the heat to their air-conditioned bedrooms, or cooled down in the pool. Lady Constance was among the latter, and even managed to get a gallant trio to join her for a desultory foursome on the tennis court as soon as the sun had begun its downward path behind the trees, whose shadows sprawled listlessly across the lawns.

It was not until seven-thirty that the whole party met for the first time. Bryce Trevelyan took Simon by the arm and led him over to a wizened little man who was engrossed in a book he had just taken down from one of the bookcases lining the walls.

'James, I'd like you to meet a fellow-academic, Dr. Prestcott. Simon, this is Professor Emeritus James Lebrecht.'

Lebrecht held out a bony claw and fastened his bright and still clear eyes on Simon, who was somewhat nonplussed, as he had been under the impression Lebrecht was long dead.

'I'm very honoured to meet you, Professor,' he said, with sincerity. The history of the early church was not his strong point, but his general interest in the history of religions had brought Lebrecht's name before his eyes many times. Lebrecht motioned to him to sit beside him.

'I don't want to keep you from the charming company of that lovely young lady.' He smiled, nodded knowingly, then went on: 'Our host tells me you are an historian. What is your field?'

'I'm afraid I'm not a pure historian at all, if such a thing exists. In fact, I'm a renegade psychologist, and only turned to history when I found my own subject had become too statistical and arid to hold any more real interest for me. So now I work in a field much maligned by historians — psycho-history, the application of the so-called science of the mind to the dead and buried.'

Lebrecht stared at Simon seriously for a full half-minute, nodding his head so slightly that Simon did not know whether he was approving him or suffering from Parkinson's disease. Then he murmured: 'And what light have you psycho-historians thrown on Jesus Christ?'

Simon chuckled. 'One might wonder what there could possibly be to say that is new, after sixty thousand or more biographies devoted to Jesus. Everyone who writes about him seems to have a different purpose. We've got through the Bruno Bauer stage of thinking Jesus was nothing but the product of the collective imagination of the early Christians, that he was a mythical figure who never existed historically speaking...'

'Yes, yes,' Lebrecht cut in impatiently, 'I know about all that, but what have you to add to our understanding of him?'

'Well, this isn't really my speciality, you know, Professor. I'm not trying to duck the question, but the eighteenth century is my hunting ground, not early Christianity. I can tell you that a lot has been written about Jesus's motivations at certain times of his life. Why did he leave Galilee, for instance? In order to be killed? He must have known what would happen in Jerusalem, so he committed a form of suicide. That fits in with the view that some have taken of Jesus as a psychopathological case, even a classical case of paranoia. When he heard about John the Baptist being the precursor of the Messiah, he began to think of himself as the one who must follow. Then there are the forty days in the wilderness — wild hallucinatory stuff up there. And the way he uses "I" so much — rather megalomaniac, it's been thought.'

'But that is all old now,' Lebrecht shook his head sadly. 'I think Albert Schweitzer dealt with such interpretations many, many years ago, when I was still a student.'

Simon was somewhat abashed. There must have been more up-to-date work on Jesus, but he didn't know of it. Lebrecht saw he was unhappy with himself, and came to the rescue.

'Tell me something about your own work, then.'

Simon smiled gratefully. 'At the moment I'm trying to write a psycho-biography of Voltaire — applying explicit personality theory to certain key phases of his life. That's what makes psycho-biography different, I suppose: all biographers use psychological intuition in a more or less commonsense way, but we apply specialised psychological data and methods to the same information about the man. I think I've got a job for life,' he sighed, 'with a hundred volumes of his works and a hundred more of correspondence to work on.'

'So your real interest is in French history?'

'French anything,' replied Simon. 'I am half-French, you see, so it's only to be expected.'

'I wonder, then,' Lebrecht began, 'if you have ever heard of...'

At that moment the doors of the library were flung open. In strode Lady Constance, looking bronzed and bouncy in a white off-the-shoulder dress that she knew she wore well, holding Floris Schoenheimer by the hand.

'I'm sorry we are a bit late, everybody,' she announced, in that jagged, brassy, infiltrating voice that so many strong-minded Australian women seem to adopt, perhaps as part of their offensive against the macho put-down attitude of a lot of their men-folk. 'Our guest of honour was sleeping it off after his television interview this afternoon.'

Floris looked about him, and saw eleven other people present. His hostess began introducing him. He did not want to meet them or anyone else. He should not be here. Anna came over and kissed him on the cheek, fondly.

'Hello, Daddy. You look tired. How did it go?'

He shook his head and smiled wanly. That was all he could say for the moment. It had not gone well. He should have known better than to agree to be on a chat show on a commercial channel, but he had stupidly thought that Australian television could not be as bad as American. Gerry MacLean had to keep up his ratings, and he wasn't going to do that by seeming to take a nutter like Doctor Schoenheimer seriously before a live audience of five hundred and possibly a million viewers.

'Now, *Doctor* Schoenheimer, you work with hypnosis, right? Yeah. And you say you can take people back to, er, lives they've had before, as somebody else somewhere? Yeah. Isn't that bonza, ladies and gennlemen, you too can know what it was like to be Napoleon, owny you might meet your Waterloo while you're under the influence!'

'There are some dangers, which is why these out-of-body experiences must be supervised by...'

'You bet, and I can think of an even worse danger, *Doctor* — if you put me under, how do I know I won't wake up a cocker spaniel?'

Schoenheimer had waited till the laughter died down, then said quietly, 'That might be an improvement.'

A bad mistake, that. Gerry MacLean got the laughs on this programme. He wasn't going to forgive that one. His considerable powers of destructive ridicule, learned in the gutters of student journalism, crappy Sunday papers and creeping, crawling commercial T.V., were mustered and aimed with deadly accuracy, like a barrister taking a witness to pieces with all the skills of timing, twisting, deliberate misunderstanding, knowing looks, raised eyebrows and smirks. Fortunately, Schoenheimer had been easily able to keep his temper, but he felt he had not made a single convincing statement. The laughter of five hundred people was still ringing in his ears. He did not want to meet more of them, to have to go through the same questions, the same mockery and disbelief. But he had not been able to escape. Sir Bryce's car had picked him up at the studio, and he had been whisked away to the depths of the countryside, feeling unreal, somehow, unattached to the world around him, floating on a tide that was in charge for the time being. He knew better than to try to resist it.

Connie took Floris round the room. First he was introduced to Robert Macdonald, a neighbouring farmer, bluff, large, no-nonsense, twenty thousand acres; his wife, Sheila, tall, bony and well-scrubbed; Geoffrey Paton, smooth, dark-jowled, balding but with his remaining hair plastered over the defoliated patches, loud voice and roving eye — a National Party Member of the Legislative Assembly of Victoria, and his smart, regulation-issue politician's wife, Maree. Then came Fuad Riad, a dapper diplomat from Egypt, and his exotic, tough-looking wife, name not clear. Blake Pascoe he knew already, a rather silly but inoffensive young man with too blond hair and an excitable laugh. Then Floris's eye caught an interesting-looking, ancient relic, scribbling something on the back of a visiting card. Next to him was that young man who came with Anna. They smiled and acknowledged each other across the gentle hum. Simon had just drifted over to join the Schoenheimers and the beautiful Blake, when the doors opened again. Blake's eyebrows shot up in dismay.

'Oh my God!' he stage whispered, 'Mother's gone and invited Paula!'

'So, who's Paula?' Anna enquired, turning to see the cause of Blake's shock. It was a short, stocky woman with cropped grey hair and horn-rimmed spectacles dangling from a chain round her neck. 'She looks harmless enough.'

'I don't know what your criteria for harmlessness are, Anna, but I think they're in for remodelling this evening. I don't want to prejudice you, of course...'

'No, no! Of course not!' The three of them chorused and laughed.

'...but just bear in mind my considered opinion that she's a ...' Blake switched his thought from devastating to diplomatic in mid-sentence. '... well, an unhappy person.'

Connie went over to greet Paula.

'Paula! We'd almost given you up!'

'Sorry, Connie. Didn't get much notice, you know. You must expect ring-ins to be late. They have other things to do besides get ready for the party.'

The double doors at the other side of the library opened, and dinner was announced before any introductions could take place for Paula. Simon was chagrined to find himself sandwiched between Paula and the farmer's wife, while Anna was installed far away, next to Blake. Floris was seated opposite Simon. Good. At least some conversation was going to be easy.

'How did your interview go this afternoon, Dr. Schoenheimer?' Simon asked innocently.

Floris pulled a face. 'Not good. Not good. I was not on form, I think.'

'Are you talking about your little television chat?' Paula placed her glasses on her nose and squinted at Floris.

'Yes, I'm afraid...'

'Didn't think you did too badly. Considering what a load of old shit you were trying to put over on us. You managed to create an impressive aura of despicability around you.'

Floris was momentarily disconcerted; then his eye caught Simon's, they both thought of Blake's warning, and the tension was relieved by the ghost of a smile.

'That's very kind of you, Miss...Mrs...'

'Just call me Paula, everyone does, and it wasn't kind at all, it was the plain bloody truth. I thought that kind of thing went out with witches. That's why I was late, to be frank. I wanted to see you in action before I met you.'

'Hardly in action. Not even reaction. I was... mmm... run over before I could move.'

Simon thought it was time to change the subject, even though he very much wanted to hear what had happened.

'And do you live nearby, then, er, Paula?' he asked.

Paula glanced at him swiftly, dismissively, over the top of her spectacles, and turned her attention back to her prey.

'Yes. But really, Dr. Schoenheimer, how can you, a person with respectable degrees and proper scientific training, consent to get mixed up with that shady lot of charlatans? It's the kind of thing you expect from a silly little actress like Shirley MacLaine...'

'Oh, you know Shirley MacLaine?'

'No, good grief, course not, but I've read the fiction she passes off as fact about her reincarnations and Mayans from outer space...'

'Well,' said Floris, 'I have met Miss MacLaine, and she is far from silly — or little. An actress, yes. She genuinely believes what she has written in her books about past lives, but I can't tell you if it is all true. Even if it were all true, and supposing everything that I have said and written is completely true, you would still not believe a word of it. Is that not right?'

'Yes, but that's no argument...'

'I'm not saying it is an argument for believing me, or her, or us. I'm simply saying how hard it is to convince anybody by making statements about improbable happenings. Even if you actually witnessed an out-of-body experience, I doubt that you would believe it.'

The farmer's wife joined in. 'Are you talking about reincarnation?'

They were.

'Well,' she said primly, arching her neck turkey-wise, 'the Church certainly doesn't agree with any of that!'

They waited for her to continue, then realised that was it.

'Well, the Church bloody well ought to,' said Paula, waving her fork, 'they're all up to the same trick. Don't you see? It's all a way of making the poor and dispossessed resigned about their miserable state in this life. Don't worry if you're being exploited, my little lambs, just be good and say your prayers and everything will be all right when you're dead. Or...' — looking at Schoenheimer — '... if you're miserable and starving, it's all your own fault, it's just karma, so learn something from the situation and it'll be better next time you're back. You're all in it together.'

'I don't think that Mrs...?' Floris glanced at the turkey.

'Macdonald.'

'...that Mrs. Macdonald would agree that we are on the same side,' said Floris.

'Indeed I would not. Christ purged us from all our sins on the Cross, and we don't need to go on suffering life after life. God tells us that "it is appointed for men to die once, and after this comes judgment," Hebrews Nine, Twenty-seven.'

'I seem to remember,' said Floris, 'that the Bible also says that when a righteous man commits iniquity, none of his righteous deeds shall be remembered. Ezekiel, something...'

'Eighteen, Twenty-four.'

They turned to the source of the interruption; they had not realised that the minute Lebrecht was quietly taking in all that had been said. He went on, 'It always seemed to me that is rather unjust. I must say, as someone who is nearer than any of you to finding out the truth about the after-life, that I don't see all that much difference between the reincarnationist's belief in re-absorption into perfect being, and the Christian's hope of sitting on the right hand of God. They are images of our hope for a better life. What I find rather unpalatable is the idea that after one short spurt of life, for seventy, eighty, ninety years if we are unlucky, we can be sent down to eternal damnation'.

'Well,' sniffed Mrs Macdonald, looking down at him, 'we've all had plenty of warning.'

'But it is so much easier for you and me than for the poor man born into a criminal family with no sense of right and wrong.'

'I expect all that will be taken into account,' she replied. 'The Lord is just.'

'I suppose you know,' Lebrecht said, 'that the early Church found no difficulty with reincarnation. Origen writes that sinners go on being enveloped in different bodies until they reach a state of purification.'

'Yes, everybody knows that since Leslie Weatherhead wrote about it,' Paula cut in.

'I didn't know it,' said Mrs. Macdonald stiffly, 'but I expect it was a heresy the Church soon got rid of.'

'That would be the Roman Catholic church, would it?' Floris asked disingenuously, rightly judging Mrs. Macdonald to be a Presbyterian. She glared at him.

'One thing you seem to be forgetting,' said Simon, 'is that Dr. Schoenheimer doesn't just believe in reincarnation and talk about it: he uses the experience as a form of healing ...'.

'Mumbo-jumbo,' suggested Paula.

'... and the only thing that really matters is, does it work? If he does in fact cure people who can't be cured in any other way, then he's justified.'

'And so are witch doctors, I suppose, and Voodoo curses. Same kind of primitivism,' said Paula.

'Same kind of satanism, you mean,' said Mrs. Macdonald.

Floris Schoenheimer looked at Paula, then at Sheila Macdonald, smiled wearily, and said, 'There is something that I think you ought to give me the credit for, and those who have been given the same kind of ability as I have — perhaps it is a gift, perhaps a punishment. I often think it is a punishment. But those of us who have that gift and have had the privilege of medical training at a high level, have been assailed by all those doubts you express; we know there are many cases of fraud, that often the phenomenon we call out-of-body experience can be explained, or anyway labelled, as mere suggestion, fantasising, free association, satanism, and so on. We have thought deeply about these different possible explanations, and I personally do not think one explanation covers them all.'

He glanced at Sheila Macdonald, and went on, 'I agree with you that in some cases, evil spirits are involved, and that it is very dangerous to meddle with a force of sheer evil that can be terrifying in its power to destroy. On the other hand' (to Paula) 'I have known some cases of so-called possession that have been treated successfully by physical and chemical means. In the state of ignorance we are in at present, no one can really be dogmatic about it. We are ignorant because for hundreds of years, those who had the ability to investigate the spiritual dimension — priests, doctors, psychologists and clairvoyants — have simply shouted at one another instead of pooling their information. We have so little time left to find out anything...'

His voice trailed away, and there was a moment's rather embarrassed silence from the others. Things were going rather better at the other end of the table.

'Are you doing some acting at the moment, Blake?' asked Anna.

Blake roused himself from his lethargic concentration on a spot on the ceiling.

'Ahm, in a way, I suppose you could say I am. Nothing too demanding, but well paid.'

Anna smiled at him. 'It sounds perfect for you. Where can we come and see you?'

'You can't yet. It's a film. A thing called *Evil Angels*. Terrible title. About the Chamberlains.'

Connie chipped in. 'Ah yes, she killed her baby and blamed it on a dingo,' she explained to Anna.

'You mean she was accused of killing her baby,' Bryce Trevelyan corrected her.

'In fact, she was pronounced guilty,' said Blake, 'in one of the most botched and sleazy trials of this century. Up in Darwin. It's the beer and the climate, you know. It turns their brains into pickled porridge.'

Before Connie could make the next obvious point that if a jury had found Lindy Chamberlain guilty then she certainly must have been, Anna asked, 'So what are you playing in this film?'

Undeterred, Connie cut in. 'The dingo.'

Blake sighed and rolled his eyes.

'Yes, I'm playing the back half of the dingo. The front half is played by Sam Neill, who doubles as Michael Chamberlain. They actually wanted Meryl Streep to double as Lindy and the back half of the dingo, all full of Freudian symbolism, you know. But Actors Equity wouldn't let her do it. They said there were plenty of fine Australian actors who could play the back half of a dingo...'

'And what do you really play in this film, Blake?' Bryce asked.

'A pro-Chamberlain journalist. I'm just in the courtroom scenes, sitting behind Meryl most of the time. She's very impressive. Gets the accent spot on. But she kept getting between me and the camera.'

'Why do they call it *Evil Angels*? It seems to brand these Chamberlains as evil from the start.'

'Well, according to the author, John Bryson, who was on set and talked to us about it, the Seventh Day Adventists were called "evil angels" when they started up here.'

'And the Chamberlains are... Adventists?' asked Anna.

'Yes. Michael is even a minister of the church.'

'But I don't understand why they were called evil, then.' Anna was bewildered.

'Well, I don't know much about it,' Blake answered, 'but Bryson said it's the same sort of thing that has happened to small sects for centuries. They have always been called heretics, which is only one remove from evil. There was a famous case in the south of France...the Albi-something-or-others.'

'Truth versus goodness,' Anna murmured. The old story, she thought, looking over at her father, under siege by two formidable-looking worthy ladies.

Paula belatedly turned her attention to Simon.

'What's your position on all this, anyway, Dr. Preston? Are you on the side of the angels, the demons, or the humans?'

'Oh, the humans every time, and it's Prestcott. But then,

I think some humans are angels and some are demons.'

'I see. If you're going to be flippant...'

'On the contrary, I am being serious. Even though I'm a psychologist, I'm still searching for something that lies beyond statistics and probability theory. I don't find the existence of forms of existence beyond the material at all difficult to come to terms with. Even the Russians have now.'

'Oh, you means those poor old leftovers who croon away in the ruins of the Orthodox Church?' said Paula.

'No, I mean Russian psychologists and scientists. They are leading the world now in parapsychology. If they take it seriously, then we'd better believe there's a very good, solid reason for it. Your materialism is rather old-hat, if I may say so, Paula. Whiff of the 'thirties about it!'

Paula bridled, as Simon had intended she should, for there was a limit to the rudeness people should be allowed to get away with, under the guise of frankness.

'I'd like to know your sources,' she said curtly.

These exchanges had been punctuated by the regular intake of excellent food and wines. From his end of the table, Blake had observed the intense discussion going on round Schoenheimer, and was very glad he was out of the way. He had had to face Paula's pet hates on several occasions. One of them was himself, and another was any play that did not have a clear ideological content. Blake was more into Ayckbourn than Brecht or Howard Brenton. He turned to Anna and whispered, 'Your friend seems to be holding his own with those two dragons down there. Mother darling, you weren't very kind to Simon, sticking him between...'

'Blake,' she cut in, 'go and tell Maria we need some more red wine, would you, dear?' He realised he had been saved from making a *gaffe*, as Sheila Macdonald's husband was tuning in.

At nine-thirty, they were all out on the terrace overlooking the lake, drinking their coffee and brandy and becoming relaxed, slowly succumbing to the sheer beauty of the scene. The frogs down by the water were sending up their nocturnal messages of love, the last kookaburra had had the last laugh up in one of the gum trees, the flies had gone home for the night, and the mosquitoes were forming ranks, ready to go on duty. Bryce switched on a blue light that was supposed to entice all misguided insects to sudden, sizzling death. Simon endeavoured to make up for the enforced separation at dinner by sitting next to Anna, but Connie took him firmly by the arm, saying, 'You haven't had a chance to speak to Mr. Riad yet, Simon.' Fuad Riad looked about as pleased as Simon, for he had been on the point of engaging Professor Lebrecht. The latter, on the other hand, was clearly relieved at the intrusion. Why, Simon had no idea. One would think that since Lebrecht had spent a good deal of his working life in Egypt, ferreting out whatever there was to be found in ancient Coptic monasteries, he would welcome the chance to talk to the Egyptian. But instead, he said quickly, 'Excuse me, I have to ask our host something rather important,' and went over to Bryce with tiny steps, like a perambulating skeleton.

'You do not know my country, I think?' Riad asked dutifully.

'No, I'm afraid not,' replied Simon, watching Anna being chatted up by the predatory politician. 'It's a pity, but one can't get everywhere. Unless one's a diplomat. Then I suppose you wish you moved around the world a bit less?'

'Very true. Ah yes. *Le voyage est fatigant à la longue.*' Simon realised that a cultivated Egyptian would be more at home in French than in English. '*Quel est le pays que vous avez aimé le plus au cours de votre carrière, Monsieur?*' he asked.

Riad was delighted to chat in the language in which he had been educated, in Alexandria and in Paris. After a while, he took advantage of a pause to turn and look at Lebrecht.

'*C'est un homme remarquable pour son âge, n'est-ce pas?* You were having a very profound conversation with him in the library.' Riad paused, then went on in an off-hand way, 'Did he mention anything about the work he is doing at the moment?'

Simon felt the casual tension behind the question. Nothing at all, he told him. Surely he was too frail to be actively engaged in research still? Riad shrugged his impeccably dressed shoulders and flashed a smile at Simon.

'*Peut-être,*' he said quietly, then drifted away in a cloud of heavily perfumed cigarette smoke towards Lebrecht who, this time, could not escape.

The Steinway was wheeled over to the wide doorway leading to the terrace, and Anna sat at it. As she took off the golden serpent bracelet she was wearing on her left wrist, Simon thought how vulnerable, almost frail, she looked. Rather predictably, she began to play Debussy's *Clair de lune*. Its ripples drifted effortlessly down to the shimmering waters of the lake, and the soft rustling of the dry silver leaves on the trees merely added noteless harmonies that Debussy would have put in, had he had the instrument to do it. Then Simon realised with a jolt that Anna was going wrong. He knew the piece note for note; there was no doubt, she was muffing it... But it was absolutely right.... She was improvising so perfectly in Debussy's style that his music and hers simply melded together. Gradually, in tiny fragments, Debussy's own music returned, they formed themselves into their recognisable harmonies and arpeggios, and Anna ended the *Clair de lune* as it had been written. The polite applause that followed awoke a few understandably grouchy birds from their precarious slumbers. They fluttered briefly and settled down again. None of the listeners dared to break the silence binding them all together in a way they did not understand.

As house-guests began to move off to their rooms, and visitors headed for home, Simon was at last able to get Anna on her own. 'Care for a stroll?' he suggested. 'Or are you exhausted after such a demanding day? Driving me here. Then driving me mad with passion, then driving me crazy with jealousy with all those other men...'

'For your information, I've only been propositioned once this evening, and he wasn't at all difficult to turn down.'

'Really! Who was that? It must have been that politician bloke. Randy lot, they are. It's all that sitting around listening to speeches — gives them an overactive libido, with lingering lustful longings.'

'They're not as bad as letcherous lecturers, though, don't you think?'

'What about loving lecturers? Or love-lorn ones?'

'I'm not sure I've ever met one. But it could be interesting.'

He took her by the hand, and they descended the path towards the lake. From the windows of the house, several pairs of eyes were watching them, for different reasons, all of which would have surprised Simon and Anna.

'I thought your Debussy variations were staggeringly beautiful,' he said, when they were seated by the water's edge. 'Have you played it before, or were you improvising?'

Anna looked out at the moon's reflexion. 'I have to disappoint you,' she said quietly, 'I didn't compose it. Debussy did.'

Simon was surprised. 'I didn't recognise it. You mean you spliced two pieces together?'

'No. No... Look, Simon...' She took his hand, looked into his eyes questioningly, and away again. 'What I played was what Debussy originally composed.'

'Well I'm damned! I didn't know the old *Clair de lune* was part of a longer piece.'

'Nobody knows.'

'Except you?'

'Except me.'

'So you have an unknown Debussy manuscript. Well

done! Are you going to publish it?' (The academic's first thought.)

'There is no manuscript. He never wrote it down. He just played it. And he played it again tonight. I very rarely allow that kind of thing to happen any more. I don't want to get myself branded as a crank. It could ruin my musical reputation. But tonight, something very strange was happening, so...'

Simon felt that if he had been a smoker, he would have needed a cigarette very badly at that moment. Instead, he let out a long breath between pursed lips.

'Well, well.'

That, ridiculously, was all he could find to say.

Simon was awakened by a furious knocking on his locked door. He struggled to sit up, went over towards the door, and called, 'What's the matter?'

Bryce Trevelyan's voice came from the other side:

'Professor Lebrecht is dead. And Anna has disappeared.'

4

Sunday, 2.30 p.m. The police have been and gone again. What a mess! Initial embarrassment at having to admit that Anna was not so much missing as engaged on secret manoeuvres on the battlefield of my bed. Her father took it very well. Seemed more relieved than anything. But poor old Lebrecht. What a way to go, and all so pointless. He must have been awakened by the burglar, who cracked him over the skull with something hard. I don't think the police have found the object yet. When I dashed out after Sir Bryce to Lebrecht's room, I couldn't believe a room with so little in it could be turned into such chaos. It looked as if every bit of clothing had been torn apart. All the books, some of his and some of the Trevelyans', had been ripped from their covers. The old man was still dressed, in his shirt and trousers, anyway.

The politician chap was most cut up about being involved, as he put it, "in such a sordid affair", and tried to pull rank on the police inspector, who wasn't having any of that. Schoenheimer's reaction to it all was odd: he kept saying 'It's my fault, I could have prevented it.' The Egyptian chappie seems to be quite highpowered. The embassy car had whisked him off as soon as he had been interviewed by the inspector. He and his tough little wife, who spoke no English, provided alibis for each other. As Anna and I did too, the inspector was very discreet about that, the wink he gave me was hardly visible. The Trevelyans were very upset, naturally. By the time the ambulance and the forensic people had come, the press had somehow got wind of it, and the phone was going all the time.

Lady Connie was very level-headed and dealt with them calmly and firmly.

'The professor got in the way of a burglar, by the look of it, and the blow on the head killed him. Probably if it had been me, it would have just given me a nasty bruise, but when you're over ninety...'

That seems to be the way the police are taking it too. When they had gone, the Trevelyans, the Schoenheimers and I sat by the pool and tried to relieve the tension a bit over a bottle of Chablis. Nobody wanted to eat anything. It was then that I remembered Lebrecht had given me his card, just after Schoenheimer arrived, escorted by Lady Connie, in the library. I pulled out my wallet from my back pocket, and extracted the white rectangle:

ALEXANDER LEBRECHT
MA (Sydney), D.Phil (Oxon.), D.Litt (A.N.U.)
Professor Emeritus of Early Church History
City University, Melbourne
42 Lister Grove MELBOURNE 3099

Idly I flipped it over, and looked at the scribbled, shaky writing on the other side. Notes, no doubt. Academics never get out of the habit of making notes on scraps of paper, knowing only too well that the best ideas vanish as magically as they sprint across the mind. At first I could make nothing of the few pencilled words:

bibl.BT.
4 vert 3 hor
pres interr elec

That was the best I could do with them. They meant nothing. A reference of some sort, obviously: 'bibl.' would clearly be a Bible, given Lebrecht's speciality. Then four green and three...*hors presse* ! That meant copies of an edition not for sale to the public. Good. Then: interrupt?

And 'election' or 'electric'. I gave up, or was about to when Anna and her father came over to where I was sitting by the pool. I showed them the card.

'When did he give you this?' asked Floris (he has asked me to drop handles, which is nice). I told him, just after he came into the library. He then said quite firmly that the message was for me, personally. He had seen Lebrecht writing on the card as he came in. Anna took it and held it. She asked me what we were talking about just prior to that, and I racked my brain for something specific — there had been so much talking, most of it rather bad-tempered, during the evening.

'I told him that I was working on French psycho-history, on Voltaire... and he asked me if I knew anything about ...'

'About whom?' asked Floris.

I didn't know.

'He never finished the sentence. You came in, and ...'

'And then he got out the card and wrote on the back of it, for you,' said Floris.

I looked at the card with renewed interest.

'We did talk about psycho-histories of Christ. That could be the Bible bit,' I mused. But BT? I looked over at the deck chair which Connie had vacated a few minutes before, to organise some lunch for us all, as the staff seemed disinclined to put themselves out, and I gazed at the bathing towel she had left there, draped over the arm. In one corner were the embroidered letters **C.T.** — Constance Trevelyan. And... Bryce Trevelyan — **B.T.** Did he have a Bible? I went from the terrace into the library. For some moments I saw nothing, until my eyes adjusted from the brilliant sunshine. I went over to the spot where Lebrecht and I had been talking. In fact, I now recalled he had been looking at the books there just as I was taken over to be introduced to him. The room was very dark on that side — my eyes were still not functioning right for indoors.

So I decided to switch on the light. I looked for the switch, and the moment I put my hand on it, everything clicked. Like an electric shock. I had just told him I was half-French, so he had written to me in French! I re-read the card: *Bibliothèque Bryce Trevelyan.* Yes, I was in his library. Now, what were *vert* and *hor* ? Wait: *près*, near, *interrupteur électrique*, near the electric switch. O.K. That's were I was. Were there four green books? But he had written the word in the singular, not the plural. Not an adjective, then. Neither was *hor*. Vert...ical, and horizontal? My eye travelled up four shelves, counting from the floor. And three books in from the switch. It was a large, bound book on contract law, slightly out of place. I took it off the shelf, and opened the front cover. Inside it I saw a piece of folded paper, very thick, like cartridge paper. I unfolded it, and tried to read it. It was in French, not in Lebrecht's hand, very difficult to decipher. I shall have to work on it when I get home, with a magnifying glass. But why did poor old Lebrecht go to all that trouble to tell me where to find it? I suddenly felt rather faint as I realised why. The books pulled to pieces in his room, covers and bindings torn off... He had known someone in the house was after this paper, and he was just as determined he or she or they should not get it. But who? The only person I can be sure of is Anna. But can I? If it was her father, she must know what he was after. Was Schoenheimer capable of such a brutal killing? But the attacker had probably not intended to kill him, just to knock him out. The Trevelyans had actually got Lebrecht there, in their house, where he would be a more easy prey than in his own home. And those Egyptian people. Now then, there's a thing: Lebrecht was quite clearly anxious not to have anything to do with Mr.... what was it?... Ruad, or something. And he, Ruad, no, Riad, quizzed me about Lebrecht's work. Another nasty thought, though: if it was in fact an inside job, the attacker would have intended to kill Lebrecht, otherwise he would have identified him when he came round. Question is, what do I do with this manuscript? I quickly stuffed it in my inside pocket in the library before anyone else saw it. Should I tell the police about it? Lebrecht had intended it for me, for my eyes. I owe it to him to at least decipher it and see why he thought it so important.

*

On the Monday morning Simon was plunged so deeply into the problems of the Unit that he more or less forgot the drama of the past weekend and the manuscript, which he placed in an envelope and asked the Unit's Secretary, Margo Plumb, to place in the safe in the office, together with the petty cash and the examination papers which were to be sat the following week by the students who were, at this very moment, attempting to cram into their heads the contents of their incomprehensible notes, which they had failed to write up regularly despite repeated advice.

The Unit's problems were caused partly by internal squabbles and partly by external pressures. Internally, there was a deep rift between those who were trained as scientists and those who had received arts and humanities training. The former saw clearly which way the wind was blowing, and wanted to get the Unit quickly and solidly accepted as part of the Science Faculty; this was where all the Research Funds were being siphoned off to. The Arts people could not even understand the application form for a research grant any more — it referred to things like "unit costs for research teams". All the philosophers and historians wanted was time and an Apple Mac. They were clearly not serious; in fact, they were an embarrassment and a liability. That was one problem. Another, stemming from the first, was the matter of the next Head. Bristow was, like Simon, going off on study leave. The new Chairperson would reign for three years, and would have to represent and defend the Unit from the sniping and cannon-fire from Canberra, which, like the British government, was seeking out small and vulnerable university departments to get rid of — especially those which did not come under the general heading of "USEFUL TO AUSTRALIAN SOCIETY".

It was therefore vital, in the opinion of several colleagues, to have a head that was screwed on scientifically and had

51

been awarded the Official Seal of Bureaucratic Excellence by the Registrar, ex-Brigadier Thornycroft. That undoubtedly meant Dr. Michael O'Neddy, who was as Irish as a kangaroo, but disappeared into a cloud of Jamesons every St. Patrick's Day. He was also the ex-manager of a mine in Western Australia, and knew about geology and interfaces. Hence his rugged visage, which resembled, on its good days, a deflated football searching for a shoulder to rest on. He was not everybody's favourite, however, largely on account of his somewhat limited intellectual horizons.

The only opponent that could be found was Dr. Victorine Crow, who was using this as a lever to bolster her case, in competition with Simon, for a Senior Lectureship — since only in exceptional circumstances could a mere Lecturer be made Chairperson. The remaining members of the Unit were either non-voting junior staff or tutors or, in one case, a Reader on the point of retirement. Thus, Simon was in a rather delicate position; delicate to the point of abstention, he thought. Either candidate spelled doom and disaster to him, personally, since O'Neddy included him among the Poms, all of whom he cordially sent to hell and damnation with every visit to Jimmy Watson's bar; and the Crow, on the other hand, directed towards him feelings of great ambivalence, since she regarded him at one and the same time as utterly frivolous and a dangerous rival.

It was with considerable dismay that he found a small delegation of colleagues at his door on the Monday morning. Dr. Grace Morgan explained why they had come. She was the Reader, the next in seniority below the professor, and it had been assumed that her retirement at the end of the coming year would make her uninterested in the future of the Unit. However, it appeared not to be the case. She, and the others present, and one person who could not be present, had a plan which could get the Unit out of an intolerable prospect: that of having to choose between Dr. O'Neddy and and Dr. Crow.

'We should like you to agree to be nominated,' she said.

'But I can't,' said Simon with alarm, 'I'm going on leave in January for seven months.'

'Ah, but that does not place you beyond the pale, I'm afraid,' said Dr. Morgan with a wicked smile. 'You see, I am not altogether out of the race yet. I've been Chairman before now and I know the ropes. I'm willing to be Acting Chairman — Person if you must — while you're on leave. Then you take over when you come back. How does that grab you?'

Simon felt he was being well and truly grabbed. If he agreed, he would open himself to the animosity of both the pseudo-Irishman and the Crow, with his main support due to retire at the end of the year. He voiced his doubts.

'I think I can assure you that your promotion would have the support of the most senior member of the Unit,' she said.

'I'm sure that's very gratifying. It's a bit like being told God is on your side as you're about to be thrown into a snakepit on your way to the lions' cage. Anyway, he only has one vote like the rest. I can't see where the numbers would come from. With three contenders cancelling each other out by voting for himself or herself, or else abstaining...'

'Exactly. The other two have been depending entirely on the hope that his or her opponent is the less popular choice. You haven't been thought of as a runner till now, because you won't be here for half the year. But if I fill in...'

'Yes, well, why don't you fill in for Bristow? We could re-elect him.'

'He won't do it. He's done eight years of it and he won't stand for another term of office.'

Simon was assailed by conflicting emotions; on the one hand he was flattered that someone as sensible and experienced as Grace Morgan should have faith in him, but on the other, he was appalled at the prospect of the jealousy and animosity that would certainly ensue if he were elected. His thoughts were interrupted by a knock at his door. He went over to open it just wide enough to tell whoever it was to come back later. It was Margo Plumb, all breathless, pert and anxious to please.

'Excuse me, Simon, but I saw this lying in your pigeon-hole, and I thought it might be important.'

He took the letter. It was a crumpled envelope, with the stamp upside down. He turned it over and saw that it had been stuck down with a piece of Elastoplast. He thanked Margo, and then glanced at the front again. The envelope had been used twice. The first name and address had been scored through and his own added over... in Lebrecht's handwriting. It had gone first to the Department of History, because that is where Lebrecht had sent it to. Someone there had written 'TRY Hist. Sci. & Ideas Unit' in the top left-hand corner. Try, indeed! He'd only been in it for seven years. He put the letter in a drawer of his desk and tried to concentrate on the question of the succession.

'Look, Grace, could I think this over for a day or two? I'm very honoured to be asked, especially by you and the others here. But I need to weigh up a few things.'

'Yes, of course, I quite understand. But the closing date for nominations is Friday, don't forget.'

'No, I won't. I'll come to a decision by then. I may need to talk to you again,' he added, as they went out.

Simon immediately took out the letter. It was very strange to be looking at the writing of Lebrecht, like a message from beyond the grave. He carefully levered up the sticking plaster, and pulled out the contents. It was a cheque for thirty thousand dollars, drawn on an account with the Vicwest Bank, Collins Street, Melbourne. On the back Lebrecht had written: 'For expenses incurred on mission.' Mission! What mission! The old man must have gone a bit dotty at the end. But how on earth did he manage to send it? He couldn't possibly have posted it in a mail box that night. How did they get their mail posted at Whitegates, he wondered. He picked up the telephone and asked for directory enquiries. A few minutes later, he was speaking to Lady Connie.

'I just wanted to thank you for ... um ... a very interesting weekend, Lady Constance...'

'Connie. And please don't thank me. It was terrible. The

police have been in and out of the place ever since, asking questions about us and the staff—and the guests. Even you. I couldn't tell them much about you.'

'Just as well,' he laughed. 'Ah, by the way, I very nearly wrote to you instead of phoning, but then I thought you might only get one delivery a week out there in the wilds. How do you get mail ... and send letters out, and so on?'

'Oh we're quite civilised really, you know. We have a helicopter drop once a month and the Flying Doctor takes our mail with him. No, I'm sorry for teasing you. We just put our letters on a silver tray in the hall, and they get whisked away by one of the staff, whoever's getting stores in from Healesville that day. And they bring mail back with the champagne and caviare supplies. You townies always think we're cut off from the world out here, I know.'

He thanked her again, commiserated about poor old Lebrecht, and rang off. So he had gone down during the night and put his letter on the tray. Had he survived the night, he would have had time to recover the letter before breakfast, especially as it was Sunday, and no one would be rushing out to get supplies. But what in heaven's name was he supposed to do with $30,000? It was a whole year's salary to him. But hang on ... he couldn't take the cheque to the bank now. Lebrecht's account would have been frozen on his death. Only his executors could release money, and they would obviously want to know why Lebrecht made over so much money just before getting clobbered. Simon realised he might as well tear the cheque up. But he didn't. He put it back in the envelope, and for the first time looked at it. It had originally been addressed to Lebrecht at his Melbourne address. There were stamps under the one Lebrecht had stuck on—a 90 cent stamp instead of a 39 cent one, obviously the only one he happened to have. Simon carefully peeled off the 90 cent stamp, and revealed French stamps underneath. The original postmark had been partly obliterated by the Healesville Post Office, but he could just make out 'Montpellier'. He then inspected the Elastoplast again, and pulled it gently off the flap. Underneath was a round rubber-stamp mark: 'BIBLIOTHEQUE PUBLIQUE DE MONTPELLIER', and in the centre, the initials 'J.F.'

Just as he was about to leave his office, Simon's telephone rang. He hoped it was Anna, calling from Adelaide. It was not.

'Ah, Simon. Vikki here. I think it would be nice if we had a little chat, don't you?'

No, I don't, you manipulative bitch. 'Yes, by all means, Vikki. But not today. Possibly not tomorrow. I'm absolutely tied up for a bit.'

'Not with the police, I hope?'

'What do you mean?'

'Oh, I read in the paper you were present at a murder over the weekend.'

'Not exactly present, Vikki. Sorry not to be able to give you the gory details. You'll have to ask my accomplice.'

'I didn't mean that, silly.'

Silly sounded like a foreign word, coming from Dr. Crow. As if she had suddenly called him '*Mon chou*'. Before leaving, he rescued the manuscript from Margo's safe, and carefully put it in his inside pocket, together with the cheque. On the way home, on foot as usual, he called in at his favourite delicatessen for food to eat whilst watching television. He put down his briefcase in order to get to his wallet, and was annoyed when a couple of men elbowed past him to get to the cashier first.

'Er, excuse me, you can't push in like that. Wait your turn.'

One of the men turned on him and snarled, 'What for you so bleeding slow? We gotta hurry, you taka too long finda your money.'

The cashier refused to deal with the queue-crashers, so they dumped their purchases on the counter and walked out expostulating loudly in what sounded like Italian. Simon and the cashier agreed that it had been very odd, since friendliness and courtesy were the norm among the Italian community round Carlton. Simon paid, clutched his purchases, and bent to pick up his briefcase. It was gone.

His hand flew to his pocket. The papers were still there.

He was actually quite relieved to see a police car sitting on the other side of the road, close to his flat.

'Are you Dr. Prestcott, Simon Prestcott?'

'Yes, I am. Would you like to come in?'

'You don't seem surprised to see me, sir.'

'No, I'm really quite glad. I've just had a very unpleasant experience. It's saved me having to phone you to report it, Mr....?'

'Detective-Inspector Sherlock, sir. And spare me the humour.'

They went inside, Simon poured himself a stiff drink, Inspector Sherlock declined. Simon recounted what had happened in the delicatessen.

'This isn't really what I came to see you about, Dr. Prestcott. I'm more interested in the death of Professor Lebrecht at the moment.'

'I can understand that, Inspector. But the two things might be linked.'

'What makes you think that, sir?'

'I think they were after something they thought Lebrecht might have given me before he was killed.'

'What would that be?'

Simon took the papers out of his pocket. 'These. Or more particularly, this.' He unfolded the manuscript, which Sherlock looked at, shaking his head.

'Could you explain what this is all about, Dr. Prestcott?'

Simon told him everything that had happened to date: the card, the message, the manuscript, the cheque. When he saw the cheque, Sherlock whistled.

'What expenses? What mission?' he asked.

'My words exactly, Inspector,' said Simon. 'The answer to that probably lies in this manuscript. I haven't had a chance to decipher it yet.'

'Could you work off a photocopy?'

'A good, clear one, yes. You'll want to keep the original,

I suppose.'

'Yes, I will. The cheque and the visiting card as well, if you don't mind.'

'I don't know what to do about the cheque,' said Simon.

'You're quite sure you have no idea what he wanted you to do? He didn't talk about any kind of job he wanted done, research, or anything like that?'

'No. Nothing. At one point, he was about to ask me if I knew anything about someone or other, but we were interrupted.'

'And he never referred to it again?'

'Never had the chance, poor old fellow.'

Simon said he would like to work on it that evening if possible, so the inspector took it to the station, had a photocopy made, and asked a uniformed policeman to come back with it. As he was about to leave, the policeman said, 'Inspector Sherlock said to tell you it would be good idea to make sure all your windows and doors are properly locked.'

'Thank you, officer. Very reassuring.'

'No worries, mate. You've got our number down at the station, have you?'

Simon made a careful note of it.

When he had finished his meal, Simon began to work on the almost illegible photocopy, cursing his not being able to use the clearer original. After about two hours, he had filled in most of the gaps in his transliteration. It was, he judged, mid-eighteenth century, or a bit later on account of the style. He then translated it, for Inspector Sherlock, reflecting that it could do no harm if he owed him one. Simon typed out two copies:

certain that but for the letter of the Pasha Ismael not only my entry to this most ancient of monasteries would have remained an impossibility, but also the extreme trust and hospitality extended to me by these austere if ignorant

*holy men, I have sent away my drivers and camels, who
had been obliged to camp outside the walls, there being
no gateway into the monastery for the preservation of
their security against Muslims and roving brigands. The
monks have assured me that they will provide me and my
faithful dragoman with a safe escort back to Cairo. I
have partaken of their simple food with pleasure, and
this, together with the simplicity of my garb (which in
truth is explained solely by my fear of being robbed of my
jewellery and watches had I not left them with my friends
in Cairo) appears to have disposed the Abbot in my
favour, since he was convinced that all Frenchmen are
demons and that their desire to read books is inspired by
Satan himself. Today, however, I am to be allowed to
spend several hours in the library. It must be many years
since it was last opened, since piles of trestle tables,
benches and cupboards, are being moved in order to
discover the doorway. The Abbot himself despaired for
some time yesterday of being able to find the key, whose
great size, when it was finally found, would seem proof
against loss.*

---

*I have at last finished my visit to the library, and can
scarcely prevent the shaking of my hand, so great is the
emotion that has moved my heart and soul this day. What
revelations! What joys! I am still suffocated with tears as
I write. When the great Dom Bernard Montfaucon wrote
of the treasures still to be found in ancient places in the
Levant, little did he suspect what would be found here.
I do not speak only of the manuscripts, priceless beyond
all consideration, of Polybius, Diodorus, Pausanius,
Herodas, and above all the <u>Hypotyposeis</u> of Clement of
Alexandria, long ago believed lost, but I speak of the
ineffable mystery to which I have been a witness, I alone,
since my dragoman was so overcome that he lost
consciousness and can recall nothing. Know then — but
who shall ever read these words, for I am bound to keep*

them to myself for the rest of my days — that I was suddenly driven by the urge to remove to one side, with my dragoman's assistance, a large chest of thick wood which, judging from the dust around it, had been not been moved for many hundreds of years. Behind it, the wall was not solid, but of loose, very heavy stone blocks. There was now little light in the room, for the sun was nearing the end of its daily course, hence I was surprised to notice how light was this part of the wall. The stones themselves appeared luminous, imbued with a gentle but uncertain glow, as if from within. This became stronger, then weaker, then stronger, by turns, and it was at this point my assistant reeled and sank to the ground. Having assured myself that he lived still, and being unable to rouse him, I turned again to the wall, which by now had reached an intensity of illumination quite indescribable. I longed to see what lay behind, and the stones, which I would never ...

There it ended.

5

Does life really consist of long periods of tedium and routine punctuated by occasional frantic crises when everything seems to converge and become inextricably complex? Or is the potential for multiple crisis always with us, but most of the time we fail to respond to it? For the last two or three years, Simon's life had moved slowly and boringly from one small task to the next. And now, within a week, he had had his peace of mind disturbed, to put it mildly, by, in order of importance, the Schoenheimers, Lebrecht, and Grace Morgan. In some way, which he did not comprehend, they were connected to each other. Well, yes, they all concerned him, so of course they had something in common.

The most disruptive element of them all telephoned about half an hour after he had finished typing his translation of the manuscript. She was leaving Adelaide the following day, with her father, for Perth, and would be back in Melbourne at the weekend.

'I can't tell you how much I look forward to that.'

'So do I,' Anna replied.

'Do you really mean that?' he asked, 'because I'd rather you didn't say things like that just to be polite or say what you think I'd like to hear.'

'Simon, darling, I shall feel a whole person again only when I'm with you. You must believe that. I have been trying to put away from me the awful, numbing thought that in a week's time I shall have to leave and go back to London.'

'Do you have to? I mean, can't you stay here a bit longer by yourself? We could go over together next month.'

There was a reflective pause the other end. 'I can see a

few problems, matters that would have to be sorted out quickly. But it's a terrific idea.'

'Then we could get a ship, and go back via Sydney, Auckland, Dunedin, Brisbane, Noumea, Montevideo, the Panama Canal...'

'That's going the wrong way...'

'No it isn't, it's the best route. East to West through the Panama Canal, Hawaii, Perth, Bombay, Capetown, the Canaries, past Gibraltar to Marseilles. Then — let's see, it would be about April by then, so we'd get you another shiny BMW with a scratch on it, and drive to Montpellier, because I've got a little job to do there, then meander through the Loire valley, a slight detour over to the Romantische Strasse, along the Mosel, chase a few mosquitoes in Bruges and pose for the hartists in a horse-drawn cab, get a boat at Ostend and be in London in no time at all. It's the only way to travel.'

'Ah, I see through you now. You own a travel agency and you want more business.'

'I'd forgo half my discount, how's that?'

'I'll think about your offer. But there might be someone else who would give me all the discount.'

'You drive a hard bargain, Miss Schoenheimer. But you're worth any sacrifice. So long as you take out your insurance with me too.'

'You've no idea what risk you would be letting yourself in for. Like poor Dr. Lebrecht. If he had known the risk of going to the Trevelyans last weekend... Is there anything new about that awful business?'

Simon told her about the manuscript and the cheque.

'This is getting very serious,' she said when he had finished. 'But what was in the manuscript? Who wrote it?'

He said he preferred to show her when she got back to Melbourne. 'Otherwise, you simply won't believe it. You'll think I'm making it up or teasing you. It's... just too incredible.'

The trivial necessities of this existence demanded attention. At 9 a.m. sharp the following morning, Wednesday, he received a phone call from Michael Bristow, asking him to please see him at 2 p.m. He would not say why.

Then when his mail arrived, he found a letter from Underwood, Clissold, Pyke and Bentham, Solicitors, asking him to contact their office at his earliest convenience. He telephoned immediately, and made an appointment with Mr. Pyke (Senior) at ll a.m. Just as he was about to leave for the City, Inspector Sherlock arrived.

'I was wondering if you had had a chance to look at that manuscript, Dr. Prestcott,' he said.

'Yes, of course. Sorry, I should have brought this round for you.' He gave him a copy of his translation.

'Do you know who wrote it?' asked Sherlock.

'No idea. I wish I did. It would make a lot of things much clearer. Look, Inspector, I've got an appointment with some solicitors now, something to do with that cheque...'

'Yes, I know you have. We'll go there together, shall we?'

It was difficult to refuse, in the circumstances.

Mr Pyke was mercifully businesslike. It seemed that he was one of the trustees of the Chelbert Research Trust, which had been founded by the late Professor Lebrecht.

'I received a very brief and mysterious telephone call last Saturday evening at my home from someone purporting to be Professor Lebrecht,' he explained to them, 'asking me to write to one Dr. Simon Prestcott of the History Department at the City University. That would have been a few hours prior to his death, it seems. In view of the gravity of the situation,' he said apologetically to Simon, 'I judged it advisable to inform the police. Now, Dr. Prestcott, could you kindly tell us what this is all about?'

'Me?' There was no question of the sincerity of Simon's surprise. 'I was hoping you'd be throwing some light on this.' He pulled out the copy of the cheque and gave it to Pyke, who registered no surprise. Not the faintest levitation of an eyebrow. Very professional.

'You will have noticed that the cheque you received has 'CHELBERT TRUST ACCOUNT.' printed upon it,' he said to Simon.

'No, I'm sorry, I hadn't noticed. Perhaps in my haste I turned the anagram back in my mind to "Lebrecht".'

'Very possibly,' Pyke nodded politely. 'We are, of course, deeply perturbed by the manner of the Professor's death, and there is much to be explained.' He paused. 'Including the reason why practically his last living act was to make over a large sum of money to you.'

'I'm as mystified as you are. What is this Trust?'

'It is registered as a charitable trust, specifically for the application of science to religious knowledge. All its funds have accrued, over more than fifty years, from the proceeds of Professor Lebrecht's own investments, books and lecture tours.'

'I'd never heard of it,' said Simon.

'It is registered and listed in all the required and proper places,' replied Mr. Pyke, as if seeing a cause for reproach in Simon's remark. 'But there have been very few applicants who met the stringent desiderata laid down by the Founder. He alone is ... was empowered to approve funding, with myself or the other trustee concurring. In the case of disagreement, the third would have a casting vote.'

'Who is the third trustee, Mr. Pyke?' asked Sherlock.

'That, I am not at liberty to divulge before a candidate,' he said, looking down his nose at them both.

'But I'm not a candidate' said Simon. 'I didn't seek this honour, I had it thrust upon me. I'm not even sure I want it. Did you see what was on the back of the cheque?'

'I have a photocopy of it here,' replied Pyke, picking up a paper from his desk. 'Do you have any idea what Professor Lebrecht meant by "mission"?'

Simon paused. No one was going to believe that weird piece of writing. And it was not certain there was any connexion.

'I'd rather Inspector Sherlock answered that,' he replied.

The inspector looked startled. 'Me? I don't know.'

'Then perhaps the time has come for you both to hear the contents of the second thing Professor Lebrecht left me. If there's a connexion, I'm sure you can be trusted to see it.'

Sherlock unfolded the typescript and began to read it out. At first, Pyke was restless and impatient, but by the end he was reduced to stupefaction.

'You say Lebrecht gave you that?'

'It wasn't quite as simple as that. I had to work out some clues to get it. The inspector has them.'

Sherlock brought out a photocopy of the visiting card, front and back. They both pored over the scribbled message.

'There is no doubt that is Professor Lebrecht's handwriting,' said Pyke. 'I have known it for many years. But I confess...'

They both gave up. So Simon explained how he had worked it out, and concluded:

'I'm sorry to say that it looks as though Lebrecht realised that evening he was in a very dangerous situation, and had to make sure the manuscript got into trustworthy hands. Then, he realised no one could afford to follow this matter through unless he had adequate funds, so he provided them from the trust. I have enquired, by the way,' Simon looked at Sherlock half-apologetically, 'what would have happened to the letter. If he had got up hale and hearty for breakfast, he could have picked up the letter from the hall and destroyed it. Then he could have recovered the manuscript from the library nice and quietly, and I would never have given a second thought to the scribbles on the back of the card.'

The others looked at each other and nodded in agreement. Pyke picked up a paper-clip and began to unwind it. 'Might I ask if you understand why Professor Lebrecht should have had so much confidence in your ability to pursue this... matter? Did he know you already?'

'No. I knew of his work, I had an interest in it, we were able to talk easily about it, and he asked me about the sort of work I was doing. They're not at all close. I'm not a specialist in religions or the church or anything like that. I'm just a psychologist turned historian. He seemed to like that combination, but that's all I can say. And I'm half-French — that's why he gave me that very difficult-to-decipher piece of eighteenth-century French, I suppose,' — looking down primly — 'which was made very much more difficult because I didn't have the original to work on.'

Sherlock coughed and smiled. 'Sorry about that. Regulations about evidence, you know... After all, we are dealing with a brutal murder.'

'And theft,' said Simon. He had scarcely given his stolen briefcase a thought, mainly because it had contained nothing of value, just three books that the University Library would charge him for.

Sherlock frowned. 'That little episode begins to take on a distinctly suspect configuration now. Can you describe those two characters?'

Simon cast his mind back. 'They could have been anything Mediterranean in origin. One was quite big and beefy, the other small, with a wiry moustache. The big one had a pock-marked face. They both wore light-coloured raincoats, which is odd now I come to think of it, because it was very warm. A sunny evening. They both had dark glasses.'

'And the accent?'

'I'm pretty certain they spoke Italian. It sounded more Italian than anything else. Not French or Spanish. Nor Arabic, I'm sure. Maybe Corsican.'

'Would you recognise either of them again?' asked Sherlock.

'I can't be sure. It all happened very quickly. The girl at the cash-desk might. She seemed a bright girl. But she's dealing with faces all day long.' He mumbled something else. Sherlock leaned closer.

'What did you say?'

'I said she deals with faces...'

'No, after that. Something like, "Re Addleno". What's Addleno?'

Simon looked incredulous. 'Did I say that?'

Pyke chipped in. 'Yes, I heard something like "Riya Dilno". Sounds like a place in the Balkans.'

Simon repeated the sounds over and over. If he had uttered them, they had come from the unconscious. So he shut his eyes and sat silently for about a minute, waiting for the sounds to make sense. Then he repeated them out loud.

'Of course!' he shouted, 'that was it!'

'What was what?' Sherlock shouted back.

'Riad'll know.'

He had a very quick lunch, and only just got back in time for the appointment with Bristow. The professor was particularly affable, and apparently enjoying some private joke. Simon was not concentrating.

'...quite a surprise to us all, of course.'

'Pardon?'

'The news. About Dr. Crow's new appointment.'

'Ah. She's got the senior lectureship. Best of luck to her. That settles the Chairmanship problem, then.'

'You haven't been listening, Simon. Come on, smarten up. I said, Dr. Crow has got a Chair.'

'*WHAT! Here?*'

'No, no. Somewhere much more suitable. At the new Commonwealth University of the Northern Territory.'

'Good grief! Well... Very appropriate.'

'Quite. That was my initial response too,' Bristow said with an uncharacteristically naughty twinkle in his eye.

'They'll find the Excluded Middle useful to know about up there,' Simon said solemnly.

'Yes, I'm sure they will. Although it was her administrative abilities, powers of organization, long-term planning capacities, and so on that I stressed they would find so useful.'

'She'll probably make a good Vice-Chancellor one day,' said Simon appreciatively.

'Now,' Bristow went on, 'one of the, er, many reasons why we shall regret the passing of Dr. Crow is that they need her up there very soon. In March, in fact. Which will leave us in a bit of a fix for some of her courses. I'm afraid you are the only one who could fill in, and I shall have to ask you to postpone your leave for a year.'

Simon was stunned at the implications of this.

'I'm terribly sorry, Simon. The Associate Dean Budgets has told me we shan't get funding to take on anyone to replace her. Anyway, I couldn't get a replacement at such short notice to teach her course on "Body and Mind from Aristotle to the Beatles". You do at least overlap a bit, although your approach will be different. O'Neddy will have to be Chairman; he's much more dispensable than you as a lecturer. The history of making holes in the earth is about all he covers, as you know.'

Simon stood up. 'Would you excuse me for a moment? I should like to make a phone call.'

Bristow looked nonplussed. 'Yes, of course.'

Back in his own room, Simon dialled a number. 'Mr. Pyke Senior, please. Mr. Pyke? Simon Prestcott. Sorry to trouble you so soon. I need to have a straight answer from you. It's rather important, or I wouldn't have bothered you. What are the chances of the money Professor Lebrecht wanted to give me, being approved for me?'

Pyke made a long statement, at the end of which Simon said: 'Yes, I realise that the police might decide I murdered Lebrecht myself for the money. But supposing I didn't? What?...Right. That's all I wanted to know. Thank you very much.'

He replaced the receiver, put a sheet of paper in his typewriter, and wrote:

Dear Professor Bristow
I am writing formally to request that I be granted twelve months leave without pay, as from 1 January next. If this leave is not granted, then it is with much regret that I must resign my lectureship with effect from 1 January next.
With my thanks for your many kindnesses,
Yours sincerely,
    SIMON PRESTCOTT.

He placed it in an envelope, sealed it, handed it to Margo, and asked her to take it in to Professor Bristow in five minutes. Then he gathered up one or two things from his desk-drawer, and left quickly.

6

On his way home from the university Simon called in at the bottle shop to stock up in the expectation of entertaining the Schoenheimers over the weekend. Even before he took the key out of the lock, he sensed all was not well in his flat. Staring in disbelief at the chaos within, he relaxed his grip on the paper bag, and only by quick reflex caught a bottle of Château Tahbilk Marsanne as it neared the floor. The similar treatment that had been given to Lebrecht's room flashed through his mind.

'Do you take me seriously now?' Simon asked Sherlock, who responded to his call within twenty minutes or so.

'Of course. Unless you did it yourself to impress me,' he replied. Simon swore with a Rabelaisian variety and violence that did, visibly, impress the inspector, folded his arms, and looked at the floor.

'All the same,' Sherlock added, 'I think it's a good job you were not in when it happened. Will they have found the copy of the manuscript?'

'No. Nor the translation. I keep them in the safe at the university — but I have brought them back with me now. I don't know what to with them. I want to show them to that chap Schoenheimer this weekend.'

'I'm not sure that's wise. He's not in the clear yet, you know. None of you are, officially.'

'Well, I could have done it without telling you, you know. I just think he may be able to throw a bit of light on this.'

Reluctantly, Sherlock agreed, providing he could be present. Accordingly, at eight o'clock on the Saturday evening, they all met in Simon's flat, which he had barely cleared up. Anna was very perturbed about the break-in, which he found gratifying. Floris looked intently at the photocopy of the manuscript, and at the translation, with Anna reading them beside him. Floris looked bewildered.

'I can't do anything with this,' he said. 'I must have the original in my hand, to get the vibrations.'

Sherlock said, 'I thought you might say that, sir,' and brought out the manuscript.

'You are taking a great risk, inspector,' said Floris with a smile. 'I might destroy your evidence.'

'Don't you worry. I'll be keeping an eye on you, like a hawk!'

Floris opened it up, ran his fingers over the writing, but barely looked at it. He closed his eyes. The only noise came from the television set in the next flat, the faint sound of commercial jingles and canned laughter. Floris leaned forward, with his head slightly to one side, as if listening. Then he began to speak.

'I see an entity now. But very vaguely. Many people have held this, and there is much violence associated with it. I see water. A river. A house by a river. Entity is kneeling, holding something, a parcel, a packet of something. Papers. Very anxious. Does not know what to do. No, it's fading... I am not the one.'

He opened his eyes, and Simon found him looking at him as he had at the Cambridge Society meeting. 'Would you please hold this?' He held out the manuscript to Simon.

'Me?'

'Yes, but first I would like you to take off your shoes and lie down on the floor.'

Simon had seen this procedure before, and knew what to expect, although he not been through it himself. He complied, and Anna began to massage his ankles.

'Dr. Schoenheimer knows what he's doing,' said Simon to Sherlock, who was beginning to look rather restive. Floris began to massage his forehead with the little finger side of his fist. Gradually he felt himself relaxing. The manuscript was loosely held in his right hand. Floris leaned over and gently transferred it to his left hand.

After two or three minutes, Floris told him to visualize himself growing longer at the feet; then at the head; then expanding all over. Like a balloon. Simon felt all this quite clearly, and began to float, whilst remaining aware of everything about him. He was now looking down on the other three, who were looking at him on the floor. Good God! Was that him? He was funnier-looking than he had thought, that strange, long face with an untidy lock of brown hair over one eye. He must look perpetually drunk. He noticed to his embarrassment that his fly-zip was half undone, and felt like telling himself to do it up. Never neglect the little things in life. But Floris was talking to him: 'What do you feel now?'

'I'm floating, just above you all. Nice sensation. I can see my fly's undone, sorry about that.'

Anna put her hand over her face and tried to stop laughing. Sherlock frowned and looked as though the thought had suddenly crossed his mind that he was the victim of a hoax. Simon said, 'Don't worry, inspector, we're very serious really.' Sherlock had the sense to realise that Simon, with his eyes shut, could not have seen his expression.

Floris then began to give Simon instructions, to float outside his flat, and describe the front door. He felt himself move away, and was out in the hallway. He mentioned everything he could see about the door: the patterns in the wood, the spider's web up at the top, the crack in the wall, the broken lamp-shade, and so on. Then Floris said:

'I want you now to concentrate on the paper in your hand. That paper is just being written on for the first time. It is blank, and you see the words being written. Do you see that?'

'Yes. I see the paper. A quill is writing words on it. Many pages. Two, three hundred pages. I am writing my memoirs.'

'Look at the room about you. What do you see?'

'Lovely. Beautiful room. I love this room. It is mine, my den. No one comes in here except me.'

Floris looked startled. 'Is there a window? Look through

it and say what you see.'

Simon looked out at the green valley below, beyond a formal garden of flower-beds, pathways and statues, which stretched for half a mile or more. 'My garden,' he said, '*c'est le parc qui entoure mon château.*'

Floris quite naturally continued to ask his questions in French.

'*Dites-nous votre nom,*' he instructed. Simon felt agitated, and said that he could not say his name, they would not let him use his name any more.

'Who are "they"?'

'*Les citoyens, les révolutionnaires .*'

'Are you a nobleman?'

'Yes. No. No more. I must leave here. I must finish my memoirs and leave, very soon. The time is coming.'

'What time?'

'Fire. All gone. Everything gone now. Just a pile of stones.'

Simon felt a wave of sadness sweep over him.

Floris said, 'Move on, now. You are near the end of your life. Have you achieved what you had to do?'

'Oh no. *Hélas, non.* I must be quick. I beat him at Tilsit, the devil, now I must tell Canning. Vital news. Wrong strategy. Must get to London.'

'To London?'

Simon immediately found himself in another room, smaller and less opulent. Outside, he could see the early morning sun glinting on the river — just as Floris had said. A man came in, with his hat in his hand. He knew it was Miles, his coachman. He handed Miles some papers, and said, 'Miles, you must make certain these get to Mr. Canning. Do you understand?'

Miles was a fresh-faced young man, bright and strong.

'Yes, I will, sir. But you are going up to town yourself to see him now, are you not, sir?'

Then Simon went up the stairs, picked up a pistol from

the head of his bed, and began to come down again. Outside, he heard a terrible scream, but before he could start running, in came that new servant, Louis, no, Luigi. He started to say, 'Luigi, what is happening?', when the servant bounded up the stairs, drawing a curved dagger from his sleeve. It was already red with blood. Simon saw the dagger raised, then coming towards him, as he tried to raise his pistol. The blade struck him in the chest, but he had enough strength to pull the trigger, and he saw the ball go in between Luigi's eyes. Then blackness.

He heard Floris's voice next to him. 'You have done with all that now. You did what you had to do. Feel yourself drifting back to me now, back to your body, Simon, your live body...'

He opened his eyes to see Anna looking at him anxiously.

'Did you hear? Did I say what was happening?' he asked.

'Yes,' said Floris, 'in great detail. And you may remember more.'

'I'm not sure I want to. That was absolutely terrifying. I don't really like being murdered.'

Sherlock stood up. 'Very impressive,' he said. 'I'm not sure where it gets us, but it was quite a show. I mean,' he corrected himself awkwardly, 'not a show, very dramatic. Wherever you were, you really were right in it, up to the ankles. And no suggestion, either. Except for the bit about the river.' He glanced at Schoenheimer.

'Do you have any idea where either of the two places were?' asked Anna.

'The first was certainly in France, and obviously during the Revolution. The second, well, it must have been within reach of London. I suppose the river was the Thames. It was very wide. All we have to do is scour the whole length of the Thames from Greenwich to Twickenham.'

'But none of that had anything to do with a monastery or Egypt or the manuscript,' said Sherlock, retrieving the paper from the floor.

'Ah, yes, it did,' said Simon. 'The manuscript wasn't written in Egypt. I could see I was looking at a lot of notes, very tatty and travel-stained. I was writing up the notes I must have taken while I was travelling, quietly at home in my château. Well, not so quietly. There was a great urge to escape before someone got me.'

'Both episodes were crises in your life during that incarnation,' said Floris. 'And the manuscript was important to both. First, you were writing your memoirs; then you were trying to hide them; I visualized you kneeling.'

'Praying, I suppose,' said Anna.

'I think not,' Floris said, 'I saw you with a packet of papers in your hand. I sensed you were definitely trying to hide them.'

'Under the floorboards?'

'Great,' said Simon, 'so now we have to pull up all the floorboards between Greenwich and Twickenham.'

Floris turned to Sherlock. 'Might I ask, inspector, how is going the investigation into Professor Lebrecht's murder?'

'We are encountering certain ... diplomatic difficulties,' he replied. 'We would very much like to interview that Mr. Fuad Riad and his wife, but they seem to have gone to ground — or gone abroad, with a thick smoke-screen around them.'

Simon stood up and moved over to the window. Looking out, he began: 'I'm not sure about all this.' The others turned and gazed at him.

'Neither am I, Dr. Prestcott,' said Sherlock as he glimpsed the flicker of a glance pass between the Schoenheimers. 'I'm not sure of anything yet...'

'I mean, the status of that experience,' Simon cut in. 'We've been talking as though it was me writing and getting stabbed by a lunatic Italian servant. But we can't just assume that.' He turned and faced them. Floris was looking at the floor, nodding gravely. Anna was looking at him, Simon, wide-eyed.

'But you felt it all,' she said, 'you told it as though it was happening to you, not to somebody else. Did you for one moment sense you were an observer? Did you see the man, see his face?'

'No. I admit that. But that could be explained by telepathy, or auto-suggestion. I might have been fantasising, just imagining myself in those situations. Writers of historical fiction are doing that all the time. Dumas would never have written *The Three Musketeers* or *The Count of Monte Cristo* if he hadn't been able to do that. Perhaps I'm a novelist *manqué*, and you have released something in me.'

Floris pursed his lips and looked at Anna.

'I have to agree with Simon,' he said, 'that the experience might not have been a genuine O.B.E....'

'A what?' asked Sherlock .

'Out-of-body-experience. It might not have been a real one in your case — but *only you can tell*. The subject is always better able to judge that than the investigator or therapist.'

'Is this some kind of astral travelling you're talking about, then,' asked Sherlock, 'like the stuff I used to read about in Dennis Wheatley when I was a lad?'

'Yes, but we don't use that term now. It is judgemental, and pre-supposes a belief in something labelled the "astral body".'

Simon was not to be shaken from his feelings of doubt. 'I'm sorry to be such a spoil-sport,' he said, 'but I have a nasty feeling I'm being used, somehow. Manipulated.'

Anna recoiled slightly, and looked hurt.

'I don't mean by anyone here — necessarily,' he went on. 'But somehow it's all too neat. I mean, just look at what's happened, the strange sequence of events lately: I happen to meet you and Anna, Anna happens to invite me to the Trevelyans, I happen to meet Lebrecht, he happens to confide in me, from beyond the grave, as it were; I happen to be able to work out his clues and read his manuscript, and now you're telling me I happen to be the guy who wrote it two hundred years ago. Now, I can accept all that as a likely series of chance occurrences, up to this last bit. It could easily be depersonalisation, or day-dreaming. After all, I had had some bits of information fed to me.'

'Such as?' asked Sherlock.

'The fact that it was written in French, and was obviously eighteenth-century writing. Then Lebrecht's use of the word "mission", which makes me feel involved personally in some business I don't understand. And then you gave me the idea of a house by the river, and a sense of anxiety.'

'True,' replied Floris, 'but you brought in Tilsit. Now that is rather special. Why Tilsit?'

'Who's Tilsit?' asked Sherlock.

'It's a place,' Simon said. 'The only reason it's famous is for the Treaty that was signed there. Between Napoleon and Czar... whoever it was. An Alexander, I suppose. Hang on a minute, I'll look it up.'

He did so, and quickly came back with the information.

'Here we are. On 25 June 1807, the Emperor Napoleon and Czar Alexander met on a raft in the middle of the river Niemen. I expect they were afraid of being bugged, like bankers who do deals in rowing boats in the middle of the lake at Geneva. Anyway, Tilsit... er... the aim was to make Napoleon's brothers kings of various bits of Europe... including... you'll like this, Floris... Holland. Russia was to stop being nasty to the Turks. And Russia was to mediate between France and England. And... Ah! there were some secret articles which were very dangerous for the British, but which were mysteriously leaked to... the British Foreign Secretary, George Canning. Well!'

'Does it say how he got the information?' asked Floris.

'No, not in here. I'll have to look it up in a biography of Canning tomorrow.'

'Our man does seem to think he had something to do with it, and with Canning. Remember you volunteered the name Canning, Simon,' said Anna.

'True. But I had heard of him before, you know. And Tilsit.'

When they had all left, Simon lay down on his bed without bothering to undress. He slowly relaxed, and found himself facing a vast staircase winding upwards into mist.

7

Cambridge in January is a terrible shock to anyone who has made a sudden transition from the southern hemisphere. It was several years since Simon had even seen frost, as he never stirred from the centre of Melbourne in winter. To be faced with snow, ice, bitter winds coming unimpeded from Siberia, and the rigours of the mediaeval domestic arrangements of St. Peter's, required a deliberate bracing of the moral fibre, and firm determination Not to Give In to Depression.

Slowly, however, he became physically adapted and socially absorbed. The beauties of the town, the exuberance of the students, the concentration of intellectual activity in the colleges and societies and the ability to go and hear world-famed specialists in a whole range of subjects, all helped to bring him back to life. The harrassments of the previous month began to lose their edge.

One evening after dinner in Hall, followed by port and nuts in the Senior Combination Room, where the Master had made a nice little speech of welcome-back for him, Simon was strolling, begowned and mellow, across the court to his rooms, in the company of Adrian Wiseman, who had been his supervisor when he was writing his doctoral thesis, and a new young Fellow named Grant, who did brilliant things with computers and artificial memory.

'One has to hand it to the English,' said Simon. 'The fabric of their society may be crumbling, they may have destroyed themselves by folly and ineptitude since 1945, but this place gives one such a sense of historical solidity that one forgets for a moment how fragile it is.'

'Don't be taken in by the trappings,' replied Adrian. 'It's all changed underneath. At least half the students care nothing for the ancient stones, or the sound of the college choir drifting over the snow. They're as bright as ever, but there's a soullessness that I find alien. I don't mean a lack of religious belief, I'm not a Christian myself, as you know. But their rejection of outward forms doesn't lead them to any inner truths. It just shows up the emptiness within. You must have noticed it in Hall at dinner. There used to be a sense of occasion about it, with everyone gowned, standing for Grace, and so on. But it's like a canteen now. Sandals and jeans...'

'And women!' Simon smiled. 'Tut, tut.'

'Yes, tut you may — a few of the Fellows resigned over that. But it was inevitable. I've no objection — they're a civilising influence on the place. If only they wouldn't scream when they're being chased up the staircases in the middle of the night. I never know if they're being raped, and then I lie awake worrying about whether I should have rung the night porter to investigate!'

'I think it's just that concentration of the learning process and domestic realities, like eating, washing and sex, in one place, that is the genius of the place,' said Simon. Only here and Oxford have kept a sense of unity in the life of the seeker after knowledge. One may take it for granted, but after a few years away, I tell you, I find it awe-inspiring.'

'Bullshit!'

They had forgotten Grant was with them. Adrian turned to him.

'What is bullshit, Grant? Taking it for granted?'

'No, all this awe-inspiring rubbish. If you don't mind my saying so, it's a load of fucking romantic codswollop. What's this farting around in mediaeval costume got to do with anything? You're like a bloke who's been away from women for a few years, Prestcott. You're hot and randy for what you've been missing, dear old Merry England. But it'll wear off, don't worry about it, it's not terminal. Good night.' And with that pronouncement, he went off through the main gate to his lodgings in one of the drearier suburbs of Cambridge.

They were by now ensconced in Adrian's study, with its walls book-lined from floor to ceiling, velvet curtains only occasionally responding to the bitter wind outside, and a crackling fire in the marble fireplace. Simon was thoughtful.

'Perhaps he's right? Maybe I am a sentimental twit?'

'It seems to me to go deeper than that,' Adrian said. 'One would think that in a society with very little future — I mean with not much time to go — the young would, in the main, turn to the past and revere it. But no, most of them cut themselves off from both dimensions, past and future, and dig themselves firmly into the present. The here and now as be-all and end-all. Perhaps that's why they blast their senses to bits with drugs and noise the human ear wasn't made to withstand.'

'But how typical is Grant?' Simon wondered. 'There are some who are still alive to permanent values.'

'Values? Or forms? Empty forms and meaningless rituals, that's all Grant sees. But perhaps it's possible to put some substance back into the shadow. It calls for an innate sensitivity of some kind. Nothing to do with learning. Some people have a sense of belonging to a whole unbroken stream of life, but some — most — cut themselves off from it. I think historians used to have this sense automatically, but now that history has spilled over into sociology and political so-called science...'

'...and psychology,' smiled Simon, 'and all the other pseudo-sciences. I know what you're getting at!'

'No, of course not, perish the thought. Not in your case, anyway. A night-cap?' He went over to the sideboard and unstoppered a decanter.

'Just a small one, thank you,' said Simon. The moment had come to sound out Wiseman. 'Adrian... Do you think there is any connexion between this sense of history and ... the intuition some people have of having lived in a different age before?'

'A lot of people have had that intuition — Kant, Thoreau, Emerson, Goethe, Tolstoy, and so on. Were they just dreamers? Grant would tell us so. But I just don't know, Simon.'

'You don't regard such a belief as nonsense?'

'You ought to know me better than that. But I don't think I ever had to quote at you my favourite bit of Herbert Spencer — I reserve it for the know-all, brash young people who appear in waves, year after year: "There is a principle which cannot fail to keep a man in everlasting ignorance; that principle is, contempt, prior to investigation".'

Thus reassured, Simon recounted to him the events of the previous few weeks, on the other side of the world. Adrian Wiseman listened, and noted inwardly. Simon ended by bringing out a letter.

'Then this arrived this morning.' He opened it and handed the contents to Adrian. He read, translating as he did so to check with Simon he had understood it properly:

Public Library
Montpellier
(Hérault)

Dear Sir

In reply to your letter of 15 December, I have the honour to inform you, as a bursar... no... award-holder of the Chelbert Research Trust founded by the late Professor Lebrecht, of whose death I am profoundly saddened to learn from you, that the information expedited to M. Lebrecht on 10 October last, related to a certain minor nobleman, born in this city in 1755. M. Lebrecht wished to know if we possessed any manuscripts or memoirs of or by the subject of his enquiry, the Comte de Freyssenet. My response was negative. Please find enclosed the entry, short as it is, on this subject, in the *Dictionnaire biographique*. Please accept my most respectful salutations, JACQUES FORESTIER, Conservateur.'

Adrian Wiseman turned to the attached photocopy, and

read out loud:

'FREYSSENET, Charles Lazare Victor de Bertin, comte de: b. Montpellier 1755, d. London 1815. Emigrated to Switzerland 1792, when his *château* at Freyssenet was razed to the ground by local peasants. Led a vagabond life as espionage agent for various foreign powers, of which, finally, England. Suspected of revealing to British government details of secret articles of Treaty of Tilsit. Died violently at the hands of a servant, near London, 8 June 1815. No issue.'

Adrian handed the papers back to Simon. 'Quite remarkable,' he said. 'There's your fire, and your château. All you have to do now is go and find it!'

'There are a few details to check on here too, or rather in London. I'd like to know if George Canning really knew him. But the main thing is to find the rest of those memoirs. Without them, the monastery is untraceable. Egypt is full of them, dotted about the desert. Careering about on a camel, being chased and shot at by Riad and his mob, hundred and twenty in the shade, not my cup of tea, really.'

'By the time you get across the court and into your rooms, you might change your mind about that,' laughed Adrian.

Simon went down C staircase, but instead of going across to H staircase, where his rooms were, he turned right and headed towards the college library. It was locked, on account of the priceless chained books that had been there for five hundred years, but as a visiting Fellow, he had a key. Having found "HISTORY, ENGLISH, 18th CENTURY," he took down several volumes, signed for them in a ledger, and trudged carefully over the crisp snow to H staircase.

8

James Sherlock was not a happy man. He frequently felt that he was part of the thin veneer between civilisation and the jungle, but nobody else seemed to share that belief. He often wondered what the incidence of paranoia was among policemen. Those few joys that came his way, either in his private life or in his job, were short-lived and really no compensation for the unsung dreariness of the rest. Take that murder case in Healesville. When the report of it had come through to Homicide in Melbourne, he had personally taken it on because it seemed out of the ordinary. And so it was. But now all the most interesting witnesses had gone: first the Egyptians had fled and were apparently beyond recall, despite the efforts of the Australian National Central Bureau in Canberra and their opposite numbers at Saint-Cloud, the French Interpol Headquarters near Paris. Then there was Geoffrey Paton, a very upper-crust politician, and his very solid wife. They had detailed files on them, but nothing in the least helpful, that is, incriminating. The young actor bloke, Pascoe, was a bit of a tearaway, and sexually suspect, possibly into drugs, and would need watching. But the truly intriguing ones were those Schoenheimers. He had had quite of a lot of information through Interpol about them; again, nothing incriminating, but it came from several sources: the hypnotist was a great traveller, and his job did not always attract the approval of authorities, especially religious and medical ones. So from Holland, France, Britain, Germany and the U.S., he had been sent a good deal of faxed info' — press cuttings and Immigration reports. The girl claiming to be his daughter was closely involved in his act, if that's what it was. All her documentation seemed to be in order, but they needed to be watched.

As for the university chap, Prestcott, he seemed clean, but he was closely involved with the girl, had gone off to England at the same time as them, and he was in regular contact with them over there. Scotland Yard had sent frequent reports on him, and them. It had to be admitted that Dr. Prestcott had, in fact, been very helpful in reporting new information to Detective-Inspector Irving, of the London Metropolitan Police. But what that nineteenth, no, eighteenth-century Frog had to do with it all, he had no idea at present. There was no further link with Egypt established. None since that strange trance business he had witnessed in Carlton. How on earth could he get the French Sûreté to start delving into archives looking for two-hundred-year-old manuscripts? And the reponse he had so far had from the Egyptian police made him very aware of the political and security clout Mr. Riad had in Cairo. There would be little help from there. Come to that, what with international relations between France and Australia being at their lowest ever, as a result of Australian condemnation of the Greenpeace sinking, of the Muraroa nuclear tests, and of French "neo-colonial" policies in New Caledonia, he could understand why he was getting rather bad vibes from Saint-Cloud. He was finding it altogether easier to work through the London C.I.D. — but progress was dismally slow, and his superiors were beginning to show signs of impatience. He must either persuade Irving to move things along a bit, or send someone to London.

Simon was getting to know the route between Scotland Yard and Harley Street quite well. It was good to have two excellent reasons for going to London every weekend, although one would have sufficed, of course. Anna and he had hardly ceased talking about the facts and implications of the Lebrecht affair, during their joyous few weeks together in Melbourne over the Christmas period — which Anna found very odd, like a Looking-glass Christmas, with walks along the sand in the bright, warm sunshine at St. Kilda or Mount Eliza, followed by another outdoor Christmas party or meal with Simon's friends in the evenings. Since their arrival in London, it had been mercifully mild (that is, just above freezing) in comparison with Cambridge.

Simon had not appreciated how much in demand Floris Schoenheimer was. He managed to get through his list of patients each day only because he also lived in the Harley Street house. It had three floors. At the front of the ground floor was the spacious waiting room, whose decoration Anna had overseen: very restful, harmonious and unostentatiously modern. Behind it was Floris's consulting room and his nurse-receptionist's office. This was provided with discreet hi-fi and video equipment, the former for transmission of sound-frequencies and the latter for recording sessions.

'Is that ethical?' Simon asked him, the first time he was being shown round.

'Without the patient's permission it would not be, any more than a general practitioner making a sound recording of a consultation. I always get written permission first, and offer the patient the videotape after, for him to keep or destroy. The most interesting ones, I ask if I may make a copy. Hardly any have refused when they have seen and heard the recorded sessions.'

'What about these sound frequencies?' asked Simon. 'Are they pre-recorded on a battery of tapes, or do you create your own?'

'In fact,' replied Floris, 'I do not like to resort to electronic input, and I use this only in difficult cases. The sound patterns we have originate from a research institute in the United States, and they have a very specific effect on the brain-waves. It is similar to the effect of slow baroque music in suggestopaedic teaching methods used in Bulgaria and Canada — but much more precise and effective.'

'You mean they inhibit beta waves and enhance alpha waves?'

'Yes. Exactly. But the mix is monitored on an eight-channel EEG, and we also monitor the patient's muscle tone on EMG. None of this is important in its own right — we are not a pure research unit, but a practical healing unit.'

'Why do you go in for all the electronics, then?'

'Partly out of pride, I suppose,' said Floris. 'I don't like being, how do you say, lumped along with faith-healers and gurus, so I give myself a little scientific respectability this way. I also do find the results useful, sometimes. One day, we shall learn how we manage to recall experiences that we have not had in this life; the answer will then lie within the range of the natural, and not the so-called super-natural. It may be simply our eternal genes communicating with one another across the ages, and implanting signals into the brain, which are experienced as memories — memories of things we don't remember, from far away. It is what we call the akashic record.'

'You seem to be much more of a materialist than I had previously realised,' said Simon. 'Is there no spiritual dimension in your system?'

'One half of my brain — you know which — says "Yes" and the other half says "No",' Floris replied, as they went up to the first floor of the house by the wide stairway. 'I am quite a romantic at heart, and would hate to find that the material world is all we have, that is, I do not want to find out that all our spiritual strivings are simply illusions, the faulty perceptions of organic computers called brains, which a material universe has created by random means.'

'You mean, for example, you would like Anna to have some personal, real, direct link with musicians who are dead and who communicate with her?'

Floris paused at the top of the stairs and reflected.

'I am really too close to her to be able to say what I want that gift to be. Frankly, it worries me, and she is not happy about it, because she feels it inhibits her present identity. It has brought her anguish and doubts about herself — her Self, with a capital S. I have to watch her very carefully. That is why I feel... No.' He broke off abruptly. 'That is enough about that.'

'Please say what you were going to say,' Simon pressed him.

'I think it better not to. I do not wish to influence your relationship with her.'

Simon looked at Floris squarely 'I would rather know what you were thinking,' he insisted.

Floris sighed, and ushered Simon into the sitting-room overlooking Harley Street. No sound ruffled the antique elegance.

'I am glad she has found a friend who is both sensible and sensitive. She has been a lonely child and a rather solitary young woman up till now. Now you see why I did not want to tell you. I do not want you to feel you have taken on any kind of responsibility for her.'

It was Simon's turn to reflect. At length, he said: 'Floris, I am profoundly grateful that you approve of me. It wouldn't have changed my feelings for Anna if you had heartily disapproved of me, mind you, because I feel I was meant to meet her, and not just for a little flirtation.'

'I know that is true,' said Floris. 'But a word of warning, Simon. Don't take her for granted. She can be very rebellious, single-minded, and ... unpredictable.'

Simon remembered the feeling he had had in the car going to Whitegates.

Anna's abode was not on the top floor of the house, as one might expect, but in the converted stables at the back of the house, separated by a small enclosed garden, and with access from the mews lane. She thus had complete independence, whilst still part of Floris's establishment, connected to it by house 'phone and by the garden. The ground floor was occupied mainly by her piano. The first floor by her bed. Simon came to think of these as the equal agents of her versatility and expressivity. But he was far from happy with the balance of their relationship, for reasons that became clear in his own mind only when he visited her doll's house, as she called it, or *garçonnière*, as he called it, after seeing Inspector Irving, on the first Saturday in February. As he entered, unwound his St. Peter's scarf, and removed his gloves, he gave her a peremptory kiss.

'Are you losing interest now you've had your way with me, your lordship?' she asked, looking into his eyes with a smile that was half anxious, half teasing.

'I'm sorry, darling.' He went over to the window looking out on to the garden. 'I've just had a rather unpleasant run-in with that Scotland Yard chap, Sherlock's Watson.'

'Why? What's happened?'

'Nothing, that's just the problem. He made me go over every smallest detail of the whole business, right from the first time I met you and your father. He is very sceptical about the importance of what the manuscript says. He tried to link up the murder and my getting the award. He pretty well implied that the three of us were in cahoots and we'd better come clean because the net is closing in around us. In fact, he was thoroughly offensive. I'm afraid I lost my temper. I told him I had my own work to do, I'd already given him his most valuable clue to date — the identity of the writer of the manuscript — and he said he wasn't interested in some defunct French aristocrat from two hundred years back, but in the identity of whoever rendered Lebrecht defunct three months ago. I'm not going to see him again unless he summons me — or charges me with murder!'

Anna poured him a stiff drink and sat beside him.

'You know, we haven't really thought about what Freyssenet says he saw in the monastery. Whatever it was, it shook him considerably. But more importantly, it seems to be a clue to something that other people want very badly. We don't know who, or why. But surely you, with your deductive procedures, ought to try to get between the lines. And...' She paused. 'I think you ought to agree to another session with Daddy.'

'We can't without the manuscript. You know it's like looking for a haystack in a time warp without something belonging to Freyssenet.'

'Then we must find something,' Anna insisted. 'Look, we know he died somewhere overlooking the Thames in 1815. And we know he came from a place called Freyssenet.'

'There are loads of villages called Freyssenet or Freycenet in the south of France,' Simon replied irritably. 'I have at least checked on that. And as he got his castle knocked down, we can't even look for that. So we look for a hole in the ground in the Midi...'

'...and somewhere under all the floorboards between Greenwich and ... where was it you said?'

'I don't know. Chelsea, or Hammersmith.'

'No, no.' Anna suddenly became quiet and serious. 'That's why I asked you like that. To see if you said the same place as you did in Melbourne, that night. You said the same place, very firmly, twice, when you were still recovering from the hypnotic recall. Now try to remember.'

'I said Greenwich twice. There you are.'

'And...'

'And...' He put his head in his hands.

'No, that's no good. Lie back and relax. It's no good bullying your conscious mind.'

'I do know about conscious minds, and the others,' Simon retorted, as he lay back on the soft sofa.

'Sorry, Doctor,' said Anna softly. 'Now, I'm not going to stroke your forehead or your feet, or you'll say it was telepathic or something. Just try to get an image, to visualize something, and say it out loud.'

For a full minute, he lay there, silently. His mind was in turmoil, like a television screen left on after close-down. Then the screen began to clear, and he saw...

'I see an H. A large H. Hhhh... Harringay... Harlow... Hammersmith — there you are, I said Hammersmith. No, wait a moment. There are people moving round the letter, running very fast... throwing something... a ball...a rugger ball. Of course! Twickenham! That was it, wasn't it?'

'Yes, my clever darling. I was sure it was, but I needed you to repeat it, to be quite certain. Now, I've been doing a bit of historical research this week, in between exhausting rehearsals at the Royal Academy, while you have been ruining your liver with college port. Tell me, Mr. Historian, who would there have been a lot of in Twickenham in the early 1800s, that you wouldn't have found in Greenwich?'

'Are you being serious?'

'Perfectly. Never more serious.'

Simon thought back to the England of the Napoleonic Wars: the threat of invasion, Martello Towers, people fleeing from the south coast towns, talk of French spies everywhere, the Scarlet Pimpernel and French *émigrés* everywhere... no, not everywhere: there were a number of French *émigré* "colonies", like Richmond. And Twickenham.

Simon nodded and smiled ruefully. 'Of course. *Emigrés.* Sorry to be so slow.'

'Do you think that narrows it down a bit?' she asked.

'Well.... I think we ought to have a walk along the river tomorrow morning. If we can summon enough energy to get up.'

It was later that same evening that Simon opened a door that they had both kept shut, in the precious but curious structure of their relationship.

'I have a confession to make to you, darling,' he began.

'Ah! I knew it! Now he tells me he is still married! Or has found a pretty little undergraduette on his staircase.'

'Do you want to go on guessing?' he said, but without smiling. Anna shook her head.

'There is just one thing I don't understand about... I'll start again. One of the many things I don't understand about you is what you get out of... *us*. No, let me finish. You have such talent, you can create such beauty, you radiate beauty wherever you go, so that I simply can't see what... what I am contributing to the... affair. You could have any one of a dozen handsome, creative, artistic men, perhaps you do when I'm not here, during the week...'

Anna swung round and slapped his face, very hard. He gasped. Piano-playing certainly gave a girl strong arms and shoulders. For several minutes, neither of them said anything. Then Anna said: 'I'm not going to say sorry. I think that was the only way to react to your last statement, so as to convince you that you are wrong. But as for the rest... Only a non-artist can know how boring other artistic performers can be. They are totally self-centred, threatened by others in the same field. We know how fragile is the musician's talent. Tomorrow I might simply find it impossible to play. Look at John Ogdon or Jacqueline Dupré. World class, then collapse. Or Cyril Smith: one needs two arms, and they may not always be there, dangling from our shoulders. A writer can go on so long as he can speak into a tape recorder, paralysed from the neck down. But the singer fears a sore throat, the actor fears his memory will fail — even Laurence Olivier went through that — the painter fears blindness, the composer deafness. Poor Beethoven. Just imagine the sheer hell Delius went through, with all that wonderful music going through his head, but blind, with no way to write it down until Eric Fenby was sent to him by an all-seeing Providence.'

Anna took Simon firmly by the shoulders. He got ready to duck. But she went on, reassuringly quietly: 'Dear, dear Simon, with you I feel no threat, because your YOU-ness responds to mine, just as my MY-ness responds to you. Even if we spoke different languages, we should feel drawn to each other like this. If you are afraid I shall be bored by you, the answer is, yes, you can bore me, by saying you are afraid you bore me. That's the only possible way.'

Her warm, soft lips on his, his hands gently feeling the suppleness of her, her body pressing with rhythmic urgency against him, were the prelude to a new phase of giving and forgiving, understanding, trust, confidence, passion, and finally oblivion in each other's arms.

It was only with great difficulty that they summoned up enough energy to drive to Twickenham the next morning. In fact, by the time they found their way into a charming riverside pub, it was lunchtime, and they revelled in piles of spaghetti bolognese and a bottle of Chianti. By the time they began to walk along the towpath, the sun was already thinking it had done its best for the day, and the Thames gloomily reflected the grey sky and the leafless trees. One or two brave scullers scudded along, glad to be alone for a while, no doubt. Simon and Anna were not too engrossed to keep an eye open for houses that might have been there in 1815, on both side of the water. Every now and then, they stopped to make notes and look at the *A to Z*. They came upon a row of delightful old houses of varying size, set back from the river and barely visible from the tow-path because of the flood wall. Simon shook his head. The picture he had firmly in his head was of a path running straight down from the house to the water's edge. They had just passed the whole length of the wall when he turned. 'Bloody fool!' he said under his breath. Anna raised her eyebrows at him, and followed his gaze. 'That wall isn't more than fifty years old. Let's have a look the other side!'

They climbed over to the road, which was still quiet and secluded. By now it was almost dusk, and lights were appearing in some of the windows, making the interiors look very warm and cosy. Anna shivered. 'I think we ought to go back,' she said. 'The car must be a couple of miles away.'

'Yes, all right, darling.' Simon was suddenly dispirited. He stopped, in order to get out his map and notebook, looked at the house opposite them, and darted forward, narrowly missing being hit by a cyclist with no lights. Anna saw him looking up, over the front door, and then doing a strange little dance on the pavement. He turned and waved to her to come over. She did, looking both ways.

Together they read the old, black nameplate over the door, with lettering that may once have been white, or gold:

FREYSSENET

9

'So what do we do now — ask the owner if we can pull up the floor?'

'Well, we can at least see what sort of a reception we get,' suggested Anna.

They had crossed over the road again to deliberate, and were now looking at the house in the fading winter light. It was early eighteenth-century, with a central door and windows each side of it. Above there were two floors, the top one under the eaves.

'Come on then.' Simon approached the gate, feeling like a small boy about to ask for his ball back. His knock was answered almost immediately by a frail-looking lady of considerable age.

'Yes?'

'Um. Good evening. I'm very sorry to trouble you, but we happened to notice the name of your house, and we're interested in the comte de Freyssenet...'

Even before he had finished, she had opened wide the door.

'Do come in,' said the little old lady, 'I have lots I can tell you about him.' Almost as if she had been expecting them, Simon thought.

She showed them into the sitting-room to the right. He recognised it straight away. Anna looked at him and he nodded imperceptibly. They introduced themselves to her; she was, she said, Mrs. Emily Greaves.

'I expect you'd like a cup of tea. Perhaps you'd care to look at these while I'm getting it.' She opened a cupboard and pulled out an album, which she placed on the large, shiny table.

'Can I help you?' Anna asked.

'No, my dear, you look at these with your friend. I can see you're both interested in the murders.'

Murders? They opened the album. Inside were several press cuttings, some from 1815, some about the house, and a photograph of a portrait. Simon began to read one of them:

THE MORNING CHRONICLE
11 June,1815.
DREADFUL MURDERS

The Count de FREYSSENET, French noblesse, was murdered yesterday morning at eight o'clock, at his summer residence overlooking the Thames at Twickenham, together with a devoted companion, Mlle. Amélie ROUSSIN, who had emigrated with him to escape the Terror. No cause is yet known for the atrocious act, which was committed by their servant, one Luigi, who had recently come into the household.

The Count was about to set off for London, to see his friend, Mr. CANNING, now on leave from Lisbon, where he is Ambassador, when Luigi left his station beside the awaiting coach, took out a knife, and finding his way barred by Mlle. ROUSSIN, he stabbed her in the left breast, whereupon she fell to the ground, screaming piteously.

The murderer then ran into the house, and drew his dirk upon the Count, who was descending the staircase. Seeing that the wound had not killed the Count, Luigi attempted to run up past the Count, who was a man of immense stature, but the Count drew his pistol and fired at the assailant, killing him instantly. The Count then collapsed upon the stairs, and died some thirty minutes later, despite the offices of a surgeon, Mr. Drew.

The Count had distinguished himself in the troubles which have convulsed Europe for more than twenty years.

'Poor girl,' Anna sighed, 'to go in that horrible way after following her master like a faithful spaniel all those years.'

Emily Greaves came in with a tray bearing cups and a large silver teapot. 'My family have lived in this house since the 1820s,' she said, 'and this Freyssenet story has almost been part of my family history. Now tell me how it is you are interested in it.'

Anna was about to launch into an account, but Simon cut in with a warning look. The less the old lady knew, the less the possibility of any danger for her. Simon had never underestimated the violence of Lebrecht's death, and the ruthlessness of the going-over applied to his own flat.

'I'm a historian, Mrs. Greaves, writing about the Revolution and Napoleon. I'd heard Freyssenet might have left some unpublished papers about somewhere. And that's what we historians are longing to find. Something no one else has published. Get in there first, sort of thing, you know.'

'Yes,' she replied sweetly, handing him his tea, 'I can see it must get frightfully boring re-hashing what others have discovered. Papers, now... It's odd you should say that. You are the second person who has asked me about papers by Freyssenet recently. Nobody else has ever asked about that. They just want the gory details, you know!'

'Oh? The second? Who else... Could you tell me who it was who asked about the papers, Mrs. Greaves? It might be a colleague, or a rival researcher, you know how it is. Cut-throat business, researching, these days, publish or perish and all that!'

Mrs. Greaves thought for a moment, then said: 'He was very polite. Foreign, I think, but you never can be sure nowadays. Indian, perhaps. Now, what did he say his name was? He was terribly religious, I remember, because when I came back with his tea, he was kneeling on the floor, praying. He said he had to do that four times a day. It must be very embarrassing for him in the middle of Oxford Street or on the Underground.'

'The name wouldn't have been Riad by any chance,

would it?' Simon asked.

'Riad? Riad.... That sounds something like it. But I can't be sure. My memory isn't what it was. I do remember his wife was frightfully interested in the architecture of the house, and wondered if it all dated from the same period or whether it had been added on to. She went round tapping the walls. I think I mentioned that my son wants to sell the house and have me to live with him in Spain, it would be so much nicer for my old bones than this freezing weather here. So they said they might be interested in buying it, and... and I gave them the agent's name, yes that was it.' She suddenly remembered she had not yet given Anna her tea, and apologised profusely.

'It would be a lovely house for us, wouldn't it darling?' Anna said. 'Do you think, Mrs. Greaves, we could have the name of the agent. I didn't see a board outside.'

'I don't want everyone to know I'm leaving. I should have people dropping in to look over it all the time. I remember what happened to my neighbours. But you can have his name, of course.'

She found a card on a shelf. 'There you are. Manningham and Ripley, Kensington High Street. They telephoned me yesterday to say a surveyor wants to go over the house tomorrow morning, so someone is apparently interested.'

'I can imagine who that is,' murmured Simon.

As they were about to leave, Simon turned to look up the staircase.

'Do you think I could go up a few stairs?' he asked. 'I'd just like to get a view of the... of the space in the hall. I suffer from claustrophobia, and I can't live in restricted spaces.'

Slightly puzzled, Mrs. Greaves stood back, and he slowly ascended. With each stair, his head pounded more strongly, until at the seventh he thought he would faint. He had never felt like that before, never. Not even climbing in the Alps. He turned round. Anna and Mrs. Greaves were no longer there. The door was open. Outside, the sun was shining. He knew what would happen then. The scream. The running steps. In through the door came Riad, with the shape of the curved knife showing under his coat. The raised arm. Pain. Pistol shot. Blackness.

'*SIMON!*'

It was Anna's voice that brought him back. She had bounded up the stairs, and caught him as he was about to fall, pushing him backwards so that he sat with a bump. Strong shoulders, these pianists — the thought flashed through his mind again, ludicrously. Mrs. Greaves proved to be a very sensible person. 'I used to be a Queen Alexandra's nurse, you know, picked up many a body by myself behind the lines.' Together they helped Simon back into the sitting-room.

'You saw something, didn't you?' asked Mrs Greaves. Simon nodded.

'I thought so. That's always the worst spot. It gets very cold, even in summer. I should have warned you, but I didn't want to put you off. A lot of people don't like the idea of a house being haunted. Never worried me, mind you.'

It was clear that she would have to be put in the picture, to a certain extent anyway, whatever the risks.

'Mrs. Greaves,' he began when he had begun to feel warmer again, 'we ought to tell you that something very unpleasant is going on. It involves the comte de Freyssenet, and this house, and some lost papers. And one person has already been killed by whoever is looking for the papers.'

'But... but you are looking for the papers, aren't you?' she asked.

'Yes,' Anna said, 'but we are working with the police. Shouldn't we ring them, darling?'

'This is a terrible nuisance for you, Mrs. Greaves,' said Simon, 'but I do think you may be in some danger, and probably from that man who came about the house. He may have killed a nice old gentleman, a professor, in order to get the papers. And...' — he looked at Anna — 'he tried to kill me on the stairs just now.'

Mrs. Greaves was not in the least put out by this. 'I'm afraid this place does have that effect on a few people, usually young girls, if you don't mind my saying it. But don't apologise, I haven't had so much excitement for years.'

It was over an hour before Inspector Irving arrived. Between them they quickly sketched in the sequence of events.

'That was very clever of you two, to find this place,' he said. There was a mixture of reluctant faint praise and condescension in his voice that irked Simon.

'Nonsense,' he retorted. 'The others are already ahead of us, God knows how.' He told Irving about the surveyor. Irving pondered. Then he said: 'I think we may let them do a little work for us tomorrow. May I use your telephone, Mrs. Greaves?'

'You are quite sure it was Riad?' asked Floris. He had responded to Anna's telephone call, and arrived at Mrs. Greaves's house soon after Irving had left.

'Quite sure, but that could well have been hallucination, a logical confusion of villains. On the other hand...'

'I think you are right, in a sense,' Floris mused. 'Even if Riad is, or was, Luigi, the servant, it is most unlikely that they would resemble one another physically. You must have superimposed his face on Luigi's... but that does not rule out the possibility they are one and the same.'

Simon protested that the coincidence was just too absurd.

'Not in the least, I'm afraid, Simon,' Floris replied. 'Time and time again, over thousands and thousands of reported cases, well documented ones, we find that groups of people are thrown together in successive reincarnations. Like recurring characters in Balzac's *Comédie Humaine*. But it gets really confusing when the same person experiences two or more lives with the same characters in totally different rôles. You may have had a little foretaste of that just now...'

'Do you mean to say, you and Anna might have been part of that incarnation too?' He shook his head in disbelief. 'I'll probably find I was your grandfather, Anna.'

'That is quite possible,' Floris said seriously.

It was midnight before they left.

'First right, then first right again she said,' Anna instructed her father. Quietly they drew up behind what had once been the stables. Mrs. Greaves was there waiting, with a small case in her hand. Simon kept a careful look out to see they were not being observed or followed. At the other end of the rear lane, they turned left and sped away.

On the Monday morning Simon had to return to Cambridge for a research seminar at 3 p.m., but not before he had heard from Irving what had happened when the surveyor turned up at the house. He was surprised when the door was opened, not by Mrs. Greaves, but by a young woman in a house coat and curlers, who apologised and said her aunt had had to go away unexpectedly, but had left her to let the surveyor in. Once inside the surveyor and his assistant produced guns, tied the young woman up, and locked her in the attic. Soon after, she heard the sounds of sawing and banging from the ground floor.

When she had been in the attic for about ten minutes, she heard the door being quietly unlocked.

'About bloody time, Murphy,' she complained, as he removed her gag and bonds. 'I was beginning to think you'd forgotten me. Where are our friends, tearing up the ground floor?'

'Yep. Taylor is in the larder.'

'They're armed.'

'So are we. Irving saw to that.'

Slowly they crept down from the top floor, cursing every creaking stair. But the noise from below was now at the level of indiscriminate destruction. They were in the room to the right of the hallway. Mrs. Greaves had told them before she left with the others how the sitting room linked up with the kitchen behind the staircase. They went first, then, to the larder *via* the sitting room, to reassure Detective Constable Taylor they were in position. Then Murphy moved quietly back to the door opposite the sitting room; Taylor stood ready at the door leading from the back stairs to the room which was being apparently taken apart. Murphy threw his door open, gun in hand, a split second before Taylor burst through his door. The two men kneeling on the floor had no time to drop their saw and chisel to pick up their guns. It was over very quickly.

'Will you please apologise to Mrs. Greaves, they did her floor no good at all, I'm afraid,' Inspector Irving said to Floris. 'I hope her insurance will cover it.'

'I'll explain,' he promised. Mrs Greaves was still fast asleep after what had, in her view, been a most enjoyable evening. Simon and Anna were poring over the packet of papers they had brought back from the house.

'It's lucky they didn't start in that room, or they would have spotted right away that the old floor-safe had been lifted,' Simon said. 'You know, I really didn't believe it was there. In exactly the spot where I had felt myself kneel, back in Melbourne. I felt extremely odd when I saw it.'

'What we have to decide now,' Anna said, 'is when we tell Mr. Irving that we have them. We are suppressing evidence, or something, I suppose.'

'I want to get a good look at them before the police get their hands on them and produce photocopies for me to work on,' said Simon. 'I'll take them with me to Cambridge and go through them there tonight.'

Anna tried to dissuade him. It was too dangerous. Riad was still at large. He had unknown accomplices. They might be watching them all at that very moment. Simon cursed the need to leave London that morning, but there was no way round it. He did not like the idea of leaving Anna —

or Mrs. Greaves. Riad presumably thought the packet of papers was still in the house, in which case he would attack there again. Or he thought Simon or the Schoenheimers had it, in which case they were prime targets.

'We could give them a bit of disinformation,' Simon thought aloud. 'Suppose we leaked to the press that the papers were in police hands, or in the Tower or something.'

Anna thought it was worth a try; but Irving was very much against it. 'The moment any of this gets into the press, they'll be round us, and you, and the house, like flies on a turd, Dr. Prestcott,' he said when Simon telephoned him. 'I agree there is some danger, so I'll post a man at the house. As for the Schoenheimers, the young lady had better move into her father's house.'

'And what about me?' Simon asked. Irving replied something like 'Hm,' and that was that. Stuff him, thought Simon. He can have the papers when I've done with them.

At 5.15 that afternoon, with the grey light scarcely reaching his desk in his study at St. Peter's, Simon settled down to read the Freyssenet papers. They were numbered from one to two hundred and nine, and were headed 'MES MEMOIRES'. Simon skimmed through them as fast as he could, gradually getting accustomed to the difficult scrawl, and noting down pages he wanted to return to — descriptions of Paris, of Versailles, and of the countryside round his château; there were conversations he claimed to have had with people of note such as Rousseau and Voltaire. There was a break of some years between 1790 and 1808, then the memoirs started up again when he was apparently living in London. Simon wrote down the numbers of the pages which mentioned Tilsit: Freyssenet stated quite clearly that he was responsible for informing Canning about the secret clauses signed between the Czar and the master of Europe, Napoleon, and that it was he who persuaded the British government to order the navy to sail into Copenhagen to capture the Danish fleet before it could do any harm to

England. For which, Freyssenet complained, he had received scant recognition from the British authorities. Simon moved on to the final, hastily penned pages, in the hope of finding some reason why their writer had regarded them as so important as to hide under the floor — almost his last act. The final paragraph read:

'10 June 1815. Coded dispatch from Fouché, through Paris network, must pass it on to Canning today. Bonaparte is moving his army Eastwards, and Wellington expects to dance with Lady Witherbourne in Brussels until the end of this month.'

All that made complete sense to Simon. The failure to get the dispatch to Wellington might explain his lack of activity until it was almost too late, at the Battle of Waterloo, which began on 16 June. But that was of purely historical importance; there was, to Simon's great chagrin and disappointment, no reference to the journey to Egypt or the visit to the monastery.

At least there was no doubt at all why Freyssenet had been murdered — or rather, assassinated, on the orders of the Emperor Napoleon I. But the murder of poor old Lebrecht now seemed utterly pointless. There was a curious parallel, though, which struck Simon as he laid his head on the pillow at last, just as a distant belfry chimed four across the sleeping colleges: Freyssenet had been killed for a piece of paper, and so had Lebrecht. Odd... very odd... never mind... think about it in the morning ...

Suddenly the telephone blasted his head off. Cursing, Simon fumbled in the dark, not able to orientate himself. Finally his hand found its way to the receiver and lifted it.

'Is that you, Dr. Prestcott?' Irving. Bloody insomniac.

'Yes. Inspector? What time is it?'

'Eight-thirty. Sorry. Bit early for you academics, I expect. But the real world must go on...'

'What do you want, Inspector?' Simon responded testily. 'I was working till four in the morning, so I'm not in the mood for homilies about ivory towers and the real world.' He had already spotted Irving as an academic dropout.

'Well, here's something to wake you up. We finished interrogating the pseudo-surveyors this morning. They were a couple of small-time crims, third grade con-men. When we started talking about accessories to murder, they got frightened, and reckoned they were into something deeper than they were being paid for.'

'But they had guns themselves,' Simon interjected.

'Not real ones. Pea-shooters would have been more use. So they put their little cards on the table. They'd been told to get hold of — I quote — "a box of valuables". Nothing about papers at all.'

'But papers have been known to be valuable, inspector. A letter signed by Napoleon would fetch thousands...'

'Is that enough to do a murder for? I doubt it. No, they definitely had the impression it was a smallish box containing some very precious treasure of some sort. They'd worked out it must be jewels. Anyhow, here's the crunch: they weren't working for your friend Riad.'

It took a moment for this to sink in.

'You mean there's someone else after whatever it was Riad was after? But that doesn't make sense. I mean, excuse me saying so, inspector, but it was Riad who said he was sending a surveyor, and that's what happened...'

'Ah, but they stopped Riad's men getting there, and turned up themselves. That's what they are telling us, anyway. The estate agent unwittingly told their boss — we don't know who it is, yet — that Riad was so interested in the property he was sending a surveyor round the next day. However...' Irving paused and heaved a great world-weary sigh down the telephone. 'However, they didn't find anything, did they?'

'I don't know,' Simon replied truthfully.

'No, of course they didn't. Because you already had it, didn't you?'

'Er... oh?... What do you....?'

'Dr. Prestcott, let's not waste time, eh? Mrs. Greaves is a grand old lady, but she easily forgets what she's supposed to know and what she isn't. She didn't mean to give you away.'

Simon pushed back the bedclothes, suddenly feeling hot and sweaty, then realised with a shock that the temperature was sub-zero out of bed, and covered himself up again. The move seemed to sober him up, bring him round, clear his brain, sweep away the mists of Lethe.

'Are you referring to the object or objects I removed with the owner's permission, inspector?'

'I'm referring to evidence in a murder case which you removed, Dr. Prestcott.'

'Well, it's all a question of point of view, isn't it, inspector? If you want this object or objects, you'll have to get the owner's permission, and a warrant or something. The thing is,' he went on hastily, before Irving could cut in, 'I'm the only one who can easily make sense of it, and I was not willing to wait till some clod-hopping policeman had messed it all up, making photocopies I wouldn't be able to read.'

'Clod-hopping!...'

'I don't mean you, inspector, I'm sorry, but I am getting bloody cheesed off. When are you going to accept that we are on the same side? I want very much to find out who killed a nice, gentle old man, even though I barely knew him. You want the same thing. I also have a research interest in the papers, so I can't afford to have them tied up in custody...'

'Impounded.'

'Impounded. I need to go through them again...'

'Again?'

'Again. That's what I was working on till 4 a.m.'

'That's clod-hopping policeman's hours, that is, Dr. Prestcott.'

'O.K., O.K. There are over two hundred pages of very difficult handwriting. You wouldn't have got anyone else to decipher that lot in a month.'

'So, speaking as an expert witness, what have you found out?'

'Nothing of interest to the case, I'd say. Quite a lot of historical interest. Nothing about Egypt, or a monastery, or strange lights. The Lebrecht page didn't come from this bundle at all. There are gaps in this lot of memoirs, and I'm afraid the context of the Lebrecht page must be somewhere else — if it still exists.'

'Are you levelling with me, Dr. Prestcott?'

'Yes, inspector, I am. If you want to get anywhere, you'll just have to trust me. Sorry. And you'll have to trust the Schoenheimers too. I'm quite sure they have no connexion with the matter.'

Inspector Irving thought for a moment.

'I'm willing to take your word for yourself, but not for anyone else. You don't *know* any more about them than I do. And I suspect you're not very objective about them — I'm sure I'd feel the same in your shoes.'

'But I can't go on getting them to help me if I have to treat them like suspects, keeping information from them, and so on.'

'Then you'll just have to be as discreet as you possibly can, won't you?' said Irving. 'Just keep in mind that it might be in your best interests too, in the long run.'

Simon put the phone down. It was now 9.15. No wonder the police force was so expensive to run, all those S.T.D. calls waking people up before breakfast. Just as he was about to deforest his face, the wretched thing rang again. A fruity voice came through.

'Good morning, Dr. Prestcott. Crankshaw here.'

'Who?'

'Timothy Crankshaw. Trinity. I was at your seminar yesterday.'

'Oh yes, of course. Sorry. I didn't get to bed till very late, still feeling a bit fuzzy.'

'Not at all. I was wondering if you'd be free to come and dine with me this evening? You can? Splendid. Let's say 6.30 in my rooms for sherry.'

Crankshaw is a lucky devil, thought Simon through the foam. Research professorship at Cambridge. No lectures, no undergraduate teaching or tutoring. Just a few Ph.D. students and the rest of the time on research and writing. Something to aim for, he supposed. Ah, well. In the meantime, he had better start transcribing the memoirs, before Irving changed his mind.

And before an angry Riad got wind of the present whereabouts of the papers. Simon found himself reading them now with a different interest: two lots of people desperately wanted to get their hands on these memoirs. In heaven's name, why? And why did Crankshaw come to the seminar yesterday, he suddenly wondered? Not his field. Never mind. Get on with it...

Freyssenet had been in Carcassonne only two days, he read...

I had been in Carcassonne only two days when I chanced to make the acquaintance of Madame de Crécy, a noted beauty of the town...

10

... At our very first meeting, at a Ball given by Madame de La Luzerne, she made it clear to me that she would welcome my attentions, that her husband was too busy and far away in Canada to be of any use or danger, and that all the pleasures so ardently desired by a young soldier bored by army life were mine for the taking, in exchange for discretion and loyalty which I...

— Good morning, inspector. How can I help you? You must excuse me if I seem a little rushed. I'm catching a plane to Singapore in a couple of hours time.

— I shan't take much of your time, sir. I was wondering if we could just go over a bit of information once again. Now, where did you say you first met this Fuad Riad?

— In Melbourne, at a party given by the director of the Banque Nationale de Paris.

— And that was about what date?

— I can look it up again precisely in my diary... Yes, here we are, it was on the twelfth of October.

— And you invited him there and then to be one of your guests for the weekend of the twenty-ninth?

— No. Oh no. It was at the lunch he gave for me and my wife later that week. Connie mentioned we were having a house party...

— And did she mention who was going to be there?

— Yes.

— He was pretty peeved to start with.

— I bet he was. Is he going to put you in prison, darling?

Shall I have to come and talk to you through a glass panel like the post office?

— He seems more interested in seeing you behind bars, actually, darling. Do you think they'll give you a single or double bed in your little cell?

— Why me?

— Ah! That rattled you, didn't it? Because he thinks you're a shady character, and I shouldn't talk to you till I'm a big boy...

— It's little Amélie, isn't it?

— *Oui, monsieur. Excusez-moi, monsieur, mais ...*

— But you're shaking like a leaf, *ma petite*. Come in and I shall get you a glass of wine...

— No, monsieur, thank you, but there is no time. I must get back to my mistress, or she will suspect.

— Suspect what? That you have come to see me?

— Ah, monsieur! You are in grave danger! Madame hates you and is plotting to have you killed because of the things you have said about her.

— But she has betrayed my confidence, Amélie.

— I do not know the rights and wrongs, monsieur, but you must believe that she is without mercy if one crosses her. That is why I am so afraid...

— I told you we should not have used these local amateurs. Now everyone knows we are in the game, both Riad and the police.

— They do not know who we are. The two clowns who got themselves caught have no links with us.

— Not directly, but through Fabrizio...

...Madame de Crécy, having failed in her attempt to have me assassinated in the crudest of ways, by a couple of hired ruffians, then progressed to more subtle methods...

—You failed in Australia through your bungling brutality.

—I did not intend to kill him, you know that. He had such a thin skull, and he slept so lightly.

—And now you use a couple of idiots who allow themselves to be decoyed by the simplest of means... We should have dealt with the old woman there and then, before that interfering academic and his girl friend got there.

—That is easy to say now. We did not know they were so close.

—We must move quickly. We have not only the police, and Prestcott, against us, but also these other bandits, whoever they are. Do they have the box, or the police?

—I know who would know: the girl.

—Just try not to kill her this time.

—Excellent dinner. Thank you. You are still very civilised at Trinity.

—Are you not at St. Peter's?

—Oh yes, tolerably. But the silver is decidedly inferior. The best stuff was deftly removed by the Bursar in 1428 when he retired to France. Unfortunately, he hadn't paid the insurance premium, I believe.

—That is a combination of iniquity and inequity one would associate more with Oxford. So your work is proceeding apace? The godless Voltaire, isn't it?

— Only a Roman would say that: they don't know the difference between a deist and an atheist even today.

— Careful. You speak of the Church I love...

— Forgive me. It's strange, but even though I was brought up among Catholics in France, I always think of Church historians as being Protestants.

— Like Lebrecht?

— Oh, was he? How did you know I knew Lebrecht?

— You... you mentioned him, I think, didn't you, to one of the other Fellows in Hall? I happened to overhear you.

— Ah. Really?

...In the middle of the night a thunderous knocking came on the door. Amélie was frightened out of her wits and jumped under the bed. My servant, grumbling, took a candle to the door and shouted 'Who is there?' It was my old comrade Briand, who warned me that Madame de Crécy had informed the police that I was to fight a duel, and the police were on their way to arrest me. Quickly we gathered up clothing, which we donned in the carriage as we sped out of Carcassonne. But I could not flee, as that would brand me as a coward for ever. I sent Briand with a message to the unfortunate Estève, my unwilling opponent, that I would await him at six outside the town...

— Not there? Strange... No, she's not in her studio, I've been ringing all day and this evening. I expect she's at a concert. I'll try again about eleven.

— But there are only four of them. All we have to do is arrange for each one to be investigated surreptitiously by an agent in Egypt.
— Is that all? Have you ever tried to arrange for a prison to be investigated, in a foreign country, surrounded by wary voluntary internees with nothing better to do than watch every visitor like a hawk? And then all we have to do is walk out with the treasure and get it to Cairo or Alexandria. It's so simple. So you do it, and come back and tell me how clever you are...

— I hope, *professore*, that you are quite convinced how unfortunate it would be if a phenomenon of such extraordinary mystical force were to be authenticated, in a church which has always prided itself on pre-dating that of St. Peter. We may think we are the rock, but they still think of themselves as the primitive bedrock.
— I fully appreciate that, eminence. St. Mark was a great

and holy man, but the practicalities of keeping the Church together require that he remain secondary to St. Peter.

— And Paul. The primacy of Rome may have been a political act rather than a spiritual one, but if primitive Christianity had gone on with Jerusalem or Alexandria as its centre, it would have been stillborn.

— Clearly it was God's will that we should have heard about this before Professor Lebrecht had a chance to do anything about it. But we must move fast and find the rest of Freyssenet's account. It would be extremely helpful, if you could find out what the Egyptians are up to. There is a man by the name of Fuad Riad ...

— If you cannot do better than this, we shall have to recall you and send someone more efficient.

— Please be a little patient. We are in the process of interrogating the girl. She knows where are the papers now, and we shall soon have a complete success.

— You do realise how important this is, Riad? The state simply cannot have such a strong mystic force operating within the Coptic Church. They are enough trouble as it is, the sworn enemies of Islam...

— Despite hundreds of years of oppression.

— What did you say?

— I said despite years of correction...

— I tell you I don't know what you're talking about. Now let me go!

— I think one or two tiny adjustments might improve your memory. I mean adjustments to your fingers. So pretty and agile; I remember how they sped over the keys that evening in Australia. It would be a pity to spoil them, like butterflies with broken wings...

—All right. I'll tell you. They're in Cambridge. With a... a Professor... Crankshaw. That's his name. Trinity College. *(At least that will take them a bit of time... I hope that's the name Simon mentioned, the man who took so much interest in his seminar... He sounds sensible and solid, and he might mention it to Simon if they call on him about the manuscript, then Simon will know there is trouble...)*

— We shall make enquiries. But you stay here until we know you tell the truth.

...It was well on into the night when we heard the singing and the shouting coming from the other side of the valley. Amélie looked out of the window and called me. I saw lights, held in the hand, a hundred of them or more, from the direction of Saint-Cirgues. So, the rumours we had heard, and had so foolishly ignored, were true, then. Citizen Gambin had stirred up the local *jacquerie* and they were about to add another jewel to their crown of shame. My dearest, faithful Amélie wanted to stand and fight them with musket and pitch-fork, but I could see there would be no chance, even if my servants remained loyal to me. We had no more than fifteen minutes. Swiftly we dressed, I gathered up the most precious of my belongings, those I had not already sent to the comte d'Andreoli in Bellinzona, by which time the coach had been made ready. Taking the reins myself, I urged the horses over the bridge and away from the approaching shouts. Fortunately the rabble were making so much noise, they did not hear the sound of our wheels or the clatter of the hooves as we set off towards Montélimar. Amélie sat within the coach, sobbing. At least I had with me one of my two most precious possessions, my adorable, faithful Amélie. But alas! The other, I had had to abandon: what treasure lies in that box bricked up in the family vault! I pray to God that the Godless shall not discover it, and that I may one day return to behold it once more, for no man could wish for any greater reward in this life.

— Two gentlemen from London here to see you, Professor Crankshaw.

— Really? From Sotheby's, I expect. Send them across, would you please, Norman?...

— We are doing our best, Dr. Prestcott.
— But it's been two days now, inspector. We can't have people just disappearing from their own homes in the middle of London.
— Can't we just! Happens all the time, unfortunately. Usually we find the ones who don't want to be found...

— Good day to you, gentlemen, do sit down. Now what can I do for you?
— I'll come straight to the point, Professor. We would like to talk about the Freyssenet papers.
— Ah, yes. Well, I was speaking last night to our friends in Rome, and they know how difficult the situation is, I hope. Now, how can you help me?
— We help you? I do not advise you to be frivolous, professor. We want the papers. Now. Please give them to us.
— You must be joking! Look here, who the devil are you?

— Just stay by me, Simon. You will have nothing to do, except make sure the tape recorder keeps on working. I can put myself into a hypnotic trance very quickly. Hand me Anna's hairbrush, will you? It may seem a funny thing to use, but the hairbrush is close to one very often, and picks up many vibrations from the head...

— Seen returning from Cambridge last night? Jaguar, EFT 185Z. That's the one. Never mind, you did your best. Where is it now? It's more important to know where it is now than to have the occupants in a cell. Yes. Good God.

In Earl's Court Road any one house could have fifty people living in it. We'll keep the whole block under surveillance. What's that? Interesting. What was his name? Crankshaw? How badly? I see. Has he made a statement? Doesn't want to? Sounds a bit fishy. The two men do sound familiar. I'll get mug-shots of Riad and fax them to Cambridge.

— Was not very nice of you, little miss Anna, to make us waste our time.

— Don't blame me! You just didn't find what you are looking for, that's all. He must have hidden them. He knew about them, you said that. So how could I be lying?

— But you knew he no longer had them.

— Of course I didn't. He could have dumped them in the river for all I know.

— Or given them to your friend, Dr. Prestcott.

— Well? Did you see him too?

— We tried. But he was not there. We searched.

— Oh? He'll recognise your visiting card, I expect.

— We ought to bring in her father. He will not like to see his little Anna being hurt.

— And vice-versa. Wait till it is dark...

— High up, a tall building. Six floors up. Not a good house. But a noble name coming through. An aristocrat.

— King's Road? Kingsway? Regents Park?

— No, no. Wait. Caught.

— Caught who? What with?

— Earl. Earl's Court. A number. 71 flashes through my mind.

— But that's a whole district, Earl's Court, not a street.

— There is no Earl's Court Street?

— I don't think so. There's an Earl's Court Road.

— Yes. That is it.

114

— It was reassuring that we all ended up at the same address, anyway, inspector. Perhaps I shall be getting a lot more police work to do now?

— Hrrmph. Well, it was quite impressive, I must admit. But we got the same result by routine methods, didn't we? Slightly ahead of you, in fact, luckily for you.

— Yes, but our way was a lot cheaper, wasn't it, inspector? Dr. Schoenheimer didn't have to sit in a car outside all night.

— I don't know about that, sir. It depends on what Dr. Schoenheimer's fee is.

— I tell you what, inspector. For getting back my Anna unhurt ... almost... I give you my services free for one year.

— We're acting as though it's all over and done with. Let's not forget there are others with an interest in Freyssenet. They're not going to give up. And I'm fed up with having my rooms turned inside out. Incidentally, you'd better have these papers, inspector. I'm going to have to do some research in the south of France. Awful deprivation, of course. Terrible bore and all that.

11

Fed up was the understatement of the academic year. When Simon surveyed the wreckage of his study at St. Peter's, he was moved to new heights of Rabelaisian invective. Even Thomas, his gyp, found it impressive, and he was used to the uninhibited vocabulary of the current brand of undergraduate. Thomas remembered Simon from seven or eight years back, when he was a graduate student. Like most old-style gyps, he took a pride in recalling the names and faces of those who had been his charges; not for nothing did he do for them, act as valet, butler, cleaner, friend and adviser — a kind of underpaid Jeeves. He was a dying race, and he knew it. He would be pensioned off next year, and he was dreading the thought of it. Day after day in a little terrace house on the outskirts of Cambridge, with no one but the old woman to talk to. Give him the company of these bright young things any day, spoiled though some of them might be. So, being involved in the lives of some of the men on his staircase, Thomas was genuinely upset when he found the chaos in Dr. Prestcott's rooms. And now the two of them were standing, surveying the residual mess.

'I done a bit of clearing up after the police left, doctor, put the books back an such like, and your clothes and the bed, cor, you should a seen it, like the wreck o' the bleedin' 'esperus it was an' no mistake. But all them cards in the little boxes, I din know what to do with them, so I put 'em in little piles on your desk there, I 'ope that's all right?'

'Yes, of course, Thomas.' Simon looked at him, smiled ruefully. 'I'm very grateful to you, and I'm sorry you had so much trouble.'

'I dunno if they took anything, sir. The police want to ask

you about that.'

'Thanks. I'll get in touch with them.'

Thomas left, and Simon began the task of putting three thousand index cards back in order — the fruit, so far, of his work on Voltaire. He realised he was coming to the end of the Cambridge resources. The University Library was well stocked so far as printed material went, but he now needed more manuscript material. Most of it was in Leningrad, very closely kept by Russian scholars who had been saying for fifty years they were going to publish critical editions of Voltaire's works including all the manuscript notes; but nothing ever happened. Recently, however, there had been a cultural break-through, and the Voltaire Institute in Geneva had managed to get microfilm of all the notes and variants written by Voltaire himself, in the volumes kept in the Saltikov-Shchedrin Library. These were essential to Simon if he was to be able to follow the creative process right through. The changes a writer makes in the course of composing a text are a vital clue to the self-censorship process. For most literary scholars, these changes are of stylistic interest, but Simon was trying to interpret them in a psychologically-based way, to reveal the underlying structures of the mind that recur over a large output of works, and over many years.

During that day, a couple of young policemen came along and took a statement from him about the break-in. He told them that so far as he could see, nothing was missing, though a fair amount of damage had been done to books and clothes.

'Any idea what they were after, sir?' asked the detective-sergeant. He told them he had no idea — money, he supposed. They thought that very likely. He was glad he had followed his hunch about the transcription and notes he had made from Freyssenet's memoirs. He had at first been strongly inclined to take them with him to London, but decided it would be best to keep the transcript separate in case of accidents, as if there were such things. So he placed them in a sealed envelope and asked Adrian Wiseman to look after them for him. Adrian was vaguely amused by this.

'I see the paranoia of the big city has got into you,' he said through the cloud of pipe-smoke that habitually surrounded his head. 'I don't think I've ever locked my door, except when I'm out of town. However, whatever you say, my dear chap. Shall I put them under the mattress or under the floorboards?' Simon replied that floorboards were too obvious, and the mattress would do, or even under the pile of essays on his desk.

When he went to collect his envelope, Adrian was in a sombre mood. 'Frightfully sorry to hear about the burglary, Simon. Anything missing?'

'I don't think so.'

'Was it this they were after?' Adrian asked cannily.

'It might have been. Academic espionage, perhaps.'

He went off, leaving Adrian shaking his head sadly over what things were coming to. It was only the following day that Thomas brought him news of the strange goings-on next door, at Trinity. On the gyps' grape-vine he heard it, you know how things get about, well his best mate worked there, and a certain professor had had his rooms ransacked and all, but he was kicking up no end of a fuss cause he don't want to call in the police or tell anyone. Just paid his gyp ten quid to help him clear it up and keep his mouth shut. The Bursar had had words with him, summat about the college insurance, but this professor said nothing had happened he couldn't manage himself, and he didn't want the police brought in asking all sorts of stupid questions.

Simon knew immediately who it was, and why, thanks to Anna's inspired gut-reaction, Riad's attention had been deflected away from him towards Timothy Crankshaw. But why was he so adamant about saying nothing to the police? Taking this little mystery together with the slip of the tongue about Freyssenet, Professor Crankshaw seemed to be less of a benign figure than your average college Fellow. Then Simon thought of Cambridge's reputation for breeding espionage agents, and ceased to be surprised. Whatever dear old Wiseman would have said about Simon's thoughts at that moment, paranoia was top of the bill.

The afternoon post brought him a letter from Geneva:

Institut Voltaire
Les Délices
Genève

Monsieur

In reply to your letter, I have to inform you that the Director of the Institut is at present in England, and would be glad to meet you at a mutually convenient time. Would you please write to Dr. Leverson at The Grange, Nr. Saffron Walden, or telephone him at the number given below.

Please accept my most distinguished salutations

M. Le Nôtre, Secrétaire.

Seeing the address there, on the letter-heading, Simon found it quite poignant that the Institut was in the very same house in which Freyssenet claimed to have met Voltaire. This had been one of the *philosophe*'s retreats from the enmity and oppression of the police state of France's *ancien régime*. What would a young aristocrat like Freyssenet find in common with such a radical thinker? The more Simon read of Freyssenet's own writings, the more he found he failed to fit in with any preconceived notion of the French aristocrat.

'I just thought you ought to know, Inspector, even though it's off your beat, as it were.'

'I'm very grateful to you, Dr. Prestcott. So if I've got it right, you think there may be a link between the two attempted burglaries?'

'Well, it's not just that, Inspector: I'm more concerned that there might be a link between Professor Crankshaw and Freyssenet. But I don't know what it could possibly be.'

'I'm not sure that's my concern,' Irving replied.

'I see. Um... do you know who Riad is working for yet?' asked Simon.

'He's proving very difficult to deal with. Fortunately we've tightened up a good deal recently on so-called "diplomatic privilege", and we are able to hold him for the kidnapping charge. If your Cambridge professor will volunteer to identify Riad and his accomplice, we've got him on two counts.'

'What about Mrs. Greaves? She saw him in her house.'

'That in itself isn't a crime, you see,' said Irving with a new-found patience. 'We're still trying to trace the people behind Riad and the couple of crims who nobbled his "surveyor". They are all being very uncooperative, I can't think why.'

'In the meantime, there are a couple of people, three in fact, who can expect more action to come their way: Miss Schoenheimer, Mrs. Greaves, and me? Is that right?'

'Yes. That is a trifle worrying,' Irving admitted.

'Just a trifle, yes.' Good old English phlegm, makes you sick. 'Well, look at it this way, Inspector,' Simon went on with the sort of half-suppressed sarcasm he normally reserved to jolly up Faculty meetings, 'if anything mildly serious, like being placed upside down in a barrel of concrete, happens to any of us, you're going to lose a witness or three, aren't you? So you can't just leave us to it, now you've got your man. Even if you're not interested in our staying alive and well, we certainly are. The moment Riad is out on bail, we'd better go to ground, I think, till you've got all your ends knotted.'

The thought behind his last words was not lost on Inspector Irving, as Simon banged down the receiver.

Professor Timothy Crankshaw felt he was a marked man. What a fool he had been to jump to the conclusion that those men had come from his own control centre. He had, he thought, missed a literally heaven-sent chance of counteracting the work of Satan. Centre thought so too. He discovered, when he made another of those ISD calls that kept Telecom so profitable, and his own telephone bills so mysteriously massive, that he was not going to receive a gold star that week.

'I really must protest, Eminence,' he whined. 'We have learned something very valuable. We now have proof that another party is interested in what lies behind the Freyssenet phenomenon. If I might respectfully suggest it, you should instruct your security people to find out who this man Fuad Riad is working for.'

The smooth voice replied, 'But we know, *professore*.'

'You know!'

'Of course. We have had dealings with him before. But it was only when he revealed his interest in you, and got his name in the newspapers through that stupid attempt at kidnapping, that we put two and two together.'

'So? Is it the Communists? Or Islam?'

'Communists! They are no threat to us. They have never tried to replace spiritual belief by another spiritual belief. It is Islam's persuasive alternative faith that threatens Rome, and Riad is one of their agents. He used to be good, but he is losing his touch. I have to warn you, however, of an even greater threat.'

'Ah! The Coptic Church! I fully realise, Eminence, that the Egyptian mystical phenomenon must never become public knowledge. To re-establish the ancient Coptic church of St. Mark would discredit Rome.'

'Precisely, *professore*.' The voice had taken on an edge. 'But if you will kindly let me explain: imagine an enemy as potentially strong as the KGB, the Gestapo, the IRA, Saddam Hussein, the PLO, Gadaffi, the Red Guard, the Islamic fundamentalists, and any other fanatical terrorist group you can think of, and what do you get?'

Crankshaw thought quickly. 'The Holy Inquisition?'

'No! No... Forgive my anger. I forgot your English sense of humour. The Holy Inquisition was an institution of charity and mercy, compared to what we find ourselves faced with now: the Square of Eskar. They make even

Islamic fanatics look like the Society of Friends.'

Crankshaw was dumbfounded. 'What! But I thought they were a monastic brotherhood, a *bruderhof*, retired from worldly concerns.'

'That is their public image. Everyone believes that. But in reality they have in place a network of religious and political agents, highly trained, very secret.'

'But how are they a threat to us?'

'Their aims are basically racist, neo-Nazi. Militantly hostile to Christianity. And to Judaism and Islam, but that is their problem. You see now the meaning of their emblem —a square round a circle. Their square enclosing the earth, completely and hermetically. Their belief is unwavering, their hatred for all other systems is implacable. As if we did not have enough anxieties with our own reformist priests, with Islam, and now the Copts.'

Crankshaw was now thoroughly confused. 'Why then, exactly, are we trying to suppress a mystical occurrence that can only enhance Christianity, Eminence?'

'You have been listening to too much ecumenical romanticism, *professore*, in your ivory tower. It may be good for Christianity, but it would not be good for Holy Mother Church. And she is our prime concern at all times, is she not?'

'Of course, Eminence. At all times.'

Professor Crankshaw slowly replaced the heavy black handset in its cradle, wishing he was merely what he tried to appear to be: a harmless, innocent scholar, a humble seeker after truth.

12

There are unwilling heroes and unwitting victims. Simon had no desire to be one of the former, and felt he was being dragged into the rôle of the latter. He fervently wished, at times, that the whole Lebrecht-Freyssenet business would go away, but without taking Anna with it. That was the trouble with his wishful thinking. He would suddenly wake up — only to find that Anna had joined that insubstantial pageant too. She had even more reason than he to feel she was an undesirable alien in a world of intrigue she did not understand and did not want to be involved in. The danger of mutilation had been real and horrible, and she could no longer take any of the pleasures of life for granted. She became anxious, moody, afraid to leave her father's house by herself. Floris tried every way he knew to re-assure her, through meditation and self-awareness, but it was no good. She was constantly afraid for Simon as well.

Whenever they talked over the telephone during the week following the Earl's Court arrest, he tried to keep his own anxiety under, but he knew she was not fooled. He felt he was a target about to be fired at by unknown marksmen from directions he could not guess.

As he was about to lift his telephone to speak to Dr. Leverson, it rang.

'Is that Dr. Simon Prestcott, late of Koala and Kangaroo Land?'

It took Simon just a brief second to place that deep, resonant, friendly Yorkshire accent. 'Only if that is the late and utterly unlamented Lord Plod of Pest Control.' He grinned for the first time in days.

'The very same!' came the roar from the other end.

'Great heavens, man, fancy hearing you! Where are you?

123

How did you know I was here?'

'Ah, you can't escape the eagle eye of your friendly English bobby for long.'

'I've seen too many of them in action lately to be completely convinced of that,' Simon retorted.

'Aye, so I gather, my lad. Let's have a drink.'

'Sure. Why don't you come up to my rooms in half an hour?'

'Done. And don't expect me to bring a bottle, Australian style! You owe me one from seven years ago.'

Seven years! Was it that long since he and George Plaidy had been inseparable buddies, when Simon needed sensible and amusing company after the divorce? George had been a brilliant classics student at St. Peter's, and had been expected to go on to read for a Ph.D. But out of the blue, he had given it all up, to join the police force. Simon could not understand it then. He could now. Occasionally he used to see George on point duty in the middle of Cambridge as he dashed past on his bicycle, but to his shame had allowed the friendship to lapse. Even so, it was George who organized the farewell party for him when he decided to move to Melbourne. He did indeed owe him one...

'Yes, of course, I've been expecting to hear from you, Dr Prestcott,' said Gustave Leverson's precise military voice. 'I must tell you that I view your psycho-biographical approach with the deepest scepticism, but that said, I should be glad to talk to you. And you are welcome to work at the Institut whenever you like, naturally. Now, let me see, I have to be in New York for most of next week. You're not going to the American 18th-century Society meeting, I suppose?'

'No, I'm afraid not, Dr. Leverson.'

'Sensible fellow. It will be extremely boring, but they have asked me to give a paper, so I must go, alas. It's being organised by a bloody awful professor of history who treats reviewing as a means to destroy reputations, so it's best to keep on the right side, then he might just kick me in the backside instead of the groin for my next book.'

'I'm sure I know who you mean,' said Simon. Or one of several such emotionally insecure people like him who haunt the world of historians.

'So would this coming weekend be convenient, if you could get to the Grange for lunch on Saturday?'

'That would be fine, thank you very much.'

'Do you have a wife?'

'Er, no, not exactly.'

'Well, do you have a companion you would like to bring? It would have to be someone who doesn't mind dogs. I know New Zealanders think dogs should be treated like farm animals, but to me they are civilised beings, and they share the house.'

Simon had not tried Anna out on that one, but thought she would regard this intelligent species with respect.

'I'm not a Kiwi,' Simon assured him, 'not even an Aussie, plain old Anglo-French. Thank you, then. I hope Miss Schoenheimer will be able to accompany me.'

'Schoenheimer?' Leverson asked abruptly. 'That's a name I seem to know. Right then. Midday on Saturday next.'

Simon just had time to get some wine and beer from the college buttery before George came thumping up the staircase, to be met with a rapturous welcome from Simon.

'I gather you're off duty,' Simon commented as he refilled their glasses. 'Would you like a ham sandwich with that?'

'Sure, thanks. No, I'm always on duty. Never sleep. Uniform's a thing of the past. I didn't spend long on the beat after you fled to the colonies.'

'I'm not surprised they realised pretty soon what a bright boy they'd got in you. Mustard?'

'Yes, lots. You've been doing quite well, for an academic,' George proferred. 'Do you regret not being able to lie young ladies back on your couch, ask them about their sex lives, and then charge a fee for it?'

'Not at all. Sex is very boring to talk about when you've heard the same frustrations a hundred times.'

'But still retains its fascination in practice after ten thousand times. Odd that, isn't it?'

'Yes, it's a great old urge. Think of the crimes and murders that sex has caused throughout history,' Simon mused.

'Tell me about it,' said George.

'Sorry. I guess you've had a few cases you wouldn't tell your mother about?'

'True enough. But it's no different, basically, from other emotional reactions that override reason, is it? I expect you've got a technical word for it, super-ego or something, the bit of the mind that tells you what's right and wrong. Fanatics all suffer from a failure of the braking system. So the emotive engine goes on trundling down the hill, killing and maiming and thinking it is doing the right thing.'

'Have you never come across a justified murder?' asked Simon.

'Not really. But I can think of one or two hypothetical situations where it might be justifiable for the sake of, say, a greater ideal. But that's dangerous moral ground I wouldn't like to stray on.'

After their predominantly liquid lunch, Simon and George walked it off along the Backs. It was good to be retracing steps, so often taken deep in earnest discourse when they were younger men, first to the left up past the lawns of King's, then back to the ornate wedding-cake of St. John's. As they dawdled past Trinity College, Simon turned to his companion.

'George, why would a Fellow of a college not want it to be reported to the police if his rooms were ransacked?'

George thought for a moment, kicked a stone into the river, to the consternation of a moorhen who was minding

126

her own business, hidden, she had thought, in the long rushes.

'I suppose you're thinking of Crankshaw?'

Simon froze. So George's visit was not just for old time's sake.

'Yes, I was actually. I suppose that means you know about my little problem too?'

'I think you have more than one, Simon. And not little ones either. That's really why I'm here — but it was only because I recognised your name on the report, and wanted to help. I volunteered and had to push like mad to get on this case.'

'What case? Some oaf turning my rooms over?'

'Oh, come on, Simon, my lad. You know what I'm talking about. The whole scenario ever since Lebrecht's murder.'

Simon whistled. 'So, Irving has put you in the picture. I must say, I'm relieved, because I was beginning to think we'd been abandoned the moment they had the guy who did Lebrecht in. That Egyptian bloke.'

'Riad? Yes, he's put away, safe and sound for the moment, but there is a lot of diplomatic pressure being applied to get him bail, and to prevent extradition to Australia. He may be set free next week.'

Simon was appalled. 'But that will place Anna, Miss Schoenheimer, in great danger. They've already tried to kidnap her and threaten her.'

'Yes, I know. Bad business. But you're at risk as well, Simon. We seriously think things are going to hot up. You've opened up a Pandora's box here, and there seem to be quite a few unsavoury parties wanting to dip their fingers in it.'

'Who, we? And who they for that matter?' Simon looked round and lowered his voice. 'Look, you see, I'm getting jittery even talking about it, in Cambridge of all places!'

George gave a hollow laugh. 'Doesn't this strike you as the ideal place for intrigue on a grand scale, what with Blunt and Co.? Which brings us back to Crankshaw. Fortunately, he doesn't have a direct line, so all his overseas calls have to go through the college switchboard. Discreet enquiries have revealed a strange habit he has developed. He's going to get a shock when he gets his phone bill.'

'Phoning whom? Not the Kremlin?'

'No' George laughed. 'The Vatican.'

Simon could not bring himself to be surprised. 'After all, he is a world authority on ecclesiastical law; twelfth-century decretals, I think. The Vatican Library must be stuffed with them. Perhaps someone is after his manuscripts too, that'd be a change.'

'Does that explain why he's so coy about the break-in?'

'No. And it doesn't explain how he knew I had met Lebrecht.'

'Did he, by Jove?' George stroked his characterful chin, and came to a decision. 'Look, Simon, if you don't mind, you'd better run through the details of what's happened, just for me. There might be something we're overlooking. We really have got to move rather fast, I think.'

'But hang on, hang on, George, we're not in the middle of the Wars of Religion. Not against Rome, anyway. I wouldn't like to get tangled up with Teheran at the moment, but Christ Almighty, Rome! With that benign old Pole running things there?'

'Does he?'

'What?'

'Run them? Did Kennedy or Reagan "run" America? Or Mitterand France? Once you get used to thinking of human society as a game of chess, you're a tenth of the way there. But think of it as three-dimensional chess. Or if you like — you know how much I used to love Sophocles and Euripides — think of it all as a whole lot of dramas going on, on different levels, with the characters drifting from one to the other, sometimes in the same rôles, sometimes with different masks on.'

'Three-dimensional Calderón, you mean?'

'Calderón?' George's broad brow furrowed. 'Er..., let's see... *Life's a Dream*?'

'No doubt.' Simon's mind flashed back to Bristow's question: Whose? God's or mine? 'I was thinking of *El Gran Teatro del Mundo*, the Great Theatre of the World where God gives out all the parts to the actors, like you or me, but we don't know what the plot is or what our lines are.'

'Yes, O.K., and this great universal drama goes on in many places, on different levels, all at the same time...'

'And maybe at different times, simultaneously, with infinite intermeshing plots and sub-plots...'

'Not just three-dimensional, but four?'

George's northern common sense suddenly took him over.

'All very well,' he objected, shrugging his heavy shoulders, 'but hardly realistic, is it, this "All the world's a stage" stuff?'

'Nonsense! What about the Celts, for instance? Haven't you ever been to Ireland?'

'Yes, of course.'

'Well then!' Simon spread out his arms, as if calling on the heavens to bear him witness, 'They're all honorary members of Actors' Equity improvising unwritten Shaw and Beckett and Joyce plays.'

They smiled at each other, briefly elated at the way they had been able to bounce off each other's imagination, as they had so often as students. Then their smiles faded, and the reality of the situation crept into their minds again, like a chill wind ruffling the still waters of the Cam beside them. To each, his own reality.

When Simon slid between the cold sheets that night he felt more at ease than he had for weeks. For the first time since that ill-fated visit to the Trevelyans, he felt the situation, as it now involved him and the Schoenheimers, was being taken seriously in hand by someone able to unravel mysteries instead of being simply carried along by them. George Plaidy had been well briefed, or had informed himself fully, from Melbourne, London and Cambridge sources, but these were, inevitably, somewhat light on detail regarding the more arcane implications of reincarnation regression and the validity of the "mystical" experience of Freyssenet at the monastery. He laid out for Simon a series of hypotheses based on the interests of the parties apparently vying with each other for possession of the Freyssenet manuscripts, or other supposed contents of the box. He agreed with Simon that they did seem to be after different things, but was against any adventuring in France to find the box which the comte claimed to have bricked up in a vault of his château, because there would be no way to protect him once he left England, and because the site was so much closer to Italy, whence at least one of the parties was operating. Simon, for his part, refused to believe in any international conspiracy theory, and clung to his belief that they were up against a couple of rival gangs who had wrongly got wind of some kind of "treasure". Nevertheless, he agreed that they could and would be quite ruthless if anyone got in their way nearer their own territory, wary though they might be of further attacks on British soil now that they had shown their hand, albeit ineffectually.

George, it appeared, was not working for the Cambridge C.I.D., as Simon had originally assumed. He had, he said, been seconded a couple of years before to a special section which liaised between police and military security services, set up to facilitate concerted action against terrorists, those modern equivalents of knights in shining armour, as he put it, devoted unto death to vengeance, the redressing of wrongs, the defence of the highest ideals, by means of a whole battery of methods from blown-off kneecaps and machine-gunned women and children, to self-righteous rhetoric. Simon was unsure about George's blanket condemnation of terrorists.

'But "terrorism" is just a label, surely,' he objected, 'for activities we don't happen to agree with? The *maquis* in Occupied France were terrorists to the German soldier who got a knife between his ribs.'

'No,' George countered, 'that's not a fair analogy. At the first international conference on terrorism in Jerusalem, in 1979, terrorism was defined as "the deliberate and systematic murder, maiming and menacing of the innocent to inspire fear for political ends". Now, you wouldn't claim that the soldier following Hitler's orders was innocent?'

' No. Though he would. So some terrorism is justified, and some not?'

'Exactly.'

'But the IRA would say they are justified.'

'Ah yes, the IRA,' George smiled. 'They prove a point: but for the IRA, there wouldn't be one British soldier in Northern Ireland. Terrorism is not only bad, it's counter-productive.'

'Not a stepping-stone to power?'

'If it's done intelligently,' George conceded. 'But putting bombs in kids' Christmas toys doesn't win friends or influence people.'

When Simon's feet finally came to terms with the sub-zero conditions at the lower end of his bed, he drifted off to sleep with two thoughts in his mind: *primo*, that he must, but *must*, get round to buying an electric blanket tomorrow; and *secundo*, that Anna always had a remarkably warming effect on a bed, so perhaps he should concentrate more on this source of warmth...

It was whilst he was still quite decidedly conscious that he became aware that all was not normal. He was not asleep, he knew, because he felt his left upper arm and squeezed it between finger and thumb, and it hurt. But even in the darkness he knew that everything was different. Gingerly he raised his left hand and felt his face. He gasped as he encountered a fully-grown beard. His pyjamas had become a long shirt. His felt his brow beading with sweat, but it was not through fear — he felt quite at ease — it was because the air temperature round him was hot, humid and oppressive. At first he did not dare to move, as he was sure he would fall off whatever he was lying on: everything was moving under him. Slowly he pushed the covering off him, not blankets but a single cotton sheet, and slid his feet to the ground. Not carpet, but rough matting. Holding on to the wall at the head of the bed, he slowly levered himself up, and quickly fell down again as his head hit something, solid wood. He cursed aloud, and realised without surprise he had cursed in French. Then his instinct took over. He knew what to do. He knew this place. He reached out with assurance and found a candle and tinder-box on a small table beside the bed. As though he had done it a thousand times before, he lit the candle and looked round, now feeling quite at home, in his bedroom. It was not a bedroom, of course, but a cabin, on a ship. Hence the rolling. Not a big ship. With a carefulness that came from experience now, he stood again, and without hesitation went over to the opposite wall. He moved his right hand to a circle in the wooden planking at eye-level, about one inch across, and pulled out a plug of wood. Through the hole came a dim light. He peered through, and at first saw nothing. Then his gaze travelled downwards, and came to rest upon the most heavenly vision ever bestowed upon him in his short but full experience of the varieties of feminine comeliness.

She was lying with her head furthest away from him, innocent of all vestment, with one arm behind her head in the guise of pillow. The soles of her small, pretty feet were pink, but the rest of her skin, her legs, thighs, slightly rounded belly and the impeccably formed globes of her bosom, were uniformly golden. One leg was slightly bent, out to one side, leaving him with a view that many men would willingly die or commit murder for. The bed was surrounded by a fine gauze hanging, upon which his eyes had originally focused, thus giving him the impression that he was seeing nothing. But this gauze was intended to keep away importuning insects, not inquisitive eyes. Reluctantly, he raised his eyes to her face, and was immediately rapt with wonderment, for the perfection of form of that shapely bow, slightly curved into a smile, the delicate texture of those firm but softly-moulded cheeks, and the nobility of her brow, beyond any beauty he had seen before, paled into mediocrity when his eyes met hers. For she was not asleep. She was looking steadily, unwaveringly, at the hole in the wall which formed the tunnel linking their love. Love. This was not the first time he had seen her. This display of her every charm was not that of a wanton, but an act of devotion. He cast his mind back to remind himself how this had come about, and was immediately stricken with grief. She was the newest acquisition of the Pasha Ismael, having been purchased at great expense as an exotic beauty of a kind rarely seen in the Levant: an Oriental, not Japanese, not Chinese, not Indian, but from a far country which his interpreter had not been able to define, since those waters were hardly known in the year 1778.

His sorrow came from his certain knowledge that this gentle creature was to become the plaything of a voluptuary who would force her to the most degrading practices, and then cast her aside along with the rest of his numerous concubines. Not only that, but when the ship arrived in Alexandria, he would never, never see her again. His rêverie was shattered by a knocking at his door. Swiftly he replaced the wooden plug, and called out, '*Entrez* .'

But the door did not open. Instead, he was again in semi-darkness, save for a glow of light coming from above his head. As his eyes became accustomed to the obscurity, he observed a small step-ladder next to him, with soft cloth tied round each rung. He was in a large cupboard, or wardrobe, and round him hung female clothing from which emanated a heavy odour of sweat and aromatics. He knew why he was there, and was aware that he was in extreme danger. When he had arrived in Alexandria, he had confided his despair about the beautiful concubine to his dear friend, Princess Elena, who was a favoured visitor at the court of the Pasha, and an intimate acquaintance of his senior wife. Seeing his sorrow, and feeling pity for him, for she too was keenly aware of the ravages of love denied, she agreed to enter into a little intrigue that could, if discovered, result in violent death. She would invite the ladies of the harem to her palace, having installed him, the headstrong, passionate young Frenchman, in a secret place. The Princess would suggest to the ladies a new game, called *cache-cache*. When it was the turn of his beloved to hide, she would guide her to his hiding-place, where they would have a brief but no doubt intense time in close proximity.

So now he was waiting. He had gone through a moment of terror when the Chief Eunuch had demanded that the cupboard be opened, when he was doing his round checking security, but the Princess had told him it contained only religious objects sacred to her faith, which no one else could see without incurring the wrath of her god. This the eunuch understood without difficulty. From the top of his ladder, through the glass above the door of his hide-away, Freyssenet could observe the arrival of the ladies as they went, faces masked, across the doorway into the salon next door. He caught the briefest glimpse of his beauteous Oriental, and all but fell off his ladder in a swoon.

For what seemed an eternity, he listened to the peals of laughter and giggles that filtered through the wall. Then the door of the salon opened, and there was a scampering all over the house. The game had begun. The first to hide was ushered to a distant place upstairs, and was eventually found. Then he saw his own object of devotion, the jewel of his heart, being led quietly and quickly into his room. Princess Elena swiftly unlocked his cupboard with the key nestling in her bosom, and pushed the girl forward. There had been no time to warn her or explain, and when she saw a man standing there, she was on the point of screaming, but the Princess firmly placed her hand over her mouth. As the identity of the man before her dawned on her, the girl relaxed. Freyssenet fell to his knees and gently took her hand, placing his lips to her fingers. Knowing how short their time together would be, the Princess gently pushed the girl into the cupboard and locked the door behind her.

There we were, in each other's arms. Had we wished not to

134

have our bodies pressed tightly together, we could not have avoided it. There ensued a brief eternity of passion that will remain forever with me. I quickly ascertained that the girl, whose name I now knew to be Min-ha, was no longer a virgin, for had I robbed the Pasha of his right to the girl's intactness, she would have been tortured and beheaded. We then proceeded to that act which honours and glorifies all creation. The ladder proved an invaluable instrument, as I was very tall and my beloved was exquisitely petite. But in the middle of our exertions, some of the other women entered the room in search of her, and rattled the door of the cupboard. It would be difficult to describe the agony of suspense, as we stood there, scarcely daring to breathe, but our kisses and movements silently continued, she with one foot on the padded rung, the other round my waist. Eventually the women went away, we completed our act of fervent love, and the Princess came to unlock the door. With what tears did we look upon each other for the last time! With what impatience did the Princess finally drag away my beloved Min-ha! I confess that I was on the verge of betraying us all by shouting "Let death come! We shall not be parted!" But the thought of the punishment that would be inflicted upon these two brave women dissuaded me. Quickly, Min-ha was hidden in another place, and I was left to weep in the darkness of my solitary repair.

When Simon returned, he found that his pyjama trousers bore the traces of passionate outpourings such as he had not experienced since he was a white-dreaming young teenager. He got up, still smelling the pungent odours of the cupboard and, above all, the fragrance of Min-ha's smooth and supple body. He could feel it again, nestling, trembling, up against him, and her rapid tiny breaths against his lips, warm and sweet. Even with Anna, it was nothing like this; even the memory had a kind of electric immediacy that no erotic dream ever produced. He glanced at his watch, and noted that four to five hours had passed since he went to bed. So the slices of time he had gone through corresponded with the passage of time in his bedroom at St. Peter's. Then he recalled another clue he had picked up: 1778. Freyssenet would have been twenty-one years old. That is about how he had felt, fifteen years younger than Simon Prestcott.

13

The similarities were obvious; they just hoped there were going to be marked differences, such as no murders and no burgeoning plots. There were double gates, but they were wide open. It had been no problem to find The Grange; it was on the B184, the Cambridge-Saffron Walden road. Anna had taken the train from King's Cross to Cambridge the previous afternoon. After lunch with Gustave Leverson Simon would drive back to London with her. This avoided the necessity to return to Cambridge, and also meant that Anna would not have to drive alone out of London, which she was now very nervous about. They would be back in London in good time for dinner with George Plaidy, who was very keen to meet Anna and Floris.

Gustave Leverson was much as Simon had imagined him: very dapper and military in appearance, precise and no-nonsense in his discourse, with a slight foreign accent which Simon could not place: neither German nor French. He was deferential and immensely courteous to Anna, and slightly headmasterish towards Simon, who found this amusing rather than intimidating. He had every reason to feel intimidated, or at least over-whelmed, by Leverson's accomplishments: he had inherited a fortune partly from his father and partly, it was rumoured, from his first, now deceased, wife. He then proceeded to put these immense funds to the service of his personal passions — not the kind of passions commonly resorted to by free-wheeling millionaires, but individuals (alive and dead) and organizations devoted to combatting injustices in the world. Rather than set up a single Foundation, with committees and administrators, he created bodies for each phase of his many enthusiasms. He had begun by founding the

Paranormal Research Foundation in the 'thirties, and had employed several young investigators of guaranteed sceptical turn of mind, to check the claims of any "psychic" who volunteered, and of many who did not. Arising from this, he started a publication called **PROOF**, first as a vehicle for his team's investigations, which destroyed the reputation and trade of a number of frauds (for a while, until they set up under new names), and then as a scientific journal with contributions from scientists, psychiatrists, and psychologists from all over the world. He was thus one of the factors that encouraged the development of the new science of parapsychology.

Leverson's next venture, after the Allied defeat of Germany, was the foundation of a research centre devoted to that period which he saw as the beginning of our anti-superstitious modern era — the eighteenth century. He had thought first of calling it "The Enlightenment Centre", but opted to commemorate the name of the man who, in his view, personified the struggle against humbug and oppression: Voltaire. The obvious place for this was the haven of neutrality, Geneva. By one of those strange coincidences that litter history, Voltaire's house, *Les Délices*, became available at the same time, and Leverson offered to pay for its restoration in return for sole control of a research centre to be housed there, incorporating his own vast personal library of eighteenth-century editions. It was an offer the City of Geneva could not refuse when it had calculated its financial value, even though the idea of appointing a foreigner to head it stuck in the gullet of many members of the City Council and newspaper commentators.

As one would have expected, The Grange was an eighteenth-century house; but unexpectedly, it was not a classically symmetrical and formal design, but in the style of Horace Walpole's Strawberry Hill: rather zanily Gothic, with battlements and turrets. As Simon eased his little red M.G. to a halt, the welcoming party appeared through the porch at the corner of the house. It consisted of a very large St. Bernard, which placed its front paws on the top of

Simon's car door, thus preventing any attempt to get out. It then simultaneously sniffed Simon's right ear and dribbled copiously on to his shoulder. The same ear then received the full force of the kind of bark that was meant to summon rescuers across several Alps. The benign giant loped back into the house, no doubt with important news about the visitors. In the meantime, Anna had been treated much more gently by the other member of the advance party, a very bouncy black cocker spaniel, who cleared the door with one leap and landed neatly on Anna's lap.

'Do you think this is them?' Simon wondered. 'Perhaps Leverson has been translated, like Bottom, into a four-footed creature as a punishment for getting his karma wrong.'

Anna was still considering how to extract herself and thirty-five pounds of dog from the car, when the next contingent arrived from inside the house. One was a girl of about eight, plump and very dark, and the other was a boy, maybe a couple of years younger, who in startling contrast was fair, with blue eyes. They ran over to the car, and the girl picked the spaniel off Anna's lap.

'Sam is very naughty and bounces on everybody,' she said. 'It's because he hasn't grown up yet.'

'That's all right, I don't mind. Hello, I'm Anna.'

'Hello. I'm Willemina, but in Switzerland I'm Guillaumine. That's my brother, Harvey, only he's Hervé in Geneva, but I call him Harvo after my favourite yummy sticky bread.'

Harvey-Hervé-Harvo had gone round to Simon's side, and lisped sans-toothily, very quietly, into his ear, as though he were inviting some terribly indiscreet admission, 'Are you the man from Thtraylia?'

'Yes, that's right, Harvey. And are you Mr. Leverson's children?'

They both assured him they were; Simon had not thought of Leverson as having a family, certainly not one as young as this. After all, he was in his seventies. Still, look at Bertrand Russell... A female voice came from the entrance hall, and Simon's heart stopped as a young woman stepped out into the pale sunshine.

Without any shadow of doubt, it was Min-ha. As if this was not enough shock, she called out to the little girl: 'Mina, take Sam inside, there's a darling. We can't have him treading all over people.'

As she came towards the car, Anna opened her door and stepped out to take the proferred hand. Unobserved, Simon gazed at the golden fingers, the perfect oval face, the warm, dark eyes.

'I'm Sara Leverson. You must be Miss Schoenheimer.'

'Yes. Anna. How do you do?'

Anna and Sara looked at Simon, who appeared to be rivetted to his seat. He looked into Sara's eyes. Not the slightest glimmer of recognition there, just faint amusement at his stunned look, which she put down to the effect of the St. Bernard.

'Don't tell me François sat on you!' she cried, coming round to Simon. He pulled himself together and got out. Took the hand. The one he had knelt down to kiss, the one that had caressed him so lovingly.... Really, this must stop, it was ridiculous.

As they entered, Leverson was just coming down the stairs, apologising for not being there to greet them earlier. Simon felt much more at ease now, knowing the legendary man was human enough to have a beautiful young wife and children and two eccentric dogs who were treated like intelligent beings.

They had an enjoyable and eventful lunch, in the course of which the Spanish couple who acted as cook and butler had a stack-up row in the kitchen that ended in a slammed door, no more cook, and a butler who resorted to the best dry sherry in the cellar by way of consolation. It could have been a disaster, but Sara handled it all with such resignation that Gustave's natural testiness was mellowed to something less than sarcasm. The children thought it was all huge fun, and kept up a commentary for Simon's sake, as they thought someone from as far away as Thtraylia would not be acquainted with such domestic complications, which were apparently a frequent occurrence at The Grange.

Anna and Sara made friends instantly, and while they and the children went out to stroll round the garden and its adjacent copse, Gustave took Simon into his study.

'So you would like to do some work in Geneva?' Leverson opened.

'Yes, if I may. The Leningrad manuscripts of Voltaire are what really interest me.'

'Yes, we are lucky to have copies of them at last. Might I ask what you hope to learn from them — you're not a literary man, are you?'

The question surprised Simon, for modern textual studies knew no boundaries between the "literary" and the "non-literary". Simon explained his plan, to use the changes made in the process of writing as part of his overall psycho-biography of Voltaire. 'So I'm not writing literary history or criticism *per se*,' he explained. 'For the purposes of my work, Voltaire is a socio-psychological entity. My aim is simply to use the creative process as a means of understanding better the structures of Voltaire's mind.'

'Simply?'

'Well, I know it's not simple. I mean, I don't just want to do what Van den Heuvel has done already, in showing how much there is of Voltaire in his stories. I want to apply more rigid psychological principles, and apply them to a wider range of works — especially the plays and the correspondence, since they have a broader interface with people, characters, and less with abstract ideas.'

'Interface? Hm.' Leverson grimaced. He had some helpful ideas about sources, showed considerable approval for Simon's intention to be as scientific and objective as possible, and then suddenly quizzed him on Barthes' Theory of the Disappearing Author. Simon, in lecturer mode, linked reader reception theory with relative perceptions of reality. Who creates the work of art, the author or the reader? Who creates reality, God or ourselves? Are we our own dream? Or the Disappearing God's dream? 'There is an object made of paper called, say, *Candide*, but we'll never know what Voltaire's personal *Candide* was. I know what mine is, and it's very different from yours, I've no doubt.'

'But tell me, if it's not the author who informs and organizes his text,' said Leverson earnestly, 'then who does? God? Voltaire the Divinely Inspired? Saint Voltaire!'

Simon was tempted to laugh with Leverson and leave it at that, but something egged him on. 'That's not too improbable, is it? You'd agree he was constantly under some kind of urge to combat evil in society, much of it inspired or condoned by the church — Calas, the chevalier de la Barre — at the expense of his own peace and welfare?'

'Yes, of course, but the sense of what is decent and right came from within him. We don't have to suppose any outside force was urging him on.'

They both found their widely divergent views stimulating, and learned much from each other. When he thought the moment ripe, Simon asked, 'Have you come across any mention in Voltaire's correspondence about a chap called Freyssenet?' He watched Leverson's expression carefully, and was certain his mention of the name came as a complete surprise.

'Fress... how do you spell it? With a "c" or "ss"?'

Simon spelt it. 'A minor nobleman from the south of France, whose memoirs give details of a visit he claimed to have made to Voltaire at *Les Délices*.'

Leverson's expression betokened both interest and scepticism.

'Ah, yes, I recall the man now. Also claimed to be a close friend of Rousseau, who never mentions him. Bit of a fantasiser, wasn't he?'

'In this particular case, I'm not sure,' replied Simon. 'You see, he gives a lot of very circumstantial detail about things that were happening in Voltaire's entourage at the time, things that were certainly not common knowledge. As he didn't even like Voltaire — until he visited him — he would hardly have taken the trouble to ferret out details so as to invent a visit, would he?'

Gustave Leverson admitted that Simon had a point, and promised to read an article on the purported visit if he cared to write one. As Simon had almost finished writing one, he was pleased.

Again, Simon ventured to move away from purely Voltairian matters. 'I do hope you don't mind my asking, but where did you meet your wife? She's very beautiful.'

'Far too beautiful for an old man like me, you mean?' Leverson laughed. 'Yes, it must be a bit galling to you young chaps, but it's been a second youth for me, especially having the children. In some ways I pity them, having such an ancient father — I'll be dead by the time they leave school. Anyway, what did you ask? Oh yes, we met in Paris. Her father was a Vietnamese diplomat at the time the Vietnam war started, and he just didn't return there. Stayed in Paris. Plenty of money. Mother's a princess, father's a sort of lord, I didn't care much for that. But she never got on with young men, found them a bit silly, I think. So I was very lucky. Never thought I'd take the plunge again after my first wife died, many years ago now. An old man's folly, I suppose you'd call it.'

'On the contrary. I think it was very, very sensible.'

'It wasn't all sense, you know: I must tell you, between ourselves, I was absolutely bowled over by her. Couldn't believe it when she said Yes. Her parents were not too pleased, which spurred me on a bit. They thought I was too old, and not blue-blooded enough for their Sara.'

Simon paused, wondering whether to ask the next question. Finally: 'You don't know if their family had any connexions with Egypt in the eighteenth century, do you?'

'Egypt! Good God! No idea. Shouldn't think so. Better ask her yourself.'

Gustave Leverson stood and looked through the wide bow window at the returning group. 'Since we're asking personal questions,' he said, 'tell me, is Anna connected to Floris Schoenheimer, the hypnotherapist chap?'

'Yes. His daughter. But why didn't you ask her?'

'Because I didn't want to spoil the pleasant atmosphere. I don't approve of what he's doing at all.'

Simon had no wish to get into an argument with Leverson over this particular matter, so he left it there.

Mina and Harvo, as they insisted on being called by this time, took Simon on one side as the Leversons were talking to Anna about the history of the house. Mina looked up at him and beckoned to him to stoop down so that she could whisper in his ear.

'Have you ever seen the High Garden?' she asked.

Simon shook his head. So, one on each side, they led him out to a lawn, from which there was an unbroken vista, as far as a hill, perhaps two miles away. Mina pointed to the hill.

'There,' she said, 'isn't it lovely?'

Simon looked into the distance. 'Yes, lovely view,' he said, knowing he had not said the right thing.

'But the High Garden, there, see?'

Simon bent down so as to follow her chubby pointing finger more exactly, and saw, just below the top of the hill, a walled garden, with trees in blossom. As he focused on it better, it grew brighter under the rays of the setting sun. The hill must have been due East of the house. The effect was such that the garden seemed to drift closer and closer, so that he could see the branches, the leaves, and the flowers, in great detail. The old brown brick wall round the garden seemed to have no gate or opening. It was like the centre of a vortex, so still, so calm.

Finally, Mina said, 'We can only see it at sunset. We've tried ever so many times to find it, but we never have.'

Harvo nodded gravely. 'I'd like to go and play in it, but we can't find it. Do you think you could find it?' He looked up at Simon.

'Oh, I think one would have to do something rather special to do that,' he replied. 'It would be even harder than going through a looking-glass or the back of a wardrobe.'

They nodded, understanding. Hand in hand, they went back to the house.

The day was drawing to a close as they took their leave of the leaping dogs, the laughing children, and the odd combination of beauty and age. Simon was inwardly warmed to see Min-ha looking so relaxed, contented, fulfilled. At least it has made up for that other terrible time she had. He never had an opportunity to ask her about Egypt. Just as well, perhaps, he reflected.

'You had another *déjà vu* experience, didn't you?' asked Anna, as they sped towards London.

'Tell you about it this evening,' Simon replied. 'I want to know what your father thinks about this one!'

14

Only when Anna, Floris, and George were feeling relaxed and receptive in the warm cosiness of the sitting room overlooking Harley Street did Simon relate what he had experienced.

'And you are quite certain that none of these details were in the memoirs you read?' Floris Schoenheimer asked.

'Absolutely positive,' Simon replied.

'And you are sure about the date — 1778?' asked George.

'Yes. Mind you, it's the sort of year that would have occurred to me anyway, I suppose: both Voltaire and Rousseau died in 1778. If anyone asked me for three important dates in the eighteenth century, that would be one of them.'

'Now tell us about your *déjà vu* feeling when we arrived at the Leversons,' said Anna.

Simon tried to express the feeling as well as he could. He had omitted quite a lot of the physical detail of his experiences in the ship's cabin and the Princess's wardrobe. It was partly his English puritan instinct, and partly his fear of embarrassing both himself and Anna that made him less than frank about this, and he was surprised at himself, even at the time. This made the intensity of his feeling on seeing Sara Leverson difficult to communicate.

'But that doesn't really explain why you were so completely stunned when you saw Sara,' Anna objected.

Simon sighed. He should have known better than to expect to get away with a half-truth with Anna. He supplied the other half. George whistled appreciatively, and Simon was grateful to him for providing a bit of comic relief.

'I reckon you're on to a good thing there, Simon.'

146

George stretched his long, powerful legs out in front of him. 'Two love lives, one here and one there — or one now and one then — and you don't even have to get on your bike. But what happens if you get up to three or four a night, eh? Be pretty exhausting, wouldn't it?'

Floris returned them to more serious matters. 'This kind of uncontrolled regression can be a problem,' he said. 'But the control is simply a matter of experience and technique, and I will help you with this, Simon. It is very good that you have been able to accomplish a spontaneous regression. It shows sensitivity, and should be developed. But you must learn to discipline it now, or you will find it dominating your life. Because it can happen any time, you know, not just in bed. You might be driving along a motorway at the sort of speed Anna drives at, when Pfuit! — over you go.'

'And crash! — over we go,' said Simon thoughtfully. He had heard of this sort of thing happening, but had never taken it seriously.

'As if you haven't got enough to worry about,' George reminded them. 'I think the time has come to make a few decisions, if I may suggest it, as a relative outsider.'

'You are quite right,' said Floris, 'but we have not known how to do this. Simon is away in Cambridge most of the time, Anna and I also have our work to do. And,' he added, looking at Simon, 'in a way it is not our concern. I mean, not our business. We have to take our lead from Simon, since he has been given this ... how shall I say ... assignment, from beyond the grave, by Professor Lebrecht.'

'You mean, you want to get out while you're still alive,' said Simon gravely. 'I don't blame you.'

'No, no! Not at all! I have not said it very well. I think we, the three of us, are all *involved*, in a way we could not escape even if we wanted to. But *you* are the link with Freyssenet, Simon, and you must say how much you want us, or me at any rate, to be active. For example, I have never suggested that we should use controlled regression again, because you have not wanted it. The choice must be yours. And now you have brought your friend in to help us, you may feel more like solving the mystery through official channels only.'

There was friction in the air. Floris had not objected to Inspector Irving; why was he getting tense about George's involvement, Simon wondered. He had noticed him looking intently at George over dinner, and had seen him surreptitiously take George's table napkin after the meal and hold it firmly in his hands. Something was afoot that called for a little diplomacy.

'Well,' said Simon and George together. Simon held up his hand. 'Hang on a moment, George. I agree that the Freyssenet mystery has been landed in my lap in the first instance. But I couldn't, and can't, do anything without your moral support, Floris, and Anna's. You have both suffered because of it already. We don't have the ability to defend ourselves against invisible and unknown enemies. So it seemed to me a heaven-sent opportunity to get the sort of help we need, when George turned up, because, let's admit it, the police aren't interested any more. We were on our own. The question is, how far can George help us. He has a job to do as well. He can't be a guardian angel to all of us.'

George stared into space for a half a minute or so, then said: 'Three points I'd like to make. First, the question of whether I get involved in this doesn't depend on you. You have stumbled on something that is bigger than you suspect, and I have been assigned to it, just as Simon has in his way. Second, I can't stand guard over you, but I can make life safer for you by some fairly routine methods, if you want to help yourselves: security, not going out alone, and so on, especially Anna. Third, if we are going to do something about the situation, instead of just hoping it will go away, we have to work out a plan that uses the expertise of each one of us.'

'But I don't have any useful expertise in this affair,' Anna protested. 'What do I do, charm them into submission with music? I feel I'm a target, a burden that has to be protected, rather than a useful member of a team.'

'That's nonsense,' said Simon. 'I wouldn't have had the

courage to do anything about this so far, without you, your trust, and companionship, and common sense, and sensitivity about situations.'

'Perhaps you were Don Quixote's Sancho Panza,' suggested George, 'Sancho Anna.'

'Thank you, George. But I don't have the figure for Sancho.'

'How about you, Dr. Schoenheimer,' George pursued, 'do you want to continue contributing your psychic expertise? I might say that I think it's the biggest trump we have.'

'Yes, of course. There's no question of my backing out now. Besides, it is a most interesting case study.'

'So long as it's published under both our names,' smiled Simon.

'Of course,' replied Floris, serious as ever, 'I should be honoured. But none of this has taken us on to the really important ground, if I may say so. Whatever you, Simon, and you, George, may believe, I have to make it clear that it would go against karmic law for any us to back out now.'

George looked at him, then at Anna, quizzically. 'You'll have to explain that to me. I know the word, of course, everybody talks about karma. But what's it got to do with this situation?'

'The popular idea of karma is that it is a kind of punishment for evil done in a previous life, or a reward for some saintly act. But it is not like that, so far as I have been able to find out over many years of study. It is a process of learning, of self-correction — or self-abasement. The rule is simple: as ye sow, so shall ye reap. But that seems to imply that bad acts will be punished. Not so. One is one's own punishment, which is very different. For example, George, did you get on well with your mother?'

George looked startled. 'No, I can't say I did. She looked after me all right, but somehow I never felt real affection for her. My fault, I expect. She did her best.'

'Not your fault at all,' Floris went on. 'I have been getting flashes about you all evening, and I knew that relationship was strained. It will shock you to know why. Do you want to know?'

George looked half uncomfortable, half incredulous. 'Yes, well, O.K.'

'In your previous incarnation, she was your murderer. But she has chosen now to be placed in a caring relationship with you. Not as a punishment, for *she chose it*, in order to live through, and learn from, the experience of bringing you into the world and providing you with life and sustenance and love. But you must help her too. It is her desire to atone, and you will benefit from the compassion and forgiveness you bestow on her.'

George was quite overcome by this. 'By Christ, that makes sense of a lot of things that have happened over the years between us two,' he said. 'Whether it's true or not, I feel ... somehow my feelings towards her have changed. As if I'm seeing her in a new light.'

'Does this mean,' Simon asked, 'that if I am Freyssenet we have to look for something in his life that will explain my life now?'

'Just so. But,' Floris warned, 'it may be connected with some other entity who has not yet become part of your present life — say, an unborn son or daughter.'

George was puzzled. 'But so far as I can gather, entities, as you call them, can look quite different each time round, and even have a different sex. That makes it a bit hard to recognise your mother if she did you in a thousand years ago, doesn't it?'

'No,' he replied, 'you would have no difficulty at recognition, if you were in a recall mode, to use the modern terminology. But just by looking at her, you would never know. Each one of us here,' he went on, looking at all three, 'has been brought together fo reasons connected with Freyssenet and Lebrecht — though they are only stepping-stones, as we are. Just think back at all the apparently random steps that have brought us together in this room tonight. If you think they are accidental, you are deluding yourselves. The last step has been George's turning up, when we needed guidance and help towards our purpose.'

'Yes, but what purpose?' cried Simon. 'It would be awfully nice if we could be granted one solid clue as to what's expected of us.'

'Life in a nutshell,' said Anna. 'But we might be looking clues in the face and not know it.'

Floris recommended patience. Other parts of the pattern had to be woven, by other people elsewhere, he suggested: a pattern going back a long way, and extending into the distant future. 'Here again, George,' he concluded, 'I have the clear sense that you took the vital step that led you to us, about six years ago. You could have resisted...'

'And I'd now be teaching English to immigrants, there being no more jobs for classics masters. It sounds a nice, safe job...'

Simon was still preoccupied by the Min-ha episode, and asked: 'How is it — I don't understand this — how is it that she and Sara Leverson are identical, in every way. You said entities don't keep the same appearance.'

Floris stood up to stretch his legs, and Anna's attention became firmly fixed on his reply. 'Yes, this case is rather different. The *déjà vu* experience often has an element of premonition. You may have superimposed Mrs. Leverson's looks on your Min-ha *before* you actually saw her — but only because they are the same entity. Min-ha may have been a Circassian or Nubian girl in fact, which is much more likely. But the sheer power of your attraction for each other was enough to pre-project Sara's image on the face and body of Min-ha.'

'But I'd never seen Sara Leverson before I had the re-encounter with Min-ha,' Simon objected.

'Who was the last *new* acquaintance you made or spoke to just before you met her again?' asked Floris.

'Let me think... It was George, I think.'

'No, he was not new.'

'Oh. Then it was... yes... I spoke to Gustave Leverson for the first time.'

'Yes. That would be it,' said Floris. 'His thoughts would

have been strongly impregnated with her, enough to enable you subliminally to pick up some inkling of her appearance, her face and body.'

'Let's not dwell on Min-ha's body, do you mind?' Anna squeezed Simon's thigh until he yelped. 'Why didn't you project me on to your little concubine, Simon?'

'I don't know — ask your father!'

Once again, Floris took a throw-away remark as a serious one to be dealt with — one of his endearing, but occasionally infuriating stolid Dutch habits.

'Something about that does puzzle me slightly. With Min-ha you were in a negative situation that could not be resolved. You were forced apart. And now you appear to be in a similar scenario, whereas one would expect the opposite, a situation in which love could flourish. But this may be explained by your having had one or even two incarnations in between.'

George intervened, making Anna's next attempt to divert attention away from Min-ha/Sara superfluous.

'Do you mean that one incarnation is the opposite of the last?'

'Only if there is a balance to be redressed. That is how karma works.'

After more coffee and liqueurs, George called them to order.

'As I see it,' he said solemnly, 'the main object of this evening's meeting has been served: to re-assure each other, and particularly me, that there is a real sense of purpose among you, a well-motivated desire to carry on with this investigation. I'm very glad about this. But I warn you you may want to think again when you know what we are up against. The important thing is, that if we are going to press on, it is time for us to take the initiative before one or other of the opposing sides stops us for good.'

'I gather you know rather more than we do,' said Floris. 'Would you enlighten us?'

'This is the game-plan as we understand it at present,' George continued. 'There are four interested parties. Let me take them in order of appearance: first, there is Islam, of course. Their main objective is the destruction of Christianity throughout the world.'

'That's Fuad Riad and Co.?' asked Simon.

'Right. Then we have the *tombaroli*, who nobbled Riad's surveyor at Mrs. Greaves's house. They're a part of a network of rival mafia gangs who specialise in tomb-robbing. They have made vast fortunes by denuding ancient Etruscan and Roman tombs of their treasures, but they are looking further afield now. Somehow, they have got wind of some kind of valuable treasure left by Freyssenet, but they're not sure what or where, so far as we know. Our job is to keep them guessing.'

'And third?' asked Anna, relishing less and less what she was hearing.

'Third, believe it or not, a faction within the Vatican, who think that any psychic phenomena relating to Christianity should be strictly Kosher, sorry, I mean, Catholic.'

Simon gasped. 'I don't believe this!' George ignored him.

'And fourth, possibly the most dangerous because we know least about them: a nasty bunch called Eskarites, the Square of Eskar. They're a neo-Nazi group implacably hostile to all religions that have originated in the Middle East. They have a new prophet who calls himself Barclay Borg. He says God told him He had made a great mistake in using Jews and Arabs as go-betweens, and wants to start again with the Nordic races. So they're dead against any more mystical revelations in the Middle East.'

'So the Mormons are O.K.?' asked Simon.

'Oh no! They claim their Bible came from Egypt.'

'What's so dangerous about these Eskarites?' asked Anna. 'They sound like another little set of cranks.'

'Originally they were,' George explained, 'but five years ago they had injections of funding on an unbelievable scale. We don't know the source, and they're run so intelligently we can't find out much about their organisation.

No office, no publications, no uniforms, no parades. We do know they are planning some very unpleasant surprises for Jewish, Christian, and Islamic leaders. But we are first in line for immediate action.'

A gloomy silence ensued.

George, undeterred, went on: 'Now let me come to the good news.'

'Don't tell me,' said Simon, 'Superman has taken off his specs and is at this very moment streaming across the Atlantic.'

'Almost right,' said George. 'You don't have Superman, but you do have me.'

'Great. I think I'll go out and wait till the cartoons come on,' Simon mumbled.

'Well, not only me.'

'You mean you *and* Batman and Robin?'

'That's pretty good, Dr. Prestcott, old chum. You see, I'm not just a one-man band. I have two agents at my disposal, highly trained, hand-picked to mingle with you in your worlds, who will become part of your lives, if you agree, and will give you as much protection as anyone has a right to expect against kidnapping. That's our main fear. None of the opposition is interested in killing you. They want information, and they'll get that either by forcing it out of you, or by following you. That's why I was very strongly against you going off to France by yourselves.'

'You mean we're to have bodyguards?' asked Anna.

'Yes.' George looked at his watch. Nearly midnight. 'You're not going back to Cambridge tonight, are you Simon?' he asked.

'No, I was hoping to stay here.' Anna and Floris nodded in agreement.

'May I use your phone?' George tapped out a number. 'Skyrocket. One front, one back,' he said, and replaced the receiver. 'Anna, would you come with me and show me the rear way in? Dr. Schoenheimer, in a moment, a man answering to the code-name of Galileo will ring at your front door. Let him in and bring him up here, please.'

Anna went through the garden with George, and unlocked the gate leading to the rear lane, just as a girl approached from the right. George beckoned her in. Not a word was spoken until they were back in the warmth of the sitting-room on the first floor. The others were already there.

The two newcomers were rather a surprise. One was a man in his early twenties in jeans and leather jacket. His real name was Leo. The other was a strapping-looking girl of about the same age, with fair hair and a sad smile, also in regulation jeans and pullover. Nicola.

'I think life is going to be simpler,' said George, 'if we adopt first names, because we're going to be one large happy family for a while. Leo will go back with Simon to Cambridge. I'll fix up his accommodation right alongside you, Simon, and he will follow you like a shadow: a student-shadow.'

'So long as nobody gets the wrong idea about our relationship,' said Simon. 'Perhaps I'd better have Nicola?'

'That's a very good idea,' said Anna enthusiastically, 'and I'll have Leo to guard me all night long.'

'And who guards me?' asked Floris. 'Or am I not worth it?'

'Of course you are,' said George. 'At night, Nicola will cover the house as a whole. When Anna goes off to college, she will go too, looking like any other student. And I will arrange for either myself or another agent to cover you, Floris, during the day. We'll do your reception-work, and very discreetly vet everyone who comes in.'

'I'm not sure what Miss Briscombe will think of that,' said Floris. 'She's a pretty formidable guard-dog herself!'

Anna suddenly put her hand to her brow.

'We're forgetting somebody in the midst of all this. Poor old Mrs. Greaves. Who's looking after her? She's in as much danger as any of us.'

George nodded. 'You're darned right she is. Completely defenceless. That's why we started with her. She's had the most sophisticated alarm system available installed in the Freyssenet house — it sets off bells everywhere except the

155

Prime Minister's bedroom. And since you mention Mrs. Greaves, that brings me to the first step in our offensive strategy plan...'

As Simon and Anna climbed to the top floor of the house, their temporary quarters whilst Anna's annexe was not in use, they felt more secure than they had for many, many weeks.

'Good old George,' Anna murmured as she snuggled under the duvet.

'Good old Nicola,' Simon whispered sleepily.

'Good old Leo.' She bit the ear that heard her.

'Ouch. And good old you.'

'Good old you, too, darling.'

They put out the light and in each other's arms, quickly, momentarily, forgot the unpleasant situation developing round them.

15

For the next two weeks Simon was rarely seen by anyone other than the staff of the Cambridge University Library, the British Library, or the Public Record Office. He searched through all the catalogues of manuscript holdings in French and British libraries, and through volumes of letters and bulletins from Freyssenet to the Russian and British governments. Most of these were held by either the P.R.O. in Kew or the British Library in Bloomsbury, except for the memorandum which he had written to George Canning in 1807, which proved that he had, indeed, leaked the infamous arrangement made between the Czar of Russia and the Emperor Napoleon at Tilsit, thus enabling England to be one move ahead in capturing the Danish fleet in Copenhagen. This was in the Leeds Record Office. Nothing, however, was of any assistance in his search for references to Freyssenet's activities in Egypt, either in harems or monasteries.

The arrival of George Plaidy on the scene had an immediate effect on Anna. Her anxieties and fears, after the uncomfortable episode at the hands of Riad, had been having a disastrous effect on her work: she had a large repertoire to commit to memory for a public recital in March — Beethoven, Chopin, Rachmaninov, Scriabin — and she found to her dismay that for the first time in her life memorising was proving very difficult. Not only that, but she found her fingers would suddenly seize up and refuse to obey her brain. Floris diagnosed this as the inevitable result of the threats made by Riad. He treated her under hypnosis, and this was improving her condition, but too slowly. With the new sense of security that came from being minded by Nicola, who was showing herself to be a tough and intelligent young lady, Anna found herself freed from trauma. The music stayed in her mind and flowed from her fingers like silvery cascades, joyfully and effortlessly. She was able to practise for hours at a stretch and engage in prolonged concentration. Even at weekends she was working too hard to see much of Simon.

It was imperative, George said to Simon, to move the action along; not only in order to find out what was behind the treasures and mysteries that interested the curious variety of rival investigators, but also to bring them out into the open: otherwise they would remain a permanent, hidden, and dangerous presence in the lives of Simon and the Schoenheimers. Simon had made arrangements to work at the Institute in Geneva during the Easter vacation. He therefore agreed to George's plan: Simon was to drive with Leo to Montpellier, and from there they would visit the various villages named Freyssenet or Freycenet in the region. If and when they found the right one, and the ruins of the château, they would contact George, who would join them immediately, for added security. Simon found this a cumbersome way of going about things, but could find no alternative. He would dearly have loved to be driving through France, in the early Spring, with Anna, or Sara, rather than the stolid and very unfeminine Leo. However, he was glad to be doing something other than poring over lists in indexes and catalogues, hoping to spot the name "Freyssenet".

The drive south, along the wide white ribbons of autoroutes, in his zippy little M.G., was exhilarating. The air got warmer and fresher, the skies bluer, as they sped past the signposts to the familiar places he had no time to see again this trip: Fontainebleau, Montargis, Auxerre and Beaune, Tournus and Mâcon, Lyon, Valence, Montélimar, Orange and Avignon, then Nîmes and Montpellier, the birthplace of the comte de Freyssenet.

On the morning after their arrival, Simon had the bright idea of visiting Jacques Forestier, the *conservateur* at the Montpellier Public Library who had replied so promptly to his letter about Lebrecht. M. Forestier received him warmly, and on hearing the name Freyssenet, warmed to the visitor even more.

'*Eh, mais oui, mon cher Monsieur, le comte de Freyssenet est né tout près d'ici, dans la maison de sa famille maternelle*... He inherited a number of baronies from his mother's side, in addition to the title of comte from his father, who was not very well liked. All the villages around his château at Freyssenet were part of his *fief* .'

'You seem to be very knowledgeable about him, M. Forestier. Are you a historian?' asked Simon.

'Only in an amateur way, about our region, that is, La Provence. But the comte de Freyssenet is a particular interest of mine, since one of my ancestors, on my father's side, was the *avocat* of the comte, and dealt with all his legal affairs, even after he emigrated.'

'So you know where the remains of his château are,' asked Simon.

'*Evidemment, Monsieur: à Freyssenet* .'

'Yes — but which Freyssenet? There are several.'

'Of course. How stupid of me. I know it so well, I did not think of the others. Here, let me show you on the map...'

He did so. There it was, not far from Aubenas. It would mean going all the way back to Montélimar, but they would at least be going to the right place.

Jacques Forestier's helpfulness did not end there. He wrote Simon a letter of introduction to the present owner of the land that once formed part of the estate of the comte de Freyssenet, Gabriel Frémont. As Simon was leaving, the keen, bespectacled eyes of the librarian fixed him firmly. 'Might I permit myself to ask what is your interest in the comte, Monsieur?'

Warily, now, Simon replied, 'Ah, well, he claimed to have an acquaintance with Voltaire. Anyone who knew Voltaire is of interest to me.'

'In that case, Monsieur, I think you will be disappointed. You will find nothing to remind you of the comte up there now. Even the village people have not heard of him, and care even less. He is part of the bad old days of the *ancien régime*, so far as they are concerned; something they like to forget.'

Simon went back to the main square of Montpellier, known as The Egg, and telephoned London. George would be on the next plane to Lyon, and would meet them in Aubenas that evening.

There was nothing to link the little red M.G. with the Renault 11 with French number-plates which entered the village of Freyssenet at 11 a.m. the following day. The sole occupant of the M.G. got out and asked at the Post Office where he might find M. Frémont. He was directed to go out of the village, up towards the mountain, called Bayzac, alongside the valley of the river Volane. About five kilometres along there he would see a signpost to Paunas, and M. Frémont would be found on his farm on the left, just before the church.

The Renault went on to the church, and parked outside the main entrance. Simon got out of his car and walked to the farmhouse. His knock was greeted by a loud barking and a scraping of chairs, then the weather-beaten door creaked open. A stocky, hearty-looking peasant in overalls stood before him.

'*Monsieur Frémont* ?'

'*C'est moi-même.*'

'I have a letter from Monsieur Forestier.'

'Monsieur Forestier?' He looked momentarily puzzled, then nodded. '*Ah, oui, bien sûr, de Montpellier* .'

M. Frémont opened the letter, read it, gave Simon an quizzical look, then said: 'So you want to see the ruins?'

'I should be very grateful, if it is not too much trouble,' Simon replied.

'It is no trouble to me.' He walked out, and pointed over towards the valley which lay below them. 'If you follow that lane between the line of trees, *là*, you will see a few mounds of stones. That is all that is left. There are some vaults underground. One of them was opened by vandals recently. Be careful, it might fall in.'

Simon thanked him, and set off along the tree-lined lane. About fifty yards on, buried in the long grass, he saw the remains of two pillars; the entrance to the château, no doubt. Then he climbed up a steep rise, until he stood on top of what might once have been a parapet, from which he looked down the whole length of the beautiful valley, which shaded into a blueish mist in the distance. This was the ideal site for a stronghold. The mounds of stones recognisably formed, in part, the bottom of thick walls. Briar and gorse made it difficult to move forward, and squadrons of angry wasps swarmed menacingly. Soon he came to a clearer patch, and saw a hole in the ground, edged with blocks of stone. The bright sunlight did not penetrate. Simon took his torch from his anorak pocket, and shone it down. There was a sheer drop of some twenty feet. Right below him, recent footprints. Had they found anything? How had they managed to get ahead? There was no way he could get down there by himself, so he turned to see if there was any way to get back to the church and to George and Leo in their car, without going past the farmhouse again. It seemed possible. He began to push his way through the gorse, which had developed a prickly defence system far in advance of its English counterpart. A flight of wasps took particular exception to his intrusion, and began to attack him; they were *frelons*, like hornets, very nasty. He saw a clearing in the gorse to his right, and moved towards it. Suddenly, his foot touched nothing, he had nothing to hold on to, and he fell through an aperture in the ground which had, in fact, been the reason for the clearing in the gorse. The hole was quite small, about three feet across, and he was able to grasp the edge briefly, and managed to fall on his feet and knees. The landing was soft, on a thick mat of vegetation. But when Simon looked up, he saw that the roof was a good fifteen feet above him.

He lay still to recover, and checked that he was still whole. Nothing sprained or broken. He pulled out the torch, and was relieved that it still worked. Thus reassured, he stood up. Too fast. The back of his head made contact with something very hard, very solid.

His first sensation was that he had knocked himself out, but he did not lose consciousness. Several details, however, did change, rapidly. The vault was illuminated by several candles; there was no hole in the roof — *mon dieu*, how was he going to get out? — and he could see clearly what were lining the walls. Coffins. Stone coffins. There was grandfather, grandmother, the father he had hardly known. Not his mother, of course; she was still alive. He looked down at the box in his hands. This was what he had come to do. He knew his grandmother would not regard it as sacrilege, for she had been such a loving, affectionate old soul, who had understood him. Not like his mother or father. Without hesitation he went over to one of the tombs, and tried to lift the lid. The extreme weight of the solid stone was beyond his strength, and he leant on it, weeping with frustration. Somehow he must make sure the box and its precious contents were safe, for ever. His eyes searched for something to help with the raising of the stone, and were arrested by an irregularity in the stone wall behind his grandmother's tomb.

Swiftly he drew his dagger, the one he had so recently brought back with him from Constantinople, and prised away the loose material round the ill-fitting stone. As it came out, he saw behind it a hollow which would just take the box, allowing the stone to be replaced. When it was back, he scraped up some mud from a damp corner, and packed it into the cracks. Then he knelt and wept afresh, for the sadness that was upon him weighed on his heart. Guilt and grief gnaw like rats and feed each other from the heart that imprisons them together.

He stumbled back along the passage, close, dark and airless. After what seemed like an eternity of walking, he came to the end of the narrow passage and looked up. Just above his head, within easy reach, was the trap-door.

Simon's head was thumping, and his hand came away wet and sticky when he felt it. A brief flash of the torch was enough to reveal the culprit: a thick timber beam, running from wall to wall. Reinforcement, no doubt, for the walls or roof. Perhaps he could stand on it and reach the hole in the roof? Unlikely; it was about six feet to one side of the hole. He must shout for help, he told himself. Then he paused. No; there was something else he had to do. His head was splitting and refused to think. No rush. Best to sit and wait till the old brain patched itself up. He flashed his torch at each of the stone tombs around him. No names. There should be. No weathering down here. Not like English gravestones, flaking away under the rain and snow and wind. Look on the top. He got to his feet painfully, and walked over beside the tomb he had been looking at. The top was thick with dust, which he scraped and blew away. Slowly some numbers materialised: 1698-1776. He felt sadness, as at the passing of an old friend, for he knew this was she, his dearest grandmama, who had crooned over him and wiped away his tears and sung him songs and nodded wisely when he told her of his first love. Instinctively, he turned the torch-beam to the wall, and saw what he knew he would see: dried mud round one of the blocks forming the wall. Resting the torch on the top of the tomb, he took out his penknife and prised away the loose material round the loose-fitting stone. As it came out, he saw behind it a hollow in which lay a small box. He gently withdrew it, afraid it would disintegrate in his hands like a Dead Sea scroll. It looked like a jewel-box, made of wood, but very solid, with iron bonds, hinges and clasps. A faint flicker from the torch warned him not to waste the battery. He switched off, and thought seriously about what to do next.

George and Leo would be trying to find him, so all he had to do was listen out for them, and shout back when he heard them. He began to be conscious of his thumping head again,

163

and drifted off to sleep. He was immediately alert, though, when he heard the sound of scrabbling through the gorse, with mumbled curses. He was on the point of calling out when something about the intonation gave him pause. As the first words became audible, he realised they were Italian. He closed his mouth again. Quickly he realised there were three things he had to do very fast: replace the stone; get the box out of sight; and hide himself. These things he did, even forbearing to swear when he jammed his fingers in the hole with the block of stone. The problem of where to hide, clutching the box, resolved itself as he flashed the torch in the only direction he knew he could possibly go: with grandmama's tomb on his right, straight ahead, in the far left-hand corner. The beam could barely pierce the multiple gossamer of spiders' webs, but the passage was there all right. He started off along it, allowing himself the briefest of light-flashes, but was appalled to see, only thirty or so feet in, that the passage was blocked. It looked as though the roof had fallen in. Now sweating profusely, in the foetid air, he listened as the Italians, the *tombaroli* no doubt, came closer. They were at the edge of the hole, he saw a bright beam of light probe round the vault. Then he caught sight of the slow snake of rope as it descended. Down it slid one man, then a second. It would not be long before they discovered the passage. Simon quietly placed the box on the ground and began to dig a hole in the collapsed earth to hide it. His hand went almost straight through. The pile of earth, apparently, reached only about two-thirds of the way up.

Silently, pushing the box ahead of him, he wriggled over the mound, hoping he would not dislodge more. His feet were barely over with the rest of him when there was a shout from the other side, as one man exclaimed that he had found a passage. Quickly, Simon moved ahead, after turning his beam on for the briefest second, and reached a slight bend in the passage. It was undoubtedly this that saved his life, for he had no sooner gone round it when there was an ear-splitting report, and the wall to his left was hit by a bullet.

Then there was pandemonium behind, a crumbling of earth, voices muffled, desperate, silenced. He did not go back to enquire about this, but moved, unmolested, ahead. At the end of the passage he found a trap-door overhead, but it would not budge. Exhausted, he sat down with the box beside him, and shone the torch upwards. The reason why the trap would not open was immediately clear: it was bolted from *underneath* ! Whoever had last used it must have got out another way, if he got out at all. The great iron bolt was stiff but eventually he eased it back, pushed up the door again, and felt it give. A minute later, he rose, as if from the dead, into the old church.

16

'I still don't understand what took you so long.'

'That's because you've had a bang on the head and you're not concentrating,' said George.

The air about them was still fresh; up in the hills of the Ardèche, spring looked back upon the winter it was leaving, rather than towards the summer it was heralding. Simon found the cool breeze slowly reviving him as they sat in the car outside the church.

While Leo applied iodine to Simon's head, despite the latter's injunctions to him to lay off, George went over the salient points of their recent movements again, realising that Simon was uncharacteristically slow of comprehension because of the cut, which might, he thought, need stitches.

'Leo and I went straight up the church tower. Great view from there. We watched you through the glasses going over towards the valley, and gathered that French chap must have directed you to the ruins. That was fine — we'd agreed you would make no contact with us. We tried to keep you in view, but the bushes got in the way. It would have been counter-productive to show our hand before the other side had shown their presence, if they were there. We had to draw them out, Simon, O.K.? That was just as important as finding the box of whatever it is.'

'Where is it?' Simon began to look round anxiously.

'Don't worry. It's safe. And unopened. We'll need a tool-kit to get into it. Anyway,' George went on, 'when you began to push towards us through what looked like impenetrable bush, we saw we were not the only ones observing you. On the far side were two men, over on the rise before the drop into the valley, and one of them was keeping you in sight through glasses. Then they moved, very quickly. They'd obviously sussed out the terrain already, and travelled faster than you. You'd disappeared — we didn't know then it was through a hole in the ground. We decided to approach the spot where we'd last seen you in a direct line from this side. In other words, they were coming at you from the east, and we from the west. O.K.?'

Simon's head was throbbing wildly, but he nodded for George to go on.

'Leo ran ahead of me, he's younger and faster, but still had to keep as quiet as possible. We didn't want to scare them off. Tell him what happened then, Leo.'

'Well, fortunately, the two guys were very chatty, and it wasn't hard to home in on them. First glimpse I had of them was as they were lowering a rope into a hole. One went down, then the other. I didn't know if you were there. So the moment the second one got down, I slid over and took hold of the rope to pull it up. Then there was the most god-awful row from down there. First, there was a shot from a gun, very loud because of the enclosed space, and I thought Oh my God, they've got you. Then there was shouting and screaming and the ground under me began to tremble. I looked back along the track I'd taken, and saw it simply disappear, bushes and all. Fell in. About ten feet of it. The shot must have caused an earth-slide down there.'

'I'm not surprised,' said Simon, 'the passage was almost blocked already when I pushed through it. So where are they now?'

'Under a few tons of earth, I imagine,' Leo smiled happily. 'Better than up here popping off at us, eh?'

Simon was not entirely happy about that, but could think of no urgent reason why they should get involved in a rescue attempt. It would have been pretty futile, by the sound of it, and would not have been appreciated by those being rescued. So his befuddled mind reasoned and rationalised a "No Action to be taken" decision.

George took up the story, and rapidly told Simon how Leo had gone down through the new hole in the ground to follow the passage along behind Simon, expecting to come across his body at any moment.

'Then I came up through the trap-door and there you were, sitting in a daze by the side of it.'

'Thanks,' said Simon. 'If I'd known you were coming, I'd have saved myself the trouble of pushing the door open!'

George suddenly became business-like. 'Right now, Leo, you take Simon into Aubenas and find a doctor to look at his head. The outside, I mean. In the meantime I shall find out more about the goons who were after you. They may not have been alone. They got here by transport. Someone is expecting them back. A few ends to tie up. We'll meet at the *Trois Couronnes* at seven. If I'm not there by seven-thirty, Leo, you know the procedure.'

'O.K., boss. Come on, wounded soldier.'

'Leave me the keys to your M.G., Simon, please. I've always wanted to drive one of those things.' George held out his hand, then got out and began walking in the direction from which the Italians had first been seen coming. Leo started the Renault up and moved off as quietly as he could in the opposite direction.

Hôtel des Trois Couronnes
Aubenas

My dearest Anna

At the moment I am reduced to inactivity, so I am filling in the time by dropping you a line. (That's not very flattering is it? Sorry. I'm not thinking very straight.) You would be very impressed if you could see me: my head is swathed in bandages. Well, a bandage. And the doctor has told me to stay in bed all day tomorrow. The way I feel, it will be a pleasure. But George is very anxious that we move away from here. So at dawn tomorrow, Leo will take my car, and I shall lie in the back of George's hired Renault, resting my poor head.

I'll tell you about that in all its gory detail when I see you. For the moment, I just want to tell you that we, or frankly I, have found the box. In an underground vault. There was some opposition, which Providence dispersed, but the box is ours. Last night, with Leo on guard at the door, just like a T.V. movie, George and I managed to prise open the lid of the box. It was not made for opening without a key, with its irons bands and locks, but all defences are only as strong as their weakest point, and this applies to boxes too. The wood was pretty soft. We opened the lid expecting to find at least a million pounds worth of diamonds.

What was inside was another box — a lead one, with an opening at the top which had been sealed with wax. I insisted on doing the honours, and got to work with my penknife. It did not take long. As the top came off, there was an odd smell, a bit like a butcher's shop. I immediately felt a bit queasy, and retired, but George pressed on, and with the help of one of the hotel forks, extracted the contents.

At first, we couldn't make it out at all. It looked most unpleasant, like a small dead animal, but without any fur. We gazed at it on the table for some time. George gingerly turned it over with the fork. I could feel myself beginning to pass out and begged George to put it back in the box. He did that, sealed it with sellotape, and there it remains. Very strange. And those tumbodumbos wanted to kill me for that? And got squashed by a vast chunk of ancient ruins for that? I don't get it, and neither does George. Clearly they were expecting something very different.

Tomorrow we move off, then. I shan't say where, for the sake of security. I hope your music is going fine. Tried to ring you a couple of times, but no luck. Love — Simplissimus.

P.S. I really do wonder what I'm doing all this for. *Boys' Own Paper* adventures are not my scene at all.

It'd better be worth while in the end. — S.

Professor Bristow, freshly, wearily back in harness after his abbreviated study leave, took up his position, coughed into the microphone, and set about the task of introducing the speaker to the audience packed into the Public Lecture Theatre of the City University of Melbourne.

'Chancellor, Vice-Chancellor, Ladies and Gentlemen: it gives me genuine pleasure this evening to welcome our speaker, Dr. Pierre Bernard, who has been invited jointly by the Association of Commonwealth Universities and the Government of Australia to deliver a number of lectures and lead several seminars, on subjects which are, I think, admirably summed up by the title of the talk he is to give us this evening: "Does Mankind want to survive?" Dr. Bernard was born in Lausanne, and studied literature at the University of Geneva before going on to the Sorbonne, where he gained a doctorate in a discipline which is, alas, unknown to us in Anglo-Saxon institutions of learning: Moral Sciences. He has applied typically Swiss scientific rigour to problems of human behaviour that straddle psychology, ethics, logic, aesthetics, and physiology. His list of publications is impressive. This is partly accounted for by the fact that Dr. Bernard has never occupied a university teaching post, and has not had to waste his time and talents on humdrum bureaucracy *[murmurs of assent from staff present]*, partly by his total commitment to an overall vision of ideal human behaviour, and to the discovery of reasons why we fall so far short of that ideal. Will you please welcome Dr. Pierre Bernard...'

It was a career break-through for Anna. To have been invited to step in at short notice for John Auden to play the Grieg Piano Concerto in Manchester, with the London Philharmonic under Sir George Bolto, was already something; but to have done it well, and to be highly praised for it by the *Times* and *Guardian* critics, was a very valuable bonus. Nicola had thoroughly enjoyed herself, to her great surprise; her musical education had been carried way beyond the rock, soul and reggae which she had thought was the only music that existed, till her "babysitting job" (as she called it to herself and to colleagues) had obliged her to hear hours of Anna's playing every day. Floris had gone up to Manchester with them, at Anna's request, both for security reasons and because he wanted to be present at her first big concert.

Pierre Bernard was warming to his theme, and his audience was attentive:

'It is tempting,' he said, 'to sit back like an anthropologist and merely observe the ravages of mankind's self-made tragedy. To accept the tragic powerlessness of humanity, and the inevitability of the destruction of this world. It is no mere chance that human thirst for destruction, on all levels, from vicious muggings in quiet streets and pouring acid over old ladies' eyes, to genocide and nuclear holocaust, is reaching a frenzied climax at precisely the time when we have the technology, for the first time in history, to bring about the complete and utter annihilation of the human race. Perhaps that is our destiny.'

A voice from the back of the hall shouted, 'What about glasnost, then?' Bernard, unused to the robust combativeness of Australian students, was thrown off balance for a moment. Then he smiled, and said, 'You are quite right to question the scenario I am painting. Things seem to be improving. Glasnost, peristroika, German re-unification, Strategic Arms controls and treaties, dismantling of Soviet military power. Unfortunately, when the big bullies put down their arms, or disintegrate, the little ones come out of the woodwork. And an irresponsible fanatical demagogue with ex-Soviet nuclear weapons can hold the world to ransom very effectively when the major powers have no teeth any more. However, I think the biggest danger is not of millions of people being massacred by nuclear bombs, but the escalating deterioration of the ecosystem by nuclear winter, far worse than the smoke of thousands of burning Middle East oil wells, in addition to the everyday damage being caused exponentially by the destruction of rain forests, overpopulation, and atmospheric pollution. I know gloom and doom are not pleasant to hear, but I see no evidence that this drift can be halted, despite repeated warnings by ecologists.'

As they neared the Swiss frontier at Annemasse, Simon began to wonder if there would be trouble. Had the French police been alerted? Had three Englishmen been connected with the abandoned Italian car which George had pushed into the bushes on the far side of the Freyssenet ruins? Would M. Frémont have heard the shot and the collapse of several tons of earth, and would he have assumed he, Simon, might be buried under the rubble? He voiced these fears to George, who merely grunted and said they would have to see. In Annemasse itself, they stopped by the central Bureau de Poste, and waited for Leo, now driving the M.G.

'Do you feel fit enough to drive?' George asked Simon.

'Yes. Well, I could do with a bit of food and some coffee. But where are you going?'

'Nowhere. But you'll have to drive your own car through the *douane*. Otherwise, they'll assume Leo has stolen it.'

They lunched at a small restaurant from where they could keep an eye on the cars, then drove to the frontier...

'And what do you 'ave in zees box, Monsieur?'

'Oh, just a piece of ancient offal.'

'It is not permitted that one should import uncooked foodstuffs into Switzerland, Monsieur. It must be impounded.'

That dialogue ran through Simon's head as he waited for his passport and papers to be returned to him by the Swiss customs officer. But he gave the little M.G. a perfunctory look-over, as if to make sure it had four wheels, then handed back the papers, smiled, and said '*Faites bonne route,*

Monsieur.'

They had telephoned ahead to book rooms in a small hotel on the outskirts of Geneva, the *Cheval blanc*, in Chênebourg. It had a secluded car park off the road, and would not be the obvious choice for foreign travellers. Simon had stayed there once before, and found its modest comforts and cuisine quite adequate. He began to relax. George inspected his head, and dressed the wound, which had not required stitches.

'Seems to be mending all right, you lucky devil. Damned sharp corner you must have caught it on.' George placed a square of gauze over the cut, and attached it with sticky tape. 'You'll have a bald patch there for a bit,' he laughed, 'like a tonsure. Fancy yourself as a monk?'

That evening, they walked by the side of Lac Léman. A mist was beginning to form over the water, and from across the lake twinkling lights sparkled. The chug-chug of the last steamer from Coppet grew louder, then ceased as the trim white craft glided into port.

'This is the first time I've ever seen a Swiss lake, you know,' said Leo. 'I never got abroad when I was at school — we couldn't afford it. I used to look at an old pre-war copy of Cook's tours in my bedroom. Out of the window there was nothing but little back gardens, you know what the suburbs of Wolverhampton are like. Well, perhaps not, but you can imagine it. Flat, dull and foggy.'

'Like the accent,' Simon thought, but didn't know Leo well enough to tease him about it.

'Anyway,' Leo went on, 'I'd look at this book, it gave you all the train times for Europe. I'd go on imaginary journeys from Paris to Rome, and Berlin to Geneva. And there were pictures of the lakes in Switzerland and Austria, blue they were, with little white steamers like that one, and mountains going down to the water, and snow on the tops of them. Interlaken I remember. And a place called, er, Montrose, I think...'

'Montreux,' said Simon. He suddenly began to realise what a privileged youth he had had, travelling from Europe

173

to England several times a year, but he had not thought so at the time.

'I used to envy boys who had a fixed address and didn't have to leave their toys and friends all the time to go abroad. Funny, you never appreciate what you've got, do you?'

'I can see Leo's point, though,' George interjected. 'The "Poor little Rich Boy" idea smacks of self-indulgence to me. Often as not, he's just plain bloody spoilt. You can't say that about a "Poor little Poor Boy," can you? The less you've got, the less you have to appreciate.'

Simon cogitated for a while. Then said: 'First, let's clear the air. I wasn't rich, by any means; and I suspect that Leo was never poverty-stricken. So we're talking about hypothetical situations. I'd say that whether or not the child of a richer family is better off depends on himself. He might lack ambition. If you've got a full plate, you don't seek ways to fill it.'

'You mean, if you've got an empty plate, you're justified in clobbering someone else and getting his?' Leo waited for an answer from one of these highly educated men.

George finally volunteered. 'I'm strictly a law and order man myself. And so are you, Leo, or you wouldn't be in this job. But I don't think we can go on expecting the poor of this world to go on saying "Please" and "Thank you" for scraps while the big boys squabble over their share prices and take-over bids.'

Simon raised his eyebrows in surprise. 'That's dangerous talk, coming from you, George. One minute you say you're a law and order man, and the next you're saying violence is only to be expected! You can't be as anti-terrorist as you say you are, and then claim terrorism is inevitable.'

George stood up and walked towards the edge of the water. 'I don't think I'm being inconsistent,' he said. 'Very little international terrorist activity is intended to improve the lot of the poor. It's all about power, not poverty. Gadaffi doesn't care a penn'orth of shit for the starving of North Africa. He's moving into New Caledonia to get his own back on the French, not to help the Melanesians. But what

I was talking about was civil disorder. I reckon there'll be civil war in Britain within ten years. Probably the North against the South.'

'I must say I do worry about England,' said Simon.

'Gee, thanks, Simon. That makes me feel much better,' muttered Leo. Simon had the grace to laugh.

'I mean,' Leo went on, 'I've got three brothers, and they've all been out of work for a couple of years or more, so it's nice to think someone is worried. Apart from us, I mean.'

'But what can you expect?' asked Simon. 'Britain is reaping the harvest of forty years of incredible errors at the highest levels of government and trade unionism. Massive over-population. Gross mismanagement on both sides of labour relationships. Result: the wreck of a whole industrial state because of class warfare and confrontation. It didn't happen in Germany. It didn't have to happen in that antiquated way, did it?'

They sat in silence, staring across the lake. Leo shivered, and said, 'Nice spot this.' He looked at the outlines of the stately banks and elegant jewellers' shops, the calm restaurants and impeccable hotels by the lakeside. The gentle hum of affluence.

They paused, suddenly conscious of the fact that this was the first time they had talked about anything other than the Freyssenet affair. The reality of their unfinished business began to make itself felt again.

'Let's think about our next move,' said George. 'We can't solve the little mystery of the lead box, so let's leave the world's problems to...'

'To our betters?' Simon cut in. 'To the experts? God help us!'

As Anna was cutting out the review of her Manchester concert from *The Independent*, her eye fell upon a headline near the top of page three:

DARING ROBBERY:
HISTORICAL MATERIAL
STOLEN FROM TWICKENHAM HOUSE

The report told in graphic detail how two intruders, believed to be a man and a woman, had brutally forced the owner of a charming period house overlooking the Thames at Twickenham, Mrs. Greaves (79), to reveal the hiding-place of a box containing papers of great historical significance, which had once belonged to a former owner of the house, a comte de Freyssenet, who had acted as an espionage agent working against Napoleon. The couple had escaped with the papers and with other unspecified objects of historical and monetary value. The police were viewing the matter with great concern, as they believed this to be the work of an international gang of thieves. Anna telephoned Mrs. Greaves to ask her if she had seen the paper.

'Yes,' she replied excitedly, 'isn't it fun? All my friends have been ringing up to see if I'm all right, so I tell them the same story, but it seems to get longer each time. Perhaps I should have been a novelist? And how's that nice young man of yours?'

'Oh, he's in Europe, working. We don't see much of each other at the moment.'

She promised to send Simon Mrs. Greaves's best wishes.

17

The following morning, Simon Prestcott telephoned Gustave Leverson at the Voltaire Institute.

'Dr. Leverson?'

'Speaking.'

'Simon. Simon Prestcott.'

There was a long pause.

'Good heavens. Where are you ringing from?'

'Here. In Geneva. I wrote to you to say I'd be coming this week.'

'Did you? Are you sure? I'll speak to my secretary, but I'm positive no letter came from you.'

Simon was quite sure. He remembered clearly putting the envelope on the porter's desk at St. Peter's College, and Clem, the Head Porter, had promised he would put it in the post box for him.

'In any case,' Leverson was continuing, 'that doesn't matter at all. I was only surprised because I have this very minute finished dictating a letter to you, with an interesting enclosure. Now I can give it to you. Can you come to the Institute at two o'clock? I'm rather tied up this morning.'

Simon had insisted to George the previous evening that he must get some of his Voltaire work done, and that he thought he had done (and risked) enough for the Lebrecht Foundation to be satisfied for a bit. George was rather restless, saying that he and Leo could not be spared for much longer. Therefore he, George, would return to London the following day. Leo would stay to shepherd Simon until the end of the week. Simon promised to take Leo to Montreux, to see if it looked anything like the picture.

After lunch, Simon drove through the centre of Geneva, and at 1.55 p.m. pulled up outside the austere façade of

Voltaire's residence, *Les Délices*, now surrounded by blocks of apartments. He had never been there before. The brass plate beside the door announced the days when the Institute was open to the public for guided tours, and when the reading room was open for visiting scholars. This was one of the latter. He was surprised when the door was opened by Leverson himself, dressed in a maroon smoking jacket and looking very dapper. His keen glance immediately darted to Leo.

'My temporary research assistant,' Simon explained.

Leverson nodded curtly, and invited Simon to pass in front of him, through a door off to the left at the end of the hallway. Simon stopped in his tracks. There, three feet away, was Voltaire himself sitting at his desk, quill in hand. Leverson gave a delighted little laugh.

'It's remarkably life-like, isn't it? Some people think it's a bit childish of me, but I have tried to make the place look as lived-in as possible. So why not include the one who lived in it and did so much good work for humanity in it?'

'Including writing *Candide*,' said Simon.

'He'd never get it published today!' Leverson laughed.

'Oh? Why not?'

'Because it can't be categorised. Publishers and booksellers need to label a book as either a thriller *or* a romance *or* popular fiction *or* science fiction *or* a social satire. I can just imagine a publisher...' — they were now going down to the cellar, packed with eighteenth-century books and pamphlets — '...a publisher writing to Voltaire nowadays: "*Mon cher Monsieur de Voltaire*, thank you for sending me the manuscript of your story, *Candide*. We should like to publish it, but it will require much editing. You have written an amusing adventure story that will sell, but all that extraneous matter about theology and optimism must go. Perhaps you can use it in a philosophical essay?"'

Leverson took them round the rest of the permanent exhibition of memorabilia evoking the life and times of the creator of *Candide*, exiled here from his beloved Paris by the fearful monarch of a France that had become a police state. *Après lui, le déluge*. Leo tried not to look too bored, and perked up visibly when Leverson brought out a set of beautiful and explicit engravings illustrating the works of the Marquis de Sade.

Finally, they came to the reading-room. Two wide tables ran the length of it. The walls were lined with leather-bound books from floor to ceiling. Two or three researchers looked up briefly as they entered, and turned back to their labours, like monks devoted to their illuminated manuscripts. They went into an office at the far end, where Leverson picked up an envelope addressed to Simon at Cambridge.

'I owe you an apology,' he said as he handed it over. 'You'll see why when you read it. Now, if you would like to install yourselves at this table, I shall leave you to digest the contents.'

Leo had spotted a little restaurant across the street, and thought he would go and get a cup of coffee there. Simon opened the envelope.

Institut Voltaire
Les Délices
Genève

Dear Dr. Prestcott

I recall with pleasure our meeting at The Grange, and thank you for your kind letter to my wife, who also received an appreciative note from Miss Schoenheimer. It is good to know that this old-world courtesy has not been entirely forgotten by the young, despite all the evidence one sees to the contrary.

In the course of your visit you made some mention of that doubtful character, the comte de Freyssenet, and I expressed the gravest doubts about his ever having visited Voltaire here at Les Délices, as you say he claimed. It is with some regret that I have to retract my outright rejection of his claim, since I received this morning, among the latest batch of very poor quality photocopies from the Saltikov-Shchedrin Library in

179

Leningrad, a *carnet* kept by Voltaire just prior to the time of his death.

I was surprised to find, within the notebook and bound in with its pages, a few manuscript pages not in Voltaire's hand. In fact, not in any hand I recognised. I should have remained in the dark, but for the fortunate poor quality of the paper of the original holograph. It was so thin that some writing on the verso of the last folio had seeped through. This had not been noticed or photocopied by the inefficient technician in Leningrad, whether in error or by design I would not care to devine. I was obliged, therefore, to resort to a mirror, which revealed the following words, indubitably in Voltaire's own hand: "*à retourner au Cte de Freycenet*".

The pages were obviously not returned to him, no doubt because Voltaire died shortly after. One can assume that they were gathered up and transported to Russia by his rapacious niece, Mme. Denis, as part of the deal she had concluded with Queen Catherine the Great, for the acquisition of all Voltaire's library and manuscripts.

In case you are interested, I enclose a copy of the copy, in the hope that it will add to the piquancy of the article which you are, I trust, preparing.

I hope to have the pleasure of seeing you here in Geneva before too long.

Yours sincerely

GUSTAVE LEVERSON

Feverishly Simon turned to the enclosure. It was certainly in Freyssenet's writing. On the final page, he could clearly pick out Voltaire's note, with its use of the common alternative spelling of Freyssenet's name. There were three pages of manuscript:

'pu soulever tout seul sans la force extraordinaire

dont je me sentais doué et qui semblait émaner de
l'autre côté du mur dont les blocs solides aurient
constitué un obstacle infranchissable même pour un
lutteur arabe...'

The pages led on directly from the end of the page
Lebrecht had had in his possession in Healesville. Simon
did not have his copy with him, but his memory of its
wording provided an exact link. So, the complete text ran:

I longed to see what lay behind, and grasped the
rough edges of one of the stones, which I would never
have been able to lift by myself, but for the
extraordinary strength with which I felt myself
endowed and which seemed to emanate from the other
side of the wall whose solid blocks would have
constituted an insuperable obstacle even for an Arab
wrestler....

Simon now read on in the monastic silence of the reading
room:

The space left by the displaced block was just
large enough to allow me to pass my head and
shoulders through. The brilliance of the light was
such that my eyes were blinded for several minutes,
and I did not proceed further until being sure of what
awaited me. Figure to yourself my astonishment, my
dear Princess, on finding the room or cell before me
completely empty. It was without windows and yet it
was full of light which seemed to come from no source.
Perhaps there was one spot which seemed brighter
than the rest, like a lantern behind a glowing white
sheet. I remained before this strange spectacle for a
time which I could not measure, perhaps seconds,
perhaps hours, unable and unwilling to separate
myself from the contemplation of that light which shed
itself upon me not just as light for my eyes, but as a
kind of healing power [force guérisseuse] *which*
harmonised all things and answered all questions.

At last I heard voices approaching, and awoke
from my rêverie. With the same ease I replaced the

stone, and the light through the wall faded as two of the monks came through the trap-door leading to the library. They indicated that they were anxious about the prolonged absence of myself and my dragoman, who was at that moment regaining consciousness. He told them that we had both been overcome by the heat and stuffiness of the library, and so they took us back to our quarters and gave us cordials to revive us.

I then found that the bad cut on my forehead, caused by the lowness of a stone archway and by my unusual height, had completely healed, leaving no trace.

How is one to explain this occurrence? I do not know, Princess. Being, as you know, a sworn enemy of all systems of repressive religion, of which I count the Church of Rome to be the worst (one of the few points upon which M. de Voltaire and I are in agreement) I shall not tell of the strange room and light to anyone but you, whose discretion I trust without reservation. However, I wish that some of the harmony and wisdom with which I found myself briefly endowed whilst under the influence of the mysterious light had remained with me. For I have today entered into the most violent disagreement with M. de Voltaire, on the subject of my dear friend Jean-Jacques Rousseau. I was led to anger, provoked by his sarcasm, and I have locked myself in my room, ignoring the knocking on my door. No doubt it is Mme. Denis, his niece, pleading with me to rejoin the company.

At last, dear Princess, these few hours of solitude at Les Délices have enabled me to find time to tell you of my travels, since I left Egypt and you, to Constantinople, Vienna, and Switzerland. This constant movement has left me with little time to brood about my separation from that person close to you whose memory lies embedded for ever within my heart. If you see that person, please assure her of my

So there it was. Simon sat back, and blew his nose as if testing the echo in the reading room. Perhaps it had all simply been the effect of the heat and stuffiness, as Freyssenet had in fact wanted to believe, with his rationalist mind. Did he really remove the great block of stone? Or was that part of an hallucination? There seemed to be no clue as to the identity of the monastery, but there were still several lines to be deciphered:

The knocking at my door was caused by a footman bringing me your parcel, from Constantinople. I have read your terrible account of the abominable events that occurred after my departure, and have not yet had the courage to open the box you have sent me. I am so overcome with grief that I can scarcely write, but I must reassure you that I have received your envoi.

It is beyond understanding that such inhuman beings as the Pasha are allowed to exist. I can understand his jealousy on being told by an envious fellow-concubine that Min-ha had been unfaithful. But his cruelty and savagery towards her are beyond pardon. To have killed her outright, even, I could forgive. But slowly cutting out her heart before having her beheaded, forcing you to observe this horrible act, and then instructing you to send that still palpitating heart to her lover...all that is the work of a depraved beast, not a member of the human race. However, if he thought that by sending me that beloved heart he was punishing me, he is very mistaken: for in this box before me lies the most precious gift I could ever imagine possessing. I shall treasure it, weep over it, and keep it forever in a safe place, in the vault containing the remains of my respected ancestors. Perhaps one day, in some world we cannot imagine, she and I will be reunited in our love, whose strength

*grows daily, instead of diminishing. Distance could
not weaken it, and death shall only make it greater.*

Feeling completely dazed and very sick, Simon was
folding the pages to stuff them into the envelope, when a
suave English voice close behind him said, 'Good afternoon,
Dr. Prestcott. Have you hurt your head?'

It was Professor Timothy Crankshaw. Momentarily,
English politeness got the better of him.

'Ah, Professor Crankshaw. Excuse me, I feel rather ill.'

Simon thrust the envelope into his briefcase and lurched
out of the reading room into the hallway just as Leo was
coming back in from his coffee break. Simon wheeled him
round, handkerchief to mouth, and pushed him outside
again. Leo was trained never to be surprised, and waited
alertly for an explanation. When Simon had deposited most
of his lunch in the bushes, he nodded towards the entrance
of the Institute.

'In there... chap called... Crankshaw... he got his room
done over... in Cambridge... when I did... but wouldn't
report it... I don't trust him... What the Hell's he doing
here?... not his scene at all... Leo, wait out here and track
him when he comes out... We must know what he's up to,
who he's contacting.'

'O.K. But what's he look like?'

'Fat, balding, fifty-ish, awash with lavender water to
cover the perspiration.'

Leo took up a position, newspaper in hand, on a seat in
the park with a good view of the entrance. Simon went back
in, cleaned himself up in the toilet, and returned to the
reading room. Crankshaw was nowhere to be seen. Simon
stepped towards Leverson's office and was about to knock
when he heard Crankshaw's voice coming from within.

'...quite a surprise to see him here. I thought he'd gone
back to Australia. Surely he's working on a chap called ...
er... Freycinot, or Freycigny, isn't he? I didn't know he was
interested in Voltaire.'

'Didn't you? Oh yes, he's doing some interesting work

on Voltaire.' He left it at that, Simon noted with relief. He knocked on the door.

'Ah, Dr. Prestcott,' Leverson beamed, 'I hope you're feeling better? This is Professor Crankshaw of the Vatican... which office was it?'

Crankshaw cut in, embarrassed. 'We have met.'

'Yes, of course, how foolish of me. It's just that I associated you with Rome, rather than Cambridge. It's always quite amusing to receive scholars in Voltaire's house from that institution which kept him on the Index Prohibitorum until a few years ago.'

Simon turned to go. 'Look, I didn't mean to interrupt...'

'Not at all, Dr. Prestcott. Professor Crankshaw was about to leave. And I should like a word with you about a new acquisition.'

Crankshaw took the hint and bowed himself out. Simon saw him pick up his briefcase and leave. Leo would take over.

'Can't bear those Inquisition chaps,' said Leverson, 'but one has to be polite. Some very high-powered grey eminence from Rome wrote to me asking for special permission but I told him any reputable scholar can come and work here. Now, the odd thing is, Simon, that almost as soon as he came into my office he popped in an innocent little question: did I know of anyone working on French *émigrés*? I told him there were dozens, hundreds. Then when he started in on Freyssenet the moment he came back after lunch, and told me you weren't feeling well, I got a bit suspicious. I hope I did the right thing?'

'Absolutely. I'm most grateful to you. I have good reason not to trust him.'

'I thought he was a bit of a creep. Oh dear; my wife's always telling me off for being prejudiced about people. I can't help it, I either take to them or I don't. She only takes *to* people, not everyone of course. She was very taken by you, by the way. She doesn't show much, in that inscrutable oriental way of hers, but you were the flavour of the day, with the children too. I gather they told you about the High

Garden?'

Simon was on his guard. 'Yes. They pointed it out to me.'

'Well, let me tell you, you're very, very privileged. It was months before they even told me!'

Leverson went over to a carved wall-cupboard. 'A bit early for an *apéritif*, but you look as though you could do with a pick-me-up. Whisky?'

Simon nodded. 'Thank you. I found the Freyssenet stuff... well... a bit of a shock. I think you'll see why when you read it yourself. I'm all right now.'

'Well enough to come and have dinner with us tonight?'

'Yes, of course, I'd love to. Where?'

'Here, of course. We have an apartment upstairs. There is someone I'd particularly like you to meet. Cheers.'

'Cheers. I'm afraid I shall have invite a friend...' Simon began to explain.

'Ah, the delightful Miss Schoenheimer, I expect?'

'Alas, no. She's in London, I think. No, it's an old Cambridge friend of mine, first-rate classicist.'

'Splendid. That will make a good table. See you at eight sharp.'

Outside, there was no sign of Leo or of the car. He got a taxi back to the *Cheval blanc* to find George confirming his flight for the following day. Simon indicated to him by sign language that some important new factors had occurred, and George said he would ring back.

'What's happened? You look a bit whacked, old chap.'

Simon reported quickly, and pulled out the copy of the Freyssenet pages.

George expelled a deep breath when Simon had finished. 'That's pretty grisly stuff. And I don't like this Crankshaw chap turning up one bit. Trouble is, we're still no closer to knowing which bloody monastery it is.'

He looked at the manuscript pages. 'What's this?' he enquired, turning one of the pages sideways. They both peered at what looked like hieroglyphics, written vertically in the margin.

'Arabic? Hellenic?' asked Simon. 'Come on George, you're the decoder. Linear A and Linear B and all that stuff...'

'Shut up a minute and hand me a magnifying glass.'

Simon went to his briefcase and took out the powerful one he always carried when working on manuscripts. After about thirty seconds, George leaned back and muttered, 'Bloody fool'.

'Who is?'

'I am. We both are. It's obvious now. The photocopier has cut off the top half of the writing. You can see a very faint line going right through it, with the lens.'

He began to copy out the symbols carefully, under a line he had drawn on a sheet of paper. Then by extending the letters upwards according to Freyssenet's own handwriting quirks, Simon quickly completed the words.

'St. Macre. Well I'm blessed!'

'O.K., Simon, so you're blessed. When do you tell me why?'

'Sorry.' Simon snapped out of his daydream. 'Makros.'

'Who the blazes is he?' He jumped up. 'Not the Makarios bloke who gave us all that trouble in Cyprus?'

'George, George... Just calm down. It's a place. The Monastery of St. Makros the Great. Saint-Macre in French. Makros was an early Coptic saint. Lived for most of the fourth century, I think. I've made notes on several of the Egyptian monasteries, and this is one of the most famous. You'd have approved of Makros, George: he didn't have any time for men of power, so he took himself off and settled in the desert. A very simple man, full of charity and goodness. Proper Saint, in fact.'

'So, there we are at last. The last clue solved. We now know the nature of the phenomenon Freyssenet saw...'

'And we've had grisly confirmation of the existence of Min-ha, and we know what's in that box...'

'But,' warned George, 'we have a problem.'

'Crankshaw?'

'Him too. Where the devil's Leo? But I mean a problem about this Princess he apparently wrote all that stuff to. Did he really write to her, or is this "Dear Princess" lark just a literary device?'

'I think he really wrote to her. In Freyssenet's espionage reports at the Public Record Office, I've frequently found he kept copies of his own letters, or wrote a report and then incorporated the same wording into a letter to an ambassador or a minister. I think our friend always wrote with one eye on posterity. I guess this letter was written to Princess Elena — that was the name that came to me during that incredible dream-vision I had.'

'Right,' said George, 'so we do have a problem! There could be a copy somewhere — the one he sent to the Princess.'

'But Lebrecht somehow got hold of the first page of the Leningrad one... No, wait a minute.' Simon reflected. 'Not necessarily. They could have become separated way back at the time Freyssenet left Les Délices in 1778. He took one page with him and forgot the rest, which eventually went to Leningrad, I mean, St. Petersburg. I'm not surprised he forgot things, considering the shock he had when that casket arrived. I can tell you, George, when I read about it, I threw up all over Voltaire's rhodedendrons.'

'Somebody, then, may have the complete version of the letter?' said George.

'Which is more than we have,' Simon agreed.

'We don't have the beginning of it, right? But does it really matter? We have the operative bit about the strange light or force. Others may have this as well. But we have a bit of the letter which the Princess wouldn't have had.'

'The bit in the margin!'

'The name of the monastery! Good boy.'

'That clue exists in two other places,' resumed Simon. 'Leningrad: no one's going to pinch that one! And the Voltaire Institute. Question: did Crankshaw see what I was reading? Would he have known what it was? And could he find it again? Even the Russians didn't pick out it wasn't just part of Voltaire's own notes.'

'Leverson?'

'Sound. He doesn't like Crankshaw and wouldn't tell him anything, except the next flight back to London.'

'Then we're laughing!' George roared. 'But where the devil has Leo got to?'

'With my car.'

Simon looked at his watch. 7.22. 'We must get a spurt on. I need a shower. You put on a tie and look like a respectable Cambridge classicist. We'll leave a number for Leo, in case he needs us.'

George's Renault pulled out of the exit on to the main Chênebourg road just as the M.G. came into the car park *via* the side street.

18

Simon found it very satisfying to be dining in Voltaire's house, perhaps in the very room in which he had slept, or had written *Candide* in 1758. It domesticated the great *philosophe* and made him less of a literary abstraction.

The other dinner guest was Dr. Pierre Bernard, fresh, in a manner of speaking, from his lecture tour in Australia.

'How long were you in Melbourne, Dr. Bernard?' Simon looked at the tanned, rugged face of the man sitting opposite him, and decided he had probably spent more time on the Gold Coast or in Fiji than in Melbourne.

'Not long enough, I am afraid. I liked the atmosphere there; very civilised. But I had to go and speak in Darwin after only two days, at the new university. There I met a friend of yours.'

'Really?' asked Simon, 'who was that?'

'A Professor... Rook? Corbeau? Corneille?'

'Ah! Crow, of course! Hardly a friend. She hates my guts.'

'The English language is so physical. Be that as it may, she asked me to thank you.'

'What on earth for?'

'Some ideas she used in her inaugural lecture. What was the topic now?' He pulled out a small black notebook and consulted it briefly. 'Yes, here it is: "Reality and Appearance: Plato, Swedenborg, and the Quantum Theory". Rather heavy stuff. Quite Swiss, in fact!' he laughed. 'She had some strange ideas about earthly existence and the after-life being a hologram created by individual mentalities, but nevertheless real. I don't recall much about it, I'm afraid. I was, how do you say, knocked for sixpence by the heat and humidity.'

Well I'm buggered, Simon thought. Crafty old Crow. I wonder if I'm part of her nightmare, or vice-versa.

'In Geneva', Pierre Bernard went on, 'we are not

accustomed to such tropical conditions, and I do not leave Suisse Romande very often.'

'You don't like travelling, Pierre?' asked Sara.

'Not fleeting visits,' Bernard replied. 'I think six weeks is the minimum to make it worth while. I spent six weeks in the United States a few years ago. Strange and wonderful people I met there. Very positive. But so afraid. It seems as though they are fed on paranoia from birth. In New York, one feels the world is about to burst into flames every day. Always a crisis. No wonder psycho-analysts do so well. I spend a day a week just walking in the mountains. One might get caught in a thunderstorm up there, but you know it will pass, and the sun will come out.'

'But I gather you aren't very optimistic that the storms we humans are creating will leave much sunshine?' said Simon. 'I must confess, I don't quite see why you have spent so much time working out ways of making mankind a viable species, if you are so sure we won't survive?'

Bernard was about to respond when George broke in. 'Yes, well, I don't know much about this Suzuki-type one-minute-to-twelve scenario, but there's not much point pressing the obvious point that the ship's going down if there's nothing we can do about it. People will say open the bar and let's enjoy the last few seconds doing what we like. It's a recipe for anarchy.'

'Oh dear, I have not expressed myself very clearly, I am sorry.' Bernard smiled apologetically. 'I do not think mankind as it is at present will survive very much longer on this tired little earth-ball. But we must look beyond that. I am certain that a certain sort of humanoid will — or could — perpetuate the species elsewhere. I disagree with Jean Giraudoux, who in a moment of discouragement wrote that mankind had missed the chance to evolve into a species superior to itself. They exist all over the world, examples of that species of the future! We can work out the recipe, it is known quite well. But there are so few. However, we shall not need many. Only a few can survive, but they must be the ones who can produce a species that will not simply make the same mistakes we have, all over again.'

'And are you one of these rare people?' Leverson asked with a smile.

Pierre Bernard laughed. 'Not at all! I am like the trainer, the, er, coach, of a tennis champion. I am not a champion myself, but I know how to make one out of the right material. We must prepare to evacuate those who will be selected and trained to act as the new humanity, not like the present one.'

'So how do you do it?' Simon asked.

'No,' Pierre Bernard responded, 'how do *you* do it? My time is nearly over. But you and your children have a heavy responsibility: to be realistic about the world as it is, and to be hopeful about a better world. Frankly, I am glad I am an old man. Well,' — he looked round — 'older than most of you, anyway!'

Gustave Leverson had been following the arguments almost as quietly as his wife. He had heard them before; he had heard Pierre Bernard before; they were old friends. But he had never before felt the sense of urgency and commitment that he had experienced round his table that evening. He was also aware of the mutual attraction that existed between Sara and Simon. A kind of mute understanding had been immediately established between them. Knowing what he did, he was pleased.

'Why didn't you ring us?' George asked grumpily.

'I tried to — but there was no bloody answer,' Leo whined. 'You know how it is at that reception desk, like as not the porter was cooking the dinner. This isn't exactly four star, is it?'

'O.K., O.K., so you followed his taxi to Carouge, on the outskirts. Then?'

'Well, an M.G. sports car with English number plates doesn't merge very well with Volvos and Citroëns, so I had to be careful. He must have spotted Simon's car outside the Institute anyway. So I didn't see where he went when he paid the taxi off. I parked the M.G. out of sight and lurked around till another taxi turned up about an hour later. He came out, must have been watching for it, and I heard him say "Ar lar ayroport". Off we went ar lar ayroport. I guessed he was going international, got there first by miles, nippy little thing, your M.G., and waited for him to turn up. Which he didn't. So either I'd missed him, which I don't think, or he'd rumbled me waiting outside the house, and put me on a false *pissed* as I hear the French say. So here's the address. Sorry I took so long, easy place to get lost in, Geneva. Everything's smaller than the map, somehow.'

'Very unfortunate, him turning up like that,' said Simon.

'Somebody must have tipped him off,' George sighed.

The letter left on the porter's desk suddenly flashed into Simon's mind. 'I'm afraid I may have left an obvious clue.' He told them.

'If that's true,' said George darkly, 'then he's very determined and single-minded. Not good. Not good at all. We must move out.'

'Where to?' asked Simon.

'Anywhere. Lausanne. Lyon. We can't possibly take that box with us by air to Egypt. They'd bring out every security device in the country. I think Leo had better drive back to England with it. Let's face it, Simon, it's only got sentimental value, to you. Same with the contents of the manuscript. You don't need to keep them. Or if you want to keep a copy, you could send it to someone trusty — in Australia!'

The next step was still not clear to Simon. 'Are you saying we should now go off to Egypt?'

'Well, we do know where to go, and that's what we were wanting to know,' George replied. 'But what about a visa? Have you got a visa?'

'Yes, on both passports — British and Australian. But if that bloke Riad was official, or semi, they'll stop me as soon as I front up at Immigration control. They might even like me as a hostage, in return for Riad.'

'I don't think they'd go that far, if it is the kosher

Egyptian authorities — excuse my mixed metaphors. But I suspect Riad is working for a very semi-official gang who happened to have a lot of influence. So the authorities could always plead impotence.'

'Let's pause a moment.' Simon lay back and stared at the ceiling. 'Apart from curiosity, why do we want to go to the monastery? Do I really want to risk having the same kind of mind-blowing experience as Freyssenet? Won't his account of it do? Thank you very much, yes of course we believe you, *Monsieur le comte*, most interesting. I'll publish a paper on it.'

'I thought you had a kind of contract with that Australian foundation, to follow through the investigation the old chap had started.'

'But he got bumped off by an Egyptian thug or two. Exactly my point.'

'Well, you knew it was risky before you started any of this. Not going to get cold feet now, are you?' George managed to look disdainful.

'I'm quite capable of that, George. I wasn't destined to die a hero, like you. You'll get a medal. I haven't even got tenure.'

George rose. 'I'm going to get a good night's sleep. Tomorrow, you move on along the lake, to Vevey. You can show Leo Montreux from there. I'll give you an address to go to, not a hotel. In Vevey, Simon, you ring Leverson and tell him it's vital he keep that notebook under lock and key — in a bank vault if possible. No shortage of those here. And ask him please to stonewall Crankshaw if he asks any awkward questions. Tell him it's a matter of life and death, if you like. It would be an understatement.'

'What are you going to do?' asked Simon.

'Contact some good friends I have here who might help us.'

'I thought the Swiss were incorruptible.'

'That doesn't mean they're unhelpful.'

The drive along Lac Léman to Vevey, at sunrise, was magical. Simon had great difficulty in keeping his eyes on the road as the mists turned pink and slowly dissolved, revealing row upon row of snow-capped mountains in the distance over the water. They arrived in the little town of Vevey in time for breakfast at the Hôtel du Lac, which Simon had been longing to see ever since reading Anita Brookner's sad, haunting novel, and he found she had captured to perfection its genteel and seedy opulence, like a melancholy echo from a time gone by. As he and Leo munched croissants, piled up on a silver platter, and sipped their scalding coffee, the steady chug-chug of a white steamer came faintly through the double glazing. Above it, a solitary seagull wheeled and soared. Leo looked blissful.

'This'll do,' he said. 'No need to go to Montrose.'

It was five in the afternoon before George Plaidy rang through to the quiet empty house by the lake at Vevey. It was a weekend residence belonging to one of his colleagues in Swiss security. When George considered the standard of living of his European counterparts, he often felt like defecting. But who would have him, with the reputation British intelligence security had?

'All set,' he announced.

'What, exactly, is set?' asked Simon testily.

'We're off to Cairo tomorrow afternoon. Three-fifteen flight.'

'Would you like me to say "Hurrah" or "Oh shit", old chap? And what am I supposed to be doing there? Buying camels for the Melbourne Zoo? And what's Leo going to say about a lead box full of a very illegally acquired item of historical Oriental anatomy? Say it's a sample of dehydrated Australian sheep? I do hope you've thought of these things, George, because frankly I've been too busy entertaining our friend here. Very demanding. Wants to watch boats going by all the time.'

'Finished?' There was a truculence in George's voice

that made Simon pause.

'Momentarily, yes.'

'Right. Then get this. I shall say it only once! You, Simon, as an associate of the late Professor Lebrecht — who was well known and revered in Egyptian academic and cultural circles — will be the Australian delegate on an Ecumenical Commission for Comparative Religious Studies, under the auspices of UNESCO. I'm your assistant. Leo will drive your car back to London for you, with the box. He won't have any trouble.'

'Thank you, George. Is that all?'

'Yes. No. Not quite. I've saved the best till last. The British delegate representing the Catholic Archbishop of Westminster, is unfortunately Professor Crankshaw. See you at Geneva *airpo*rt tomorrow at one-fifteen p.m. Don't be late.'

19

...very glad when it was over. If I'd been by myself I'm pretty sure the young immigration officer would have shoved me on the next plane back to Frankfurt. It was all an unholy mix-up at the Egyptian end. George had told his contact we should be going to Alexandria via Frankfurt, but they had failed to pass that on from Cairo straight away. I don't know if all the cloak and dagger stuff was necessary, but anyone expecting us on the Cairo plane would have been rather puzzled to see us shuffling aboard a Swissair flight to Frankfurt at 10 a.m. I had been less than pleased when George turned up at 6 a.m. in Vevey to hustle us about and get us to Geneva in time. Leo was left with the job of returning George's Hertz car and getting mine back to England. At one point he will clearly have to be driving both cars at once, but that's his problem.

During the hour and a half we had to wait at Frankfurt, George condescended to let fall a few snippets of information about his connexions, which had enabled him to get me transformed from *persona non grata* to *grata* so fast. 'Egypt,' he said, 'is extremely anxious to avoid getting drawn into the bitter fighting between racial and religious factions in Lebanon, Israel, Jordan, Iran, Iraq, and so forth.' So, for that reason their security service is very keen to cooperate with European countries, and George had had frequent dealings with his opposite numbers. He told me he had stressed the urgency of our getting access to the Wadi Natrun monasteries (without specifying any particular one) in order to counter the activities of Fuad Riad and his cronies. Apparently, Riad had been running a very lucrative business in the sale of Egyptian treasures for some time, using his diplomatic status and immunity from customs inspection to further his main aim in life, personal enrichment. He was also suspected of dealing in drugs as well, but had been extremely clever up to the point when he got interested in Lebrecht and Freyssenet. Since then he had managed to botch practically every move, to the fury of his mafia syndicate, the embarrassment of his friends in high places, and to the joy of George's security colleagues, who were delighted to see Riad discredited and, for the time being at least, out of the way. However, no one was sure if there were hidden elements of the Riad faction still in operation for us to worry about. Egyptian security are also, apparently, anxious about the spread of activity by the Italian tomb-robbers, those *tombaroli* chaps; they are moving into Greece and Egypt, attracted by the big money to be made from sales of antiquities to multimillionaire collectors. They may still be under the impression that there is treasure of monetary value at the monasteries — the Makros one did have a fabulous library, by all accounts. I don't know what's left of it now. We shall see, if we're lucky.

Because George's message didn't get to Alexandria before we did, the immigration people hummed and hawed about letting me through. We waited for about an hour in a hot, stuffy office, then one of the *douaniers* came in, wreathed in smiles and holding a magical piece of paper. 'All is O.K. fine,' he announced, 'you go in now. Change your dollars into lovely Egyptian pounds. Welcome to Egypt!' And we were waved through into the arms of the chap who had presumably brought about this miracle. He goes under the improbable name of Mr. Mut, a bland, roly-poly little chap with a cigarette permanently glued to his mouth, which makes it even more difficult to understand a blind word he says. We gathered from him that his office had not had time to organise the monastery visit with the Coptic Orthodox Patriarchate, but he would go to their office in Nebi Daniel Street first thing tomorrow morning and fix things up. In the meantime, he had booked rooms for us at the new Sheraton Beau Rivage.

'Bloody nuisance, that,' George mumbled to me, 'the

faster we get to Makros and out again, the better I'll like it.'
Nevertheless, he smiled back at our saviour, and we followed
him out into the balmy Mediterranean evening. He whisked
us quickly and hair-raisingly in his battered Mercedes to the
hotel.

And that is where I now am, my dearest Anna, reclining
on my bed (having caught up on some sleep and wishing
you were beside me), trying to make sense of all this, and
mugging up my notes for the next step tomorrow. I have a
feeling this is going to be even more, how shall I say, not just
dangerous, I'm not trying to be melodramatic, but more —
significant? (no, awful word); I'd like to find the equivalent
for 'awesome' or 'fearsome', applied to adrenalin:
adrenalinsome — than the Freyssenet *fracas*. Now I have
to talk to George about Copts and things; he's a glutton for
information, a real beaver. He can even bring out some
effective words in Arabic — 'Just picked it up alongside
Greek, somehow' — you know him. Good night, dear, dear
friend. I wish we could curl up together now and talk about
all this. It would be a comfort.

At least you are now in the picture, regarding everything
that's been going on. Sorry I have been so remiss about
writing, but as you can see, we have been moving from one
crisis to the next at disconcerting speed. To think I once
thought university life was full of crises! I can now see
those storms as the piddling little ripples they really are. Is
this the beginning of wisdom, do you think? I'll have to look
it up in Lao Tse.

Kindest regards to Floris,

Love, Your ever affectionate Simplissimus.

Simon addressed the envelope, and was just wondering
what to do for stamps when a knock sounded on his door.
Normally he would have simply called, 'Come in', but
something warned him not to this time. Instead, he tiptoed
across the room and quietly opened the door connecting
with George's room (George's request that it be opened had
caused a little lifting of the eyebrows at reception). George

was dozing, and sat up abruptly as he entered. Simon put his fingers to his lips, and whispered to him. George moved swiftly to his own door and quietly opened it, then peered out. He was just in time to see a female high heel disappearing into Simon's room. He motioned to Simon to count five then go back into his own room via the closed interconnecting door. George went out into the corridor. On five, Simon gently opened the door. He saw a girl standing by his wardrobe, her hand raised, about to open it. The wardrobe was to the right of the interconnecting door; the corridor door was directly behind her.

'You won't find anything in there,' said Simon.

The girl was not in the least thrown off her guard. 'Good evening, sir,' she said with a charming smile. 'I was just checking to see that everything is in order for you.' Her accent was a mixture of Arabic and French, as was her appearance, which Simon's mind was giving him flashing signals about, but which made no sense to him. He did not quite manage to prevent his eyes refocusing on George as he silently entered.

'Allow me to present myself,' she said, opening her shoulder-bag. The gun was in her hand just as George came within range. Without turning she said: 'Mr. Plaidy, you should teach your friend to lock his door. Stay where you are unless you want a dead friend.'

'He wouldn't be any use to you dead, would he?' said George.

It clicked in Simon's head. Of course: Anna playing the piano, Fuad Riad trying to engage Professor Lebrecht in conversation, the cicadas in the trees by the pool — and this girl, with longer hair, posing as Riad's wife. It was probably she who cracked poor old Lebrecht's skull. Simon felt a wave a hot anger sweep over him.

'Then we can dispense with you instead. We know you brought in no weapons, so don't try to frighten me.'

'I wouldn't dream of it,' said George. 'There are two things I dislike doing. One is frightening a lady, and the other is shooting her in the back. So drop your hand, and turn round slowly.'

Simon thought George was taking bravado a bit too far. The girl obviously saw the advantages of getting rid of George rather than Simon. Stepping backwards, slightly to her right, so as to be able to keep an eye on them both, she swivelled her revolver slowly round through an arc. When it was pointing roughly at the head of the bed, George's right hand moved from behind his right buttock, very fast, and revealed that it was holding a much more business-like weapon with a silencer on it. He hissed at her: 'Drop it! *NOW!* Don't move.'

She obeyed. Good training saved her life. Simon could see that George was in no mood for arguments. So that was what the Mercedes man had passed to George on the front seat.

George picked up her gun and made her lie face down on the floor. Then, with his own gun pointing at the side of her neck, he interrogated her. At first she refused to say anything at all, but gradually, expertly, he managed to goad and gently lead her to respond to his questions.

What particularly undermined her resolve was the spontaneous reaction from both Simon and George when she said that she and Riad were inspired by purely religious motives. After some genuinely derisive laughter, they simmered down, and George asked the girl, whose name they had established along the line as Zaina, what she really thought her friend Fuad Riad was wanting to achieve, she said: 'You cannot know the problems we have here with Christians if you ask that. Always they are causing problems for the one and only true religion, Islam.'

'Even if we admit,' said George, 'that Islam is the only true religion, Zaina, do you really think that Riad's purpose is, or was, to prevent some sort of Christian uprising in Egypt?'

'Of course! What else?'

George shook his head sadly — not relaxing his hold on his revolver; he had come across several beautiful, seductive but totally ruthless and deadly female terrorists in the past few years.

'You won't believe us, but Riad's implication in tomb-robbing, illicit sale of national treasures, and probable connexion with the drug trade, is well known by my security colleagues in Cairo, Paris, London, Washington, Rome and Canberra. You notice I said "probable" drug connexion, so I'm not exaggerating for effect. His religious interest was just a cover, as his diplomatic status was. Are you trying to tell us you didn't know this, Zaina?'

For some time she said nothing. So George said: 'What is it you think we are trying to find?'

'There is some remnant of evil infidel power you have found a clue to. I do not know what it is, but it is not desirable it shall be made known to the world.'

'But supposing it is a genuine sign from God?' asked Simon.

'There is no God but Allah,' she replied firmly.

'That means there is no God but God. No one who believes in God would argue with that. But what kind of Moslem are you? A Sunnite? A Shiite? Or a Murjiite, perhaps? Or what about a Kadarite? Or a, what is it, an Ahmadi?'

'Ah! Ahmad proclaimed the doctrine of *jihad*, of holy war against you unbelievers.'

'Oh, did he? I thought I read that *jihad* really means *striving after righteousness*? How can it be right to persecute believers in Jesus, when Ahmad himself believed that Jesus was taken down from the cross while still alive, and that He went and taught and healed in India, right?'

'Yes. To Kashmir. But what is the point of all this?'

George was beginning to wonder too, and made an impatient gesture to Simon, who indicated he had nearly done.

'All right, Ahmad doesn't matter, even though he claimed he had come, only a hundred years ago, in the spirit and power of Jesus, whom he adored because of His gentle spirit and peaceful teaching. And he, Ahmad, was one of you, a Moslem! Would he have wanted to kill people just to prevent the revelation of a mystic sign from God, in a monastery devoted to Jesus? How can you be so certain you are right that you can murder and assassinate?'

'You filthy Christians are as bad!' she screamed. 'You have killed and murdered for centuries — not only during the Crusades, but each other in your Holy Wars of Protestants against Catholics...'

'Good. At last we are in agreement. You say the Christians are as bad. Conversely, that means Moslems are as bad. You have persecuted the Copts, this pious, simple people for centuries. Did you know that the Nazi practice of branding Jews was a Moslem idea? Yes, they branded the Coptic monks with their name and a number. They demolished churches, made the Christians wear degrading dress, imposed heavy taxes on them. And you have the nerve to complain that you are having trouble from the church of Jesus? Oh, I *am* sorry for you!'

'I don't need your pity, you Christian pig!'

'You're wrong there. I'm not a Christian. But I would defend to the last anyone's right to be one. Or to be a Moslem. You all kill one another because you have the Truth. Did anyone ever kill to defend a doubt?'

As George moved to ease his aching arm, Zaina quickly brought her legs up and tried to kick him in the groin. But he was too quick, and hit her kneecap sharply with the barrel of his gun, heavy with silencer. She lay back and moaned, looking very hurt and furious.

'Have you done with the comparative religion debate?' he asked Simon. 'Good. Then lift the telephone and dial this number.' He gave Simon a slip of paper. He recognised the close-lipped tones of the voice at the other end as Mut's and relayed George's message: they had one of Riad's thugs, and would he come and collect her? The man sounded quite excited, and said he would be straight over.

When Zaina had been marched, handcuffed and sullen, down to the waiting car, *via* the emergency staircase, George was irritated with Simon.

'What the blazes was all that religious argument for?

You surely didn't expect to make her change her mind or her ways, did you? You might as well try to convert the Pope to Marxism.'

'I'm sorry, George. I did go on a bit. But I was trying to get something straight in my own mind. About these Copts. I wanted to see if she had any real reason for wanting to suppress this ... phenomenon. It struck me that she might know something about it we ought to be aware of. You see, the Copts are devout believers, and by that I mean pretty uncritical. They've had a bundle of so-called miracles over the years, and this might be just another one.'

'All right. Now: let's try and prepare ourselves mentally for whatever we might come across tomorrow. I've tried to cover the material things, so fill me in about this mystical stuff.'

'First, George, I'd be glad if you would level with me.'

George looked slightly startled. 'What do you mean?'

'You know why I'm fascinated by this phenomenon — and I have a job to carry through for the Lebrecht Foundation anyway. But you've bagged your baddies, so why don't you just want to move on to the next case now?'

George went over to the well-stocked drinks refrigerator, extracted a couple of bottles of beer and glasses, and sat down heavily. 'This is how it is, Simon, old chap. First, locally: you know the Egyptian government had the Coptic Pope under close arrest for a long time — and eight bishops — all without trial.'

'He was kept in a monastery, wasn't he?'

'That's right. They ringed it with troops to make sure he didn't get out. It was a good job they were all incarcerated, in fact. Someone had fed the Egyptian secret police with false information, that they were plotting against the government, so they were put away safely — and Sadat was assassinated! So none of them could be blamed for it.'

'This Pope of theirs, was he really a subversive?'

'We...e....e...l..l..., in a sense, I suppose he was, in a mild sort of way. He told the Copts all to have nine children so that they'd outnumber the Moslems, and loony things like that.'

'So the government was oversensitive?'

'Yes. Same as English governments were oversensitive to Catholics right up to the eighteen-thirties. And oddly enough — I only made the connexion while we were in Geneva — one Copt was a friend of Sadat and an opponent of the Patriarch, or the Pope as they call him.'

George took a long swig of his beer. Simon snorted. 'Well, come on then! Talk about milking an audience.'

'It was the Abbot of this place we're going to, the Makros monastery.'

'He's *persona grata* with the government?'

'Well done, got it in one. So guess what his answer will be if we try to reactivate some mystical force in his manor.'

'A little tact and diplomacy will be required.'

'And stealth, and some downright lies, come to that. Now,' said George, 'you explain to me why this place should have been singled out for supernatural visitation.'

'No, wait a minute. You've only covered the local interest. What else should I know?'

'Yes. Well then...This phenomenon, if it is still extant and accessible, might have international repercussions, because it's not like the Virgin Mary appearing before a few adolescent schoolgirls. Freyssenet says clearly it was a force of some kind that can affect the mind and induce a changed perception of reality. Fill one with *agape*, universal love. Now,' George went on rapidly, 'a few years ago, no one would have given it a second thought. Hysterical rubbish. But things are different now. E.S.P and parapsychology are the new post-nuclear weapons. Billions of people with their television sets on for hours a day — sitting targets, vying with each other for the title of Apathetic Moron of the Year. Several international political and commercial groupings have the expertise to exploit this before we could say "subliminal". If Mankind had been built like that at the start, we wouldn't have got past the first generation. We'd have wanted to shake hands with the crocodiles.'

Simon found himself saying out loud, quite spontaneously, 'The wolf also shall dwell with the lamb, and the leopard shall lie down with the kid; and the calf and the young lion and the fatling together...'

'...and the cow and the bear shall feed...', George responded.

'...and the lion shall eat straw like the ox...'

'...the spirit of wisdom and understanding...'

They looked at each other, stunned. Simon said, 'I had no idea I knew those verses. I haven't looked at the Old Testament for donkey's years.'

George pondered, then said uncomfortably: 'No, neither have I. It must be the atmosphere here.'

'Seriously, you may be right. Here we are in Alexandria, where St. Mark was martyred; he'd been the first to preach the Gospel in Egypt. Christianity in Egypt spread from this very spot. Clement of Alexandria and Origen were the greatest of early Christian thinkers. And it happened *here*, George, not in Constantinople or Rome. Of course,' he went on, 'that in itself doesn't explain why we both suddenly recalled those words. It's almost as if... oh, I know this is probably pure fantasy... as if the monastery is already exercising some sort of influence...'

'But what is it about that particular monastery, Simon? We need to know, to come to terms with what we are dealing with there.'

Simon went over to his case and brought out a folder. He needed to refresh his memory about a couple of points; it was getting late and his mind was weary.

'Briefly, what I think is this: that monastery is one of the holiest places I've ever read about, outside Jerusalem. First, because of the piety of its founder, in three hundred and something. He said that Cherubim guided him throughout his life. In the year 444, forty-nine Elders were murdered there by the Barbarians. The relics of these martyrs were placed in a chamber within the monastery. It's said the Barbarians washed the blood off their swords in the well, which gave it healing properties. So, that's two sources of, what shall we say, spirituality in the place. But then there's the chrism...'

'Ah! *Khrisma*. Unguent.'

'Good to see the modern world hasn't knocked all your ancient Greek out of you, George. But this chrism, they reckon, is or was rather special: a watered-down remnant of the four hundred pounds of myrrh and aloes and other spices the disciples used for the embalming of Jesus. And finally, the head of St. Mark was kept there for about forty years, in the eleventh century. If all that doesn't add up to a holy place...'

'It's certainly way ahead of the Baptist Chapel in Wigan,' George nodded. 'But how can we be sure Freyssenet actually came here? Could he have imagined it all?'

'Well,' Simon flipped over some pages, 'here are a couple of small circumstantial facts, the kind that often impress policemen. One: he describes how he was hauled up over the surrounding wall in a chair, on the end of a rope, because there was no gate into the monastery — a simple defence system against Bedouins and suchlike. Now, listen to what Lady Danvers Pasha wrote in 1963, in *Medieval Egypt* : "The gate of St. Makros resembles all the monastery entrances: over the door, at first rarely used, is the opening through which visitors used to be drawn up in a basket, in former times." O.K., now, secondly, he says he went through a trapdoor to the library, remember?'

'Yes, yes.' George was getting impatient again.

'She writes this: "The second room on the right leads in to a small chamber, in the floor of which is a trap opening into the secret room in which the library of the monastery was concealed".'

George calmed down, and agreed this was impressive corroboration. 'But let's consider the phenomenon itself,' he went on. 'He admitted the heat had overcome his dragoman, and perhaps even himself, so it could have been a hallucination. Did it, in fact, have any permanent effect on him? Do we know that?'

Simon shuffled a few pages, photocopies of the Freyssenet

memoirs. 'All I have to go on here is what he says about himself. He admits that before he went on this journey to the Levant, he was a spoilt, licentious, selfish aristocrat. But when he got back to his estates, he became a model landowner, read up about the new agricultural methods of Thomas Coke and Jethro Tull so as to improve the lot of his peasants — as well as himself, no doubt; he despised the Court and welcomed the Revolution — until he saw how quickly it turned sour. He was disgusted at the hatred and violence of the citizens, and tried to make them more moderate. For that he was branded an enemy of the people, and he fled just before his château was burned down. The servant-girl who had saved his life in Carcassonne fled with him, and remained his companion — but he never married her, because his mother didn't approve. Pretty wimpish, that. The girl was murdered when he was: on the pavement outside their house in Twickenham. She just got in the way of the chap with the knife, apparently. Poor girl. So, the short answer is, he was a different man when he came back, and fought against what he saw as two régimes based on hatred and tyranny: the one that led to the Terror, and the one that ended at Waterloo.'

'Good,' said George. 'No proof, but at least nothing that contradicts the theory that this phenomenon did have a powerful effect. With luck, we shall know tomorrow.'

It was midnight. Simon felt as though he had gone through a lifetime since George's thumping on the door had awoken him at six that morning.

Back in London, Floris Schoenheimer was also trying to sleep. But he drifted into what he recognised, automatically, as a second state or trance, and visualised Simon, with his hands bound, face to face with a vigorous, stocky young man, in the uniform of a French general, with a shock of hair over one eye. Floris knew the soldier was General Bonaparte, but the face was not the one he had so often seen in portraits. He knew it, but it eluded him... who was it?... who was it?... He drifted off to sleep.

20

They were up, breakfasted, and ready by 8.30. At 11.30 Mr. Mut, wreathed in smiles and smoke, finally arrived.

'Very sorry for lateness, gentlemen,' he said, in his disarming way. 'Late work last night, disposing of the young lady. At that hour, nobody was very interested to fill in forms in triplicate and prepare charge sheet. So I had to find private accommodation for her in rather dark cellar and make official transfer this morning.'

'No problems with her?' asked George.

'Problems? She is one big walking problem. Very confused. Apart from that, no. Then off I go to Coptic Patriarch's office, open at 11 a.m. only. So I was on the step of the door when they took in the goat's milk, yes? Ha, ha, ha.'

'No problems with them?' asked George.

'Problems? No, no problems. Name of Professor Lebrecht seems to be very powerful with Copts. What is he, a bishop?'

'He's more like dead, actually,' said Simon. Mut did not know whether this was a peculiar English joke or not, so he merely smiled and nodded knowingly, gazing into the distance through his permanently half-closed eyes.

'And what about the Hertz car?' asked George, trying to keep his voice patient.

'No need,' said Mut, with a gesture of finality. 'I have permission to drive you where you want to go, and make sure you have no problems.'

George was visibly annoyed by this, but could think of no way to get out of it. 'Bang goes our private tour,' he muttered in Simon's ear, 'bugger the interfering sods!'

Ten minutes later they were rattling off south on the road

to Cairo. They were quickly through Alexandria, which is all length and no width. As they roared along the desert road, Mut kept up an endless stream of monologue, which no one else could hear because of the engine, which seemed to have been fixed at full volume. After sixty miles, he turned off right, and they were on the way to Wadi Natrun. The car's air conditioning was fitful, and Simon just thanked his stars it was not July.

'Now,' announced Mr. Mut, 'only ten kilometres to monasteries. Which one do we go to first?'

George looked round enquiringly at Simon, and said, 'Oh, I don't really know. How about if we go to Makros, Simon?'

'Yes, George, that is a good idea. I'd like to go to Makros. It sounds really interesting.'

Mut gesticulated with both hands. A bump in the track nearly took the car off into the shallow lake. Wadi Natrun was, in fact, a whole chain of lakes, seventy feet below sea level, and full of salt and soda. Very good for mummies, if that is what one is into. And soap.

'You don't want to see the famous library at Deir-es-Surian?'

'Not today, thank you, Mr. Mut,' said George.

'Just as well you don't, it's not there any more, ha, ha, ha. Very good stucco-work though. No?'

'Makros would do very nicely, thank you,' Simon shouted.

Soon it was there before them: long, formidable castle walls stretching out across the sand, with a solid, square-looking keep, a large dome, and a slender tower reaching towards the heavens. They drew up at the gate in the east wall. A voice came from above, and Mut answered multisyllabically, including the word *ingleezi*. The monk replied, '*Istenna hena!*'

'We wait,' Mut announced composedly, lighting up a cigarette.

Not for long. The gate was opened, and a peal from the belfry seemed timed to welcome them.

Down the steps to the cool walled garden of the monastery, shaded by palm trees and bushes; on the drawbridge, they paused, and the monk said something to Mr. Mut, who turned to George and Simon. 'Over there,' he pointed towards the north-west corner, enclosed by walls three feet thick, 'is the ancient holy well, and the Cell of the, how do you call, *krisma*, you understand?'

'Yes, thank you, we understand,' Simon replied, and looked. Then he turned his gaze upon a great dome, which he guessed was the Sanctuary of Benjamin. He felt a fit of awe coming on, despite himself. The monk was ushering them on.

Mut turned to them again to interpret: 'The Abbot will receive you soon. We wait.'

George whispered to Mr. Mut : 'I hope our stuff is all right in the car. You left it outside, didn't you?'

'No problem, 'he replied, 'monks push the car inside. Here, it will be safe as an Englishman in his castle.'

The interview with the abbot was short and in French. Simon said he would be particularly interested to see the old library, of which Professor Lebrecht had spoken to him.

'*Ah, le professeur Lebrecht, comment va-t-il?*' the Abbot asked. Simon explained that he was, regrettably, dead. The Abbot was visibly distressed. Simon did not add any details. He simply said that La Fondation Chelbert — he showed him Pyke's official-looking headed letter — had given him a grant of money to finish some of the research in which Lebrecht had been engaged in the monasteries. And Professor Lebrecht had particularly mentioned the library, accessible through a trap-door.

The Abbot, whose long, venerable beard and kindly, saintly demeanour contrasted with his alert, sharp eyes, shook his head slowly. 'But do you not know?' he said, 'we now have a new library. It is this you must see, with the ancient books and manuscripts — the few we have left.'

Simon was caught with his mouth open, not knowing whether to push further his desire to see the old library. Casually he asked: 'So the old library does not exist any more?'

The Abbot raised his arms. 'It was not destroyed. But it is never used. It was too difficult to arrive at, to enter. An inaccessible library was good in the old days when the monks were ignorant, pious men who did not read. But now, we have many scholars here, and they must have good conditions for working.'

Inwardly, Simon applauded this. But it was shattering news.

'*Mon père*,' he went on, hopelessly improvising, 'my interest lies more in ancient architecture than in manuscripts. My assistant, Monsieur Plaidy, is a Greek scholar, and wishes to examine your books. But I should very much like your permission to explore the older parts of the building, and take photographs of them, before modernisation makes them disappear for ever.'

The Abbot looked at him gravely for a full minute. Then said: '*C'est bien.*' He turned to the monk who had brought them in, standing like a still shadow against the white wall, and spoke to him— in Coptic, Simon supposed. The monk smiled, nodded, and looked at Simon and George. Mr. Mut interpreted for them.'You are to be the guests of the Abbot, and you (he turned to Simon) are allowed to see what ancient parts of the monastery you wish, to continue the work of Professor Lebrecht, whom the brothers here greatly revered.'

They both bowed, out of courtesy saying the little Arabic they knew, '*Mshakreen awwe, mutashakir geddan,*' to thank him, and backed out of the Abbot's study.

Their guide beckoned to them to follow. George asked Mut where they were going. 'To be shown your cells,' he replied. 'You are expected to be here for two, three days, at least.'

'You'll need them, to get through all those Greek manuscripts, won't you George?' laughed Simon. 'While

212

I clamber over the old stones with my Olympus, flash, zoom and all.'

'You may not have thought, Simon, old chap,' said George, 'that you are going to need some assistance. We'll talk about it later...' He realised Mut had his ear discreetly bent in their direction.

Their cells were next to each other, overlooking the inner garden, which was entirely surrounded by walls, keep, church, and other cells. 'Just like Cambridge, really,' Simon commented.

When they had recovered their luggage from the car, and had expressed their profound appreciation to Mr. Mut, who promised to come and fetch them in two days time, George reclined on his narrow bed, and Simon asked:

'You see some problem about the search, do you?'

'Well,' said George, staring at the white ceiling, 'we have first to find the wretched library, then the chamber alongside it, then make some kind of scientific assessment of the light, or force, or whatever, if it manifests itself.' He got up and went over to his case. He lifted it on to the table, with difficulty. 'Now you'll see why I've been paying for all this excess luggage.'

He pulled out an armoury of equipment: very small video-camera, geiger-counter, high-performance mini tape recorder, thermometer, P-K counter, infra-red camera, and packs of film. 'This is special sensitive film for taking kirlian photographs,' he explained.

'Good. That was bright, for a policeman. You mean the sort that can photograph the shape of leaves when they have been cut off, and things like that?'

'Saucy bugger. Yes — it reacts to minute electrical emissions. Now, you're not going to be able to manage all this lot by yourself. And we must have some kind of tangible evidence to take back, or we shall be looked on as nut-cases.'

Simon said he would try and explain the exigences of modern technology to the Abbot.

'But don't mention the infra-red and kirlian stuff, or he

213

might begin to think it's not just the bricks and mortar you're interested in,' warned George. 'He's no fool.'

Simon quickly began to feel very much at home. Home was, for the moment, his simple cell, which was of the traditional primitive pattern: an outer chamber, with an inner sleeping chamber leading off it. The sheer serenity began to envelope him; the austere devoutness of the monks had already shown itself in the little he had seen of their style of living. With a pang of regret he remembered all this would be over in a day or two. But for the moment... He entered the cool, silent bed-chamber, and lay down. Just forty winks. It had been a hard and stressful time. He began to relax for the first time in weeks. But there was still work to do. The purpose of the whole affair... He must keep going... keep going...

He saw himself, without surprise, down there on the bed, head turned slightly to the left, right leg slightly bent, eyes heavy but not quite shut. He willed himself outside his cell, and he was there, looking at the closed door. One of the monks came along and passed right by him, unaware. It occurred to Simon to look at himself, and again he was not surprised to see that the now familiar costume of Freyssenet was upon him, and the beard upon his face. Across the courtyard, a number of things were different. Every building was ancient; no modern accretions; but his image of what constituted modernity was changing by the second as the eighteenth century re-asserted itself upon his being. He now knew exactly where to go, and was about to set off across the courtyard when a voice came from behind him: '*Monsieur, vous allez à la bibliothèque?*'

He knew it was Adam, his drogman, interpreter and guide.

'*Oui, mon ami. Tu m'accompagnes?*'

Without hesitation he mounted a stone staircase to the first landing. In front of him was the winch that wound the drawbridge up and down. Then he turned into a small tunnel running the full length of the landing, above it. There were doors leading off this tunnel, and he went into the second one. He was now in a small room, in the far corner of which was a trap door. He bent and opened it, with Adam's help. Below, it was pitch dark, and a dry, musty smell rose up. Beside the trap were candle and flint. By the light of the guttering wick, they descended, and from that candle lit others below, until they could pick out the rows and piles of ancient manuscripts around them, all in disorder. He picked one up; it was in Greek. His old tutor would have been proud of him, he thought, as he worked out the title page: *HYPOTYPOSEIS*. Underneath, he read the name **CLEMENT**. He stared at it in disbelief: this thick tome — about two hundred pages, he judged — was supposed to have been lost for ever, according to the greatest authority of the time, the Benedictine scholar Dom Bernard de Montfaucon, whom he had dutifully consulted before setting out from France. Yet, here it was! He put it on the bottom step, and looked around. Dust, dust everywhere. There was only one piece of furniture, a heavy wooden bookcase, about four feet square. For no reason, he began to pull it away from the wall, Adam helped him, but the effort seemed to overwhelm him, for he went over and sat on the steps, with his head in his hands. So he turned again to the wall which was barely visible at first in the dim candle-light. But slowly it began to glow of its own accord...

Simon deliberately, gently, drew himself back to his cell, as Floris had taught him to. He knew he must be able to recall exactly where he had been. He got up, quietly opened his door, and breathed in the cool evening air. It was still light enough for him to be able to picture where he had been. Pulling his diary and pencil from his pocket, he sketched in what he could see and what he could remember, in a composite drawing. He could see the problem now: the landing no longer existed. But the tunnel above it? Was there another way into it, apart from the landing? He felt he must find out, before the details began to fade. He quickly rummaged in his bag for his camera and electric torch,

215

checked that it worked, and set off up the staircase. At the point where he as Freyssenet had turned off to the landing, there was a slight discolouration in the stonework: more recent. He went on up, another dozen steps, and turned on to the first floor. But it was really the second. Underneath, the tunnel and the chambers off it must still be there. He decided to walk along what he imagined would be the roof of the tunnel, going the whole length of the building. From the other side of the courtyard, a bell began to peal — calling the monks to prayer or their evening meal, no doubt. The thought struck him that he would be missed if they wanted him to eat, so, reluctantly, he retraced his steps to his cell, just as one of the monks was about to knock at his door. He looked rather startled as he saw Simon appear, but bowed his head, and said in very halting French that the Abbot would be honoured if he would join him for the evening meal in five minutes. George would have his meal brought to him in his cell, as the only meal taken in common was the midday one.

The Abbot, Bishop Matthew, received him with a grace and calm that immediately put him at his ease, picking up their conversation from where it had left off.

'So you are an architectural historian?'

Simon knew there was no point in telling anything but the truth to this wise old bird. 'Not exactly, *mon père*. I am a historian, but to this discipline I have added the science of the mind, psychology.'

The Abbot quickly proved himself to be *au fait* with Freudian and Jungian analyses of religious experience, and Simon even more quickly dropped his habit of talking with some condescension to people who were not psychologically trained.

'Many of us here know how difficult it is to maintain spirituality in the modern world,' said the Abbot. 'Unlike most monks of former times, we have lived in the world, and have found our peace in the intermingling of solitude and community in this holy place. It has a remarkable atmosphere, you know. Even you, who I sense not to have any deep Christian faith, will feel differently in a day or two. That is why I wished you to stay.'

'How do you explain why it is remarkable,' Simon asked.

'I think it is because of the depth and the length of the divine love that has been concentrated here, for sixteen hundred years. The only law we have here is love, both *caritas* and *agape*. All our actions, endeavours and thoughts are inspired by the monks' love of God and of their fellow-men. The brothers, you will notice, conform to the ancient tradition of monastic life, and have a very united spirit, but each is left free to develop his own personality and vocation. They are led spontaneously by the inner light of the Spirit. Ah, if only there were more men in the world like this, how much less suffering there would be.'

'And yet you have cut yourselves off from the world, where you might do so much good,' said Simon.

'We might say the world has cut itself off from us. If we cultivate our garden, it is not in order to keep others out. This monastery has a precious tradition of welcoming every visitor, of whatever race, creed, or social class.'

'Does this not conflict with your desire for solitude and a life of prayer?' asked Simon, who had read somewhere that as many as a thousand visitors a day came to the monastery at the height of the tourist season.

'This is part of our service to the world, and we do it with joy,' he replied. 'And we are not inward-looking on the material plane either, for we have agricultural experts among us who are helping to solve the country's food supply problems. Tomorrow you may see our new farm buildings, our stockfarming experiments with new breeds and strains. We are helping to bring the desert to life with new wells. And all this is the work of God, which He has put into our hands, and we are so full of joy when we can offer this proof of His beneficence. This work is part of our message of love to the world: this is our humble way of creating universal love. With genuine openness of heart and spirit to all people, discord collapses, conflict disappears. Only in this way can we create the "new man" we read of in Paul's letter to the Ephesians, and...'

The Abbot paused and lowered his head, smiling. 'I am sorry, I am giving you a sermon, and I wanted so much to hear about your work, and about my poor friend, Professor Lebrecht. Tell me how he died, and how you knew him.'

As Simon recounted those events, now so far away in space and time, the Abbot became more and more still and gravely concentrated. But Simon did not tell him about the secret cell in the library, the mystic light, the healing power that Freyssenet had found there. For some time, the holy man facing him sat staring at the table between them. Then he said: 'I think you have not quite told me everything.' He looked up into Simon's eyes, as he had done when he had asked for permission to roam over the buildings. Simon had the grace to blush.

'I am sorry, *mon père*. I have not lied to you, but I have not told you all Professor Lebrecht wished me to do. I do not know why he chose me for this task, but I am sure his motive was pure. He passed on to me, after his death, in fact, a manuscript in which...'

When he had finished, the Abbot sat back, dabbed his lips with his napkin, folded it and placed it carefully on the table.

'I have heard of such a... *phénomène*... here, but never before have I encountered a description by a person who had witnessed it. I am at the same time exalted and appalled.'

Simon started. 'Appalled? Sceptical, I can understand, but why appalled?'

'Because of the responsibility of such a concentration of God's power, here, where we have always thought our witness was one of quiet simplicity. But tell me,' the Abbot went on, 'why are you interested in this if you do not have the Christian faith?'

Simon found it very difficult to say what he said next.

'I have never been able to associate myself with any

church I found in France, England, or Australia,' he said, 'but not because I had anything against them. They simply never said anything real to me. To put it bluntly, I could not imagine Jesus himself belonging to any of them. But already I feel quite different about Christianity here. It's almost as though I am seeing for the first time what it is really like, and returning to my roots. But to answer your question: I am greatly disturbed by the power of destruction in the world, and the increasing tide of hatred and violence behind that power...'

'Or created by that power, perhaps?'

'Yes, if you believe that evil comes from outside the collective human mind. I'm far from sure, at this point. But this light Freyssenet saw did appear to have an enormous potential, for reducing the basic flaw in mankind which produces all the forms of evil in the world. Anything which could have that effect on the mind must be of interest to a psychologist.'

'So your interest is purely scientific? You would want to explain it, not use it for good?'

'That was true until I met a man in Geneva, a Dr. Pierre Bernard, who is working on the theory that Mankind as a whole will destroy itself almost totally in the not too distant future, and before then we have to create a new mankind...' — he paused — '... who will be trained and educated along quite different lines, so as to live by love and compassion, instead of by hatred and aggression. I found his ideas fanciful and impractical at first, but somehow they all make urgent sense now. And they link up in a very strange way with... with this place, and... the light...'

His voice trailed off. Suddenly he found it all too much. He was part of something he did not understand, it was too big, too complicated, too impossible. An unknown rôle in a drama with no script and no plot. A wave of intense vertiginous panic welled up inside him. The Abbot leaned over the table and took his hands in his, saying nothing. Simon suddenly found that all four hands, clasped together, were bathed in his tears, but he did not attempt to wipe them away. He knew there was no need, so great was the understanding between them. It was as though all the tensions of the years had suddenly been released. Never a weepy man, he had been perturbed by his tendency to lacrimate during past months, but from now on, he suddenly knew, he could be at peace.

'You have a task to perform, my friend,' the Abbot said eventually, 'and you will now be able to do it with God's blessing. But you must do it alone, and there will be those who will wish to stop you. Beware. Move wisely and with circumspection. I will help you in the only way I can, by showing you, tomorrow, ancient plans of the monastery as it used to be before our restoration work. But to investigate that cell, if it exists, will be for you alone, for you were chosen. Finally,' he said, 'tell me about your friend.'

'Oh, I knew him many years ago when we were students...'

'Not so many years ago, I suspect,' the Abbot smiled in the shaggy depths of his long, grey beard.

'Well, relatively. He is now involved in trying to stop terrorism on an international scale.'

'But what is his interest in coming here?'

'Mainly, to increase my chances of survival. There have already been people trying to do unpleasant things to me.'

'I see. So he is not a Greek scholar?'

'Oh, yes, he was a brilliant classicist at Cambridge, but he decided his vocation lay in the here and now, rather than the past. I can't say I blame him.'

'And you have confidence in him?'

'Absolutely. He saved my life in Alexandria.'

The Abbot stood up and went towards the door. Outside, it was very dark. He explained that the generator supplying electricity to the monastery was shut down at ten o'clock, and gave Simon an oil lantern to light his way. Like a shadow, a monk came to escort him. The Abbot held out his hand, and unselfconsciously, Simon kissed it.

Some time during the night he heard the great bell calling

the monks to prayer; an hour later, as he was dropping off, again the bell rang out. He looked at his watch. Four a.m. But it was worth being awoken, for the chanting of the monks began to filter through the thick walls, such ancient harmonies and intonings that somehow made the pompous tunes and grand prissy sentiments of so many Hymns Ancient and Modern seem irrelevant to Christianity. This is how it must have been, only a hundred years or so after Christ himself. Much closer to the chanting of Jews and Moslems than he would ever have guessed, never having thought about such matters. But it sounded *right*.

George knocked on his door at 6.30, looking spruce in a clean white shirt and shorts. 'Time for breakfast and a cold shower,' he announced. 'There's something for us out here.'

Simon struggled out, blinking in the bright sunlight streaming through his open door. On the table was fruit, bread, and coffee. And several rolls of ancient-looking paper.

'Splendid!' he called, as he gently unrolled them. 'The Abbot said he would let us have some plans of the place as it was. See if you can make sense of them, George, while I dash down to the ablutions.'

When he got back, George was fully engrossed in one of the plans, orientating it from inside the doorway. He pointed towards the keep, and said, 'That's probably where we should look.'

'Yes. You're right. Well done...'

'... for a policeman, I know. But how do you know I'm right?'

Simon told him of his psychic walk and his real one, along the corridor. 'Below it has to be the tunnel. But where in heaven's name is the way into it?'

An hour later, armed with their accoutrements, they set off, plan in hand. They went into every chamber, cell, and passage on that floor, but could find no evidence of a way down to the floor below. Simon put his head out of a window, and looked down. Ten feet below him was a smaller window, the only one in the vast expanse of wall.

'Look here, there is another floor just below this. But how could we get into that hole?'

He looked up, and saw a winch, of the sort used to haul up grain or flour in ancient times. 'What's the good of a winch without a rope? 'asked George despondently.

Simon saw he would just have to ask, but he certainly was not going to bother the Abbot. Down by the entrance to one of the three churches in the garden he saw the monk who had acted as his escort the night before, and who, he knew, spoke French and a little English. The monk quickly understood, and took him along to a workshop, where coils of rope hung from the ceiling. The monk asked what it was needed for, and Simon felt he had to tell him. The monk responded with something like horror. Very dangerous, he said, winch no good at all, rotten wood, very old. Simon insisted, but was far from happy at the prospect of hanging out over a forty-foot drop on a rotten old winch. He went back with the rope less than enthusiastically.

'Let's have one last scout round,' he said, 'before I commit suicide.'

Torches in hand, they went over the ground again. Nothing. Then George stopped, tapping his head. 'We haven't looked underneath!'

They went out again into the bright sunlight, shielding their eyes against the glare of the sandstone, relieved only by the green of this oasis garden. Past the gleaming new library with its colonnaded portico, and into the chapel dedicated to the first saint of Egypt, St. Mark, whose head had been kept in this very place for forty years. Inside the chapel, they looked up at the beautiful frescoes which some dedicated artist had painted in the eleventh century. Simon focused the small but powerful Japanese prism binoculars he had round his neck, marvelling at the detail of the Wise Men at the birth of Christ, and the Angel of the Resurrection.

'Anything there?' asked George.

Simon concentrated. His glasses swept past a painted medallion showing the Virgin Mary, and then went back again to her eyes. He passed the glasses to George.

'Have a look at the eyes in the round painting.'

George did so. 'They look... as if they're hollow. Black holes.'

'So there might be a space behind them. But it's the same problem — how do we get up there?' A thought struck him. 'Wait a minute; sometimes, in order to get up a church tower, you start off in the crypt.'

Down twelve steps below ground level, and sure enough, at the base of the wall, behind a painted screen, was a small door. Its hinges complained bitterly as they were brought into action. Inside was a narrow staircase going up along the width of the wall. As they ascended, faint patches of light filtered through other holes they had not noticed, in the chapel. At the top, Simon recognised the tunnel. As if in a dream he walked straight to the second door on the right. Into the small chamber, over to the trap-door. Their excitement was bubbling inside them. They were nearly there. The trap was open, and George shone his torch down.

The wooden steps were no longer there. They had crumbled away. But they had the rope. George fastened one end securely to a beam, and slid down. Simon followed. They were now in the old library. Visualising his recollection again, he went over to the far wall. There were the remains of wooden shelving still, made of heavy, thick planks. With some effort they slid it aside, and looked at the stones. With his fingers, Simon felt along the joins. One stone seemed to stand out about half an inch. 'I think I've got it,' he whispered. 'But it would take a heavy crow-bar to shift it.'

They had only a penknife between them — the very one, Simon reflected, that he had used to prise out the stone at Freyssenet. But it was no use here. They sat and pondered. The air was getting stuffier, and their heads began to pound. Sweat began to pour down their faces as they waited, not knowing what to do next.

'The sensible thing would be to go and get some tools,'

Simon said, 'but somehow, I don't want to leave it.'

'Neither do I.'

After an indeterminable time, Simon thought he heard a faint sound; not quite a hissing, or a whistling, or a humming, but something of all three. Like wind through trees.

'Hear that?'

'Yeah. Passing aircraft?' George suggested.

'Could be. We wouldn't hear it in here though. No sound could get in here from outside.'

'Or vice-versa,' said George.

He opened his pack and took out his equipment, at the ready. He switched on the tape-recorder. The sound was now registering quite strongly on the tiny dial. Because he was focusing the infra-red camera on the wall, he was the first to notice that it was changing its appearance, becoming almost translucent, and steadily, unwaveringly, getting lighter.

'Let's try moving the stone again,' Simon suggested. This time, their fingers could get a grip on the great solid block, which was much lighter, and seemed to be helping them pull it out. One inch, three, ten, eighteen inches thick. It was out. Carefully they laid it on the floor, avoiding crushed fingers. There was a gap about fifteen inches by two feet.

'You'd better get your head in,' said George, 'I'm too big to get through there. Take the camera.'

Simon put his arms through first, then head and shoulders, hips just about made it. For one panic-stricken moment, he irreverently imagined himself stuck like Pooh, and George would have to hang his washing on his legs for a week until he got thinner. With a push from George, he was in. Just as Freyssenet had experienced it: it was glowing, every square inch of it, with the most delicious light, not glaring, but perfect white. And the concentration of light was over there, to the left. He edged towards it. It had no substance, no feel about it at all, but was infinitely more powerful, like a visible magnetism, benign yet absolutely itself, without reference to anything or anyone else in the universe. George now had the video-camera through the hole, and was telling Simon to verbalise what he felt.

'I feel as if I'm floating, as if I have no body, no weight. Nothing frightening about it. Perhaps this is what it's like taking a trip, I don't know. But this is pure good, pure beauty. I feel like lying down now. On this spot.'

He lay down, and George tried to keep the camera steady as Simon was levitated about two feet above the floor, slowly rotating. 'It's playing with me, George,' he shouted with glee, 'like a seal or a porpoise in the water, it's pushing me round for fun!'

He started to move horizontally now, slowly, and roll over at the same time, all in slow motion.

'Pity you can't try this George. Go out and lose a stone or two, and come back in!' But George was fiddling with his instruments, getting complicated readings about the nature of this light-force. His psycho-kinetic recorder was noting and storing complex data. This piece of equipment was straight from the E. S. P. Intelligence Research Centre in Florida. If anything could analyse the light, this could. The kirlian film would reveal electrical currents and their direction. The infra-red film, any manifestations slower than light.

This went on for some time. Simon was deliriously happy, and did not want it ever to stop. George had nearly all the information he wanted.

'Simon, *old chap*,' he said reassuringly, 'tell me how you feel. Any different?'

He hardly recognised Simon's voice when he replied. It was deeper, more musical, more harmonious, like a Russian choir reduced to one voice.

'I feel as if I have been through a psychic sauna,' he said. 'Everything is so wonderful and right, I just want to love it all, open my arms and embrace it all. I feel drunk, and yet I'm sober; light-headed, but never clearer; excited, but never calmer; without thought, yet all-knowing; here, yet everywhere; myself, but everyone. I'm you too, George, and you are me, we are all one, drifting along at different rates to one point of perfection. It's beyond words. Beyond thought. Beyond self. If only everyone could have this. Everything we do and think would be out of pure love. There would be no conflicts to solve, no hurts to heal, no wars to fight, no enemies to kill.'

George switched off his meters and other equipment.

'You're quite happy in there, are you, then?' he called.

'Happy isn't the word. Pure joy, George.'

'Good. Because that's where you're staying, Simon, my boy.'

'What do you mean, George,' he asked blissfully.

George was with great difficulty lifting the stone, and had placed one end of it into the gap.

'Awfully sorry about this, Simon old chap, but we couldn't have any more miracles coming out of the North African wog cauldron.'

Simon was too euphoric to understand what George was revealing to him. George went on: '...and then, just think, whoever gets hold of this force can render the rest of the world utterly defenceless. It's like taking all the teeth out of a tiger.'

'Don't be silly, George,' said Simon, still not able to take him seriously. 'That sort of thinking will blow the world up soon — what's the good of that to any country?

'Better than being peaceful cattle grazing mindlessly.'

'But we're old friends, George. How could you do this to me?'

'Friends!' George laughed derisively. 'You've got to be joking! I liked you when we first met, Simon. I found you amusing. But later I came to see you as you really are. You're superior, arrogant, condescending, snobbish. Every time you come out with that jibe about me being a policeman I could break your neck.'

'But that's just fun, for heaven's sake.' Simon had now returned to the floor, and was trying to crawl over to the gap, which was now very small.

'Your fun, maybe. But you don't realise I know how much misery your callous sense of fun caused for Muriel

226

too.'

'*Muriel!* Who the blazes is... You mean *Muriel*?'

'Yes, *old boy*. Once your wife, and now mine. You realise you have never once asked me about my private life? Whether I had married, or had a family? You're so bloody self-centred.'

Simon realised with a sickening jolt that George was absolutely right. He had been too single-minded, too intent on viewing George in terms of the task to be accomplished.

'God, I'm sorry, George. I'd no idea... But I didn't cause Muriel misery! Honestly, we were just not made for each other, not on the same wavelength at all.'

'That's not what she says. You went in for a lot of mental cruelty on her.'

'Now you sound like her lawyer. Look, accept my apologies, and stop this rather bad joke, will you? It's getting very hot and stuffy in here.'

'You don't understand. I took this job on for political reasons. But when I found I could get rid of you too, it was a Heaven-sent opportunity. This is the perfect way. All the world will know is that you disappeared mysteriously, and that the so-called phenomenon was a load of nonsense.'

'But you've got all that information about it on your equipment!'

'For strictly limited consumption. Goodbye, Simon.'

He pushed the stone back in, with a great heave of his fifteen stone. No sound could be heard from the secret chamber within. He slid the shelves back, picked up his equipment, and walked over to where the rope was dangling.

21

Floris usually left a gap in his appointments book after lunch, for meditation. Today, however, he felt the need earlier in the day. Fortunately, the work for the morning could be done by his assistant: writing up cases and analysing some results. He went quickly to his bedroom and lay down, with a peculiar sense of urgency he could not explain, but which he knew better than to resist. After a few minutes he achieved complete relaxation, and he received the unmistakable impression that someone close to him was in distress. To his surprise, however, instead of being enlightened about the cause, or the person, he went back again to the scene he had previously witnessed: Simon, with hands bound, before a high-ranking officer. But this time, the scene moved and developed. It was clearly Freyssenet now, and the soldier was equally clearly General Bonaparte. The General was saying: 'I have been awaiting this moment for some time, Citizen Bertin...'

'I am the comte de Freyssenet. Kindly respect my title. Or do you wish me to call you corporal, general?'

'Your insolence only makes your execution more certain. You would do well to understand that I detest you for what you are and for what you represent. Your arrogance, your haughtiness...'

'Call it rather a sense of dignity, nobility if you will, *général* — something you will never have. You are a little man. That pettiness of spirit comes from within you. If you were a king, you could not change.'

'Do not give me sermons!' Bonaparte shouted.

Floris found himself no longer a detached witness, but a participant. He was seated in a chair in the far corner of the room, which seemed to be a modest palace — in Italy, he sensed. He looked down at his body, and saw without surprise (being used to this kind of experience) that he was a young female with long, dark hair. *I am Amélie, Freyssenet's devoted mistress. I shall die with him, by the Thames, on the orders of this general.*

Bonaparte raised the whip on his desk, and went to strike the aristocratic sneer off Freyssenet's face. The girl bounded across the room and threw herself at Bonaparte, shouting abuse at him. She was a strong peasant girl, and took some shaking off. The soldier on guard outside the door dashed in.

'Take her to a cell to cool down,' said the general, 'while I finish with this citizen.'

As he turned back to Freyssenet and fixed his eyes upon him, Floris realised with a shock that it was George, and was immediately aware that Simon was in great danger, at that very moment. Composing himself again, he willed himself to detach and travel. He did not know which monastery he was in, but he followed the force emanating from where Simon was in trouble. Over the desert now, towards a tall tower in a garden surrounded by high walls. Into a chapel, up... The light was momentarily blinding. Then he saw Simon prostrate in the airless chamber. He watched, appalled, as Simon's etheric and astral bodies began to loosen and detach themselves from his physical body. The process had to be stopped, but Simon seemed to be in a semi-conscious state. Exerting all his will, Floris silently called out to Simon: 'Don't give in! Push the stone! It is light, you are strong! Push the stone!'

To his relief, he saw Simon stir and open his eyes. Now the light centre slid across to Simon and enveloped him. Floris was at first puzzled why the force had not revived Simon itself, but then he realised that it could not alter the course of events; it could only help when the human will was already active. The light grew stronger again, and was now shimmering brilliantly round Simon, like another aura. Floris had never imagined anything like this. It seemed to join Simon and the stone that blocked his passage back to life. Simon lifted his feet and drove them into the stone. It moved out and dropped on to the dusty floor outside. Immediately the light-force streamed through the hole, as air flowed in.

Floris moved to the other side of the wall, and saw George climbing the rope, having tied his pack to the end of it. He looked utterly startled as the stone fell out and the light sped towards him like a fire-ball. With a cry, he let go of the rope, and was beginning to fall to the floor eight feet below him. But the light caught him up, twirled him round like a bobbin, so fast that Floris could no longer see anything of him but a blur. Then it gently deposited him on the floor. Simon had been watching this, open-mouthed, through the hole. He now began to scramble out of the chamber. But the light-force had not finished with the world...

Professor Timothy Crankshaw was far from happy as he sat, gently perspiring, in the bus. As it clanked along the tarmac road towards the Monastery of St. Makros, he made perfunctory contributions to the conversation of his fellow delegates, but his mind was really elsewhere. Suddenly, the bus jolted to a halt, and the driver began to shout incomprehensibly in Arabic, pointing ahead. Crankshaw looked, blinked, and looked again. On the horizon, perhaps five miles away, he recognised the tall tower of the monastery of St. Makros, on the top of a rise. But above it, in the sky, was a strange sight. At first he thought it might be a firework display, but that was unlikely in broad daylight in the desert, he quickly reasoned. Was it a tornado? Did they have tornados in this part of the world? As they all looked, ooh-ing and aah-ing, the white light, quite clear against the dark blue sky, changed its shape: first it was a cloud, then a mushroom. Good Heavens! Had the Egyptians let off a nuclear bomb? The word ran round the bus, then silence fell again as the shape changed quickly to the Cross, then the Star of David, the Maltese Cross, then a Crescent, a circle in a square, and a dozen other spiritually symbolic shapes, one after the other, sometimes repeating in apparently random order. Cameras clicked and whirred. Those who had got off the bus to get a better view now began to run towards the tower and the strange forms above, forgetting how far away they were. Finally, the light-force gathered itself together in a vast circle, like a corona, and moved upwards, slowly at first, then with increasing speed, until it was a mere speck in the heavens. Then it was no more. Everyone was reduced to absolute, awe-stricken silence.

An hour later, the assembled delegates were in the cool new library of the monastery. The Abbot entered, accompanied, Crankshaw observed to his chagrin, by Simon, who was looking disgustingly well and pleased with himself. The Abbot spoke into the microphone.

'It is a great honour to have here today the delegates of the Ecumenical Commission for Comparative Religious Studies. You must have thought we simple monks had overdone your welcome as you approached. Alas, I have to tell you that such spectacular sights are beyond our budget and also beyond our imagination. It is, however, more than a remarkable coincidence that that incredible phenomenon occurred whilst you representatives of the religions of the world were able to witness it. I cannot explain it. There is someone here who, perhaps, can. But I am convinced that the reason why this community of religious men was chosen has nothing to do with the particular religion which we practice here. You will have seen the shapes which the light assumed before our eyes. They were the living symbols of all those systems of belief to which you adhere. By the very fact of your being here, as members of this Commission, you have shown your desire to find ways to ensure the peaceful, harmonious reconciliation of our different faiths.'

Simon saw Crankshaw shift from one foot to the other and look at the ceiling. The Abbot went on:

'The fact that this great mystical experience took place here does not mean that the monastery should become a shrine or a place of pilgrimage. The unbroken history of pure devotion we have is shared by many other places in the world. But this concentration of spiritual force, of which you saw part today, is with us no more. It revealed itself to us. We saw it. We acknowledge it. We thank God for it. But we must put its message into action in the world, not just here. I beg you, when you disperse throughout the world, to remember that all religion must bind us together in love, whatever symbol we follow. Now, I would like to ask someone to speak to you, who has just now borne the brunt of the release of spiritual or psychic force we have had here today. He is a psychologist, and will try to explain rationally what he had experienced. Dr. Simon Prestcott.'

The assembly applauded politely, the half a dozen reporters and press photographers present got their tape-recorders and cameras at the ready. Simon gave a carefully edited account of what had brought him there; in fact, he only needed to say he was continuing the work of Professor Lebrecht. When he came to describe events in the secret chamber, however, he began to feel it was beyond him.

'I don't know if you have ever tried to tell someone what it is like to be in love, or describe a rainbow to a blind man, or a Beethoven quartet to a deaf-mute. That is a bad analogy, because the lack is not yours, it is mine. You ... most of you would understand what I have just had revealed to me if I could tell you. Perhaps...'

He suddenly had an idea, and went over to the pack which George had abandoned. He took from it the tape-recorder George had switched on as he, Simon, went through the hole. He rewound it.

'Perhaps the best thing I can do is play you what actually happened. Now, it will give you no idea of what it looked like, but I don't think that matters. It's the effect that counts.'

He switched it on, and placed it close to the microphone on the dais. At first there was nothing, and he feared George must have failed to press the record button. But then he heard his own voice coming through clearly: 'Let's try moving the stone again...' He switched off just before the moment George showed himself in his true light.

When the recording finished, the delegates thought that was it, and began to applaud, this time more vigorously. But Simon put up his hand.

'That experience, in itself, is pointless, in my view. What remains is to give it meaning. I feel ill-equipped to do this. I was not the right person for it, I'm sure. It should have been Professor Lebrecht, but I was the only person around when he... died, suddenly, and he entrusted the task to me. So what effect has that strange experience had on me, that is of any use to anyone? I have hardly had time to assess it yet. It happened less than two hours ago. But something very profound has happened to me, in that I now see the problems of our world in a new light. *In* a new light...yes'

He closed his eyes and tried to relive those moments, then went on in a low, quiet voice, barely above a whisper, and yet it was audible to everyone there: 'When I was within that light, I did have an intuition of the perfect state of being, which gurus and hermits take a lifetime to know. So I am very, very privileged. What have I learned? That the only work really worth doing is work that enables us humans to evolve into a moral and spiritual species that can be worthy of continuing to exist. Worthy of Jesus, of Mohammed, of the Buddha, of the other great living symbols of something greater than our poor fallible selves. I now know what we must aim for; I didn't before. I was all bound up in systems and techniques, just as many of you are still bound up in your particular systems of belief and distort them for your own ends and your own power...'

Restless rumbles told Simon he had hit a few raw nerves. Undeterred, for he had nothing to lose, he went on: 'I am not here to flatter you, but I think ecumenism — which is the still struggling ideal that brings you here — is one positive step in the creation of the pluralistic humans of tomorrow, who so love the world that they will die rather than cause pain, hurt, deprivation or suffering of any kind to others. There are splendid people in the world, including some of you, trying to find ways of preventing conflicts, wars, terrorism, poverty, tyranny, bigotry, intolerance. But those are just the symptoms of a deep-seated design-fault in humans: the aggressive use of intelligence. Once, that enabled this physically weak and insignificant creature to survive and become lord of the earth. But it has got out of hand. It is now applied on a vast scale, not for survival, but for destruction. Not to provide food and shelter for our families, but to force beliefs on others. If we all resolutely adhere to the principle that no ideal that excludes love for fellow humans can be a genuine ideal, then we can begin to isolate the psychotics and the pathologically sick, and make sure they never get into positions where they can hurt the innocent. Can this ever be achieved? No. But if we stop trying, the end of humanity will come faster than any of us suspect...'

Simon then gathered up the pack and recorder, and escaped to his cell, beyond the reach of reporters and of Timothy Crankshaw. He wanted time to think, especially about George. When he tried to remember what he had said to the assembly, he could not. On the table in his cell was a cable, addressed to him care of the Ecumenical Commission. He opened it, and read:

'REGRET INFORM YOU DEATH GUSTAVE LEVERSON GENEVA TODAY STOP PLEASE CONTACT URGENTLY HERE STOP RETURN VIA GENEVA IF POSSIBLE KIND REGARDS PIERRE BERNARD.'

22

Anyone who has attempted to make an international telephone call from Egypt will appreciate how low Simon's reserves of patience became (despite his newly acquired sense of benevolence towards mankind) before he heard Pierre Bernard's voice at the other end.

'You received my telegram?'

'*Oui, Monsieur, je vous remercie.* I was very sorry to hear about M. Leverson. How did it happen?'

'Very peacefully. He had a heart attack. It was during the night, and he was alone. It was not unexpected, apparently, but he had insisted that Mme. Leverson return to England to deal with some problem there, two days before.'

'Where is she now?' Simon tried to sound casual.

'She is back here in Geneva. I should like to speak to you about an rather important matter. Can you come to Geneva?' asked Bernard.

Simon was only too glad to have the excuse. 'Yes, of course. I can be there tomorrow.'

'Excellent. I shall expect you for dinner tomorrow evening at seven, if that is convenient?'

Mr. Mut, who had returned to the monastery the moment he heard the radio report of strange goings-on there, had extracted Simon from the attention of reporters and other curious witnesses of the strange happenings in the sky above the tower. Not before Timothy Crankshaw had buttonholed him, however, and plied him with questions about what precisely had happened inside the monastery. Simon pretended to be suffering from a liberal dose of amnesia, and was very vague about details. He did assure the professor, however, that the only evidence of what had happened was the tape-recording which he had made public at the meeting. (In fact, Simon had no idea if George's other instruments, and the video-camera, had registered anything.) Crankshaw seemed moderately satisfied with this, and with the Abbot's assurances about the desire of the Coptic church not to make any propagandist capital out of the fact that the most remarkable psychic-spiritual manifestation of the century had occurred in a Coptic monastery and not a Catholic one. Someone handed Simon a cassette of his speech just as he was leaving the monastery.

At Geneva airport, Simon had to give a press conference, about the events at St. Makros, and he tried to interpret the significance of the phenomenon more clearly. He himself had not witnessed the changing symbols in the sky, of course, he explained. He was at that time still recovering from his close encounter with the light-force. He was told that one of the American delegates on the Ecumenical Commission had had the presence of mind to get his video-camera out, standing beside the bus, and had some good footage of it, which would be shown on T.V. throughout the world that evening.

When he was asked, 'Why do you think *you* were chosen to be the privileged witness of the psychic force inside the monastery?' he began to realise his danger at the hands of the media. At all costs, he felt, he must avoid being turned into some sort of spiritual guru, or allow the media to spray him with the odour of sanctity. So he played this down, insisting that he just happened to be there, looking at the ancient parts of the monastery, and accidentally strayed into a room that had not been opened for many, many years. Equally difficult was the question, 'What has happened to the other *Anglais* who was with you?' To this he replied that he had been overcome by the heat, and was being treated for mild hypertension and nervous exhaustion. This was not far from the truth.

It was only in the plane from Cairo to Geneva that Simon had time to think about George. He was profoundly shocked and upset by the enmity George had been concealing all that time; all those moments of apparent friendship had, it seemed, been cleverly play-acted. The double shock of finding the hostility of his first wife coming into his life again was intensely perturbing. He could not conceive how rancour could be stored up like that, and passed on to someone else as well. But then, if George had felt so badly about him, he would have found in Muriel's complaints justification for his own hostility. He was genuinely sorry for George, who seemed to be a broken man after his encounter with the light-force. Simon had tried to speak to him, but he had just sat there in a daze, staring into space, in his cell, to which he had been carried by a couple of the monks. The Abbot had offered to keep him there in the excellent sick quarters, for as long as he wished to stay. Simon thought this would be the simplest solution, for the time being. Muriel would have to be informed, of course, but Mr. Mut promised he would get a message through, as Simon was not anxious to talk to her.

When he had escaped to the Hôtel du Cheval Blanc, with the aid of a resourceful taxi-driver who took him round the narrow, winding one-way streets of the Old City, Simon played back the tape of his speech. He was appalled. Shocked by his arrogance, astounded by his self-righteousness and sententiousness. He telephoned Cambridge.

'Adrian? Simon Prestcott.'

'Ah, I've just been looking at you on the box. I see you've been having fun.'

'Not altogether. Look, Adrian, I'd like you to do me a favour. Soon you'll hear or read the speech I gave to the Ecumenical Commission, and I want you to believe it wasn't me.'

'Good heavens! Someone impersonated you?'

'No, I mean I wasn't in control. I can't recall a word of what I said. It must have been the effect of something extremely disturbing that happened to me. I assure you I've not been transformed into another Billy Graham. So I want you to promise me that if I ever start to turn into a sanctimonious, garrulous old bore, you'll tell me. Will you?'

Adrian Wiseman promised. Simon then telephoned London.

'Floris? Simon.'

'Thank God. Are you safe? Where are you?'

'In Geneva. Yes, I'm O.K. It's been a rather odd experience. I'm looking forward to telling you about it.'

'You English with your understatement never cease to astonish me!' Floris replied. 'I know about your experience, and it was not just "odd".'

'Oh, it's been on radio or television, has it?'

'Simon, listen to me: *I was there*.'

Simon was stunned into momentary silence, which Floris found gratifying. It had sunk in.

'There? You mean...?'

'Precisely. Light, stone block, George, I saw everything. It was, er, how would you say, a bit curious.'

'*Touché*. But you must not, repeat not, tell anyone you witnessed it. Not even Anna, if you can help it. Have you told her?'

'No. She is at a master-class in New York at the Juilliard. I expect she will ring as soon as the news breaks over the Atlantic in a few hours time.'

'Look, Floris, tell her not to answer any questions about me, or the monastery, or Freyssenet, or anything, O.K.? I think the affair is blowing over now, but I can't be sure.'

'I don't think it is blowing over at all. The repercussions are about to begin. But they may not be so dangerous for us. It all depends on how George is. He may be paranoid, and that is dangerous. We must see what effect the light-force had on him. The strain may have been too great, I cannot tell yet. And your ex-wife seems unstable too.'

'Singly, they may not be a problem. It's the effect they have been having on each other that worries me — feeding each other's hatred. Like terrorists reminding one another what they are fighting for, in case they forget.'

Simon sat by the telephone for some time before making his next call. Finally, he dialled.

'*Madame Leverson, s'il vous plaît.*'

'*C'est de la part de qui , Monsieur*?'

'Simon Prestcott.'

'Ah, it is you, Simon. I didn't recognise your voice, it has changed. I have just been seeing you on the television.'

'Madame Leverson... Sara... I have heard about your husband. I am so terribly sorry, for you, for the children...'

'I know. Thank you. I have a very large hole in the centre of my life now. He was still so full of ideas about his next plans, his new project, it is very sad. But he did not suffer. I am above all sorry I was not here. Somehow, I think he knew something. He insisted I should go to England, but it was not really necessary. He did not want me to see him die. He went through the narrow gate all alone, as one must.'

'Do you really believe that we pass through only once, Sara?'

'I was brought up as a good little Catholic girl in Vietnam, Simon. So that is what I am supposed to believe. But I don't know really...'

'How are the children?'

'Still back in England. Perhaps I should have brought them back for the funeral, but I felt I wanted to shield them from death.'

'When is the funeral?'

'Tomorrow morning at ten, at the crematorium.'

'May I come?'

'I should be very sad if you did not.'

It was only when setting out for dinner with Pierre Bernard that Simon realised he did not know where he lived. Hopefully he looked him up in the telephone directory, and found his name there. It was, by good fortune, quite close by, in Grange Canal, but he thought it wise to ring for a taxi. He was ten minutes late when he arrived at the tall wrought-iron gates. He eyed the large notice —

ATTENTION! CHIEN MECHANT!

— with some apprehension, and rang the bell. The clanging within set off a storm of barking from the other side of the gate, together with a clanking of chains. He just hoped the chain was short. Light streamed out from the front door, and he heard Bernard instructing the dog to be quiet, which reduced it to a reluctant whimper. The bolt on the gate was withdrawn.

'Ah! Monsieur Prestcott! I was just ringing your hotel to see if you were coming.'

Simon wondered how Pierre Bernard would cope in Egypt, or India. Bernard seemed to be reading his thoughts.

'You must excuse me; my grandfather was a watchmaker. It is in the blood!' He laughed. Simon laughed nervously as he edged past the large kennel. Bernard said, low into his ear: 'Do not worry; there is no dog. It is a tape recording. I will explain why when we are inside.'

There were no other guests for dinner, which surprised Simon, who had imagined he had been keeping a royal party waiting. Madame Bernard, whom he had not met before, greeted him pleasantly, and with obvious relief that he understood French. She appeared to be somewhat older than her husband, still with traces of ancient prettiness. Simon could imagine them both as a young married couple: he, tall, strapping, able to cross an Alp a day; she, small, round, fluttery, complaining that he was walking too far too fast. The maid brought in soup, which was extremely good and welcome, and the wine began to flow; a very agreeable, unknown Swiss wine.

After the *escalope*, Mme. Bernard excused herself, saying she was *fatiguée*, but Simon realised that her withdrawal had another reason, for no sooner was she out of the room than Pierre Bernard began to talk in earnest.

'I have to speak to you seriously, *mon ami*,' he said. 'Have you spoken yet to Mme. Leverson?'

Simon did not know what the thrust of the question was, and replied cautiously that he had telephoned to offer his condolences. Bernard then asked him if she had mentioned anything about her late husband's plan for a new centre.

'No. She did mention something about plans, or a project, but nothing in particular.'

'Then it's for me to tell you. Gustave Leverson knew some time ago that he had very little time left to live. He and I have had many meetings and discussions over the past few months. On many things he and I did not agree, but on one thing yes: there is an urgent need to establish an institution for the *formation*, the creation, of enough people capable of carrying on the human race after the total destruction of this planet.'

'Yes, of course I remember you talking about this.'

'But you have not heard the detail. I shall go into this very carefully with you if you prove to be interested.'

'Why is this urgent for me? The world isn't going to be blown up tomorrow, is it?'

'No, I hope not. If it is, we shall all have deserved it. But you are wanting to return to England, so I must tell you everything while you are here.'

'I'm not in any hurry to leave Geneva. But everything about what?'

'First, please,' Bernard spoke with such intensity now that Simon restrained his questioning, 'explain to me about the experience you had at the monastery, of which I heard tonight on television and radio — has it changed your attitudes in any significant way?'

Simon looked at him for a moment, thinking back to his conversation with the Abbot, the light-force, his speech to the Commission's delegates.

'Yes. It has. I used to be a serious frivolous person. Now I'm a frivolous serious one. I can't curb my tendency to see the comic side of things. But underneath it all, I feel so deeply about the problems of this world that I just don't dare to think about them for too long.'

'That could just be the onset of depression,' Bernard replied. 'I must know if you see any point in ensuring the continuation of the human race. Now, please think carefully, and seriously, before you reply.'

'I don't have to think,' Simon replied. 'At that monastery in Egypt, I had two experiences which convince me that man must go on existing. One was meeting the Abbot of the monastery, who is the nearest I have ever come to a saint, in his simplicity, understanding and compassion.'

'And the other?'

'The other was being totally immersed in that force of absolute good. It hasn't transformed me into a better person, I don't think, because I'm too fallible; but it gave me the first-hand knowledge — and I mean *knowing*, not just hearing-about or reading-about — of perfection. If human beings can be as saintly as the Abbot, and can be receptors of such sheer beauty and goodness, then they are worth preserving. We *may* be the only species in the universe capable of receiving the message, who knows? If I can do it, millions ought to be able to. That's the marvel of it all: if the experience had been reserved for the Dalai Lama or the Archbishop of Canterbury, I should have thought it was a bit beyond the common run of humans. But it isn't. I find that immensely comforting and encouraging, don't you?'

'Tell me,' said Pierre Bernard, ignoring his question, 'do you depreciate yourself through humility or because you wish to be reassured?'

Simon opened his mouth to answer but fortunately (since he did not know what to say) Bernard went on, 'I ask because your professor in Melbourne had nothing but praise for you, and predicted a very successful future for you.'

'He spoke to you about me?'

'He knew you would probably be coming to do some work in Geneva, and thought we might find common ground. When do you return there?'

'I don't know. At the end of the year, I suppose.'

'And your work there pleases you?'

'Some of it. I like teaching, although much of it is elementary, compared to Cambridge. The university there seems to be run by bureaucrats whose purpose in life is to create more and more paper-work to keep academics away from their research. I'll never get used to the system of giving everyone twenty working days "leave" a year like the army. So if I need to spend what we in Europe think of as the long vacation researching overseas, I couldn't, without making a special case. I'd have to be back at my desk, ready to dash into a footling committee meeting at the drop of a hat. I'm not sure how long I'll be able to stand that.'

'You lack freedom of movement?'

'Yes, indeed. And one needs it there, if one's intellectual interests lie outside Australasia.'

'So you would not be happy living as a monk in the desert, never straying from your cave or monastery more than a few miles?'

'If I had the kind of devotion and simplicity necessary to choose that kind of life in the first place, I should no doubt be happy. How about you?'

'My life is very solitary here, as it is. Rather monastic, in a way. I walk by myself in the mountains, and meditate as I look down upon those brooding valleys, and those shining peaks that try to pierce the heavens. I meet a few chosen friends, occasionally travel to Paris or accept an invitation to lecture abroad.'

'And your wife?'

'She is a gentle, settling influence,' he said affectionately. 'She has never tried to understand my ideas, although I spent many hours discussing them with her when we were young. So now we are two old companions who give each other comfort.'

Simon thought of the contrast between them, and himself and Muriel. Perhaps if he had been more patient, they could have become the same? Too late now. Anyway, he doubted if Madame Bernard ever had the same sharp tongue and bitter discontent as Muriel. Muriel and George! Well, well!

Bernard was speaking again. '... opportunity to break away from it before it is too late.'

'Oh? What are you going to do? I expect the Americans would snap you up.'

'*Mais non, cher ami! Pas moi! Vous!* You were not listening. I apologise — you must be exhausted, all the excitement, and air travelling. We shall talk about it again tomorrow, *n'est-ce pas*?'

'Talk about what?'

'The proposal. Look, here is a preliminary outline of aims and objectives which Monsieur Leverson and I have prepared, in consultation with three specialists from the Swedish Peace Research Institute.'

Simon glanced down at the document. The front page was printed with the words :

THE CENTRE FOR FUTURE
ENLIGHTENMENT STUDIES
Proposal for Foundation

He turned the page and read the list of Foundation Committee members. They were vaguely known to him, through newspaper reports of United Nations and other international agency advisory committees — a Swedish statesman, a Swiss jurisconsult of the International Court at the Hague, Richard Jensen — one of the close associates of Douglas Hofstadter, whose work on the nature of human thought processes was well known to Simon, and Raymond Blindon, whose work on the logic of false ideas and the tyranny of ideologies was throwing new light on human behaviour.

'Quite a high-powered team,' Simon said.

Bernard laughed. 'Perhaps, after all, your British understatement will be a characteristic of the human of the future! Yes, we have assembled *quite a team*. Every one is dedicated to the idea of preparing a curriculum that will ensure a type of human who will not only survive, but will create a society without conflict. We think you should join us.'

Simon was startled. 'Join you? But who? Where? You're not getting all these people to come and staff your Centre, are you?'

'No, of course not. They are the advisers for the establishment of the Centre. It is still an idea, an ideal in our minds. But you would bring it all together, make it real, make it exist. We need someone young who is willing to devote himself completely to working for the Centre.'

Simon found it hard to take this seriously. 'You are being serious, are you?' he asked. 'Because if you are, I must ask a question which is not inspired by insecurity but by frank certainty that I am not your man: why me?'

'All right, if you insist, I shall admit we could be making a big mistake. Does that make you feel better? But at the same time, Leverson and I came to the conclusion — after a good deal of checking up on you, your personality, your capacities, even your healthy scepticism towards pretentiousness and humbug — that unless you reveal some quite unsuspected weakness before you meet the appointments committee, you would be the right man for this job. It is obvious that your experience at the monastery has increased your attractiveness to us immensely. Your speech to the Ecumenical Commission showed you possess great powers of leadership...'

'That's a load of...' He repeated more or less what he had said to Adrian Wiseman.'

'Do you mean you repudiate the ideals you expressed in your speech.'

'No! Not all! I just wish they hadn't come out in such a hectoring and pompous manner. It's most embarrassing.'

'I think your genes are having a great battle inside you,' Pierre Bernard smiled, 'the French ones urging you to be as humourlessly committed as Sartre and the English ones urging you to wear your mantle lightly.'

'Voltaire managed the compromise all right.'

'Then perhaps he should be your model. You will just have to put your new rôle down to inspiration. If you were a channel, a medium, perhaps you should accept it humbly.'

'I don't like the feeling I'm being used,' Simon complained. Then it dawned on him that this was only one more step in a whole process of "being used", ever since that damned Cambridge Society meeting in Melbourne.

Bernard went on: 'Your reservations do you credit, they show you have no thirst for personal glory; but as you said, you have had the direct *experience* of perfection. That is vitally important. Instinctively you know what we are aiming for — even if you yourself will remain imperfect because of your personality traits and education.'

'Ah, thank you. That makes me feel better.'

'Let me draw a simple analogy: who was the piano teacher of Daniel Barenboim? Or Kant's philosophy teacher? Or Einstein's physics professor? Need I say more?'

'No. All right. One last question. Who is funding all this?'

'M. Leverson. It is — was to be — his last enthusiasm. At our last meeting together only three days ago, he signed all the necessary documents for the transfer of funds to the Foundation Trust. Several million, all safely invested.'

'What about his wife?'

'She approves entirely. And she will be very well off too, if that is what you are worrying about.'

'Well, I shouldn't like to see her thrown out on the street.'

'In a sense she will be, of course. She will have to leave *Les Délices*. But she has a beautiful house in England, you know.'

'And where will the Centre be?'

'We are negotiating for premises here, in Geneva. I hope you will be able to bear it. It is a very dull city.'

'The attraction of any place depends on who lives there,' Simon responded. '*Un seul être vous manque, et tout est dépeuplé...*'

'Have they found the High Garden yet?'

'No, Simon, they have not spoken of it since that day you came to see us, with your young lady.'

They were seated in the director's apartment at *Les Délices*. The funeral had been simple, short, well-attended. The number of people who took the trouble to fly in from various parts of England and Europe attested to the esteem in which Gustave Leverson had been held. The reception at the Excelsior Hotel in the rue Longemalle had passed sadly but, at the same time, joyfully, since those who were there were at the same celebrating the very varied achievements of a remarkable man who had never gone out of his way to be popular, but nevertheless had inspired something approaching affection among many people. As he was about to leave the hotel, one of the waiters had come up to him.

'*Monsieur Prêtecotte?*'

'*Oui, c'est moi.*'

He had handed Simon a note. It read: 'If you are by any chance free after this, I should be grateful if you could come to *Les Délices* for a short while to talk. — SARA.'

The waiter had taken back his reply: '*Avec grand plaisir.*'

'I hear you will have to leave here.'

'Yes.' Sara smoothed a non-existent frown with a small, delicate finger. 'The tidy-minded City of Geneva has already sent me a letter reminding me that my tenancy ended with the death of my husband, but they will kindly grant me one month to make other arrangements.'

'I don't suppose there is anything I can do?'

'You? But why should you?'

'Forgive me. I didn't mean to intrude.'

She put her hand on his arm. Left it there. Tears began to well up in her eyes.

'Please, do not misunderstand me. You do not intrude. Far from that. I have many acquaintances, here and in England. But very few people I am close enough to to ask for help in this situation. You see, Gustave did not make close friends. I think it was because I saw what a lonely man he was that I married him.'

'You were ideal for him. He needed someone warm and loving.'

'He gave me two beautiful children, and a very pleasant life, and all the affection he was capable of. I am very fortunate, I know that.'

'But...' *careful, Prestcott* '... are you saying... you never loved him?'

'Not with what I would call love. I feel guilty for that, *mais l'amour ne se commande pas.*'

'By the way...' He hesitated. 'Miss Schoenheimer is not precisely "my young lady".'

'I am sorry. Did I use the wrong word?' Sara looked slightly embarrassed.

'No, not at all. But she isn't. Not in that sense. We are very fond of one another, but we're not in love.'

'Fond...' Sara played with the word. 'That is a lovely word: fond.'

Simon was very aware of the delicacy of the situation, and said he thought he should go. He hoped Sara would ask him to stay, but she merely nodded. As he stood looking out at the rhodedendrons he had once so dramatically disgraced, his mind full of the things he wanted to say but knew he must not, he said: 'I may be staying in Geneva, you know?'

'I had understood Gustave and Pierre wanted you to work here. Do you think you will?'

He hesitated. 'I'm not sure at the moment. It depends on... an unknown factor. Can we talk again before you leave Geneva?'

'But of course. I have to stay to clear up many things — papers, lawyers, another place to live. '

'But you have your house in England. Will you not return there?' Simon asked.

'It is too big, too difficult to keep up with impossible servants. I cannot live in two countries. It may be simpler to live here. The education will be better for the children. English schools are either deplorable or snobbish.'

They agreed to meet for lunch the following day, by the lake.

23

A week later, Floris Schoenheimer answered his telephone in between two appointments.

'Simon! I was beginning to wonder if you had returned to Australia! Where are you?'

'I have just got into London, from Geneva. Some rather unexpected business kept me there. May I come and see you?'

'Me, or Anna?'

'You or both of you.'

Floris invited him to lunch at the house. He and Anna embraced warmly. Over lunch, Floris soon turned the conversation to George.

'I was as profoundly shocked as you by the violence of his hatred,' he said, 'but I understand what is behind it.'

He told Simon about the confrontation between Freyssenet and General Bonaparte.

Simon was, by this time, beyond surprise. Instead, his mind began to work on an explanation for the joint hatred of George and Muriel. Perhaps her past was linked with his. But there was no chance of getting her to agree to an O.O.B. experiment with Floris.

'That is not essential,' said Floris. 'Now think: do you still have anything that belonged to her, that was close to her? An article of clothing or a letter?'

Simon thought, and remembered the pack he had taken from George. The major contents — the video camera and other equipment — he had left in a large safe deposit box at a bank in Geneva, on Pierre Bernard's advice. He had also found a letter written to George from Muriel. He had recognised her handwriting, but had not read it. On the other hand, he had not known where to send it. He searched in his case for it, and found it in a jacket pocket.

Floris took the letter and went to the couch. Anna gently massaged his temples, and his face relaxed, became younger. After a short while, he began to speak.

'I am in an ancient castle on a hill, battlements round it, very large, a fortified town, yes. I am moving to an elegant house slightly on the outskirts, built much later, inside a bedroom, a beautiful lady walking up and down, very angry, saying "*Il m'a insultée, ce cochon de Freyssenet, je l'aurai, je l'aurai!*".'

'How have you insulted her?' Floris asked.

Simon knew straight away. It was Madame de Crécy, the vitriolic lady in Carcassonne, who had tried to have him killed in a trumped-up duel. He felt beads of sweat forming on his brow. The combined hatred of Bonaparte and of Mme. de Crécy was a formidable force. Why had they been brought together again? Was it in order to finish him off?

When Floris returned, Simon voiced his fears, and all three agreed the situation was not good. Somehow, they must find out what had happened to George.

'If only he would let me treat him, and confront him with his past anger, it may be dissipated. The same for your former wife. Otherwise, I fear you have not heard the last of them.'

Simon felt justified in asking Inspector Irving to find out what had become of George, and learned later that day that he was on sick leave, at home as far as anyone knew.

'The trouble is,' said Floris, 'we do not know what he remembers. He went through a traumatic shock from that light-force. But it is a bad sign that he has not tried to find out how you are.'

Simon reflected. He could not simply leave things as they were. Finally, the three of them agreed what to do...

'May I speak to George Plaidy, please?'

'Who wants him, he's not very well,' a sharp voice

replied.

'Floris Schoenheimer.'

'Florry Who?'

'Just say Floris, would you please?'

There was silence for two or three minutes. Then Floris heard George's voice, sounding as though he had a bad cold.

'Hello, Mr. Plaidy? You remember me, Dr. Schoenheimer?'

'Yes, of course. How can I help you?'

'I was wondering if you had had any news of Simon? He seems to have disappeared.'

'I've no idea. I haven't been too well since I got back from our trip. I fell down some old steps and damaged my head.

'I am sorry to hear that. Do you have headaches?'

'I'll say I do. Life is one unending headache.'

George put his hand over the mouthpiece, and Floris heard him say, 'It's all right, Muriel, I know what I'm doing. Leave me alone, for God's sake!'

Floris paused, then said casually, 'You know, George, chronic headaches are quite a speciality of mine. In view of our past collaboration, I should be very glad to treat you free of charge.'

George began by saying he couldn't possibly do that, but did not take much persuading. He was clearly in a bad way. But then Floris added: 'It will be necessary for your wife to come as well—I presume that was your wife who answered the telephone?'

'Oh? Why?' George asked, defensively.

'Because it is difficult to treat the individual psyche in isolation. I always like the spouse to know quite clearly what is happening, so that he or she can continue the treatment afterwards if necessary.'

They agreed to come that afternoon, George was so desperate. Simon and Anna went off to her studio, to talk

251

together for the first time in ages. They had much to say to each other. Neither felt it was going to be easy. It would have been easier if each had known in advance what the other was going to say, but such an arrangement is rarely possible in human relationships. They both started in the dark, and edged their way towards the light of their present situation, which was so different now.

'You have been through a lot since we last met, Simon.'

'It's been quite exciting, yes. Well, since I've been told off for understating, I'll admit it's been bloody terrifying at times. And you too — great success, I hear. That's marvellous. How was New York?'

'I learned a lot in a short time at Barenboim's master class.'

'Do you happen to know who Barenboim's piano teacher was?'

'Mmmm... I suppose I should know. He probably had several.'

'Yes, but he probably wasn't as brilliant as Barenboim, or you would know straight away, wouldn't you?'

'He may have been brilliant, but I can't recall who taught Barenboim , that's the difference. What's the point of all this, Simon?'

Simon laughed. 'I just needed some reassurance about something that I am being asked to do, and I don't think I'm good enough for it.'

'How exciting. Tell me all about it.'

'First, Anna...' He took her hand. 'I should like to talk about us. We've moved apart, haven't we? You are totally engrossed by your music, and I... well, I've been preoccupied too.'

Anna put her arm round his neck and kissed him warmly. He felt the old stirrings. 'Simon, my very dear Simon, we have come to mean a great deal to each other, and I think we shall never lose that close bond. I feel we must have been brother and sister once. But...'

'Let me tell you something before you get embarrassed,' Simon interrupted. 'Min-ha is free. I think, in time, we may be together at last.'

'You mean Sara?'

'Yes. Gustave Leverson has died. All that's happened so far is that she finds I am the only person she wants to have around in this difficult time. It's a sign, at least. I've declared nothing, told her nothing — she's still mourning for a man she was very attached to. I'll respect that, but I had to find out if we were on the same wave-length, and we obviously are. So I am just hoping.... And I was so afraid you'd be hurt. You know me better than anyone in the world, Anna. I have been desperately torn between you, but you know why Sara is the one.'

Anna pulled his head towards hers, and held their foreheads touching. 'Of course I know. One cannot fight that. But in any case, I'm in love too... with my music. It's all going so well. And when I'm not emotionally involved, I feel I can channel all my soul into my playing. That is my purpose in life, for the time being, anyway.'

The import of the manifestation was only just beginning to be appreciated; it had happened in such a remote part of the world, and so few people had witnessed it. But the amateur video-recording made from the ecumenical bus was now being telecast internationally (all proceeds to the Seventh Intercostal Church Inc. of Eureka); the B.B.C. and the commercial television channels were trying to find out where Simon was, to interview him. His speech had been printed in most national papers, with copious errors, and was being interpreted in wildly different ways. Simon was a commie, a wet, a saviour, a crazy loon, the conscience of the world, a heretic, a dangerous megalomaniac, a New Age hero, an Antichrist. A German Greenie group wrote to urge him to stand for the European parliament. Several interviews he had never given were published. The World Council of Churches was attacked for spending so much money on a lavish firework display when millions were starving...

Floris had to remember that he knew nothing about the animosity of George and Muriel towards Simon, and that he had no knowledge whatever of events at the monastery, apart from what everyone had seen on television. By four-thirty, Floris had induced a state of relaxation in George sufficient for an attempt at therapy to be made. Floris found Muriel to be in an even worse state of tension, partly because of George's condition, partly because of unresolved inner conflicts. An unfortunate conjugation, these two, thought Floris, bringing out and nourishing each other's negative emotions. Muriel had clearly been a good-looking woman, in a slightly horsy sort of way. But she was a heavy smoker, which gave that characteristic drawn and sallow quality to her skin.

'You say you hit your head, George, and that caused the headaches?'

'That's right.'

'Just show me the spot you hit, will you?'

George felt his head gingerly. 'About there, I think,' he said, with his finger on a point near the back of the crown. Floris parted the thatch of dark, wiry hair and inspected the area carefully.

'What other symptoms do you have?'

'Other?'

'Yes. The headaches are not the only thing you feel.'

He said it with such confidence, George could not lie.

'Well, there's nothing else specific. It's a general sensation. How can I describe it? Of being pulled in two. I'll tell you what I thought I was feeling like, it came to me last night in bed: like an insect that has to break out of an outer case — what is it called...?'

'Like a pupa breaking out of a cocoon?' Floris suggested.

'Yes. Or a snake sloughing off its skin. I felt sort of split right up.'

'It was the bread and butter pudding,' said Muriel, 'I told you you shouldn't have a second helping.'

Floris smiled, and found to his surprise that she smiled back.

'The pudding may have helped, Mrs. Plaidy, but I don't think it's the first time George has felt like that, is it George?'

'No. To be frank I feel like it all the time.'

'That is very helpful,' Floris said. 'Now, to put it plainly to you, I am sure your problem is not caused by hitting your head. There is no evidence of tissue damage. You are, how shall I say, you are at war with yourself, George. You expressed the condition very well — you are trying to break out of an outer form you don't want any more. Do you want me to help you to achieve this? I shall need your trust and co-operation. I cannot do it otherwise.'

George did not hesitate. He did, and he would. He lay down on the couch, agreed to having the session video-taped, and Floris persuaded Muriel to massage George's ankles, gently overcoming her protests that it was stupid, while he did the same circular movement with his outer hand to the centre of George's forehead. George proved to be a good subject. He floated, described details he could not see from his lying position, in such a way that Muriel was visibly impressed. Then Floris started to direct him back in time to the incarnation that was causing the conflict.

'You know the comte de Freyssenet?'

'Yes.'

'Are you his friend?'

'Certainly not. He is my sworn enemy, a traitor, an aristocratic terrorist.'

'You know how he died?'

'Of course. I gave orders for him and his little peasant trollop to be executed.'

Floris switched into French, and to Muriel's astonishment, so did George. '*Comment se fait-il que...* How is it that you have so much power?'

'*Je suis l'Empereur*. My power extends over the water.'

'Why did you want to kill them?'

'That dirty spy had received a report of my strategy for the battle at Waterloo. It was no good killing just him. She would have delivered the message to the English government if she had been left alive.'

'And you succeeded?'

'Of course.'

'Go now to the end of your life, your Majesty. Have you succeeded in your ambitions?'

'No. Failure. A dream destroyed. Because of traitors like Freyssenet.'

'But Freyssenet was dead. He never got his message through. He was not to blame.'

'Is that true?'

'Absolutely true. You beat him. Your assassin stopped them both. They died a horrible death, in their own house.'

'Excellent. I'm glad to hear it.'

'He was punished, and so was she. You do not need to pursue them any more, do you?'

'You are certain they did not succeed in betraying me before the battle?'

'Yes. The message has been found at the comte's house. It was never delivered.'

George gave a deep, contented sigh.

'Will you not let the matter rest now?' asked Floris. 'You are an Emperor. One of the world's outstanding men. You have no need of petty revenge on enemies you have already beaten. A sign of the truly great is their generosity in victory.'

'You are right. He deserved to die. He is dead. Let him be in peace.'

'Will you forgive him, let him go in peace?'

'I will.'

'And you will be at peace with yourself. You will no longer be torn between friendship and enmity.'

'I am glad.'

Floris gently brought him back. He had only a vague memory of what had transpired, and Floris played back the video-tape.

'Do you really think that Simon and I...?'

'I know, George. I was there. The light, the stone you tried to put back, the force that pushed it out again and enveloped you...'

'Is that what happened? Every trace of memory of what happened, from the moment I stopped videotaping, has gone. First thing I remember after that was waking up in a sick bay in the monastery.'

Muriel had been watching and listening fretfully to all this, smoking incessantly.

'Now look here, George,' she said firmly, 'you and I have always agreed that Simon was a rotten sod. Don't you let this Emperor nonsense get the better of you. I don't know what he's done to you, this man, but you'd better snap out of it.'

Floris gently ignored her outburst. 'How's your head, George?'

George thought, got up, moved about, shook his head, breathed deeply. 'I've never felt better. Like a new man.'

'You are, in a sense. And it will last. This hasn't been some sort of hypnotic game, Mrs. Plaidy.' He turned to her. 'You would be surprised how many of our ills are caused by unresolved conflicts from a previous incarnation. Very often groups of entities go on interacting through several reincarnations, until peace or union is achieved between them. I believe the same is true in your case.'

Muriel backed away. 'Don't you start on me. I don't want anything to do with this sorcery.'

George went over to her, took her hand, and began to speak to her in a low and urgent voice. Floris did not interrupt. After a few minutes, she slowly turned round.

'All right. If George says it's genuine. But I'm not convinced, by any means, Mr. Scheimer.'

Floris, with George's assistance (which helped to relax her) went through the same procedure. It was far from easy in her case, because she was so resistant and fearful of letting go. Floris had rarely seen such a knotted-up aura. The extent of blotchy red in it showed how much raging, repressed emotion there was in her. Brown patches indicated the bad digestion she must be plagued with. Slowly, she consented to float, and found it pleasant. With great discretion, Floris took her back to Mme. de Crécy. The first time Floris mentioned Freyssenet's name to her, George started violently and muttered, 'Good God! So that's why...'

The festering resentment Mme. de Crécy felt towards Freyssenet, for the social humiliation she felt he had caused her, needed very careful handling, because she could not see that Freyssenet had paid for his actions. The way through, he found, was *via* the girl, Amélie, her maid.

'Do you know what became of her?' asked Floris.

'I'm not interested in the fate of a skivvy, *la petite putain*.'

'She stayed with the comte, shared his life and miseries, and it was she who was stabbed through the heart before his eyes, on Napoleon's orders.'

'Good riddance to bad rubbish.'

'*Oui*. She got her true reward for betraying you, didn't she?'

'*En effet!*'

'But her death was agony to Freyssenet. He suffered greatly, seeing her there, her blood running into the gutter. He was punished too, wasn't he?'

'He was. I am glad.'

'Both of them together, violently murdered. You didn't know that, did you?'

'No, I didn't.'

'Do you think they suffered enough, for the humiliation you suffered, Mme. de Crécy?'

'Yes. Enough.'

'You will not harbour feelings of hatred towards Freyssenet in your unconscious memory?'

'There's no need to any more.'

Unlike George, she remembered everything that had happened when she returned. Visibly shaken, she opened her arms to George, who held her tight while she wept copiously, releasing the emotions she had for so long kept in.

Floris felt that Simon would be safe now.

24

The interview was well under way. They had got down to organisational details. Richard Jensen indicated to the chairman, Raymond Blindon, that he wished to put a question.

'Dr. Prestcott, considering that the primary aim of the Centre will be to elaborate educational and behavioural programmes capable of creating a race of agapons or agapoids, how would you select those capable of succeeding?'

Simon had thought a good deal about this problem, and had discussed it with Floris; for if Floris was correct in his theories and beliefs, there must be some connexion between the innate qualities needed for the future post-human race and his or her spiritual development.

'What I am about to propose,' he replied to the committee of four, 'may not seem very scientific to you, but I assure you it is worth pursuing. We are agreed, I think, that moral perfectibility has nothing to do with intelligence (as measured by current testing procedures), educational level, heredity, or social environment. Therefore none of the criteria normally used for selection will do for the Centre. But there is a method which takes no account of the variable factors I've just mentioned. A method of assessing the spiritual nature of people. That is, by auric readings. A few months ago, I would have treated any such suggestion with disdain. I can only ask you to believe that my recent experiences have so widened my perspective in these matters, that I am able to speak to you of the apparently unbelievable with equanimity and confidence.'

'I think we are not unaware of the field of investigation you are referring to,' said Jensen. 'But how could it be useful to us?'

Simon outlined his project: to set up a technically sound way of recording and testing the validity of auric readings, to ascertain on a large, statistically significant scale whether the colour configuration of an aura did in fact coincide with the personality and spiritual potential of the subject. Only those whose spiritual, emotional, and mental attainment was of a high order, through repeated refinement over countless thousands of years of past earth-time, would be sufficiently free of those flaws that were in the process of destroying humanity. But this did not mean creating a race of hermits and gurus, he said. They would have to be practical, well-balanced, social creatures, infinitely adaptable to new conditions on another planet. And if they were to survive, their potential psychic powers would need to be very high, for their self-defence.

Another member of the committee put up his hand. 'Dr. Schultz has a question,' said Blindon. Schultz, a German-Swiss medical researcher, began to speak, his abominable German-Swiss accent performing on the French language a most un-Swiss degree of violence.

'Dr. Prestcott, you have so far failed to provide us with a precise account of the methodology you would establish, and a scientifically rigorous description of the results you will achieve.'

Simon gave him a look that the Crow would have been proud of. 'Herr Dr. Schultz,' he said, 'one of the reasons *imaginative* scientific research is becoming impossible is that research-funding bodies insist on knowing the answers before researchers even know the questions. All I can say is that it would be necessary to use the best available knowledge regarding educational programs, based on Montessori methods, Yoga techniques, Tao, the ideas already developed by Dr. Bernard and by Dr. Edward de Bono. But none of these would achieve the level of perfection and psychic power needed for Agapons, if they are to survive and create a viable Utopia based not on social or political theories, but on moral and spiritual qualities within each individual.'

Dr. Blindon looked round the table, saw there were no more questions, and smiled at Simon. 'Thank you, Dr. Prestcott. You have told us in great detail what you experienced at the monastery of St. Makros, and the value of that experience in gaining a privileged insight into what is meant by a perfect state is clear. I think we all respect that, even though it has been dubbed in some unsympathetic quarters as a form of hysteria. Your ideas on selection, training, aims and objectives have been most interesting. I have one further question to put to you: are you not concerned that the aims of the Centre — to provide for the salvation of a small number of highly privileged beings in order to ensure the continuation of humanity in the universe — do you not feel this is very élitist, or very risky? It could be perverted into a neo-Nazi Superman cult, couldn't it?'

Simon looked at the smile on Blindon's face and realised he was being invited to step into a trap. After some reflexion he replied.

'First, élitism. Yes, it is élitist, and will be attacked for this reason. There are those who wouldn't allow the lifeboats on a sinking ocean liner to be used if they couldn't take every passenger. I would want the women and children to get off first, for the usual sentimental reasons, but...'

'...but we are not dealing with an ocean liner?' Blindon interjected.

'Exactly. More like Noah's ark. And the species to be saved must be chosen on a rational, scientific basis, if we're able to do it. As for perversion... This is a very real danger — I've had first-hand experience of it, as you know. I could well still be walled up in that monastery, and very dead, with the light-force in the wrong hands. We mustn't underestimate the utter ruthlessness of those who'd like to use these methods as a way of producing an acquiescent population incapable of dissent.'

'Thank you, Dr. Prestcott.' Blindon seemed satisfied, but it was difficult to tell. 'Now we must consider your candidature along with that of a small number of other short-listed candidates who responded to our announcement some months ago. We shall be in touch with you very soon.'

Simon went out, with no idea whatever of how the interview had gone. The reference to unsympathetic responses to the reports of the St. Makros episode had been most unsettling. He ought to have expected that, of course.

During the next six months Simon's life was gradually transformed. From being a disenchanted university lecturer he blossomed into a leader with both vision and an eye for detail. At the same time Sara preoccupied him, sometimes joyfully, sometimes with anxiety lest he might lose her. One afternoon, as they were sitting in her new apartment, he unwittingly created a barrier between them which he could not have foreseen. She had asked him about Anna again, and he admitted that they had been lovers. She reacted with a chilliness that astounded him — as though he had been unfaithful to her.

'But you can't be jealous of Anna!' he protested, 'I've told you, that is all over now.'

'But if you can be so quickly "over" Anna, perhaps you can quickly be "over" me too.'

Simon began to realise that there was a unsuspected cultural gap between them that could prove disastrous if he were not very careful. He stood up and looked out over the lake of Geneva, *le lac Léman*. Far above it, in the distance and as if suspended, the glistening cap of Mont Blanc was catching the sun's rays. He turned, sat, took Sara's tiny golden hand in his, raised it to his lips. Her eyes were fixed on his, questioning deeply.

'Sara, I want you to listen very carefully. There must be no misunderstanding between us about this. I never told Anna I loved her. Not once. Neither did she say it to me. When I told you we were fond of one another, I thought you knew what it meant....'

'I did not know it meant being lovers.'

'It doesn't. Anna and I were physical lovers who were

and still are fond of each other. We feel affection for each other. We trust each other. We care about each other. But she knows that I am completely, totally in love with you. She is not jealous. She longs to see you again, to be your friend. That may be strange to you, perhaps, but to twentieth-century Westerners it is not difficult or extraordinary. Only one thing matters to me now, and that is my love for you. I live for you, I would die for you, I would die if I lost you. Please don't let Anna come between us. You and I are meant for each other this time.'

'You are holding my hands too hard, you know,' she smiled. He realised how tightly he was gripping them, and apologised. Sara placed her fingers upon his lips, leant forward, and kissed him with a strength that told him all he wanted to know.

Simon felt is was time to broach the subject of their previous history, but feared he might come up against another barrier. Would she be shocked because of her catholic upbringing? Or regard him as dotty and unreliable, after all those years with the ultra-rational Gustave? He had to risk it. When he came to the scene between them in the cabin of the boat, her eyes grew wider and more disbelieving, and she asked him if this was not some kind of joke, or a male fantasy perhaps. He reassured her so earnestly that she allowed him to go on, until the episode in the cupboard. Then she burst into peals of laughter — the first time Simon had heard her express amusement so heartily.

'We made love in a cupboard?'

'Yes. I can see the funny side of it too, with you on a ladder because you were too short for me. But the next bit turns from farce to tragedy. You were later killed for it. Your heart was torn out by your jealous husband. I, Simon, found it, exactly where Freyssenet said he put it. I still have it. When we get back to England I can show it to you.'

This sobered her up. When he had finished his account, she sat silent for a long time with closed eyes. Then she said: 'At least it explains why I found it so pleasant and natural to kiss you.'

At Sara's request, they did not sleep together until after they were married. That took far longer than Simon wanted. Not only did Sara wish to avoid indecent haste, out of respect for Gustave, but she also had a very strong family sense, so her parents and brothers had to be brought from various parts of the world where they had settled — one of them as a doctor in Melbourne. Then there was the question of where to have the wedding. Simon had no problems about this: an anvil in Scotland would have been fine. But family pressure, and Sara's own preference, was for a Catholic ceremony. Simon had no great love for the idea, as he could not prevent the picture of Professor Timothy Crankshaw oiling its way into his mind's eye.

Then he had what he modestly called a brilliant inspiration. While clearing out his papers to move from Cambridge, he came across a photocopy of a cutting from *The Times* of 13 June 1815, relating the murder of Freyssenet, which stated that he and Mlle. Amélie Roussin were buried alongside each other in the churchyard of St. Pancras Church, where many French *émigrés* lay. Simon took Sara to see it, now dwarfed by high rise flats and grimy from a hundred years of smoke-belching trains. They searched for the graves, but fruitlessly as most of the headstones had long ago been jammed together liked sliced bread to make room for the railway line to St. Pancras. However, the interior of the Church was charming and well looked after, and Sara was happy since it had once been a Catholic church. Floris was overjoyed at the elegance of the solution.

Harvey and Mina were excited, bright-eyed, smiling, but serious as page-boy and bridesmaid. To Simon's great surprise, Anna had said that if she was not allowed to be maid of honour, she would be eternally offended, and Sara agreed, after some initial hesitation. Simon toyed with the idea of asking George to be his best man, but Floris warned him to be cautious about opening up relationships with him again, so a cousin stepped into the job. The ceremony was intensely moving for Simon; a sudden and unexpected wave of pity came over him for devoted little Amélie, whose bones lay just outside in an unmarked grave.

When they were finally on their own, in a cosy little hotel near Saint-Sulpice, and they had closed the window against the dull roar of the Paris traffic, Simon and Sara embraced amid the suitcases and found they were surprisingly embarrassed. Fortunately they both began to laugh about it.

'I feel like a virgin,' said Sara, giggling with her hand over her mouth.

'So do I. I think a little Dutch courage is required.'

He pulled a bottle of Moët et Chandon out of a duty-free plastic bag, and gently eased the cork out.

'You're very skilled at that,' said Sara. 'I always make them dent the ceiling. I even broke a window in Geneva — a genuine eighteenth-century one.'

Simon took her hand and cupped it in his own. It was as smooth and tiny as a young girl's, not made to span octaves. He couldn't imagine it was strong enough to extract a champagne cork, and made the mistake of saying so. Sara's eyes glinted in a new way. She took his wrist and tightened her grip on it, her face still smiling and relaxed. Without any effort, she made the bones crack and the blood stopped. She had put pressure just where it was most painful, and he tried to pull away, but she held on, laughing now. He took her other arm and fell on her on the bed. He feared he might wind her, but she lithely slid away and lay on top of him, still holding his wrist. With the other hand, she grabbed his hair and brought her mouth towards his neck, just below the left ear. He thought she was going to kiss him, but she bit him, not very hard.

'You little tiger!' he gasped, 'you've asked for it now!'

'Yes,' she whispered, 'I am asking for it now.'

They lay still. He felt her slight body begin to move slowly on top of him. She looked deeply into his eyes.

'Simon, I do love you. For the first time in my life, I know what it is to be passionately in love. I feel just like that champagne, longing to pop the cork.'

'And we haven't even started yet,' said Simon. He began to undo the buttons on her white dress.

'No!'

'No?'

'No. They are false.'

He cupped her breasts with his hands. 'I don't believe it.'

'Not those, silly. The buttons. There is a zip at the back.'

'I have a zip at the front, and it's not false.'

'Thanks for telling me. I should hate to waste my time.'

Sara stood up, turned her back to him, and he undid the long zip. The dress slid noiselessly to the floor. He unhooked the satin bra as well, and shuddered slightly all over as he felt her nipples rise strongly, like hard silken buttons, against the palms of his hands. She gave a sharp intake of breath.

'It's like releasing doves from a cage,' she said, looking over her shoulder at him. 'But you haven't told me you love me yet.'

He had, many times, but now was different.

'No.' His hand moved slowly down until it reached her delicate triangle, surprisingly soft, like a small furry animal. 'No, I really don't dare to any more. That little word couldn't tell you what I feel for you, darling. I'm so deeply, deeply...'

His voice trailed off. He held her close to him, and kissed her bare shoulder gently.

'Yes,' she whispered. 'I know. It's like coming home.'

'It was worth waiting for,' he said, 'but by God, I've been sorely tried! For over two hundred years, actually.'

As Sara stepped out of her dress, Simon had a fleeting image of Anna undressing before him that time, but immediately he knew the difference. With Sara, lovemaking was not only a mutual and prolonged delight, as the daylight grew dim unnoticed, and in the light of the street lamp her body became a deep glistening gold, repeatedly coming to tight and trembling climaxes, beneath, above, alongside him; but beyond this soft, strong, sensual, so long-awaited pleasure, there was also a sensation of intense joy, of realisation that this was meant to be, that it had an essential *rightness* about it. For them both it was the first conjunction of profound love and of passionate desire.

> *My love, my heart,*
> *think how sweet*
> *To live together yonder,*
> *loving at leisure, in the land*
> *where, as in you, prevail*
> *Order, beauty, delight, calm and ecstasy.*

The final stages of the conversion of the house in Geneva, which was to be the home of the Centre for Future Enlightenment Studies, had been completed in record time.

Tomorrow was the official opening. Representatives from the United Nations, UNESCO, neutral countries, the Swedish Peace Foundation, churches, and universities, were due to arrive any moment. Simon went round the laboratories once again, the lecture rooms, his own office with the words **DIRECTOR OF RESEARCH** inscribed in gold, and found it all good. Many things remained to be done for the opening: sound system to be checked, catering and drinks to be delivered. He heard a van draw up outside the main entrance; the *intendant* would deal with it. He had to polish up his speech before four o'clock. Sara and the children would be arriving then to take him home.

At two minutes to four he heard Harvo and Mina calling him from the drive. He got up and saw them, hand in hand with Sara, walking just behind the parked van by the main entrance. He went towards them. How he adored them; every time he looked at them, he brimmed over with joy, and felt like skipping along like a little boy.

Two hours later, in Harley Street, Floris and Anna settled down briefly to watch the B.B.C television news. They were due to take the 10 a. m. plane from Heathrow to Geneva the next day for the opening. Anna still had some packing to do. More crises in Eastern Europe, in the Middle East, and in the Commons. Then the newscaster faltered and picked up the telephone on her desk. She replaced it and said: 'We are interrupting our scheduled programme of news to go over to Geneva, where reports are coming in of an explosion...'

On the screen came a scene of chaos. The front of a building, or what remained of it, shrouded in smoke, fire engines wailing, ambulances waiting. People shouting, crying. The outside broadcasts presenter appeared, and wiping his eyes from the smoke and fumes, said: 'What you see behind me is all that is left of the main entrance of the new Centre for Future Enlightenment Studies in Geneva, which was due to be opened tomorrow. It seems that about three o'clock this afternoon, a delivery van pulled up at the entrance. The driver was seen to get out, look at his watch, and walk round to the back of the building. No one thought any more about it. Then at four o'clock, the van blew up, a colossal explosion, the van must have been packed with explosive. Unfortunately, at that very moment, the wife and children of the new Director, Dr. Simon Prestcott, from Melbourne and Cambridge, were walking close by the van. They have... there is no trace of them. Dr. Prestcott was knocked out by falling masonry as he rushed out to save them, and is still unconscious, in a critical state...'

Floris and Anna stared, aghast, unhearing, at the picture. A hole in the ground, which must have been where the van was. And behind it, a dark red patch. Anna pressed her hands to her mouth and tried to stifle her sobs as the B.B.C. telecaster began speaking again: '...several terrorist organisations have claimed responsibility for the bombing. It is not yet known whether the device was set off by remote control, or by an automatic timer...'

— *Can we go and play, Mummy ?*
— *Of course, darling.*
— *Why don't you go over to the stream and play Pooh-sticks on the bridge?*
— *But Simon, there isn't a stream or a bridge.*

— Yes there is, Mina. If you want a stream and a bridge, they exist.

— Yes! Look Mina! I see it! Come on! Come on Sara!

— I wish you wouldn't call Mummy Sara, Harvey.

— She lets me. She's more real if I call her Sara.

— My Mummy's real anyway.'

Mina sighed wistfully.

— What's the matter, darling?

— I'm sad about Sam and François. They'd only just come out of quarreltine when we came here. I wish we had another dog to play with. He'd love to swim in the stream.

Immediately, they heard a joyful barking from over by the wall surrounding the High Garden, and a white spaniel with black patches, with one white ear and one black one, came bounding over towards them.

— How lovely! shouted Mina.

— What's his name?

— You choose, said Simon.

— Jack! said Harvey.

— Muffin! shouted Mina at the same time.

— Jack Muffin, then, if you like, said Sara. You can do whatever you want and have what you like here, so long as it doesn't hurt anyone.

— Can we stay here for ever? asked Mina . She tickled Jack Muffin's undercarriage as he obligingly waved his paws in the air.

— There isn't any 'for ever', said Simon. Everything just goes on, the same or changing, for as long as we want it to. Till then, we'll all stay together.

He put his arm round Sara, and they walked off to explore the rest of the High Garden.

— Strange, it's smaller than I thought it would be. Yet it just seems to go on and on, he said.

— It's like a dream , isn't it?

— Not a dream , my love. This is real. All the rest was dreams and nightmares.

Floris went on staring, unseeing, at the T. V. screen. The news was followed by a screening of the Australian mini-series, *Vietnam*. A newsreel shot showed an American soldier with the words **'KILL A GOOK FOR GOD'** printed across the front of his helmet. The telephone startled Floris out of his stupor. Anna had gone to the bathroom. He could hear her sobbing uncontrollably.

'Yes?'

'Dr. Schoenheimer?'

'Yes.'

'This is George Plaidy. Have you heard the news?'

'Yes.'

'Isn't it appalling? What a terrible waste. Look, Dr. Schoenheimer, Floris, we can't let Simon's death be for nothing. He was convinced that force he — we — experienced at the monastery held a power so strong he just didn't know what to do with it. But I think we were meant to do something with it. The psycho-kinetic readings were fantastic. But nobody knows what Simon did with the equipment. Do you happen to know?... Floris?...Are you still there?...'

'Yes, I'm here. I have no idea, George. Please excuse me.'

Floris wearily replaced the receiver. The enormity of the situation suddenly weighed down upon him. Something had been unleashed in the world, and he sensed how strong and ruthless were the forces of those who wished to be the first to harness it, control it, exploit it. Floris cursed his failure to uncover the true nature of the conflict they were engaged in. The moment he had singled out Simon that evening in Melbourne, he had set him on a path leading, step by step, to disaster. Floris could not accept that Simon had been saved at the monastery just to be pointlessly liquidated in Geneva. He told himself he should have delved deeper, farther back, to discover the reason why Simon had been chosen as the unwitting and sometimes unwilling agent of resistance — but against what? His intuition whispered to him, perhaps too late, that he and Simon, and all the thugs, bandits, and terrorists were mere pawns in a game that ranged far beyond this little planet.

25

Floris found the visit to Geneva physically trying and spiritually draining. First, he had gone to see Simon at the hospital, and found him in a state of deep unconsciousness from which he had not shown the slightest momentary recovery. The brain specialist in charge feared that even if he came round, there could be permanent severe brain damage. While he was left alone for a moment, Floris looked in the small wardrobe by the bed, and found what he wanted.

In the mortuary, the pitiful remains of Sara, Mina and Harvey moved him to tears: a small burnt sandal, the charred pages of an exercise book, a tattered, disfigured doll, and a half-melted gold necklace... The vibrations he received from these personal belongings retrieved from the site of the explosion were so violent that he was overcome by nausea and had great difficulty in pursuing his investigation. However, he managed to hide a small fragment of material, which he recognised as coming from Sara's skirt, and took it away with him.

Then came the long interview with the inspector in charge, who could not understand Floris's interest in the affair. '*Vous n'êtes pas de la famille, monsieur? Alors, je regrette....*'

It required a telephone call to Inspector Irving at Scotland Yard to get any co-operation. Well, one couldn't blame the Swiss, said Irving; they were very thorough, and Dr. Schoenheimer could have been anyone, after all. Simon's papers at the Centre revealed nothing helpful such as threatening letters. Indeed, Floris was not sure what what he was looking for, since he was not interested in finding out who had planted the bomb (unlike the Swiss police, who were quite passionate about it, by Swiss standards of excitability). But others, apparently were very interested too.

'We have problems, Monsieur Schoenheimer,' Inspecteur Guisan had told him. 'The family of Madame Prêtecotte, they are *vietnamiens, non*? Some of them were at the church service, and made very worrying statements which my men overheard.'

'What sort of statements, Monsieur Guisan ?'

'Revenge. Reprisals. Vendettas. They are very rich and powerful people, and they may be foolishly inclined to interfere with the law. The honour of the family seems to have been hurt by this brutal murder of one of their favourite daughters. So if you have any influence with them, *monsieur le docteur ...*'

'None at all, I fear. But if I have the opportunity to warn them, I will.'

'You can tell them that we shall do everything in our power to bring the culprits to justice; we do not tolerate such violence on Swiss soil. We are surrounded by madmen, in France, Germany, Italy — *L'Action directe*, the Red Army Faction, the Red Brigade... the violence continues and new groups are always appearing with new ideals to murder for. We can well do without a Vietnamese faction waging a private war!'

— The woman and children were not supposed to be killed. We have made more enemies for ourselves. Very dangerous ones. You shall be severely punished for this stupid error.

— It could not be helped. We had no way of knowing...

— You were instructed to call Prestcott to the main entrance by a telephone call. Why did you not do this?

— The woman and children approached the van before we could make the call. He came to the entrance, and...

— ... and you panicked!

— The potential damage to Mother Church appears to have evaporated, Eminence, now that the Coptic Church is no longer involved.

— That is true. We think you may relax your attention to this matter. It is a pity about the deaths, of course, but sometimes sacrifice is necessary for a greater cause.

— Amen.

— So how do we find out? Before anyone else?

— All I have to do is to gain the confidence of Schoenheimer. He knows I'm a reformed character. Don't worry. I can convince him that we must have the data before anyone else, for everybody's sake. Even the Russians would agree, if they can agree among themselves. We might make a joint approach to him?

— Better the Russians got it than the Iranians or the Iraquis. At least the Kremlin understands what's at stake.

— The Kremlin? What's that?

The sensation of perfect harmony with self and with loved ones close to him remained intact and unchanging, apparently outside time. Very imperceptibly Simon grew aware of his being summoned. There was no need to tell Sara about it, for all knowledge was shared, all thoughts transparent. She knew that whatever was to be, was, already, and that resistance could only delay the final joyous outcome. It had not been so on earth, where so much had to be achieved by effort of will and refusal. Here, the process was incomparably simpler and immeasurably more complex. Simon no longer needed to use a simulacrum of physical means of motion and mobility: he willed, and he moved. The result was sheer exhilaration, once he had overcome the nausea, not unlike air-sickness. This time, he simply let himself go, and drifted in the direction, no, along the frequency, required. Before he arrived, he knew who would be there, and he felt immensely relieved.

Lying quietly in his study in Harley Street, with the lights dimmed and the telephone switched to the answering machine, Floris held the piece of Sara's material together with Simon's handkerchief (which he had taken from his jacket pocket at the hospital), and quickly placed himself in a trance. As he drifted away, he was vaguely aware of a faint click from the direction of the study door, but the effect of Simon's and Sara's vibrations was so immediate and strong, he could not resist being drawn out of his body. He was pleased, for it meant that Simon, lying in a state of limbo between life and death, was receptive and anxious to communicate. Floris allowed himself to drift, upwards it seemed, but he knew spatial dimensions meant nothing. Then he was stopped. There was an invisible barrier. It did not have the function of blocking his advance, but of checking him. It entered into him, was both within and without simultaneously, ausculting every particle of his mind and being. He stood before it, touched it, and revered it because this was part of Simon's and Sara's world. They had created it as an extension of themselves. When it had made his acquaintance, it accepted him, and allowed him to pass through its insubstantial mass. Then he felt his call to Simon being strongly answered.

He was in a garden of incomparable beauty, bathed in a warm light of hyacinth and gold. Everything about it denoted order, beauty, mystical joy, and a mingling of incompatible qualities — calm and ecstasy. There was a stream gently flowing across it, and a small wooden bridge. He heard the laughter of children, but he could see no movement. Floris willed himself on to the bridge and stood there, looking at a clump of trees whose foliage gently wafted although there was no breeze.

It was just in front of the trees that Simon materialised.

He looked thin, but strong, older, but with finer features. Wiser. The state of Simon's aura shocked Floris, but he was not surprised. Simon was near death, his soul had been cast out of his body without warning, causing some of the vital forces to be left behind. The vibration and energy of his aura were diminished, and the aura had become overladen with dark yellow, the effect of the mental anguish caused by physical violence. But the curling auric wings testified to the way he had expended the latter part of his life for noble purposes. The predominant hues of green, blue and purple were wholly satisfying to Floris, for he saw from them that Simon's evolution had been incredibly rapid during the short time he had known him; they signified healing powers, spirituality, and dedicated universality. Then he was struck forcibly by the extent of the loss, and felt keenly his own place in it.

The exchange which took place between them was rapid and wordless. Floris recorded it in his journal afterwards:

MTG WITH SP

I floated gently towards him.

'Simon, do you know me?'

'Of course, Floris!'

'Are you happy to see me?'

'Naturally! Do you like our garden?'

'It's unbelievably beautiful.'

'The children and I made it,' Simon said without affectation. 'I'm glad I don't have to pay the gardeners.' I was glad he had not lost his sense of humour.

'And yet it is objectively real,' I said, 'since I am here in it.'

'But no one will believe you,' said Simon. 'They will say it is a wish-fulfilling fantasy.'

'I realise that. I feel guilty about what has happened,' I told him. 'I should have been able to warn you, but I failed.'

'You were meant to fail. They blocked you off. Ever since you foiled them by helping me at the monastery, they have

been determined to maintain a psychic cloud around you.'

'I have felt it, strongly. Like jammed radio-waves.'

'How did you manage to get through to me today?'

'I felt I was getting extra psychic strength from somewhere.'

'That could be good or bad. They might have wanted you to reach me, to overhear us. They have been trying to enter the garden, but our wall keeps them out.'

'So you are under siege?'

'Not for the time being; we are in sanctuary. But I have been given a fleeting intuition of what we — you — are up against. The dark forces are formidable, Floris. Unimaginably horrendous! If only I had known in Geneva what I know now about the closing of the gap.'

'What is the gap?'

As Simon was about to reveal to Floris the nature of the process to which the Earth was being subjected, there was a determined attempt at psychic interference. It was concentrated on Floris, who felt himself being driven inwards on all sides by enormous pressure, with a high-pitched whine, which turned into a screech, blotting out all thought. Gradually, the sound and the pressure abated, and he saw why: Simon had been joined by Sara and the children, and their combined strength had, for a short while, prevailed. Sara's glowing aura signalled her state of joy and her pleasure at seeing their friend again. Then she and the laughing children floated back to the bridge. Simon placed a forefinger on his lips and ears, and encompassed the landscape with a circular glance.

Floris was plunged into utter darkness. It was like the sun being switched off at the height of a cloudless summer's day. His eyes adjusted, and he saw the bright stars and galaxies of the universe, then afar, Earth, enveloped in swirling, black clouds, impenetrably dense. There was just one slit through which he glimpsed the familiar blue of our planet. Then the clouds seemed to gather strength, billowed and surged, and slowly filled the gap. At once the whole firmament was extinguished. Not just Earth, but everything, every single atom, evaporated into an endless Void. Then he was back in the garden.

'When the dark circle is complete round earth,' Simon said to me, *'when the two flanks join, nothing will be able to break through. Earth will be totally isolated from all the forces of light and of... not Good, that's too trite ... of Creativity. The universe will be pushed back into the state of things before Creation. Absolute, infinite, changeless black Void. But that is not all.'*

There now began another determined attempt at interference in the communication between them. Simon's thought-waves became scrambled, and at the same time Floris saw his aura begin to fade. Then it seemed as though he made a supreme effort to regain strength; he seemed to grow in stature, the auric wings became resplendent, and his thought came flooding back into Floris at tremendous speed, as though he realised time was short.

'The destructive force you saw in that visualisation has been attacking Earth by corrupting the most powerful religious institutions,' Simon transmitted rapidly to me, *'the most potent forces for Good ever conceived. This explains much that has happened in the past two thousand years. Especially the Crucifixion, the Crusades, the Inquisition, the persecution of Galileo, the conflicts and terrorism of religious groups in India and the Middle East. Jesus and Mohammed have been betrayed so often and blamed for the crimes committed in their name. That could happen to any powerful organisation — or individual — intended to bring Light and harmony to the Earth. It could have happened to me, if I had stayed alive with access to the*

light-force. It could happen to you, Floris. No one is immune. Only Jesus Christ was immune.'

'You mean the Temptation?'

'Yes,' said Simon, 'that was the first manifestation of the dark forces' massive attack on Earth. When Christ, the physical form of the creative force, entered through the psychic gap, the dark forces had to counter-attack by riding on the back of the strongest conjunction of material and spiritual power Earth has ever known: the Roman Empire and Christianity.'

I asked him what his part was in all this, why he had been chosen. His reply stunned me.

The garden round him was suddenly replaced by a sandy, desert waste. In front of him, lining a dirt track, was a row of crosses from which bodies still hung, some groaning, some dead, stinking and rotting with their eyes picked out by the birds. To the left, on a rise, were three more crosses. The body from the centre one had just been lowered, and the flimsy garment girding it fell off as it was dragged along by Roman soldiers. One of them picked the cloth up, and an old Essene monk went up to him, offered him gold, and received the garment, which he quickly carried to one of the other crosses. The naked body of one of his brother Essenes, was now being lowered. Floris recognised him as Simon. The monk wrapped him gently in the garment, and the vision faded.

Simon went on: 'This explains the strong sense of belonging I experienced at the St. Makros monastery.' As Freyssenet, he said, his function had been to witness the light-force and record it, but before he could find a safe and convincing way to reveal it, the Revolution broke out, forcing him into exile. The great ideals of liberty and fraternity were quickly degraded into the massacres of the Terror. Then he was murdered by Napoleon (who was as

278

easily subjected by the dark forces as Robespierre had been). The Coptic monastery of St. Makros had been chosen because of its multiple sacred character, and Geneva chosen for the Centre because of its religious history and its importance as a focus of international peace.

I asked him why he had been killed when he was on the point of succeeding with the Centre, and expected him to say he was the victim of the dark forces. The truth was quite different, and at first filled me with disgust. The death of Sara and the children was a human error, unpredictable because impetuous and unpremeditated. But his death, he said, had been essential to protect him. By releasing the light-force at St. Makros, Simon had provided a respite for Earth, but he had thus revealed himself as the agent of light, and had been placed under threat of subversion by those forces he could never have withstood. Hence acquiescence to the blocking of my psychic protection, and to Simon's removal from the earthly plane by means easily explicable in everyday terrorist terms. Silently prompted by Simon who read my emotions, I slowly accepted the need for this.

'Can we ever overcome these dark forces?' I asked him.

'No,' he answered, 'only delay them, so as to ensure continuation of remnants of the human race, on another planet, and so foil the closure of the gap. We humans are the only vital, organic, living, physical, spiritually-aware, intelligent link with the creative force in the universe. That is why we are being targeted with such ferocity. Our prognostication was correct, but we did not see how close the climax is.'

'Have you any advice to give me?' I asked.

'Fight for the Centre — opposition will be much stronger now. Beware of friends. Tell Anna to be very careful. They will play on her emotional nature. You must strengthen her quickly.'

'What about George Plaidy?'

'He was not involved in my death. But his ideals are not ours. He could be an ally, but the dark force is concentrating on him. You must read his aura with great care. If he is

being treacherous, his dilemma will show clearly.'

'What about Sara and the children?'

'They are still in a state of euphoria. They are wrapped up in one another, and have no thought for what is happening to the world they lived in for a brief time.'

I decided to brooch the subject that touched me most deeply, as a person.

'Simon, you know you have a choice. You can either return to your body and live, or remain with Sara. You have a duty to stay alive and continue the struggle with us. But you have a right to peace and joy with those you love. When you are certain what is best, you must decide.'

'I have made my choice, Floris. You must forgive me, but I am too weary, too weak, to go on fighting on earth. I know my body is shattered — I should never lead a normal life, I should be under constant threat, my brain may not even function properly, and I should be an emotional cripple with Sara and the children dead in that horrible way. I am far more use here, for as long as we can communicate.'

'Shall I be able to contact you again?'

'Perhaps not so clearly.'

'But reinforcements? There must be some help for us from somewhere.'

'Of course. The universe is full of it. But it cannot act unless it is called and wanted by a vastly more powerful collective will on earth than you can muster.'

'What about all that light-force at the monastery? Has it all simply dispersed? Can't it be harnessed and re-directed?'

'There is a way. The answer lies in a locked computer disk I hid away after leaving Egypt. At best, an electronics genius could produce only a very weak form of the light-force, but if it got into the wrong hands...' He flashed to me the location of the hidden disk.

'It would still be useless without the correct password, wouldn't it?' I asked.

'It's not impossible for a determined computer hack to find that out. But if you suddenly have to act under duress, just access the disk by choosing COMMAND/OPTION and

select SAVE. If there's no duress, no Option is necessary.
One mistake erases the lot. There is no second chance. So
do the opposite. Do you understand my meaning?'
'I understand it backwards,' I assured him.

Floris bade Simon farewell, and watched him glide over to
the bridge, where three small, shimmering forms awaited
him and greeted him with gleeful cries. He thought he heard
something strangely like a dog barking too, but decided that
he must have imagined it.

It was not until he was on the point of re-entering his
body that Floris became aware of the danger that had, in
fact, been slowly menacing him ever since he left the
garden. Silently, insidiously, a resistance had been building
up around him, impeding his return. He cursed himself for
being so emotionally involved in Simon and what he had
told him that he had failed to notice what he should have
foreseen: they, it, would not allow him to get back where he
could pass on the information he had regarding the dark
forces. As if caught in a net, he struggled to free himself, to
make contact with the inert body he could see lying on the
couch. It was like swimming in glue, he was being sucked
in, under, paralysed like a fly in amber. Dimly he recognised
the figure standing in a corner of the darkened room and, to
his amazement, felt a strong force of will for his return
coming from the waiting form, bolstering his own fading
strength. Audibly the voice was repeating, 'Come on Floris,
hurry up, we've no time to waste'. Finally, the resistance
abated and allowed him through.

Before opening his eyes, he said quietly, 'Hello, George,
it's good of you to come and see me.'

George was startled and stepped forward sheepishly.

'That's very impressive, Floris. I hope you had a good
trip.'

'Just visiting some old friends.'

'Simon, I imagine?'

'He told me you were not responsible for his death,' said

Floris. George said he was glad that had been cleared up, rubbed his hands together vigorously and, having regained his aplomb, said firmly: 'We have no time to lose. You know why I'm here. It's vital that you entrust the computer data to me, now, before anyone else gets at you or it. For your own sake, and Anna's, let me relieve you of that responsibility.'

Floris focused on George's aura, and made certain rapid deductions.

'You're quite right, George,' he said, rising from the couch,' follow me.'

He went to Anna's Steinway, lifted the lid, and with the blade of a knife carefully slid out a small blue computer disk from under the metal frame. George snatched it from him, but remembered to say 'Thank you.'

'You realise it's no use to you?' Floris said. 'It is, how do you say, locked, and you don't have the password.'

George clenched his jaw and tried to smile at the same time. 'Then you'd better give it to me. If you don't mind, please Floris.'

Floris demurred. 'You do promise to keep the information under the strictest security, don't you, George?'

'Of course,' George laughed mirthlessly, 'it's cost me enough to get, I'm not going to share it around.'

'But tell me — I think I have a right to know — how will you use this data? What can the light-force achieve without the work of the Centre?'

George bit back his impatience and smiled. 'Let me reassure you, Floris,' he said, with the sincerity of an insurance salesman, 'we have the purest motives. You and Pierre Bernard would approve of them. Just imagine: no more religious conflict anywhere in the world. Like the calm of an Arctic winter, after the heat and passion and turmoil of a tropical summer.'

Floris felt an inward shudder, as the memory of that total Void flashed through his mind. 'And who are "we", exactly?'

George reflected, resting his chin on his hands, meeting Floris's gaze unflinchingly, even though he was torn between the desire to share a secret and the solemn oath to keep it. Could Floris be won over, he wondered? Could he possibly help to square the circle? What an asset he would be! But discretion won. No rush. His good faith would be put to the test when the disk was unlocked.

'I can't tell you any more for the time being,' George said. 'The less you know about these matters the better for you.' He paused and lifted his eyebrows imperceptibly. 'And Anna. Where is she, by the way?'

'At rehearsal. She has a big concert tomorrow afternoon at the Festival Hall. Quite a breakthrough for her. At least, it's taking her mind off... all this unpleasantness.'

'She's been through a lot. Character-building, though. She's a grand girl. Very attractive.' George stood up. 'I might go along to hear her. Call on her afterwards, maybe.'

'That's not such a good idea, George. She associates you with Simon, and that could be very distressing for her.'

George nodded. 'O.K., I'll defer the pleasure. For the time being. Now, how do we unlock the disk?'

'Right. It's childishly simple: you just ... hold down COMMAND/OPTION and key in the word SAVE.'

'And what happens if I get it wrong?'

'I expect you get another chance. After that it's irretrievably erased.'

'Then we'd better hope I get it right,' said George.

Floris fervently hoped he had made the right choice. At this stage in the endgame, he realised that double bluff against intelligence experts could be highly dangerous. King and Queen could lose to Black Knight and Rook, with no Bishops on the board.

When George had left, Floris wrote up on his Mac SE his conversation with Simon in as much detail as he could remember, addressed a copy to Pierre Bernard in Geneva, marked "STRICTLY CONFIDENTIAL AND URGENT: BY SPECIAL COURIER", and telephoned the courier service. They were there within the half-hour. Then he felt safer. Very, very worried, but safer.

Two days later, an emergency meeting of the Executive Committee of the Centre for Future Enlightenment Studies was held in a small room in the old League of Nations building overlooking Lac Léman. The Chairman, Raymond Blindon, coughed politely, and began formally. He knew, as did Pierre Bernard, how much, for the whole world, hung on what would be said and done in that room in the next two hours.

'The Council of the Centre for Future Enlightenment has to make an urgent decision about the policy to be adopted. The tragic death of Dr. Prestcott, and the partial destruction of the Centre, have been terrible blows to the cause we espouse. It is tragic, in the real sense, that our work has resulted in terrorist violence and death, the very horrors we are dedicated to eradicate from the potential human of the future. Do we accept defeat, or do we start again? Madame Guyot?'

'*Je vous remercie, Monsieur le président*,' said the formidable lady. 'As Mayor of the City of Geneva, I have the task of ensuring the safety of its citizens. I also am responsible for maintaining the prosperity of the City, which is in no small measure due to the international community and organisations established here. When the Centre for Future Enlightenment was proposed, it seemed to the City Council to be an ideal institution for this city. But the situation has now changed. We still live under the cloud created by Hussein Ali Hariri, who hi-jacked an Air Africa DC-10 at Geneva International Airport and threatened Swiss interests throughout the world if his demands were not met. The President of the Swiss Confederation, M. Pierre Aubert, expressed the extreme resentment of the Swiss people, at being held to ransom by the Lebanese terrorist and by the Green Cells, the clandestine Islamic organisation supporting him. In the last analysis, they got nothing — but Switzerland still feels itself a target. This accords badly with our neutral political posture, and we do not wish to invite further attention from terrorist organisations, Paris style. Therefore, I have to inform you that the Conseil de la Ville de Genève is not anxious for the Centre to resume its work here.'

'That is most disappointing, Madame Guyot,' said Blindon. 'Dr. Bernard?'

Pierre Bernard, his rugged face looking pale and haggard, was visibly distraught as a result of the recent deaths of his friends. He raised his arms in a gesture of resignation and despair.

'What Madame Guyot tells us does not surprise me. Geneva has always regarded it as an almost sacred duty to hold itself *au-dessus de la mêlée*. It did the same in the time of Hitler, pushing neutrality to the point of censoring any publication that could even remotely offend the Germans, for example. But the work of the Centre is a different matter, *n'est-ce pas*? The Centre is itself supremely neutral. This means every power is a potential enemy; or at least, a potential detractor. Let us not forget what is at stake here: not the victory of one nation or political system over another, but the survival of humanity at its best, in the most perfect form possible, so far as we can surmise this to be: that is to say, totally non-aggressive, but capable of maximum self-protection. Almost a re-statement of the basis of Swiss neutrality, *n'est-ce pas*, Madame Guyot? We already have everything ready to commence, except for a front porch and a Director of Research. I do not intend to belittle Dr. Prescott's sacrifice, but he would never regard himself as irreplaceable. And I do know, from a direct source, that the work of the Centre is even more urgent than we ever imagined. Not only must we continue, but we must hurry. It may already be too late, in fact.'

'Could we know what is the source, Dr. Bernard, and the danger that threatens us?'

'I should like to read a report I have received from Dr. Floris Schoenheimer, on a meeting he had two days ago with Dr. Prescott...'

The murmurs of surprise abated, and Pierre Bernard read Floris's account of his visit to the High Garden. When he finished, no one liked to break the stunned silence. Then

Mme. Guyot spoke up.

'I do not think we can seriously take into account a purported meeting on the astral plane. It sounds like paranoid delusion to me,' said the Mayor. She had not reached her powerful position in male chauvinist Switzerland by being credulous.

'We know that this very gift once saved Dr. Prestcott's life, at the monastery,' Bernard protested.

'That is what we were told...'

'If we had not believed Dr. Prestcott's account then, we should not have appointed him. Why should we now refuse to believe these very same sources?'

'The two cases are not the same.' Mme. Guyot closed her eyes, as if pained to have to ram home the obvious. 'At the monastery, Dr. Prestcott was alive. But to go on from that to say it is possible to communicate with Dr. Prestcott dead, requires belief of quite a different order.'

'Dr. Prestcott was not in fact dead when the meeting took place,' Bernard reminded her. 'He was near death. What are you saying, exactly, Madame Mayor? That we should not trust Dr. Schoenheimer, or that he may be genuinely confused himself?'

Raymond Blindon intervened with a placatory smile at Mme. Guyot.

'We should not have believed either him or Dr. Prestcott regarding the phenomena at the monastery, had there not been so many trustworthy witnesses. I quite agree that all this is quite fantastic, by normal standards. But we are not involved in a "normal" situation at all. There is something very, very abnormal going on, and we simply cannot apply our usual sceptical criteria to any of the information being offered to us.'

'I reiterate, *Monsieur le président*, that Geneva, the peace city of the world, should continue to support the work of the Centre,' Pierre Bernard insisted. 'With greater security, the Centre can be made as safe as any other vitally important organisation. If Geneva withdraws its support, it will be failing in the most urgent international duty it has ever had to perform.'

It was Blindon's task to ask for a recommendation to take to the full Council of the Centre, and then to wind up the meeting.

'We have heard views expressed from both sides, on many issues. We should now proceed to vote on our recommendation. The motion is: "That the work of the Centre for Future Enlightenment shall continue forthwith; and that a new Director of Research shall be sought and appointed as a matter of urgency." Those in favour?...Against?...I shall use my casting vote as Chairman in favour. The motion is carried.'

'I fear I must repeat that the Geneva City Council may well refuse permission...' said Mme. Guyot, rising angrily from the conference table.

'In that case Madame Mayor, the City Council will have to face world opinion in going back on an agreement already signed and sealed. Let us leave it there for the moment.'

— You're sure he didn't suss you?

— No way. I've been in this game a long time.

— I still don't like it. It isn't usual to hold down COMMAND for a password. We'll SAVE without the complications first. We've got a second chance. If in doubt, the simplest ploy is the best.

— Aye. Simplest is best.

Floris was not surprised when he heard from Pierre Bernard that the full Council of the Centre had decided that its work was to be suspended indefinitely. The Council had been warned that in these hard times it could not expect continued international agency funding on the basis of that fantastic stuff about meetings on the astral plane. Sceptical, pragmatic, fallible, accountable Unocrats, Eurocrats, and ordinary government bureaucrats, were beset with growing ferocity by the day-to-day problems of overpopulation, the environment, the deepening world-wide depression, unemployment, social unrest, crime, poverty, Aids, famine, racial and religious conflict, and above all, the increasingly easy access to ex-Russian nuclear weaponry. They could not focus for long on anything but immediate problems. The future of humanity seemed to them a rather vague, esoteric, self-indulgent, academic matter. Things were looking black enough without the unquantifiable complication of so-called "cosmic dark forces". These odd abstractions were not mentioned in any open meetings or communiqués, even though no one believed in them — after all, they were not a factor in even the most sophisticated War Games. But if news of them got about, there could be world-wide panic, the stock exchanges would collapse, the dollar and the Deutschmark would sink through a black hole and fail to come out the other side... Unthinkable. KISS. Keep it simple, stupid.